In The Fast Lane

Lotte Moore

Hashtag PRESS

First published in Great Britain by YouByYou Books 2015
This edition published in Great Britain by Hashtag Press 2018

Text copyright © Lotte Moore 2018
Cover illustrations © Philip Hood 2018
Cover design © Helen Braid 2018

A CIP catalogue for this book is available from the British Library.

ISBN 978-1-9998053-0-2

Typeset in Garamond Classic 11.25/14 by Blaze Typesetting

Printed and bound in Great Britain by Clays Ltd, Elcograf S.p.A.

Hashtag PRESS

HASHTAG PRESS BOOKS
Hashtag Press Ltd
Kent, England, United Kingdom
Email: info@hashtagpress.co.uk
Website: www.hashtagpress.co.uk
Twitter: @hashtag_press

Wishing all the world could go a little slower.

Acknowledgements

I would like to thank:

Philip Hood for the incredible cover illustration and Helen Braid for her wonderful design work.

Kate Turner for making the inside of the book look as good as the outside.

Helen and Abiola at Hashtag Press for bringing my novel to life.

Thanks also to the ladies at Literally PR, led by Helen Lewis, for their ongoing support for all my books.

PART ONE

Chapter One

Kensington 1990

"Bye Freddie. Don't cling to me or I'll be late. It's past seven. There's a good boy."

Briefly pecking his wife, Serena, on the cheek, Lang closed the front door, hurried down the busy street and soon mingled with the early morning stream of commuters who surged down to High Street Kensington tube station.

He wasn't Freddie's daddy any more, nor Benjie's or Alicia's, he was one of the 'city suits' anxious to reach his office where deals and finance ricocheted from wall to wall, where people became single-minded in striving to achieve targets and outsmart the opposition.

As usual, the tube was stuffed with hands gripping newspapers, bad breath, perspiration, taut shoulders, and gritted teeth. The rush hour was in full spate. Bank tube station resembled an ant's nest as hundreds poured out, eager to fire up their computers and check the world markets before they opened.

Meanwhile, back home in Phillimore Gardens in West London, Serena gave a quick brush to her sleek auburn hair, then dusted Freddie's crumbs from her colourful dress and slashed lipstick on her lips. She hugged her youngest son, Benjie, before Maggie the au pair swooped him up and led him into the kitchen.

Serena got into her jeep with the children for a quarrelsome school run. Five-year-old Freddie was trying to annoy eight-year-old Alicia in his usual manner.

There was a sudden screech of brakes and Serena yelled out of the window at a bus driver, "For God's sake! You've shattered my headlamp!"

The bus driver stopped and yelled back, "I haven't even touched your fucking headlight!"

He drove off furiously with lots of cars blasting their horns at being held up. A line of chauffeurs crawled round the school block looking for a gap to drop off their little passengers. Serena finally parked on a double yellow line and pulled the children from their seats.

"I guess Daddy won't be back tonight," Alicia sighed.

"No, he's working on a big project, he won't finish 'til about ten, darling," said Serena, whilst guiding Freddie through the school gates.

Loud "Byes!" were issued from parents as they waved off their offspring. Serena added hers to the chorus, and then walked back to the car.

"Oh! That's outrageous!" She ripped off the parking ticket. "I've only been here two minutes."

"Bad luck."

She recognised the soft voice over her shoulder and turned. "Hello Vivi, darling, I don't like getting cross so early in the morning."

"Let's have a coffee to calm you down," said Vivi. "Meet you at Starbucks in ten minutes."

Vivi's serene nature always helped her sister wind down a bit.

"Two cappuccinos please," Serena ordered and then they sat down together.

"So, how's life?" asked Vivi, running her fingers through her long dark hair.

Serena rolled her eyes. "Lang's working so late every evening now. We rarely go out, but I'm having a dinner party tonight with a few friends even though he'll be late. How's Theo?"

"In Moscow, of course. He's got a new agent who's booked various concerts in Europe. Bella's given up turning down his side of the bed! Thank goodness I've got her, she's such a help with the children" said Vivi, her warm brown eyes smiling.

"How is Georgie, by the way?" asked Serena. "Freddie told me she sang a solo at school the other day." Serena's mobile rang. "Oh God, that's this awful actress complaining about the curtains I've just designed. Must go. See you later darling, at school."

After a full day working in the office of her interior design company, Serena returned home around 6.30pm to find Maggie the au pair trying to pacify Benjie who was screaming in his cot, while Alicia slopped around in a pair of Serena's Jimmy Choos.

"Come on you lot. I've got people coming over at eight."

Serena hurried into the kitchen and started preparing dinner when the phone rang.

"Hello brother dear, how are you? This weekend? Yes, that would be fun. Can't get rid of the kids though, so they'll have to come too. OK, Jonty, see you Saturday."

Serena almost hit Alicia as she turned swiftly to put a saucepan on.

"Mummy, can I have some of yesterday's apple pie?"

Benjie's screams echoed throughout the house.

"Yes darling, get it yourself and take some yoghurt if you want."

Serena dashed upstairs to calm Benjie. She held him tight and he instantly stopped screaming and snuggled into her chest.

"Here you go, darling."

She wrapped him in his favourite cuddly shawl and smiled when she saw his eyes flicker. Gently, she laid him down on the bed before creeping slowly out of the room.

The doorbell rang just as Freddie kicked his ball into a vase of freesias on the hall table. Serena groaned and opened the door to the gas-meter man.

"Can you come back tomorrow please? I'm very busy now."

"Oh, look at Harry, Mum!" Freddie said excitedly.

Serena looked through to the dining room table in horror to see the hamster cage shedding sawdust as the creature whirled its wheel frantically. Serena screamed for Alicia, who rushed into the dining room.

"Alicia, help me with the table and put that damned cage in the cloakroom. Freddie, pick up those flowers. Do not touch the broken glass."

"But Mum, I want to watch—"

"Do as I say *at once!*" Serena yelled, returning to the kitchen where a dreadful smell of burnt fat and smoke was billowing out of the oven. The turkey was sizzling as she transferred it to a new dish.

"All done. Do you need me to do anything else?" Alicia asked.

"Please tell Maggie to put Freddie to bed, I'll be up in a minute. Oh, and can you tell her to take care of the broken glass?"

"Of course." Alicia manoeuvred round the dining table, dominated by a large candelabra.

"I'm coming now, Freddie."

Turning the oven down, Serena hurried upstairs to find water everywhere as Freddie was naked in the empty bath tub, shooting his water pistol into everyone's slippers. Freddie was a rather hyperactive child, so she tried hard to accept his often difficult behaviour.

Serena sighed. "You should be in bed. Come on, jump onto my back."

There was a squeal of delight as she ran along the passage and lowered him onto his Batman duvet. Serena then stroked his brow (which he loved) for a few moments, turned out the light and quickly went downstairs. She set the table and lit the candles, and soon the room smelt of jasmine.

She was just flicking a comb through her hair when the doorbell chimed, and a gaggle of voices noisily arrived.

"Hello Dee. Wow, what a tan! Where have you been?" Serena asked.

They pecked on the cheek, leaving mild red smudges.

"Jed had a big photo shoot in Malta, so he dragged me along to help with the makeup," she replied.

"Hello love." Ash smiled as he hugged Serena. "Haven't seen you since that crazy bash in Lambeth." He winked at her.

Serena laughed. "I'll just get the Champers. Could you open it for me please, Ash? Maggie dear, hand round the olives."

They all wandered into the sitting room. Serena smiled as she looked at her friends. It was nice to have the house full of adult conversation.

"Cheers to us!" said Dee.

Soon gossip was buzzing from one animated face to another. Serena's slim body manoeuvred between them, filling glasses.

"Yes, I've finally fallen pregnant." Libby stroked her velvet-clad tummy.

"Congratulations. I'll be able to show you all the best baby fashions and prams." Serena gave Libby a brief hug as her mobile hummed. Her husband's name flashed on the screen.

"Lang? Oh, you poor thing, still at it? Remember we've got friends here for supper. I'll keep something warm for you. OK, bye darling."

Serena briefly wondered why Lang was working so late, but dismissed the thought.

"Come on, let's eat. Sit where you like."

She lifted the turkey out of the oven. Maggie meanwhile had put all the veg on a large oval plate.

After serving everyone, Serena felt soothed by the warmth of friends and wine. She was a relaxed hostess, at her happiest when entertaining. Suddenly there was a thud, then a scream from above.

"That's Freddie falling out of bed again. Excuse me."

As she turned to go upstairs she caught sight of Ash rubbing Dee's ankle with his foot. *Strange,* she thought. *I barely see them talk.*

Poor Freddie was lying sprawled across the floor with a bloody nose.

"I had a nightmare, Mummy. Three sharks were trying to eat me."

Serena dabbed the messy nose and put him gently back to bed.

"I'll leave the light on. Try and dream about something nice, like Willy Wonka's chocolate factory." She kissed him tenderly on the forehead.

The laughter downstairs grew louder. Ash was telling one of his risqué jokes no doubt. The phone in her own bedroom rang. She ran down to the hall and picked it up.

"Hello. . . Vivi, what's wrong? Oh my God, how dreadful. Did they take anything? You poor darling and Theo's away in Russia, isn't he?" Vivi was sobbing at the other end of the phone. "Is your house keeper there? And you've called the police? I'm so sorry love, I just can't come around. I'm in the middle of a dinner party and Lang isn't home yet and the kids are in bed. I'll send him a message to pop round when he's back, shall I?"

"Yes, please do," Vivi replied tearfully.

The phone went dead. Serena stared at it, wondering if she should cancel the dinner and attend to her sister but then she dismissed the thought. The police will be on the way. She sent a text to Lang explaining briefly what happened. He would be there to support her sister. There was no point upsetting her guests.

Serena went back into the dining room. Maggie was filling up everyone's glasses and the conversation was bubbling. She started to relax and enjoy the evening.

Jed stroked Serena's bangled arm and said, "This is a fab gathering."

A short while later, Lang arrived in the doorway, his weary eyes gazing at the merriment.

"Hello there, you seem to be having a good time."

"That was quick! Come and join us." Serena got up and slid an arm round his shoulder. "You know everyone here; you met them all at the Lambeth do. How's Vivi?"

Lang smiled and retreated to the kitchen feeling a little remote and shy at the boozy gathering. Serena came to join him.

"So, how is she?"

"Who?" Lang frowned.

"Vivi! I texted you to check on her. Poor thing has been burgled and she's in an awful state. Theo's in Russia."

"Oh no! I'll go and check if she and the kids are all right," Lang suggested.

"Thank you love, I mean there is no way I can go, can I?" Serena said, gesturing back towards the full dining room.

Lang felt like falling into bed, but smiled and nodded realising that this meant he could avoid being at the dinner party a while longer.

Chapter Two

Chiswick

Twenty minutes later, Lang drove hurriedly into Chiswick Mall, noticing the full moon stretched across a low tide. He parked under some huge willow trees and rang the gold Venetian bell beside a large oak door, which was opened almost at once.

There was Vivi in a deep purple gown, her long black hair falling over her right shoulder. The vulnerable pain in her eyes almost made him gasp.

"Oh Vivi, you poor girl. You must have been terrified. Tell me how it happened," said Lang, putting his arm round her shoulders.

They walked into a beautiful high-ceilinged room with richly brocaded curtains and scarlet and gold wallpaper. Lots of urns and carved tables gave the huge room an ornate atmosphere. A grand piano dominated the back of the room. He sank into a vast sofa.

Vivi, who looked exhausted, remained standing and immediately started retelling the events in a quavering voice, "I was lying in the basement Jacuzzi meditating. I'd lit candles to give a soft light. Suddenly, I saw a face at the long French windows. A man was waving a knife in the air, threatening me. I screamed and pressed the alarm bell. Bella came rushing in, asking, what was the matter and handed me a towel. I yelled at her to call the police."

"What time did all this happen?" Lang asked gently.

"Oh, about 8.30. I haven't finished. The police arrived as soon as the burglars had left. They surrounded the garden and found a single trainer." Vivi explained, with panic in her voice. "Georgie and Jago were up there while the thieves ransacked our rooms. Can you imagine what might have happened to them?" She started sobbing quietly.

Lang took her hand. "What did they take?" he whispered.

"Two very valuable Russian miniatures that came from Theo's mother and some of my jewellery."

"Have you rung Theo?"

"Yes, but I couldn't get through, so I sent a text instead."

The housekeeper, Bella, knocked on the door and came in with a tray. "Your husband rang on the upstairs line to say he couldn't get through to you, Ma'am. Is the phone off the hook?"

Vivi replaced the handset that had been knocked out of place in the commotion. Bella hastily scuttled out of the room.

"Tea?" offered Vivi.

"No thanks, but I do wish I could help you in some way," Lang replied.

She turned away. "You're very kind to have come over, let alone listen to me."

There was an awkward silence.

"This is the most beautiful room; such vibrant colours, yet so peaceful."

"Yes, I don't see my clients here. I've got a calmer room upstairs." Vivi pointed upwards, a slim arm extending from her gown. "A lot of my people seem to need me at present." The phone rang. "Hello Theo. . ."

Lang got up, kissed her on the forehead and mouthed, 'I'll ring you tomorrow,' as he left, not wanting to be in the way.

"Hello, Vivi dear, what's happening? You sounded very stressed in the text I got," Theo said.

Over the next five minutes Vivi described the incident again. "Thank goodness Lang popped over. Serena was entertaining and couldn't leave her guests. It was such a relief, just to talk to someone. I'm pretty scared here tonight. I just wish this hadn't happened while you were away." Vivi was weary and feeling vulnerable. They carried on talking; about what the police had said, about changing the locks on various doors. "I do miss you, and little Georgie wakes up asking if Daddy is back."

"I'll be home soon after the Tchaikovsky concert. Take care darling, I love you." Theo added, "And please stay safe, Vivi. I don't know what I would do without you."

Come home now, Vivi wanted to say but instead she replied, "I will darling. Speak soon."

Chapter Three

Kensington

Serena's hangover made her even more flustered than usual.

"We're going to Aylesbury this evening to stay with Jonty and Cheryl. Did I mention it last night?" she said to Lang, which annoyed him because that meant he'd have to leave work early.

The school run was ear-shattering, each child snatching something from the other. Serena parked the car outside the school gates just as her mobile rang. She blocked one ear as she held the phone up to the other.

"Vivi! How are you and the kids after last night?" She shouted over the noise.

"Not good. Georgie's come out in spots and Jago's got a cough. Could you pop in today? I'd so love to see you," asked Vivi hopefully.

"I can't. This famous actress has asked me to start a big job on her penthouse. So sorry my love, but then we're off to see Jonty and Cheryl tonight. Why don't you come down too?"

"Goodness, what fun that would be, but I've got a client on Saturday morning and the kids are too ill to leave. Give them my love. By the way, they've caught a suspect whose trainer matched the one left behind," said Vivi.

"That's quick work. Must dash, darling. I'll ring from Aylesbury. Big hug!"

Serena suddenly realised that Alicia and Freddie had crept out of the car and into school during her brief conversation. She whisked Benjie up and rushed in to see if they were actually in their classrooms. Freddie was in his class lying on the floor with five other boys, blowing bits of paper about. When Serena peeped in Alicia's class, she was sitting on a desk and locked in a gossip with three giggling girls. Serena knew she ought to tell them both to sit properly and be quiet, but really weren't they now the teacher's problem?

After a very hectic day seeing several clients, Serena arrived home around 6pm, threw various clothes into a suitcase, then packed a large box full of toys and wellies. As she finished packing, Lang arrived looking dishevelled and ashen. The children rushed up and hugged him, twining themselves round his knees.

"Good day?" asked Serena.

"Had better," muttered Lang under his breath.

Serena wanted to push for more details, because something about Lang's expression tugged at her nerves, but there were the children to round up and the car to load.

Later, she promised herself. *Once we're in Aylesbury and the children are in bed, I'll get to the bottom of this. . .*

Chapter Four

Aylesbury

Their drive to her brother's house in Aylesbury was long and tedious and they arrived at Jonty's just after 10pm. A roaring fire greeted them. Outside, the gusty April wind whistled through the lattice windows and made the low-beamed ceiling seem heavy and dark. It was a cosy room to relax in, as the steaming logs crackled and spurted in the huge fireplace.

"How was your journey?" asked Jonty, after they'd bundled the sleeping little ones off to bed. He smiled through his shaggy beard.

"Rather slow. We saw an awful accident on the other carriageway, just after Berkhamsted," said Serena.

"Have you heard about Vivi being burgled?" Lang asked.

"Yes, I've just talked to her on the phone. She sounded quite shaken, poor thing," said Jonty.

"I saw her last night. Went over to try and comfort her. She's a remarkable person. So serene. It must be the job she does—counselling people all day," said Lang.

"I tried to persuade her to come down here, but she's got clients tomorrow—so dedicated," Serena said.

Cheryl carried in a tray of glasses and some homemade elderflower wine. Lang took a glass. "This will warm you up. It's Jonty's latest brew and quite potent."

Serena settled in a chair by the fire and looked fondly at her brother. "How's the lambing, JJ?"

"Good but it's been really hectic," said Jonty

"Oh, and we're also looking after a couple of two-day-old lambs whose mother died!" added Cheryl. "We keep them warm by the Aga and bottle-feed them."

"And the pony club?" enquired Lang.

"That's *very* busy," Cheryl continued. "About twenty disabled children come to ride every day."

"Yes, she's a wonderful teacher and the kids adore her," said Jonty radiantly.

Lang and Serena felt mellow after the third glass of homemade wine.

"What about the great forest? How many trees have you planted this year?" enquired Lang sleepily.

"It's coming along well. I've planted one hundred oaks, three hundred alders and two hundred ash. Of course, I'll not see them in my time, but *your* children will." There was a sad tinge in his voice in the knowledge that he and Cheryl could never have children themselves.

A squeal came from upstairs.

"That's Freddie. I'll be off to bed when I've seen to him." Serena hugged Jonty, then Cheryl, and went upstairs. Lang had fallen asleep on the sofa.

*

The next morning, Alicia and Freddie were competing to see who could smash their eggshells into the smallest pieces. Bits were flying everywhere. Cheryl was at the back of her large kitchen preparing animal food. Serena and Lang had enjoyed early morning pleasures (uninterrupted) and were languidly getting dressed. Benjie was singing to himself in his cot next door.

Downstairs, Jonty plonked his muddy wellies by the back door.

"Would you like to have a tractor ride later?" he asked Freddie and Alicia.

"Oooh, yes please!" they cried.

Hearing a loud clattering of hooves in the stable yard they looked out of the window.

"Look, that boy's only got one leg," said Freddie in amazement. Large blobs of egg were dripping off his spoon and dribbling down his T-shirt.

"And that little girl with bunches has only got half an arm and she's riding sideways," exclaimed Alicia.

"Yes, that's seven-year-old Mandy and Olly who's eight. They've been coming here for nearly two years and love the rides. How they squeal when the ponies go through puddles and splash them," Cheryl said. "Perhaps you can help me put on the other children's hats and boots?"

Their eager faces giggled with excitement as Cheryl handed them a cloth.

"Here, wipe your hair. Egg seems to be tangled in your curls," she said to Alicia.

Jonty walked over clutching a lamb under each arm. "Would you like to see these two feeding?"

"They're so sweet! Can I hold one?" asked Alicia. She clutched a quivering lamb and stroked its forehead.

"Come on, let's go to the ponies," suggested Cheryl as she led both children out to the yard. "This is Lara who helps me every day and that's Ed who only works here at weekends. He's showing your mummy the best pony."

Serena was holding Benjie who wriggled hard, trying to pull the tail of the pony Ed was grooming. Cheryl was busy pulling on riding boots for the waiting children. Alicia handed out hats and made sure the straps were fastened tightly.

The cool sun stretched across quiet fields, which seemed to be openly waiting for spring.

Later, after the students had gone, Alicia and Freddie were helped onto the ponies. Ed led Freddie, and Cheryl guided Alicia to the paddock. Suddenly, Freddie's pony was startled by a rabbit racing across his path. He swerved to the side and Ed had to stop him sliding off. Everyone laughed as Ed pulled him from the pony, handing him to Serena to help comfort him.

Alicia was learning to trot and beamed with pride as Cheryl coaxed her on. She seemed a natural rider. After an hour, everyone wandered back to the house and tucked into shepherd's pie.

Meanwhile, Lang, who had gone for a walk, reached the edge of Jonty's forest. It was breath-taking. He gazed at the various trees, not planted in rows but scattered randomly. The oaks already dominated the whole area. The closer he got to nature the more Lang eased up. Right there, tranquillity pervaded his soul as he absorbed the silence for a while. Reluctantly, he headed back to the farmhouse where Benjie was running about the yard chasing kittens.

"Can we have a kitten Daddy?" he exclaimed excitedly.

Lang smiled and walked into the large sitting room to hear Serena on the phone to Vivi.

"Oh, you poor thing! Everything seems to be happening to you while Theo's away. Can't you persuade him to come home early? A visa problem? So, it's a torn ligament? How on earth did that happen? At her gym class. Poor Georgie. . . does it mean plaster?"

Lang intervened and took the mobile. "I know someone in the Foreign Office. Would it help if I spoke to him?"

"Yes, yes please, anything that will get him back home soon," replied Vivi anxiously.

"I'll speak to Robert on Monday and see if he can pull any strings. I do hope Georgie recovers quickly." Lang handed the phone back to Serena.

Alicia rushed in. "Daddy, I've been trotting on a lovely pony."

"And I nearly fell off because of a silly rabbit," interrupted Freddie.

After an enormous roast lunch, with no television in the house, everyone either read or played games. Cheryl took Alicia to her Arts and Crafts shop where Hilary, Ed's mum, was working. Cheryl demonstrated the process of spinning wool, then taught Alicia the basics of knitting. Alicia was amazed and began to knit slowly all by herself.

Cheryl was so clever at engaging the kids and she was especially fond of Alicia who she hoped would come and stay more often as she grew older.

On Sunday afternoon, Lang sat in the drawing room waiting for a chance to talk with Jonty who sauntered in, hay sticking out of his hair and jacket.

"The children loved the tractor ride. They so enjoy this place and we love having them," he announced. "Try this home-made brew, it's got quite a kick."

After a couple of drinks, Lang loosened up. "Can I tell you something?"

Jonty raised his eyebrows and sat down. "What is it?" he asked slowly.

"I've done something really stupid," Lang said, holding his head in his hands. "I've borrowed way over my limit and I've been trying so hard to keep it from Serena."

Jonty looked horrified. "Are you serious?"

Lang looked up and nodded. His face paler than usual. Then he suddenly asked, "You couldn't lend me a hundred thousand for six months, could you? By that time, I'm sure I'll be able to pay you back."

Jonty abruptly stood up and poured another large drink. "I'm afraid I can't possibly lend you anything like that much money because all I have is tied up in the farm and forest."

"Yes, of course, I understand. Please don't breathe a word of this to anyone, especially Serena. I shouldn't have asked," urged Lang, his bottom lip trembling.

The phone rang, making him jump. Jonty answered it, breaking the tension.

"Hello? Who? Yes, he's just here."

Lang froze in terror, hardly able to grasp the phone.

"Hello," he said hesitantly. "Yes, hello Mike. Who? Bill Yates? A heart attack?" Lang, whose face showed a mixture of relief and anxiety at this shocking news, seemed unable to think properly. "Tonight? Yes, of course, but I'm in Aylesbury so we won't get back until about 6pm. I'll come straight in."

After a few minutes he put the phone down, utterly relieved that the call didn't concern his own money troubles and turned to Jonty.

"The Chairman has had a heart attack and he's in intensive care. We'll have to leave straight away so I can go to the office and see to things. Jonty promise me, whatever happens you'll look after Serena and the kids, won't you?" Lang begged.

Jonty nodded. "Yes, of course. She is my sister after all." He exhaled hard. "I'm just grateful that Cheryl and I live peacefully with a family of trees instead of children in this lovely countryside. Our only problems happen when some sheep go missing. Mind you, I would have loved to have had kids, a son to take over the farm and leave the forest to." Jonty smiled sadly. "I guess we all have our own problems to manage. . . I won't say a word. I'll go and get some fresh eggs for you to take home."

"Jonty?"

Jonty turned round and locked eyes with Lang.

"Please don't tell anyone what I told you."

Reluctantly Jonty nodded his head, "I promised you. I won't say a word." As he entered the fresh air outside Jonty breathed a sigh of relief that he didn't have these issues—or secrets—with Cheryl.

Chapter Five

Chiswick

Theo turned the key and slowly pushed open his heavy front door. It was 4pm. There was an unexpected silence. He felt uneasy. Where were the children to welcome him? The living room door was ajar, and Bella lay on the couch half asleep in front of the television.

"Hello, there," Theo said softly.

She was startled and jumped out of her chair. "Hello, what a surprise." Bella took his coat. "There's no one here, they're all at the hospital with Georgie. She's getting better now, but she's still in traction. Oh, it's been such a worry for poor Mrs Vivi."

Bella wrote down the hospital address for him. "Shall I order a taxi for you?"

Theo was only now realising the enormity of the situation. He didn't think Georgie would still be in hospital. "Yes please," he murmured.

His tall, elegant frame stooped as if carrying a heavy load. Pushing back his thick blond hair he wandered towards the front door. "I'll wait here, Bella."

Once at the hospital, Theo looked around frantically for his family.

"Could you tell me which ward Georgie Hanover is on, please?" he asked a nurse at the front desk.

As he climbed the stairs to the third-floor anxiety hung heavy inside him.

"Here's Daddy!" shouted Georgie. "You've come home at last!"

"What a lovely surprise," said Vivi. She was smiling but it looked strained. "We've certainly needed you."

Theo hugged Vivi warmly then kissed little Jago who pulled his hair, giggling.

"And how is my little princess?" he asked Georgie.

"I'm sort of alright apart from my aching arm. I want to come home, Daddy."

"You will in a couple of days," interrupted a smiling nurse, taking the temperature in Georgie's ear.

An hour later, having left a forlorn Georgie, Vivi drove them home, handed Jago to Bella to be bathed, then settled down for a quick drink with Theo.

"So, how was Russia? I haven't even asked."

"Great," he replied. "I've had some very successful concerts and the audiences were fantastic. In Moscow, I played both of Tchaikovsky's piano concertos."

Vivi hadn't seen him this elated for a long time yet was disappointed he hadn't asked her about the burglary, so she brought the subject up herself.

"The police have suggested some safety locks on the upstairs doors and windows," she explained.

"You poor, dear girl, it must have been a terrifying experience for you. I'm sorry I wasn't here," Theo said sympathetically.

"Theo, you've no idea how scared I was, seeing this face at the window when I was relaxing in the Jacuzzi. He had a knife in his hand and was sneering at me. Bella called the police. I can't believe the other two had the cheek to get in upstairs where the kids were asleep. I've hardly slept a wink since. Must you go away so often?"

"Oh darling, I know it's hard at the moment, but Vivi, this could be the biggest concert of my life in Moscow and I'll probably have to go several more times after that," he said. "Sergei, my new promoter, has asked me to play in St Petersburg to replace a pianist who's ill next week. It's an opportunity I just can't pass up."

Vivi remained silent, amazed that he would be returning to Russia again so soon with everything that was going on at home.

"Perhaps I might come with you one time when things have calmed down?"

There was a gentle knock before Bella popped her head around the door. "Would you like to say goodnight to Jago?"

Theo readily went up to the nursery where Jago stood eagerly in his bed. Meanwhile, Vivi picked up the phone to call Lang.

"Just to let you know that Theo has returned at last! There's no need to bother your friend at the foreign office."

"I was actually meant to call you," replied Lang. "I found out today that my friend did investigate the visa thing and found there was no problem, the visa was perfectly valid." There was silence. "Are you still there?" asked Lang gently.

"Yes, you are very kind to have helped...night Lang."

Vivi put the phone down. Her hand began to tremble, so she clenched her fist to stop it. She squeezed tight, so her nails were digging into her hand.

Why did Theo lie about his visa if there was no issue? And with the burglary and Georgie's accident, what kept him so long from home when he was needed here?

Chapter Six

Kensington

The next morning, Serena asked Maggie to bring Benjie to the hallway for a quick goodbye hug. Monday mornings were always frenetic. As she drove down to Kensington High Street twenty minutes later, she suddenly spotted a notice, 'Water works begin Monday morning.' She cursed under her breath.

"God, I'm going to be so fucking late."

When she finally arrived at the school gate, everyone was battling to park. It was like dodgem cars at the fair.

"I see your brother has a page in *The Times* today," yelled Simon, another parent who Serena had only ever spoken to on the school run.

"Really, what about?" replied Serena through the car window.

"A lovely article about the forest he's planted. Page five in *Times 2,*" said Simon, now alongside in his car as they inched towards the school gates.

"Ghastly traffic, I've got to be at the office in fifteen minutes," Serena growled.

"I'll take them in," Simon offered.

"Would you?" Both cars drew up onto the pavement where Serena undid the seat belts and plonked Alicia and Freddie into Simon's large Land Rover, calling, "Thanks! Bye!" as both kids scrambled onto the back seats.

Twenty minutes later, when Serena rushed into her spacious

office in Notting Hill, Gems, her assistant, approached her looking grave.

"There's been a flood at Le Harvre's penthouse. Plumbing problem. It's ruined the new carpet you laid on Thursday."

"Oh hell! Nothing's going well in that bloody job, I wish I'd never taken it on. She's a tricky woman and I think she'll explode when she hears about this accident."

Serena's mobile rang as she sank into her favourite office chair. It was, as predicted, Poppy Le Harvre, livid about the flood.

"Look, it's not *my* fault. It's an unforeseen accident. I'm not apologising as it has nothing to do with my interior decorating! The insurance company will pay, and I'll get the floor dried out as soon as possible."

Serena threw her mobile into the rubbish bin, leaving it ringing incessantly amongst the waste paper.

"Gems, be a love and get hold of the insurance company. Then find the firm that dries out damp with their huge fans. What's it called? Blow Dry, I think. Ask them to send someone to meet me at the penthouse, 12 Moon Street, tomorrow morning at 9.00. I'm going to Peter Jones now to look through curtain fabrics for Cheyne Street. Leave my mobile in the basket till tomorrow, I can't bear any more yelling. See you tomorrow."

An hour later, Gems received an urgent call from school asking for someone to pick up Alicia. She had been violently sick, and they couldn't reach Serena on her mobile. Gems reassured the teacher that Serena would be there in about an hour. Luckily, the loyal assistant found her boss in Peter Jones surrounded by masses of samples and talking to the saleswomen.

"Sorry to interrupt, but Alicia's been sick. The school want you to collect her now," reported Gems gently.

Serena groaned and headed out of the store.

Half an hour later, with a deathly-pale-faced Alicia in the back seat, they drove home. Amidst the chaos, Lang had left an urgent message on the home phone's answering machine. Hastily settling Alicia on the sofa, Serena rang him back.

"Hello, my beautiful Fig Tree. Amazing news! I've been promoted to the board as a result of Bill Yates' death."

"Oh Lang, how fantastic. Congratulations! We can book that holiday now!" Serena replied excitedly.

"Yes, maybe, don't rush me," Lang snapped, thinking anxiously about his secret problem. "Of course, I'll have to stay late this evening and sort out my new office."

Serena felt disappointed that her loneliness every night would continue. "Try and be back by 8.30," she pleaded.

By 6pm, the office was empty except for the contract cleaners. Lang wondered what he should do about his illegal borrowing and whether they would be discovered now he'd been promoted. He sat in his new black leather armchair internally terrified and anxiously wondering how he could sustain the fraud.

The new Chairman, Bob Calder, popped his head round the door. "Pleased with your promotion? You'll find life even more hectic than usual, I'm afraid," he said, smiling.

"Mmm. . ." Lang managed in reply.

It took a couple of hours to move his things to the new office, in particular the contents of his secret drawer. As he was carefully locking them away he heard a loud commercial hoover in the corridor and quickly pocketed the key.

The cleaner backed into the office followed by her hoover. "Evening sir. You're working late. The whole place is empty 'cept for you and the Chairman." The stout African lady brazenly grinned at him.

Lang smiled tautly and walked to the lift.

*

Langs mobile jangled. "Yes, I'm almost home," he said before hanging up.

"Hello my love." Serena put her arms round his neck as soon as he walked through the door. "Have you seen the wonderful picture and article in the paper about Jonty's forest? I must ring him." She handed the paper to Lang.

"Wow! That's great publicity," said Lang impressed.

"I'm just going to check on the kids." Serena hurriedly ran down the hall while Lang lay back on the sofa. He felt like his brain was buzzing. He buried his head in a cushion, and fell asleep.

An hour later Serena was shaking him awake. Jonty wanted to talk to him.

"Congratulations about your promotion—wonderful news." Jonty's elated voice brought him awake fast.

"Yes, it's quite a responsibility," said Lang, then added, "I see you're in *The Times* today!"

"Yes, it was such a surprise *and* Prince Charles has invited me to Buck House to tell him about the project." Lang had never heard Jonty so excited. "Mind you, I don't want people wandering over my forest yet. Everything's very tender during the early growing years. Publicity isn't always good."

"Of course," Lang replied pensively. "Oh, here's Serena, I'll pass you over."

"Big hug, clever brother. I'm going to have to dash, Lang hasn't even had dinner yet. . . okay, you too. Bye." She turned to her husband. "This is an exciting day! How did everyone at the office take it?"

"Oh. . . you know. Listen love, I'm rather tired—can we catch up tomorrow?" Lang forced a yawn to emphasise the point and tried to ignore the guilt at the disappointed face of his wife.

"Aren't you hungry?"

"I'm fine," Lang said, standing up. He kissed her on the forehead before hurrying out of the room, wiping his sweaty palms on his blazer.

*

Alicia was sitting quietly in front of Serena's bedroom mirror, daubing mascara on her eyelashes. She looked like a witch's daughter.

"What *are* you doing, Alicia?" Serena asked, crossing her arms.

"I'm practising for the school play. I've got to look like a Mummy so I'm copying you!" Her serious face made Serena laugh.

"Oh, little Popsy, shall I help you?" She wiped off the mess and started to outline Alicia's beautiful dark eyes.

"Yes, Mummy, but don't make me look cross like you do on the school run," stated Alicia.

"Cheeky!"

"Can you paint me, too?" asked Freddie, dripping wet from the bath.

"Oh darling, I've only got one pair of hands. Where's Daddy?"

"Doing a poo on the loo," said Freddie.

Monday night was always chaotic because it was Maggie's day off. All the kids were enjoying Daddy being around at bedtime; a very rare event.

Just then his plaintive voice called out, "Where the hell are the loo rolls?"

Freddie laughed. "I threw them downstairs because they fell in the bath while I was making an engine."

"There's one under the basin," shouted Serena.

Eventually, Lang tucked up Alicia and went downstairs to find Serena chatting to Gems on the phone. He poured himself a large martini, sat on the sofa, and waited.

Once she'd finished, she let out a long sigh. "Sorry, I've had a dreadful day and was trying to sort out tomorrow. I had to leave the office early because Alicia was sick at school, then Poppy Le Harvre's new house was flooded so she was screaming down the phone at me to get it dried out immediately and—" Serena clapped her hands. "Pour me a vodka and tonic, would you?"

"Well, I've been busy too. The new office is big and the phone rings non-stop. Lots of people demanding meetings. I don't even know half their names."

"But at least it means lots of extra money for your Fig Tree to spend," purred Serena. "Oh! Which reminds me—it's Ascot next week. I'll buy a new outfit. Are we going in the Bentley?" She rambled on so excitedly that Lang found it hard to break in.

"Steady on darling, I don't exactly know yet *how* much more I'll earn, but we've also got quite a bit of debt, remember," he said seriously.

Serena jumped on his lap. "Come on. Loosen up a bit. You're always too cautious." She raised his chin to kiss him.

"Okay, we'll do Ascot. But not on Thursday. That's Bill Yates' funeral." Lang stroked Serena's neck and they were about to kiss when Freddie ran in.

"Mummy, I'm so thirsty. You forgot my drink."

Serena rolled her eyes, disentangled herself and picked him up.

"Night night, Daddy," grinned the boy's impish face.

Lang lay back and read the article about Jonty's forest wishing he could leave a simpler life like his brother in law.

Chapter Seven

Chiswick

Vivi and Theo arrived at the Chelsea & Westminster hospital just after midday. Georgie raced towards them as they entered the ward with her arm still in a sling.

"I'm so much better now! I'm coming home," she announced.

"Yes, she's ready to be discharged," the nurse said.

Vivi handed her a large bunch of flowers. "Thank you for all your care."

"You're welcome," said the nurse.

"You've been such a good girl. Let's buy you a pretty dress on the way home," suggested Theo as they walked down a long corridor together towards the lifts.

"Ooh yes, but where's Jago?" Georgie asked.

"He's at home with Bella playing trains," replied Vivi.

They all arrived back at the house about teatime, exhausted and happy. Jago jumped into Vivi's arms.

"There've been several calls for you, Mr Theo," Bella said handing him a list of messages.

"Right, I'm off to my study. Let me know when it's story time," Theo said and Vivi nodded.

"The children's tea is ready," said Bella.

"I'm starving. Can I have fish and chips?" Georgie said eagerly.

The doorbell rang.

"Special delivery," said a rough-faced man holding his crash helmet. "Sign 'ere." His dirty finger pointed to 'Theo Hanover.'

"Thank you." Vivi signed and shut the door. "Take this to Daddy please, Georgie, then play in your room while I see a patient upstairs for an hour."

The doorbell rang again and Vivi opened the door to see an elegant, sandy-haired lady.

"Hello Mrs Jackson, do come in."

Vivi showed her into a long room with various armchairs draped in red and purple throws. White curtains billowed softly from large open windows and the floor was covered in rush matting.

"Please sit down." Vivi pointed to a deep-seated sofa, as she took her notebook from a small desk nearby. "How've you been since I saw you two weeks ago?"

Half an hour later the delicate discussion came to an end. As Vivi opened the door for Mrs Jackson to leave, she picked up a note from Theo. He'd suddenly been called to the Academy to discuss a possible tour of Paris and Vienna after his Moscow appearance. Vivi didn't know how to feel. She was happy for him but also annoyed. *He is leaving us again.*

When he reappeared, Jago was screaming his head off. Bella handed him the boy, who immediately stopped yelling as Theo began singing funny songs.

"Ahh, you're back," Vivi said, taking Jago from him. "Georgie's just getting out of the bath. Meeting go well?" She hoped her voice sounded calm.

"Yes, it was an extremely good session," he said avoiding her eyes before bounding upstairs to see Georgie.

Chapter Eight

Kensington

During breakfast, Lang announced, "We're taking the office Bentley to Ascot on the 12th. So, it's all black for Yates' funeral on the 11th and lovely colourful dress and big hat for the Friday."

He beamed as Serena ran around the table and hugged him. The children, scoffing Rice Krispies, were too busy to react. Lang kissed each one as he left in haste.

"Come on," urged Serena.

She gave Alicia her lunch box. Freddie dropped his. The hardboiled egg rolled under the kitchen table collecting pencil-sharpener shavings.

"Oh Freddie, what a mess."

Serena wiped the egg, wrapped it in a lettuce leaf and put it back in the box. They said goodbye to little Benjie in Maggie's arms and rushed out to the car.

After the usual battle of the school run, Serena walked into an empty office to find her mobile ringing incessantly on her desk.

"Hello, Mrs Bagshot. Have your builders finished? Oh good. I've got various samples to show you. Shall we meet next week, say Tuesday at the flat?"

"Glad your mobile's working!" Gems laughed. "It didn't like being in the waste paper basket getting tangled up in all the rubbish."

"I've got to buy a dress and hat for Ascot next week due to Lang's promotion. We're going in the firm's Bentley—it's so exciting!" Serena clapped her hands at the prospect of a spending spree. "Can you answer my calls? And if Le Harvre phones tell her I'm away on business."

After three and a half hours, she arrived home in a chic red dress and a large hat with peacock feathers, but no one was in to show off too, so she drove back to the office and paraded about for Gems instead.

"Wow, now *that* is fantastic!" Gems exclaimed.

"I must ring Lang to tell him about the hat," announced Serena.

"He rang. He'll be busy until the evening," said Gems.

"Oh hell! Typical!" exploded Serena.

Chapter Nine

City of London

Lang's office

Unlocking his desk drawer, Lang read over the documents in a green folder and made some notes before cautiously returning them to the drawer and locking it again.

"Rosie, would you ask the bookkeeper to bring the last six months' ledgers in?" he called.

Five minutes later, a tall, smartly dressed accountant entered Lang's new office.

"Good day Mr Ralm. Do sit down."

The two men went through the ledgers. Mr Ralm pointed out two rather large accounts, and asked whether they should be marked 'Overdue'.

"No. I'll tell you when," Lang replied abruptly.

He spent the rest of the day meeting people directly responsible to him, and discussing various problems but no matter who he was meeting or what he was working on, half his mind was in that locked drawer and on the accounts that should be marked overdue. . .

Chapter Ten

Kensington

When Lang arrived home, Serena was arguing on the phone with Poppy Le Harvre. "I've told you they're using a special machine to dry the floor out. I'll be in the office tomorrow at 9am. Please don't ring me at home again!" She slammed the phone down and shouted to Lang, "Don't move! I want to show you something," before rushing into the next room.

She came sweeping in, adorned in the low-cut red brocade dress with a shimmering hat of blue-green peacock feathers, waving as she tottered on very high heel shoes.

"You look wonderful, my Fig Tree. Like royalty!"

Serena beamed, then suddenly said, "That reminds me. We must ring Jonty. He's got an invitation to discuss his forestry project with Prince Charles next week and wants to stay a few nights."

"He'll see his sister in all her feathers if he's here on Friday." Lang laughed.

"Let's take him to our special bistro—he'd love Bess and her fish soup. I'll ring him now."

Serena spent a good ten minutes laughing raucously with Jonty over the phone.

"Do you call him Your Royal Highness or Charlie?" she giggled. "Why didn't you accept his offer to stay at Highgrove? That's silly! You're not shy about trees for goodness sake! You know more than he does, I should think. Yes, see you next

Wednesday. Is Cheryl coming with you? Oh, of course. . . her riding lessons." After a few moments she put the phone down and exclaimed, "What a hectic time we've got coming up; Jonty's visit, Yates' funeral, then Ascot."

"I'll have to be in the office early all week, mind you," Lang said anxiously, as Alicia hurried into the room dressed as a chef carrying a tray of burnt chips.

"This is what we learnt in our cooking lesson, but the fish cake fell on the floor." She proudly handed Serena a charred chip on a fork, then gave Lang the others. "There you are, Daddy. That's your supper. Sorry there's no salt or tomato sauce. We're not allowed them at school."

"Thank you, sweet girl." Lang took the chips then hugged Alicia. "You're going to be a busy bee like your Mummy when you grow up."

"Why has Mum got that funny hat on? The shoes look like clown boots," said Alicia.

"I'm going to the races and all the ladies wear fun hats," said Serena and Alicia pulled a face.

Freddie marched into the room with a saucepan lid on his head, clacking two wooden spoons together. "I'm a guard at the palace."

Chapter Eleven

Chiswick

When Vivi arrived home, she sighed when she found a note from Theo who'd been called to yet another meeting at the Academy. Her first client wasn't due for a few minutes, so she wandered into the back garden. Jago was gazing at next door's cat chasing a bird up the tree. He was giggling and banging his chubby legs on the grass.

Bella came out with the pushchair. "It's going to rain soon, so I'll take him to the playground now."

The doorbell rang.

"That's Mr Grayton I expect," Vivi said, planting a kiss on Jago on her way to the front door.

A small thin man in his forties with a timid face stammered, "Sorry I'm late. Had a bit of trouble getting my boy off to school."

"Nice to see you. We'll go upstairs," said Vivi gently.

Having seen four patients that morning, she was mentally exhausted, and went into her meditation corner for half an hour. She wondered how Georgie was enjoying her first day back at school. The difficult problems of her patients had made her rather depressed. To take her mind off everything she went downstairs to prepare lunch.

Chapter Twelve

Kensington

When Jonty arrived on Wednesday evening, Alicia immediately tugged at his sleeve and Freddie zoomed in on his scooter. Serena mouthed 'sorry' for her excited children and Jonty smiled to show it was okay.

"Wow, what a welcome!" said Jonty.

"Where's Auntie Cheryl?" asked Alicia.

"She's looking after the ponies and baby lambs, but she sent you this homemade fudge, and some wool for you to crochet, Alicia."

"Thank you." Alicia jumped up to kiss his ruddy cheek.

"Can we come and see the lambs again?" asked Freddie, accidentally ramming his scooter into Jonty's left leg.

"Ow! Come any time. It'll be lovely to see you."

"Are you meeting Prince Charles tomorrow?" asked Serena.

"No. I'm meeting his group of forest advisers first, who are going to discuss species and show me slides of possible diseases. Then I meet Prince Charles on Thursday," said Jonty.

"Will you get his autograph please? He supports my favourite football club," Freddie asked eagerly.

"I'll try."

"Come on, bath time," said Maggie, with Benjie in her arms. "Hello, Mr JJ."

Freddie followed her out obediently.

"Alicia, go and finish your sums. I'll come and check them in ten minutes," said Serena.

Later, Jonty read Freddie a story, played draughts with Alicia, and finally sat down to enjoy a large drink with his sister.

"We'll have to wait at least another hour before Lang returns." Serena sighed.

Jonty froze at the mention of Lang's name, but Serena didn't notice.

"So, where's Lang? Does he always work late?" Jonty eventually asked.

"Yes, unfortunately it's the same every night," Serena said sadly.

"Let's have a look at your garden. How are those cuttings I gave you?" asked Jonty, changing the subject.

They walked through to the back, pushing open the French windows onto a highly scented patio where an overwhelming waft of mint reached them. Wild poppies swayed into lupins and daisies in a slight breeze.

"Your border is certainly vigorous."

"Yes, the gardeners have worked hard at it." Serena tapped him on the shoulder. "Come and see what's buzzing at the bottom of the garden." She guided him to a large shrub behind which there was a hive full of bees. "I bought it for Lang's birthday but he's never here to deal with them, so I take off the honey and Lang enjoys it. I'll give you a pot."

"You are an efficient girl," said Jonty proudly. "You ought to be living in the country like us."

Serena looked at him bewildered. *Live in the country! No way,* she thought to herself.

"Hi JJ. Sorry I'm so late." Lang walked tentatively towards them. "It's been such a hellish day. My boss—ex boss's—funeral's coming up and I've been asked to be a steward. Anyway, how are *you*? All ready to meet HRH?"

*

The funeral was rather laborious. Lang showed his business friends to their seats but knew none of Bill Yates' relatives, which made him feel guilty even though he knew he was being ridiculous. He wished it didn't have to come to this—Yates's death—for him to move up in the company. Lang sighed. For all he knew, being promoted could lead to everyone finding out his secret. He shook his head. It wasn't time to think of all that. Instead, he listened to two partners give good speeches about his predecessor.

Everyone met at the local pub afterwards, sharing stories of Yates, and he looked appreciatively at his wife, who looked elegant in a black velvet suit.

They got home to find Jonty lying on the floor pushing the controls on Freddie's train set, as engines whizzed round the sofas and tables. Freddie was screeching with excitement. Jonty hung his face round a chair.

"Hello you two. Looks like you need a big drink," said Jonty.

"Oh, I meant to ask, would you like us to organise transport for your royal do tomorrow, JJ? We've got an excellent local man called Mike," Serena suggested.

"Yes, please," replied Jonty. "How about you though? Won't you need him for Ascot?"

"Ah, *we* have other plans," came his sister's reply.

*

The next morning a shiny black Bentley arrived promptly at 11am. Waving goodbye to Benjie (clutched in Jonty's arms),

Serena slid onto the plush, white, leather seat carrying her colourful, wide-brimmed, feather hat.

"Shall I take that, madam?" offered the chauffeur, placing it gently on the front seat.

Lang slipped in beside Serena, looking very handsome in a grey top hat and tails. Smiling warmly, he put his arm round her as the car drove off.

Chapter Thirteen

Ascot

As they neared the Enclosure, the buzz of excitement increased while the jockeys paraded their horses.

"Quick, we must find our box," said Lang, anxiously pulling Serena along. Her peacock-feathered hat almost took off in the bustle and breeze. "Here we are, Number 118." He gently guided Serena up the narrow stairway.

"Hello, I'm Foster James, and this is my wife Mary," said a tall man who dwarfed Lang and Serena as they shook hands.

Everyone sat down hurriedly. The starter bell rang, and horses flew out of their stalls to excited yells. Serena found the noise electrifying and started to cheer.

Lang squeezed her hand trying to quieten her down. "People in the boxes don't yell—sshhh—you've not backed a horse yet," he whispered.

"I know, but I'm sure that grey stallion's going to win."

Serena was getting carried away, standing up and waving her scarf as the horse galloped in first.

"You seem very excited! Did you have a bet on him?" asked Foster James.

"No," confessed Serena, "I just knew he'd win. Will you put a bet on Jinko in the next race please, darling?"

While Lang spoke to the bookie, Mary James chatted to another lady, Mrs Crosby, then introduced her to Serena (who was certainly the most elegant of the three women).

"What a marvellous hat. Where did you get those divine feathers?" enquired Mrs Crosby.

"I found it at a charming shop in Richmond. The girl made it for me on the spot," said Serena proudly.

Meanwhile, at the Tote, Lang had bumped into a city colleague called Tom. During the conversation, Tom revealed a bit of scandal about a mutual friend of theirs who had been found artificially inflating his firm's profits and been charged with false accounting.

"The man is ruined, bankrupt. . . might even spend some time in jail."

Lang went white while expressing astonishment at the news. "I thought they were one of the soundest firms. I'll come back to you later—must take my wife's betting slip." He reached Serena just as the race began.

"What's the matter?" she gasped. "You look awful."

"Oh nothing," said Lang quietly.

Serena's horse, Jinko, lay fifth when suddenly it overtook all the others, raced ahead by a length, and won. The crowd erupted. So did Serena. Jinko was 30-1. Lang was really screwed up inside but tried to put on a proud grin for Serena's sake.

"In the next race I'd like to bet on Rialto. Could you collect my winnings?" enthused Serena.

Lang went back to the Tote and collected his wife's winnings but didn't see Tom this time. Luckily though, he had his mobile number.

"I'm stuck in my seat. Can't talk now. Give you a ring tonight," Tom said hurriedly.

In the next two races Serena's choices came third and fourth, but the last race was another triumph and her enthusiasm overruled Lang's intense anxiety. As he returned to the box, he found Serena jumping up and down, and just caught her feathered hat as it flew towards Foster James.

They arrived home with a crushed hat and Serena's handbag bulging with notes.

"What a wonderful day. Thank you darling."

The Bentley drove off as Serena pushed Lang onto the sofa and fell into his arms. Half an hour later, they'd just got dressed again when Alicia and Freddie bounced into the house. Vivi, who had been looking after the children in the afternoon, placed Benjie in Serena's arms.

"Did you have a good time?" Vivi said, raising an eyebrow and Serena blushed.

"Why are you lying on the sofa, Mummy?" asked Alicia.

"Come on, let's have tea," said Serena as Vivi held in her laughter.

Chapter Fourteen

Chiswick

Having said goodbye to her last patient, Vivi went through to the garden, and lay in the hammock. She tried hard to banish all the afternoon's problems following three complex patients. Shutting her eyes, she drifted off into a light sleep.

"Excuse me, Mrs Vivi—sorry to wake you, but there's someone at the door and Mr Theo is in his office on the phone." Bella stood there with bubbly Jago in her arms.

Vivi yawned and slipped off the hammock. "Give Jago a swing, Bella."

She opened the front door to find a thin, apologetic looking boy of about thirteen.

"My mum stupidly left her bag in your room—she's too tired to come back and get it," he said resentfully.

"Oh yes—is your mum Mrs Dimet? I've got the bag here. Thank you for coming."

Vivi handed the bag over, then shut the front door and heard Theo's agitated voice on the phone. "Yes, if you've got a new conductor I'll be in Moscow on Friday!"

She hurriedly went into the kitchen and made a cup of green tea, saddened at the thought of Theo leaving them again.

She was still there, five minutes later, when Georgie came home from school. "Guess what, Mummy? I'm going to be a Princess in the music show! And I have to sing one song by myself."

"You clever girl! Do I have to make a costume?"

"No, another mummy at school is going to make a long red dress for me. You look a bit sad Mummy—why?"

But before Vivi could answer, Theo came into the kitchen. "Vivi, I've just had another call from Russia. They want me to be there on Friday to start rehearsals," he said anxiously.

"Yes, I expected you'd be off again soon," Vivi replied, almost in a whisper.

"Oh Daddy, don't go away again," Georgie said tearfully.

"I'm sorry darling but Daddy needs to work. Plus, your grandmother lives out there, so I can send her your love. Would you like that?"

"I guess so," Georgie said, wiping her wet face. "Will you be gone long?"

Theo shook his head. "I'll be back before you know it."

Chapter Fifteen

Kensington

Jonty arrived back at about 8pm. "I've had some very potent Prince Charles home brew. I'm not used to so much booze on an empty stomach," he said, almost falling onto the sofa.

"What was he like?" asked Serena excitedly.

"Fascinating. Really enthusiastic too. He's going to set up a fund for new forests and find unusual species to plant. He has such knowledge."

Lang stood up grinning with a drink in hand,

"Congratulations, Jonty." Serena hugged him happily. "*We've* had a good day too." She tipsily threw a mass of £10 notes into the air. "I backed lots of winners. Whoopee!" As she jumped up her pretty red dress split down the back and she laughed. "Oh hell. Never mind, I can buy plenty more with all this."

"Let me put some of it into the bank for you," suggested Lang, eyeing the money on the floor. *It wasn't enough, but it could help.*

"What a splendid hat," said Jonty, as Serena paraded about.

"We're going to take you to Bessie's, our favourite little restaurant in about half an hour," she said.

"Maybe Jonty would prefer something more casual," Lang said, and Serena snorted.

"Nonsense!"

"What a surprise!" Jonty glanced at Lang "I'll nip up for a shower if the bathroom is free."

As he entered the master bedroom he could hear water gushing onto the tiled bathroom floor. Freddie was hanging round the showerhead throwing water bombs at a sunken rubber boat in the bath.

"Quick! Turn that water off! You're flooding the floor," Jonty called to him.

"I can't. The red tap's too stiff," shouted Freddie, leaping on to the wet floor.

"Where's a mop? I can't have a shower here," said Jonty.

"Maggie will help," said Freddie laughing.

"Oh my goodness! I thought you were in bed," exclaimed Maggie who walked in at that exact moment—her face a picture of horror.

Jonty recounted his adventures with Freddie in the car on the way to supper. Lang found it hilarious, while Serena was less than impressed.

As they were greeted by Bessie, Lang glanced around and saw Tom Calder huddled in a corner, deep in discussion with two 'city people.' He shuddered. Lang immediately suggested they sit downstairs.

"It's cosier," he said, leading them down the steep staircase hurriedly.

"I'm already drooling at the smell of roast lamb," said Jonty.

Bessie waddled round the scrubbed table handing out menus.

"We've told my brother about your fabulous lobster soup," said Serena, enthusiastic as ever. The intimate restaurant was bubbling with hungry chat. "Oh, I forgot to show you this letter. Mummy's decided to arrive this Thursday. She'll be spending three days with us, then go to Vivi for five, and then have a week with you, Jonty, for some fresh air. She hopes to get a lift to Aylesbury. In her scribbled note from Madeira she wrote, 'As I'm almost seventy, a family party might be fun! Even though most of my friends are dead, there are a few old fogies left.'

"Let's order a bottle of nice wine." Lang sighed. The thought of his bossy mother-in-law giving orders all day made him wince.

"Better let Cheryl know," muttered Jonty, picking up the phone. "Hello Cherry-Berry," he blew a woozy kiss and said in a stage whisper, "Get ready, the Queen B's coming from Madeira to stay with us. Better start polishing that desk she gave you. Oh, and it's the old girl's seventieth in a couple of weeks. . ."

Chapter Sixteen

Chiswick

Theo walked from the house into the garden. "I've got a surprise for you, darling. We've been given free tickets to Glyndebourne on Thursday to hear my friend Alena Kirova sing in Figaro. I last saw her at a recital in Moscow near my mother's house."

"How exciting! I remember we heard her sing in Cosi at Covent Garden," Vivi enthused. "Let me see what clients I've got. I'll just check my diary."

Theo went over to Georgie who was lying pensively in the hammock. He pushed her gently.

"Daddy, why do you keep leaving us? I only have half a dad and Jago has even less because he's so little," Georgie said.

Theo felt a lump in his throat. "All my concerts seem to take me abroad. I love the piano and I have to play it, like you love reading. We can't stop." He bent his head to kiss her cheek.

"But other dads don't play the piano in Russia," she protested. "Please can we go to the seaside one day?"

Just then, Vivi reappeared. "I've managed to change two clients on Thursday. What fun! I must get the picnic hamper out."

"Can't I come too?" pleaded Georgie.

"No darling, but you can play with Alicia after school instead. Won't that be fun?"

"I suppose so," sighed Georgie sadly.

"Oh, and another thing. I've just had an email from Serena

saying Mummy's arriving next week to stay at their house first, then five days here, then Jonty's. This will be her seventieth birthday. Oh, you won't be here, will you?" Vivi asked.

"No, probably not," said Theo sadly. He glanced at Georgie whose bottom lip was trembling. "But maybe I could postpone Friday's rehearsal and we could all go to Brighton for the day."

Vivi looked amazed. Georgie jumped up and hugged him.

"Granny Beady will be able to see me being a princess in the school play. Maybe you could fly back too Daddy?"

The next morning Vivi prepared the picnic for Glyndebourne, while Theo shut himself away for three hours of piano practise. She saw clients until 2.30pm, then lay smiling to herself in the hammock.

What a treat to spend all day with my husband at the opera. Fancy him changing dates so they could take Georgie to the seaside, she thought. *Maybe now he will put his family first more.*

Chapter Seventeen

Sussex

Everything sparkled as Vivi and Theo drove towards Sussex that Thursday. The countryside's lush green fields and countless different trees in all shades of green caught the sunlight. Theo didn't talk much.

As he drove, they listened to Shostakovich's Piano Concerto No. 2. The slow movement was one of his favourites. Vivi was looking beautiful in a long patchwork skirt and purple velvet top, her long dark hair flowing round her slim shoulders.

"I think Alena suggested we picnic near the stage door, so she can pop out to see us," said Theo.

Two hours later they arrived, they were sat upon a rug on grass as soft as moss. Vivi laid out the picnic while Theo strolled round admiring the beautiful flowerbeds.

"Hello, how good to see you!" called an exquisite low voice. There was Alena, already dressed for Cherubino in an hour's time. They kissed each other on the cheek three times in the Russian way. She chatted animatedly with a slight broken accent. "Oh, this place is glorious, what an unusual setting to sing in and the audiences are so enthusiastic. I'd like to perform in England more!"

Vivi stood up and joined them. "How is your family?" she asked Alena. "Is your mother looking after the children?"

"Yes, and my husband is cross because I'm away. He misses my cooking!" The mezzo laughed. "But I have quite a few concerts in Europe, and guess what? The Met in New York have offered me Aida for just a week!"

"That's fantastic. I'd like to see you as Amneris. Maybe my concert might coincide with your date," enthused Theo.

"Are you going to New York? When is that?" queried Vivi, rather surprised.

"I'll tell you later, darling." Theo turned back to Alena and Vivi frowned. "Will you have some wine? Or don't you drink before the performance?" he asked.

"No, I just gargle with it!" Alena laughed. "Anyway, if you'll excuse me, I must dash. I have to warm up before I go on." She gave a brief hug to Theo and Vivi.

"Good luck," said Theo.

The performance was wildly received. Alena's Cherubino was sung with purity, humour and a rich vocal sincerity.

"She's such a good actress," whispered Theo, putting his arm round Vivi's shoulders during the last act.

"What a lovely evening," purred Vivi, as they slowly walked to the car.

Theo suddenly swung her round and kissed her face, neck and finally lips with great tenderness.

On the journey home Vivi asked, "So, when are you going to New York? You never told me you had a concert there. You must give me an updated schedule."

"Do you remember I told you that Sergei, my new promoter, has asked me to take the place of someone who's ill at a St Petersburg concert? Well, there's another concert after that in New York that I also have been asked to help with," enthused Theo.

"I wish you had told me," Vivi muttered under her breath.

*

As he opened the front door Theo whispered, "Let's have a cosy Jacuzzi together."

Soon they were sliding over each other, their naked bodies making shadows in the soft candlelight. Theo held her perfectly shaped breast and drew it to his mouth, massaging the other with his long fingers. They were soon passionately entwined, unable to wait for the pleasures of intense arousal and satisfaction. Their sighing and gasping gave way to another united climax of breath-taking power. Vivi lay limply floating on top of Theo.

A few minutes passed before he lifted her up out of the water and wrapped her in a towel.

"That was the first course. Let's go to the bedroom for the second one," he said softly, guiding her to the stairs.

Entering the bedroom, Vivi threw off her towel and stretched out on the gold satin throw as Theo slid across the bed stroking her back and buttocks. Running his tongue down her spine, she coiled into the foetal position with both hands between her knees.

Slowly he turned her over to face him. His lips crushed hers as his tongue circled the crevices deep inside her mouth, at the same time entering Vivi whose thighs welcomed him. Every sense became one. It was a unity of complete perfection. They fell asleep utterly fulfilled.

Chapter Eighteen

Chiswick

"Seaside today!"

Vivi and Theo's bedroom door burst open at 6.30 the next morning to reveal Jago in a bathing suit, banging his bucket and spade together.

Georgie followed carrying a beach towel. The children pulled off the bedclothes and jumped into bed for a hug. Chaos followed as Theo jumped out of bed to have a shower.

"Where are your pyjamas, Daddy?" Georgie asked confused.

After a messy breakfast in which Jago sprinkled the floor with Rice Krispies, and smeared peanut butter on his face and arms, Vivi said, "Bella, could you wipe Jago down please, then dress him quickly. Theo's nearly ready to leave."

Georgie had chopped-up hard-boiled egg and spread it between two slices of buttered bread sprinkled with a thick tomato sauce that oozed onto her sticky fingers.

"Let me wrap that in foil, while you go and wash your hands quickly. Daddy's waiting in the car," said Vivi.

Chapter Nineteen

Brighton

As Theo drove along Brighton seafront, they ran into a large procession.

"What's that man doing in a tutu? Look, there are two more in miniskirts and high heels." Georgie laughed whilst Theo pursed his lips in response.

"It's just a march for people who want to dress up," said Vivi, turning to smile at Georgie, half-relieved that Jago was still asleep despite all the shouting and singing.

Theo turned up a side street.

"Shall we go to the other end, away from the pier? It should be a quieter beach for the children."

They drove slowly westwards along the promenade and out of town, Georgie jumping up and down in the back with excitement.

"There's so much water, Mummy. Is it cold?"

"Yes, it is. Oh look, there's a good stretch of empty beach, let's go there," said Vivi, pointing at the desired space.

Theo drew up behind an ice cream van. Everyone piled out with Theo carrying a sleepy Jago who woke up as the sea breeze stroked his face. Georgie raced on ahead, shouting into the wind. Vivi put up a wind-break and unrolled a large waterproof blanket. Not much use putting up the folding table as the wind would sweep everything away. The sun was certainly not hot enough for the children to need sun cream.

"I'm going to build a sandcastle. Come on Daddy!" said Georgie, pulling Theo along the wet sand. Half an hour later she called to Vivi, "Bring Jago to sit in our lovely castle."

Vivi traipsed down the beach and lifted Jago into a pool by their castle. There were squeals of delight as Theo dug a huge pit that Georgie jumped into. Vivi pretended to be a dog pawing the sand, trying to cover Georgie up to her neck. She was laughing so much she got hiccups.

A family walked by licking sticky candy floss, their faces a mass of pink gunge.

"Ooh, can we have one of those?" asked Georgie. Her sand-covered arm outstretched.

"Let's enjoy a paddle first," said Theo.

They raced towards the sparkling sea. A shallow tide swirled round their feet as they tiptoed in. Vivi glanced at Theo galloping through the water with Georgie in tow. Little Jago was swinging the bucket of water over his head, shivering as it dribbled down to his toes. This was a bonus day indeed, and after the previous night, Vivi felt radiant.

An hour later both children were bouncing up and down on a musical roundabout, Georgie waving and Jago looking rather grim.

"Hold on tight!" shouted Vivi.

On the walk back to the car, Theo relented and bought Georgie a large stick of candy floss to be shared with Jago. By the time they got to the car Georgie's hair was whirled with pink candyfloss and Jago's face was almost invisible—only his eyes peeping through the pink mass.

The sound of Vivi's mobile phone added to the chaos.

"Where are you?" asked Serena.

"We're having a fun day in Brighton en famille," replied Vivi happily.

"What, with Theo too? Has he brought the piano?" Serena laughed. "Listen, Mum's arriving next Thursday so we need to discuss a party date and the guest list. Can I come over on Saturday?"

"Yes, of course. Actually, that's good timing as Theo leaves for Russia that morning so everyone will be rather low. Come at lunchtime and bring the kids too, and they can have sausages in the play tent," suggested Vivi.

Chapter Twenty

Aylesbury

Jonty pushed open the farmhouse door and fell into an old kitchen armchair.

"Phew, I'm not used to living like they do in London. No one ever stops. Even the kids are always rushing. The pavements are like dirt tracks, cyclists race in-between pedestrians and prams, then leap off the kerb and dash through red lights. Teenagers on scooters almost shave off your toenails. As for traffic jams! It's like a circus of bumper cars. Everyone lives on their nerves. How are you, my Berry?"

He opened his arms wide to hug Cheryl as she fell into his lap.

"You certainly look exhausted," she said, stroking the side of his face. "Well, nothing much has happened in our haven except one of the lambs died and a pony bolted into the plantation. He obviously liked the smell of young bark. I had a meeting about the new equestrian centre plans. It's going to be quite a large centre, Jonty, I'll need a big team of helpers."

They sat together quietly with their arms wrapped round each other's shoulders.

"If I have a soak in the bath, will you rub my back?" Jonty eventually said.

They both smiled. His twinkling eyes always made Cheryl's tummy tighten.

An hour later, after back rubbing and more cuddles, Cheryl

went downstairs and made cheese on toast and a cup of cocoa. She riddled the Aga, drew the kitchen curtains and walked upstairs, still naked, with the tray.

*

About 5.30am there was a shout beneath their window, "Hey! One of them ponies is chasing the lambs!"

Jonty opened the window and leaned out, "At this time?" he called back to one of the workers, Jacob, then hurriedly put on a raincoat over his pyjamas and stumbled down the wooden staircase.

Jacob was waiting at the door with a torch and led Jonty to the field where a pony was frisking and trying to butt one of four pregnant ewes. Between them they managed to slip a halter over its head and slowly dragged it out of the field back to the stables.

"Looks as though she let herself out," said Jonty, pointing to the broken latch.

Cheryl was cooking his favourite breakfast when he returned and normality resumed after a chaotic start to the day.

"Tell me about Charlie. Did he have any useful advice about the plantation?" she asked.

"Yes, he's such an interesting guy. My project has really caught his interest. He warned me about various viruses that attack maples and to keep an eye open for those clusters of stinging caterpillars on the oak trees. Oh, and he said what a marvellous heritage we would leave. He wants to visit the forest within the next two months to see how we are doing."

Cheryl grinned proudly. "It must be so reassuring to have

his enthusiasm," she said. "I'm going to the site manager's office now. We need to discuss the size of the riding arena. Also, Serena asked us if the 25th is free for your mum's seventieth? Will you ring her?"

Jonty groaned and nodded as Cheryl left the room.

Chapter Twenty One

Chiswick

Theo knew that saying goodbye would be difficult, especially with Georgie, so early the next morning he left a note attached to a rose for Vivi and a comic with some sweets for the children.

He crept out of his sleeping house at 6am just as the taxi arrived to take him to Heathrow.

Tender family feelings made him almost regret the departure, but what lay ahead was very exciting: a chance to expand his repertoire and experience new audiences.

Chapter Twenty Two

Moscow

Theo's mother, Baba, was there as usual to meet him at the airport. Her tall, thin figure stood out, adorned in a long red dress with masses of beads under a black cape.

Theo was her only son and she lived for his music. His father was an English writer who left Russia to pursue his career just three years after Theo's birth, which meant that Baba brought Theo up in Moscow where he attended a musical school. He left Russia at fifteen to join the Royal Academy of Music in London where he flourished and was awarded a much-needed scholarship for several years.

Baba drove slowly through the sodden streets excitedly firing question after question at her son. "Tell me about your concerts? Will I be able to see you in Vienna?"

"Yes, of course! We must get Sergei to arrange it. I've got some lovely pictures of Georgie and Jago. You need to come over to England and see them. Now Georgie's getting older she's becoming more and more enchanting. I can't believe she's already seven. I do miss her when I'm away," said Theo sadly.

"Perhaps I could come back with you when you next go back to London?" suggested Baba. "Your Papa, Gerald, told me so much about England before he left, and his love for the country was so strong he never felt the desire to return back to me in Russia."

Theo was always amazed that his mother could talk about his father's departure so nonchalantly.

As Theo entered her small flat in the suburbs of Moscow, he saw a letter on the hall table.

See you at the Conservatoire for rehearsal 9am tomorrow.
Welcome back!
Sergei.

It gave him a jolt to be so quickly thrust into work, yet a surge of excitement also made Theo want to get to a piano immediately, but of course there wasn't one in the small flat.

He fought the urge to dash to the Conservatoire but he had to stay with Baba for a while.

"How is your arthritis?" Theo asked, as they settled on the familiar sofa.

"Oh, my hands are getting painful and swollen, especially in the cold, and I do miss teaching but the standing affected my back too much," Baba replied.

"I'm so sorry, you must miss it all. But à propos. . . can I talk to you about money?" He handed her a fat envelope. "This is to replace the ballet classes, so you can be comfortable and eat properly."

Theo put an arm round Baba and hugged her tenderly.

"Thank you, dear boy, you are so good to me." She squeezed his arm. "Come, let's have some supper, I made your favourite soup." Baba pointed to a large steaming saucepan.

They spent the evening looking at photos of the grandchildren and pictures drawn by Georgie for Gran Baba, which made Theo's heart ache. How he missed them!

Theo realised the time and made his way to his old bedroom door.

"I must get some sleep because the rehearsal begins at 9pm. Please wake me at 7am."

They hugged and Theo kissed her on both cheeks.

"It's so good to see you," said Baba, squeezing his arm.

*

The next morning, Theo rushed to the Conservatoire, arriving as the orchestra was tuning up. Sergei embraced him as he neared the piano.

"Welcome back. We've all missed you."

They held each other's gaze for a split second, then Theo sat down, ready to begin the Mozart piano concerto No. 22. He felt exhilarated to be back with his fellow musicians.

The conductor, Felix Murel, came onto the podium, baton raised. In total harmony, the glorious opening bars prepared Theo for what lay ahead. The morning involved a lot of readjustments and re-runs, which the conductor insisted on perfecting.

The lunch break bubbled with gossip and jokes, especially from one of the trombone players whose risqué sense of humour made Theo laugh endlessly. The afternoon was a serious plod through Tchaikovsky's Piano Concerto No. 2, so well-known that it had to be interpreted, according to Murel, "As if it was just composed."

Murel was a great admirer of Theo's soaring cadences, which added new dimensions to the first movement.

Chapter Twenty Three

Chiswick

Serena arrived at Vivi's by lunchtime on Saturday to find a rather gloomy house. Georgie and Jago were still getting over the fact that Theo had gone without saying goodbye.

Her own children were far more cheerful, though. Alicia, Freddie and Benjie stumped through the front door in high spirits. A few minutes later, gloom was forgotten, as Georgie caught magic bubbles blown by Freddie through a long pipe, while Jago sat on the grass pulling laces through discarded trainers.

"So great to see you," said Vivi to Serena, albeit a little sadly. "Come on, let's have a drink." As they sat down with two glasses of Pimms, she sighed and said, "I wonder what Theo's doing right now. I miss him."

Serena put her arms round Vivi and hugged her sister fondly.

"Come on, let's cheer you up by starting the party list. Oh gosh, do you remember that party we had when awful Lady Sincombe gave Ma instructions on how to look gorgeous in a Jacuzzi? And that dreadful man, Duncan, who admired her so and said, 'I'll always be waiting for you however old you are'. He had bad breath and wore those tatty open sandals," recalled Serena.

"Leslie was the worst though, in tweed trousers and sexy silk shirts. As for Bee bringing her new lover Fred from the local garage, that really put a spanner in the works, didn't it? No pun intended!" exclaimed Vivi. "And, of course, Sam, such a sweet man; gay and gorgeous. The best hairdresser she ever had!"

"Freddie smeared ice cream all over my face!" said Georgie disturbing the reminiscing.

"It's only fun," he said laughing.

"No it's not!" Georgie yelled before stomping away.

"Let's have a game of hide and seek," called Alicia, already halfway up a tree.

"Where's Lang today?" Vivi enquired.

"I don't know. He's terribly screwed up about work. I've never seen him so fraught." Serena sounded anxious.

"Do you think all's well there? He never used to be so tense," said Vivi.

"Well, I've been wondering too. He's so on edge. You're the professional, do you think I should ask him?" Serena was unusually serious.

"I think you should." Vivi began jotting down names for the party. "Who else ought we to invite?"

"Don't forget to ask Father Conway, her Sunday friend in Madeira."

"Oh yes! He absolutely *must* come!" said Vivi.

"Let's have it at my place," suggested Serena. "We'll have a marquee, and each contribute one of her favourite dishes, however eccentric it is."

"Have you asked the Ramseys?" wondered Vivi. "He's the eye surgeon who Ma quite fancied until she could see properly, and Sheena, Dad's loyal secretary. Oh, and Rose, her cousin, who I adored when I was nine. I wanted to marry her. She might be dead by now like half the other suggestions, mind you!"

"Shall we have a brass band or a chamber group?" enquired Serena.

"I think violin, flute and piano," replied Vivi. "She'll love hearing them tinkle away. Also, I think evening will be best. All the kids will be in bed and she loves candlelight. Toby's got a wine shop, so we can get the booze reduced."

Both sisters were having a good time organising the do until Serena glanced at her watch.

"Vivi my love, I've got to dash. I'm meeting Lang in town. We're off to a rather grand dinner party. Come on kids," she called. "What a lovely afternoon. Give me a call anytime you're feeling lonely."

She kissed Vivi before she gathered her children, and they all headed out of the front door, chatting merrily.

Vivi forced a smile and waved as they left, feeling as if they had taken all the cheer with them.

Chapter Twenty Four

Moscow

After the morning rehearsal finished, Sergei and Theo arrived at their favourite café. Theo was feeling exhilarated after three hours perfecting the first movement.

"It's going to be an exciting few weeks. Replacing Aranov will give you a wonderful opportunity to capture a new audience in St Petersburg." Sergei was bubbling with enthusiasm. "The Tchaikovsky is coming on brilliantly. What about Scriabin for the second half?"

Theo leaned over, arms spread wide open across the table. "Your enthusiasm is contagious. Yes, I rehearsed the Scriabin this morning. What a challenge! By the way, could you get a ticket for Baba? She'd so love to hear me play. Poor thing, her arthritis is much worse. I must take her to England soon to see the children. Also, I'm going to ask Vivi if she'd like to stay in St Petersburg for two nights."

"That can easily be arranged, it is my job, after all." Sergei smiled warmly at Theo.

After laughing and some ribaldry, they walked back to the rehearsal room, feeling very relaxed.

"As it's Sunday tomorrow, shall we go to the Kandinsky exhibition? I've got free passes."

"If it's not too early. I may go to church with Baba first. Shall we meet at noon?"

The afternoon was slightly spoilt by the orchestra leader breaking a violin string, which took some time to replace. Theo was irritated by the delay and impatiently walked to another studio next door where he practised some difficult cadences, then started on the vigorous third movement. Before he knew it, an hour had passed.

"Murel's waiting for you." Sergei put a hand gently on Theo's shoulder.

"I'll be there in five minutes," he said abruptly, continuing on the piano.

"The violinist apologises for interrupting your solo, and Murel told him off for not having a spare with him. Everyone is now ready to continue."

"Yes, yes, I know but it's stopped the flow. You don't understand, you're not an artist," replied Theo, angrily standing up to face Sergei, who still wore the same calm expression. He was used to dealing with temperamental artists. Theo stomped off to the orchestra next door.

Later, Theo was sitting on the balcony after an excellent baked fish with Baba, when his mobile broke the silence.

"Hello, Vivi darling," he murmured, as her gentle voice purred down the phone.

"Georgie's missing you terribly. Can she talk to you?"

"Yes, I miss her too."

"Hello Daddy," Georgie said. "I've got a photo of you by my pillow so I can talk to you before I go to sleep. What are you doing?"

Georgie's voice gave Theo a pang.

"I'm sitting on Granny Baba's balcony watching the sun set behind the houses and—"

"Can we come and see you play the piano sometime? Home is half empty without you," Georgie pleaded.

"I—I—," Theo stumbled over his reply. He wanted to open his arms and hug her. "How is Jago?" he asked instead.

"He tried to eat some shoe laces when we were having a picnic the other day. I'll give him a hug from you, shall I? He looks for you under the bed."

"Pass me to Mummy please," said Theo.

"Yes Theo?" Vivi said.

"Vivi, what about coming to St Petersburg for my big concert? Could the children go to Serena for two days?"

"Oh, that would be fantastic!" Vivi caught sight of Georgie's tears. "I'll call you later, about 10.00pm."

Vivi rang off, then wrapped her arms softly round Georgie. "He'll be home soon, darling. I know! Why don't we cheer you up by making some pancakes?"

"Oh Miss Vivi, what a mess!" cried Bella, as she came in ten minutes later laden with shopping, almost slipping on a well-squashed pancake that had fallen on the floor.

"Would you like one Bella?" called Georgie as she tossed another one in the air. It landed on Bella's head.

"Certainly not!" she cried, laughingly trying to retrieve it.

Chapter Twenty Five

Kensington

Serena spent Sunday contacting several of her mum's friends who were delighted and excited to be reunited with Beady. Many appeared ancient, some deaf, and one or two sounded tipsy at midday! She decided to ring Beady in Madeira to ask if there were any special people she'd like to see.

She reeled off lots of names. "How many can I have? And what food are you doing?"

"Listen, we'll talk about that when you arrive. Anyway, most of it is a surprise for you." Beady's bossiness subsided as she sighed huskily, then inhaled on her Balkan Sobranie. "It'll be an evening do. Will your older friends manage it?"

"Of course they will. If not, I'll drag them there." Beady laughed.

"I must go now, Ma. I've got to put Benjie to bed."

She found Lang lying on the floor, telling Freddie about the first aeroplane ever invented.

"Can you make one for me, Daddy?"

"Yes, let's get some paper," said Lang.

"I've just had a talk with Ma. It's going to be quite an endurance test with her staying. I must order the marquee tomorrow. We'll need chairs and trestle tables, won't we?" burbled Serena.

"God, it's going to cost a bundle. Can't we do without the marquee?" Lang said anxiously.

"Not really, darling. Besides, it's much cheaper than some awful anonymous banqueting room at a hotel. Will you arrange the wine with Toby? Shall we have Dom Perignon to start with?"

"I think that's going too far! We really can't afford such luxury." Lang was getting annoyed at Serena's extravagance.

"We've only got a few days before she arrives. What are we going to give her as a birthday present?" asked Serena.

"Oh, give her 200 of those ghastly, smelly fags of hers, or one more cerise, pearled handbag to go with her vast collection," Lang snapped, irritated by the imminent invasion of his mother-in-law.

Chapter Twenty Six

Aylesbury

"Cheryl, look at those maple leaves, they've got strange rings on the back. I hope it's not the virus that Prince Charles warned me about," Jonty said anxiously.

"Why not ring up his environmental people?" suggested Cheryl.

"I don't want to bother them."

"Come on, this could be serious and affect a lot of other trees."

Jonty walked them down towards the plantation looking for further diseased leaves.

"It seems to be only those three maples." He turned to see Cheryl looking at a different group further along.

"Oh dear, these don't look too good either, JJ," she said, holding two oddly-mottled leaves in her hand. "Do ring the office and ask their advice. That's what Prince Charles suggested, didn't he? Don't be shy about asking, love."

Cheryl put an arm round Jonty's dejected shoulders.

"Hello, can I speak to Jim Davy in Prince Charles' office for the environment?" Jonty asked, two minutes later.

"I'll put you through, sir."

"Hello, it's Jonty here. We met last week with Prince Charles. I've got a problem with several of my maple trees. The leaves have a ring like pattern on their underside. Does this suggest a virus infection?"

Jim Davy sighed. "Ah yes, that's quite a common virus called 'ring mottle.' Can't be treated I'm afraid. They must be destroyed so none of the other trees get infected. It's contagious."

Jonty was shocked. "What causes it in such young trees?"

"No one knows. Maples are prone to about five different viruses, but don't worry, it's bound to happen in a big forest like yours," Jim Davy said, trying to reassure him.

"That's kind of you. It'll be sad destroying them, but thanks for the advice. Give my regards to Prince Charles," replied a subdued Jonty.

"Let's go up and tell old Jacob about the infection," suggested Cheryl. "He's got your interests at heart and his advice is worth listening to."

She drove up the windy hill to a small cottage in the derelict grounds of an old farm. Jonty got out and leaned on a gate looking down towards his plantations in the far distance.

"It will certainly grow into an enormous forest," he said proudly.

"Hello, Mr Jonty." Jacob's wind-worn face suddenly grinned above his stooped shoulders. "I saw the car. What can I do for you?"

"We've come with a worry I hope you'll solve. Some of the maple saplings have got a virus called 'ring mottle.' I've spoken to Prince Charles' office and they said the trees must be destroyed, which was a bit of a shock," stammered Jonty.

"Ah, that's normal with such a big family of trees growing together. When I was working on a big estate in Scotland, dozens of oaks needed to come down. They'd grown so high they needed a tractor to pull them out," said Jacob with his habitual grin. "Anyway, let's get rid of them quick before it spreads. I'll come down with you now."

Jacob slipped into his grimy wellies, hauled on a muddy waterproof and slammed his front door.

"Can you drop me off at the farm?" asked Cheryl. "The children will be here soon, eager to get on their ponies."

Jacob grunted, "You do well for those kiddies."

Jonty called up a farm worker in the next field, told him to bring the tractor to the wood, and soon the first diseased maple had been yanked up. He could hardly bear to watch. It was like his own child being hurt.

Chapter Twenty Seven

Moscow

Sergei handed over the tickets as Theo walked ahead into a blazing red-walled gallery full of Kandinsky's work. They wandered through slowly, sharing different impressions about each picture. Theo disagreed with Sergei's blind passion for the artist; it almost irritated him.

"I must get in some extra practice today. It'll be a good chance to work on the Scriabin uninterrupted," he said as they went downstairs, having seen the show.

"Let's have a drink here first," suggested Sergei, taking his client's arm as they sat down at a table.

"Alright, I'll have a beer. Have you managed to get a ticket for Baba next week?"

"Yes, in the front row so she can watch her clever son closely." Sergei paused, then smiled. "You really are a most remarkable man. Such powerful feelings in every interpretation you play. It's a rare sensation to hear a well-known piece performed as if for the first time."

Theo was flattered and a little embarrassed at the same time. "I get so deep into the passion I feel for the music. I'm in another world when I play." He seemed almost dream-like, then suddenly glanced at his watch. "I've booked my room at the Conservatoire. Thanks, Sergei, for Kandinsky and the drink."

Theo tapped his arm and was gone.

Sergei watched him disappear.

Chapter Twenty Eight

Kensington

Lang almost fell through the front door, his tall frame stooped and weary. "Hello darling."

Serena took his arm. "You look exhausted. What about a stiff gin? You really must try and get home earlier sometimes." She watched him as he lay back on the sofa.

"Business is great, but being a director takes up more time than ever. The firm is anxious we're overtrading and we've got to keep enough capital in-house to sustain the turnover."

Serena frowned. "But why must everything be so worrying? The burden's affecting you. I don't want my man having a stroke. The stress has never been so bad," she said anxiously. "I think we must somehow have a holiday."

Lang shook his head. "I'm a director now. I've got greater responsibility and—"

"Yes darling, but even directors need a break," Serena interrupted. "Isn't there a law which says everyone must have at least one two-week holiday a year?" She was trying hard to weaken Lang's stubbornness. "Let's go to the Seychelles. You know we've been offered a villa there."

"I'll see, my lovely, persistent Fig Tree." Lang smiled fondly.

"This is going to be a hectic week with Mummy arriving," Serena said.

"Let alone staying in our house and interfering," grumbled Lang.

"Fat Betty's making a birthday cake covered in Madeira flowers. Alicia's going to paint meringues. Freddie's trying to draw an aeroplane card. Now, what shall we give her? Maybe a cosmetic bag from Cartier?"

"Yes, I suppose she'd enjoy carrying all that gaudy makeup in it."

Lang disliked Beady's painted face. Lipstick oozing from her lips and all that green eye shadow. . .

*

Serena had received forty-five replies for her mothers party. Even the vicar from Madeira was coming.

"The marquee's being erected on Friday, three days after Ma's arrival. Rosie Fellows has agreed to bring her charming quartet," Serena regaled over breakfast. "I've suggested Handel, Mozart, Boccherini and Vivaldi (Ma's favourites) at fifteen-minute intervals."

Lang smiled and put down his coffee cup. "By the way, you'll be delighted to hear that the Chairman popped into my office suggesting I take a holiday next month. I've earned it with all the new business I've brought in."

"Oh, whoopee!" cried Serena, hugging him. "Where shall we go?"

"Let's get over this mother-in-law drama first," Lang said rather brusquely.

"You really get irritated by Ma, don't you?"

"Just a bit," Lang said and walked out of the room.

Chapter Twenty Nine

Chiswick

Vivi had just shown out her third client of the day and was in the middle of some peaceful exercises when the phone rang. "Serena, I'm doing my yoga. Can you ring back in fifteen minutes?" she asked wearily.

Vivi found it imperative to relax after the intensity of her morning sessions. Half an hour later she returned her sister's call.

"It's about the food for Mum's party," explained Serena.

"Yes, I'm making an enormous lasagne, or would you rather fish?" asked Vivi.

"I think a whole salmon would be far more special; she does love fish," suggested Serena.

"And then how about a big meringue and strawberry tart?" went on Vivi. "Georgie could put a picture of Beady on it!"

Serena laughed. "Good idea! We're also doing a large sirloin followed by fresh fruit salad. I've spoken to Cheryl and Jonty who said they'll do *all* the fresh veg and cheese. Lang's ordered the red and white wine through his office."

"Phew! Thank goodness you're good at organising big parties."

"Yes, I love arranging events, although Mum will probably want to change things or interfere, of course!" Serena was used to 'I know better' statements from Beady. "She'll be arriving in two days and there's so much to do."

Just then the doorbell rang out.

"Oh, hang on Vivi, that'll be the man about the marquee I expect," said Serena. She opened the door. "Mum!" she gasped.

"Thought I'd come a few days earlier to surprise you!" Beady laughed as she hugged Serena, her scrawny body jangling with beads over a cerise silk shift.

As she walked into the dining room a minute later, Alicia and Freddie were jumping around with excitement, pulling presents from Granny Beady's bag. Little Benjie revelled in the tissue paper, tearing strips and throwing them into the air. Alicia sat beside Beady asking her to read some of her gift, *Swallows and Amazons.* The elderly woman's voice filled the room. Vivi could hear all this on the phone, which had been completely forgotten about, and felt very sorry for her sister.

"Hello!" she shouted down the phone, just as Serena remembered to pick it up again. "

Well, you heard her arrive!" she whispered. "It's a bit much to come without any warning, don't you think? Anyway, could you have her over for lunch tomorrow while I do some more party planning?"

"Yes, of course, I'll collect her on the way back with Georgie at midday," agreed Vivi.

As Serena walked back into the dining room, she exclaimed, "Well Mum, this *is* a surprise. What made you come earlier?"

"Well, you know me, I like to do the unexpected," she said.

Serena's hidden fury had hardly subsided before it erupted again, as a stinking coil of smoke wafted across her face.

"Oh Mum, please don't smoke while you're with the children. I don't want them inhaling that filthy tobacco."

Beady pushed Alicia off her lap, then glowered, stood up and stubbed out her the cigarette in a nearby plant pot.

"But do finish that chapter. Alicia so loves being read to," Serena asked her mother icily.

"Let's continue in the garden, Alicia. Are you coming too, Freddie?" Beady asked.

"No. I'm going to help Mummy bathe Benjie," said Freddie.

"What a pity it's Bella's day off," said Serena, still vexed at the disruption.

An hour later, bumps and shrieks of laughter drew Beady upstairs.

"Look at all that water!" she remarked, stepping over the boats and balls bobbing about in two inches of water.

"This is their fun time, Mum!"

"Hello squidgy, squidgy." Beady leaned over the bath handing Benjie a duck that he promptly squirted into her face. "Oh dear! Gran can't see now." Both boys roared with laughter. "I think I'd like a shower before supper." Beady, wiped her glasses with a tissue.

"You remember where your room is? Straight down this passage, bath and shower to the left. If you wait here with the boys I'll go and get your suitcase."

Serena hurried down to the hall, then heaved the suitcase upstairs.

"Thank you, darling, I'll be down in a bit. Let me know if I can help with supper."

"That's okay, it's all prepared," Serena quickly replied.

A little while later, on her way to the stairs, Beady popped her head round the door to examine Serena's bedroom. The spare room's new curtains, and Alicia's room which had been completely revamped into a feminine bedsit, even with a 40-inch plasma!

"How disgraceful," she murmured under her breath.

Ten minutes later, Alicia handed out crisps as Serena and her mother enjoyed their cocktails.

"That bit of the garden could do with some weeding," said Beady. "I'll have a go tomorrow. Your herbaceous border is lovely."

Serena smiled thinly. "Oh, by the way, Vivi would love to see you for lunch tomorrow. Pick you up here at midday, alright?"

"Well, I'm not sure. I'd much rather help you."

"Oh, you can't disappoint Georgie," insisted Serena.

Luckily, she had rung Lang's office leaving a warning message that Beady had arrived two days early. He reacted by arriving home at 9.00pm, even later than usual.

"Beady," Lang said stiffly, kissing her dryly on the cheek.

"Lang," Beady replied in the same tone. "You look dreadful, dear."

"Lang's been promoted," Serena said quickly, before Lang could respond. "He's running the whole company. Lang, darling, your food is in the kitchen."

Serena shot him an apologetic look. With a tight smile, Lang walked out of the room.

Beady tutted. "Really does look a mess. He must get it together."

Chapter Thirty

Aylesbury

A group of children with a range of disabilities surrounded their ponies in an enormous field as local MP Tim Brant pointed to a large white plaque.

"This is the foundation stone of Cheryl Croft's Riding School for Children with Disabilities," he declared. "We proudly announce the commencement of building today, ready for the opening of this wonderful project in six months' time."

At this point his assistant freed a mass of balloons, and a local photographer zoomed round taking pictures. The children cheered and some decided to chase them. Jonty hugged Cheryl then offered Mr Brant a glass of home brew.

"What a fantastic setting. You've put so much work into this project. I'd like to contribute to it personally." He handed a cheque for £500 to Cheryl.

"That's most generous, Mr Brant. You'll be rewarded when you see the children ride," said Cheryl.

"I hear you're planting lots of trees which will grow into one of the largest forests in the South," said Mr Brant, turning to Jonty.

"Yes. It's an exciting project. I'll gladly show you round. Prince Charles has shown a keen interest in the idea, but it's already got a few problems I'm afraid. Several maples caught a virus and had to be destroyed. I want to get the local schools involved. It would be an excellent educational subject combining the environment with future generations."

Brant nodded. "When I've seen the trees I'd like to get Gully Fox, our Environment Minister, involved. Perhaps he would sort out a grant for you." His lanky body leaned towards Jonty as they shook hands. "Must be off now to a pig farmers meeting." And with that, and his assistant in tow, Tim Brant waved and jumped into his Jeep.

"What a great occasion, Cheryl," said Jonty. He waved at the children who were on the bus that would deliver them safely back to their homes in the local villages.

"It was amazing. That Mr Brant is a good MP and it was really nice that he showed interest in both our passions—very generous of him to give personally towards my centre. Let's relax in the field while the sun's out."

Cheryl got a rug from the kitchen and they sauntered into the long-grassed field behind the house.

"Listen to that silence," Jonty whispered.

They lay totally at peace for over an hour, gazing at large woolly clouds until suddenly the silence was broken by the sound of a tractor roaring into the kitchen yard.

"One of yer sheep was savaged by a fox last night," announced Jacob, when Jonty went to investigate. "I had to kill it, poor thing."

Chapter Thirty One

Moscow

Baba was smiling broadly. "Who put up all those posters around town?" she asked proudly at dinner.

"That's Sergei. He works very hard at promoting me. You must meet him sometime. He's so enthusiastic about my playing."

"Let's give him supper here?" Baba suggested.

"Maybe when the concert's over," agreed Theo, spooning up the last of the borscht from his bowl. "The final rehearsal's tomorrow. Sergei's taking me out afterwards, so I'll be late. Remember to wake me tomorrow at 7am, will you?"

*

Theo felt excitement running through his veins as he put on a purple shirt with a mandarin collar, confident it went well with his blond hair. As he reached the Conservatoire just before 9am, he heard the buzz from every instrument as it vigorously tuned up.

A few photographers were sitting in the front row of the empty auditorium for the dress rehearsal, eager to snap the prodigy Sergei was passionately promoting.

There was a hush as Theo sat down, then Murel, the conductor, swept in. Seconds later, an explosion erupted as they raced into the first movement. Tchaikovsky was transformed through Theo's fingers. Even the orchestra was taken aback.

Bubbling voices during the break pleased Theo as did some vociferous praise from Murel in the dressing room. Eventually, though, he broke off talking to the conductor and went to practise the Scriabin, anxious about its second movement.

Sergei came in quietly and listened at the back until he'd finished, then said, "Here's a coffee." He put it on a chair. "We're very booked up for tomorrow night. How are you feeling about your big Moscow debut?"

Theo's eyes glittered. "I'm longing to show them my passion for these two Russian pieces. I must do more work before this afternoon's rehearsal though. There's never enough time. Do we meet at the Bolshoi Theatre in the morning?"

Sergei nodded. "Yes, everything will be there for you.'

Chapter Thirty Two

Kensington and Chiswick

Vivi arrived just before midday, as Serena and Beady returned from taking Benjie to the playground.

"Hello Vivi, darling," exclaimed Beady, hugging her warmly. "We've just had a beautiful walk in Holland Park."

They bundled into the house, chatting avidly. Maggie took Benjie and handed Serena some messages.

"Georgie's waiting by the car Mum, and I have a patient to see after lunch."

Vivi kissed Serena goodbye. "Hope this afternoon goes well."

Georgie gave Grandma Beady a terrific welcome and didn't stop talking during the journey home. Little Jago tottered towards them as they walked up to the house, while Bella swept up a few toys in the front garden.

"My goodness, how Jago has grown!" Beady was being pushed through the big wooden front door by Georgie.

"Come and see my garden. I've got three baby carrots, two marigolds and some parsley," yelled Georgie.

Vivi hastily prepared lunch, chatting to her mother when Georgie drew breath.

"Can we eat outside, Mummy?" asked Georgie, hugging her tabby cat.

"We can't. I've laid the table here and the spaghetti's coming now," said Vivi, dishing out on the long wooden table. "Mum, I have to see a client at 2pm. Will you relax in the garden?

Mind you, it may not be easy. I expect Georgie will want to play Snap."

"Yes, I shall enjoy being with her. Jago will be playing with his bricks no doubt."

They looked at the little boy in his high chair, winding spaghetti round one finger and grinning at the messy mince oozing from his upturned bowl.

After lunch, Georgie led her grandmother into the garden.

"What a lovely, colourful mixture of flowers. What are those red ones with long stamens?" asked Beady and Georgie shrugged her shoulders.

After a few games of Snap, Georgie jumped on the swing, swinging away and singing school songs, while Beady scanned a magazine and Bella came out to retrieve Jago for his nap.

"It's time for your piano practice, Georgie, let Grandma come and listen in ten minutes," Bella suggested.

Once everyone had gone, Beady wandered down to the bottom of the garden through several shrubs and a few old trees. On the other side of the grass was a large rockery raised against the wall with masses of big stones interspersed with tiny white and yellow rock-plants.

As she bent over to reach a yellow rose, her foot slipped on a boulder and she fell forward heavily. Beady lay there in shock for several moments before Bella rushed out.

"Oh, Miss Beady, let me help you up." Beady raised her head. "Your face is bleeding. I'll go and get some tissues."

Beady slowly sat up with her mouth hurting and her limbs trembling. Having returned, Bella dabbed the blood gently.

"I think you've lost a tooth," she said, handing Beady a mud-stained crown.

They walked slowly into the kitchen and Bella settled her into a chair.

"Can't make you a cup of tea, it might hurt your mouth. Try this water."

Beady smiled wanly, murmuring, "Thank you. With a straw please."

Vivi shut the front door as her client left and turned to see Bella, who informed her of the accident.

"Oh Mum, how awful! Are you in pain? Your mouth looks very swollen," she said anxiously.

"I've lost a front tooth. Bloody nuisance," replied Beady.

Her face looked such a mess that Vivi didn't know whether to take her to casualty, the doctor, or the dentist.

"What would you like me to do?" she asked, stroking Beady's swollen hand. Then, getting no answer, "Tell you what; why don't I ring Serena?"

Vivi went outside to tell her sister the shocking news.

"I think A&E would be safest," suggested Serena. "Drop Georgie off here. She'll be so upset seeing her Grandma like that."

"Yes, I'll come now," Vivi replied. "Good job the marquee hasn't arrived yet. We'll have to postpone the party for a week. Her friends can't see her with a swollen face and one tooth missing."

"I hadn't thought of that. Wow! This is going to be some cancellation. And all those expectant old guests too! See you shortly."

Vivi went back into the kitchen to find her daughter sitting on the floor beside Beady.

"Poor Grandma, how did you hurt yourself?" asked Georgie tearfully.

"I just fell on the rockery trying to pick a yellow rose," said Beady, cross with herself.

"Georgie darling, go and get a nightie and your school clothes. You're going to sleep with Alicia tonight while I take Grandma to the doctor."

"Mummy, can't I stay and help?" Georgie begged.

"No, you'll help me by going to Auntie Serena. Jago will stay here with Bella."

Everyone was silent in the car except for intermittent sobs from Georgie. Serena opened the car door to say hello to her mum, and Georgie rushed out.

"Oh Lord, that does look awful!" said Serena.

"I'll ring you later when she's been seen!" said Vivi.

They spent five hours in A&E. The X-ray showed no broken bones, just bad bruising on the knee and face. One tooth would have to be replaced. They got home late that evening.

"Would you rather sleep on the sofa downstairs, Mum?"

"No thanks, I'll manage. I've got to keep my independence; however painful it might be. Sorry, Vivi darling, for spoiling our time together." Beady hauled herself slowly upstairs. "I wasn't even supposed to be staying with you until next week, was I?"

"Oh, that doesn't matter, I'll go ahead and turn your lights on. I forgot to tell you it's Theo's big night tomorrow in Moscow, I must ring him now." Vivi took Beady's arm as they reached the bedroom. "Shall I take your coat and shoes off, Mum? I expect you're aching and bruised."

"Yes, if you would." Beady sounded very weary. "Thank you, Vivi dear, for looking after me. You go and ring Theo. Wish him luck from me too. I want to hear all about the performance tomorrow."

Vivi hurried downstairs and quickly dialled Theo's mobile number.

"Hello, my darling," Theo replied sleepily.

"Have I woken you? So sorry, I was just wondering how the rehearsals went?" Vivi's voice was trembling as the words tumbled out affectionately.

"I'm half asleep. I want to be fresh for the great day. Oh Vivi, I wish you were at my side," Theo whispered.

Loving words finished their chat and after putting the receiver down Vivi felt a sudden wave of solitude. She stood, letting the darkness swallow her up.

Chapter Thirty Three

Moscow

Baba slowly drew the curtains back as sun poured across Theo's shock of blond hair.

"This is my day!" He smiled at Baba, then stretched elegantly in bed. "I'll stay here and relish the music deep inside me for a while."

"What would you like for breakfast?" she asked.

"Just coffee."

"Let me cook you an omelette."

"No Baba, I'm full up with excitement."

He lay motionless looking across the rooftops, fingers moving gently across his knees.

Two hours later, Theo arrived at the Bolshoi Theatre Grand Hall, excitement bubbling inside his cool exterior. Sergei guided him to his dressing room, then onto the stage that seemed huge.

The vast auditorium was ablaze with golden plasterwork and red velvet seats. He went to the piano, pressed a note, then some chords, as the orchestra dribbled into their places, tuning their instruments and joking with each other.

Murel came in and jumped onto the podium, anticipating a vigorous rehearsal.

"Are you ready to play your heart out Theo?" He smiled as he raised his baton.

Often, during a last rehearsal in the actual hall quite a few adjustments had to be made in various sections of the orchestra. Theo disliked the interruptions to the flow of his playing.

During a break, Sergei brought coffee to his dressing room.

"These just arrived." He handed over a bunch of roses from Vivi and a drawing from Georgie.

"Ah, my dearest girls," said Theo, smelling the flowers.

"What would you like for lunch? Shall I bring something here or shall we go to our café, even though it's a bit far away?"

"Let's try something new," suggested Theo as two heads popped round the door.

"Come and join us at the Hall restaurant," said Yan, a big, burly double bass player who always made Theo laugh. Maya, the brilliant oboist, stood by his side.

Sergei seemed a bit put out.

*

The final part of the rehearsal finished around 4pm after which everyone vanished, and the hall became empty.

Theo's excitement was building inside him, purring in his guts. He wanted to start playing. He sat in his dressing room and listened to the tannoy, over which a hum of arriving concert goers buzzed in muffled tones. The sound rose and evolved into almost discernible chatter at the imminent début of a rising star.

Sergei whispered, "Good luck, maestro!" just before Theo walked into the spotlight.

The audience welcomed him with cheers. He bowed once and sat down. Murel reached the podium in a bound, raised his baton and in a second the piano exploded into a torrent of chords, Theo's fingers racing across the keys, sweeping on the orchestra. He raised the roof as his power and brilliance surged across the audience.

Ten minutes later, the adagio fell into a graceful gentleness, satiating the listeners with its beautiful phrasing before suddenly erupting into the third movement. Agile fingers rushed up and down the keys. Theo *was* Tchaikovsky rising to a gigantic climax. When he got there, hands raised from the keys, the audience stood up and cheered. Meanwhile, he stood shyly and bowed, tears in his eyes, then looked over towards Baba and blew her a kiss.

During the interval, Sergei rushed into his dressing room and gave him a bear hug.

"You've captured this audience completely. It's electrifying out there!"

Theo walked back on stage twenty minutes later to cheers and wild clapping. He played Scriabin's two piano sonatas with astounding sensitivity. The audience was so silent he almost forgot they existed until the finale, when tumultuous applause burst out at the last bar.

Afterwards, at the post-concert dinner, dumplings were handed round to hungry, eager faces. Almost the entire orchestra filled several tables at a popular Georgian restaurant.

"Ah, Khachapuri, my favourite!" exclaimed Theo.

Three scruffy male students came up to him.

"Can we have your autograph?" one of them asked as the others watched him in awe.

"Certainly, what instruments do you play?"

A tall, skinny teenager replied, "The double bass. We're in a trio at present. He's flute and he's piano."

"Keep practicing," said Theo and the students nodded eagerly.

The evening evolved into riotous singing, bottles clinking and feet stamping.

Chapter Thirty Four

Aylesbury

"Hi, Serena love. I was ringing to see if Mum arrived safely last night?" asked Jonty.

"Oh, my dear JJ, in all the chaos, I forgot to tell you of all people! I'm so sorry. She arrived *two* days early as a surprise!" Serena continued to tell Jonty the whole story, finishing up with trying to postpone the party and marquee because Beady's face looked so battered. "So, you'll be having her down there a bit later than planned," she said at last.

"Poor Mum, shall I have a chat?" Jonty asked.

"She's at Vivi's," said Serena.

After putting the phone down, Jonty went out to the stables to update Cheryl.

"Just let me finish grooming this pony. I'll meet you in the garden. Want a cup of tea?" she asked before he could do so.

A few minutes later they threw off their anoraks.

"What a lovely, warm, May morning," Cheryl beamed, sipping her tea. "What's up? You're looking anxious."

Jonty relayed everything, including the 'two days early' surprise. "Serena sounded rather impatient about it all. She's got to cancel fifty-two invitations, poor love. Mum's not an easy patient and she'll hate looking awful with a swollen face and black eye, even though she's brave. Remember how she coped with the shock of Dad drowning? She looked almost regal at the funeral, holding her tears back, but we all know how much she must have been hurting inside."

"Yes, but then perhaps that was partly because of the girls? Serena was *so* upset and Vivi looked incredibly vulnerable. Do you remember?" said Cheryl wistfully.

"Fancy, somebody who'd been in the Navy, ending up in the sea." Jonty sounded forlorn.

Cheryl put an arm round him and said, "Let's leave memories behind shall we? I know! We can pop up to London one day to see Beady if you want."

Jonty cheered up. "Let's go on Tuesday. Can you leave the riding? Jane can organise that, can't she?"

Cheryl nodded and they sat cosily together wrapped up in their own thoughts with the sun warming their faces.

Chapter Thirty Five

Chiswick

Vivi sank into a deep sofa, having finished her morning session with clients. She always felt reluctant to see people at the weekend. It seemed an intrusion into her family life; but being alone, it somehow filled a 'missing Theo' void. Thankfully Bella had taken Georgie and Jago to the fair.

Since Beady had gone back to Serena's, their big house felt even more empty and lonely. Vivi ached for Theo—just to feel him, smell him, see him. She felt engulfed in nothingness. Despair had caught her unawares. His trips away seemed to be getting longer and busier.

"We're not sharing our lives any more, yet our love is so powerful when we *are* together," she heard herself mumble aloud.

After being married for nine years, family life seemed to be diminishing. The first few years had been blissful, gentle, and sensual, but Theo was only on the edge of his career then. Listening to music for hours, their arms and legs would caress each other and the centre of their souls seemed to fuse into one. Remembering this, Vivi sat in silence, while the sunlight filtered through the curtains warming her tear-stained face. A surge of wretchedness made her tremble, and then the phone rang.

"Yes, who is it?" she whispered.

"It's me, Theo. You sound very distant. What's the matter?" he asked urgently.

"Oh, it's nothing. How did the concert go?"

"It was incredible. They cheered so long I cried. The Tchaikovsky went brilliantly. How I wish you'd been there." Theo was interrupted by a sob. "Vivi my love, what is it?"

She sighed, "I'm missing you so much. I can't go on this way. It's empty, like a void, when you're away. I put on a calm face to everyone, but inside I'm churned up and wanting you so badly."

"I'll be back tomorrow evening, Vivi darling," he replied.

"I know. I just wish you were here now."

"Soon my love," Theo said.

They said goodbye and she put the phone down gently. The long white curtains billowed out as she stood watching Jago and Georgie bounding towards the house with balloons and ice-creams, carrying their laughter towards her. Vivi ran down to greet them.

Chapter Thirty Six

Moscow

Theo rang Sergei urgently next morning. "Get me a flight to London today, as soon as possible, I have to go back."

"But you must stay for the press interviews and meetings. Everyone is—"

"I'm not interested," Theo interrupted. "They can phone me for interviews. I've given a good performance but I *have* to go home before St Petersburg in a few weeks."

Theo put the phone down sure and determined in his decision. Sergei was stunned, unable to make sense of his protégé.

Chapter Thirty Seven

City of London

Just as he was about to leave his office, Lang spotted Bob Calder walking towards him down the long corridor.

"What a coincidence. Just the man I want to see," said Calder, putting an arm on Lang's shoulder and pulling him back into his plush office room. "That Trust company you brought into the firm is doing some lovely business—very impressive. But I did just have a query about some outstanding balances. Is this one something to do with you?" The Chairman held out a sheet of paper.

Lang's face turned white. "Don't worry, I'm seeing to that." He hastily took the document from Calder's hand and put it in his pocket.

Calder checked his watch. "Drink?"

"No thanks, I've got some photocopying to do, then I must dash home and prepare for a family do."

They shook hands and Lang turned left onto a brightly lit corridor. He waited until he could no longer hear Calder's footsteps before pulling out the document and staring at it with blurry eyes. He crumpled up the paper and lowered his head in his hands.

"What am I to do?" he muttered to the empty room.

Chapter Thirty Eight

Kensington

During supper that evening Serena grew increasingly concerned, "What *is* the matter tonight, Lang?"

"It's just the office and the workload."

His weary voice tested Serena's patience. "I thought you were pleased to be promoted. Why must you be so gloomy? *I've* had a ghastly day, too, with three different customers complaining about the colour of carpets and curtains. I want to scream half the time, but I have to be calm and courteous instead." She stood behind Lang, gently fondling his hair. "Talk to me about work. What's getting you down?"

"I can't explain it to you. It's too complicated," Lang muttered.

"Please talk to me," Serena said softly but when Lang didn't respond, Serena let her hand drop to her side and sat down feeling rejected.

"Hello Lang, you *have* been working late," said Beady, entering the room. "It's almost 10pm."

"Yes, it's very hectic at present," he snapped.

"Poor Serena's had a bad day too. Shall I make you both a hot toddy?"

"No Mum. In fact, would you mind just leaving us alone please?"

Beady looked at her daughter and son-in-law, then did as she was asked. Serena watched her go, then turned back to Lang, deciding that a change of subject was called for.

"I offered the Vicar from Madeira a bed here for the night for the big party by the way. The quartet are having a run-through in the drawing room the day before."

Lang sighed. "Must they? That's all I need!"

"Well, I'm sorry, but I've arranged it now. It'll be alright on the night, you'll see. Come on, let's go up, shall we? I think we could both do with a good night's rest."

As they entered the bedroom a smell of cinnamon greeted them. On either side table a steaming toddy sat on a saucer surrounded by bay leaves. 'Sleep well' written on both napkins in silver ink.

"She just can't leave it, can she?" Lang tutted, aggressively undoing his tie.

"She's being nice," Serena retorted.

"Well, I wish she wouldn't."

Chapter Thirty Nine

Chiswick

Vivi drowsily rolled over, clutching her pillow on which Theo's shirt was draped. Suddenly she felt enveloped. The embrace almost crushed her as she felt his mouth on her neck.

"Oh Theo! You're home!"

Her body turned into his embrace. They were one again. He bent to kiss each breast, his soft hands caressing the contours of her lithe body, stroking her thighs and kissing the moist parts between them. Vivi gave an ecstatic cry of pleasure as he slipped deeply into her. Their rhythms rose soaring into places they'd never been. Every part of them gave each other sublime satisfaction, finally reaching an explosion of total unity.

The peace was disrupted by Georgie bursting into the room just after 6am with little Jago stumbling along behind her.

"Daddy! I love this Russian doll!" she cried, bounding onto the bed and hugging Theo.

Theo hauled Jago up for a hug. The bedroom was alive with laughter.

Vivi watched her husband and children, crying inwardly with joy. *We're all here*, she thought, stroking Theo's face.

Breakfast was chaotic and rowdy. Bella came in to clear the plates and plucked Jago out of his high chair. Meanwhile, Vivi got up to hug Theo.

"I can't believe you're back, it's so wonderful. You'll be here for Beady's party," she said.

"Another party?"

"No, this is *the* party—for Mum's seventieth. I did tell you it was postponed because of her accident, but perhaps you were too distracted by work. But her face isn't swollen anymore, so we've rescheduled it for a few days' time—we thought we may have to wait weeks!"

"Well, I may be rehearsing or even doing a concert at short notice," Theo replied.

"Do try and be here with us all." Vivi's appealing eyes won him over.

Theo practised for a couple of hours until Vivi came in and suggested a picnic. He played some songs on the piano for the children and they romped until the hamper was ready.

It was a beautiful sunny morning, so everyone cycled to Chiswick Park. As they arrived, Georgie grabbed Theo's arm and the two of them were running to a huge cedar tree when his mobile rang. He stopped to answer it while Georgie continued to run.

"Sergei!"

Vivi watched the excitement on his face, and momentarily felt her heart sink. She walked on and found a large grassy area among the huge cedars. As she spread out the rug, little Jago crept underneath trying to play hide-and-seek. Vivi spread out plates and cups with some wine for Theo and herself.

"Lunch is ready!" she called to Georgie, who was swinging from a thick branch of the overhanging tree.

"Where's Daddy?" she asked.

"Over there on the phone."

Georgie jumped down and raced across, pulling Theo towards the picnic. She took his phone and hid it behind the tree.

"Come on Daddy, it's *our* time with you now. We have to share you like a piece of cake before you get gobbled up."

A wave of guilt washed over him and he gently squeezed his daughter's hand.

Vivi fed Jago, who was entranced by the tame squirrels darting in and out of the trees.

"That was Sergei wanting to discuss St Petersburg," said Theo, sitting down on the rug. "He's arranged a box. Would you mind sharing it with Baba?"

"That would be lovely darling, I'm so excited!" Vivi smiled delightedly, but then caught sight of Georgie's downcast face.

"Can't I come too?" pleaded the little girl mournfully. Just then a squirrel jumped onto her plate and scurried off with a biscuit. Distracted, she got up to chase it.

"Is she too young to come to your concert?" whispered Vivi.

"I'd love her to be there, but maybe not *quite* yet. I'll get Sergei to record it for her."

Just then Georgie returned and bounced onto Theo's lap. "Can we have a pet? A cat or a dog... or a squirrel?" She giggled.

"We'll see," said Theo, wrapping his arms round her, relieved that she was no longer unhappy.

Chapter Forty

Kensington

"This is a slow old train. Why ever did you choose it, Cherry Pie?" asked Jonty, gazing out of the window.

"It just seemed a good time to arrive in London," said Cheryl without looking up from her crochet, which spilled out onto the next seat.

"Mum *will* have a surprise when she sees us. It was such a good idea of yours, even though we'll have to come back again on Saturday. Hope her face is better for the party," Jonty said. Eventually they pulled into Marylebone station. "Let's be extravagant and get a cab."

Jonty put his arm up as a taxi swivelled round towards them.

A little later, they stood outside 16 Phillimore Gardens as the bell trilled their arrival. Serena was suitably amazed.

"Ssh, we're on a surprise visit to see Mum," Jonty whispered.

"She's doing some weeding," said Serena, kissing them both on the cheek.

They walked through to the garden.

"Yoo-hoo!" called Jonty.

"Oh, what a surprise, JJ!" Beady walked towards him and they hugged. "Dear Cheryl, how are you?" Beady bent down to kiss her. "Let's all have a drink."

Serena went to make Pimm's while the others sat on the bench.

"I'm glad to see you've made a full recovery," said Jonty, putting an arm around his mother's slender shoulders.

"Are you excited about the party?" asked Cheryl.

"Yes, I'm so looking forward to seeing all my old friends. Goodness knows why Serena has ordered a marquee though. Very extravagant. I'm sure we could have got everyone into that lovely big drawing room upstairs. Mind you, she always overdoes things."

Just then Serena appeared with the drinks. "Where will you have lunch?" she asked.

"What about the pub up the road?" Jonty suggested.

Beady ruffled his hair. "That *would* be a treat. Will you come too, Serena? Or are you too busy?"

"Afraid so Mum, I have to wait in for the marquee."

Beady loved seeing Jonty over a delicious lunch in the pub garden. Cheryl made them laugh with stories of the ponies from her riding school.

Finally, the marquee arrived. Five men trundled through the house and drove pegs into the lawn, chattering to each other as they worked. It was erected within two hours, just in time for Serena to dash off to collect Alicia and Freddie from school.

"Now kids, you've got to keep out of the way while they move the tables and chairs into the marquee," Serena warned them.

"Whoa! How exciting," said Freddie. "Can I watch?"

"I don't see why not, so long as you're good."

"Mummy, I got a star today writing about polar bears," said Alicia.

Serena congratulated her, distracted by the many tasks ahead of her. They arrived to see a second even bigger lorry outside the house.

"Look at all those chairs," squeaked Freddie. "Enough for a football match."

Serena jumped out to greet the delivery men, giving them directions to the marquee in the garden. Beady, Jonty and Cheryl arrived just as both lorries were driving away. They walked through the kitchen.

"My goodness! It does look grand but aren't there too many chairs?" said Beady.

"There's enough for all of our guests," said Serena patiently.

"We must decide the place names of course," Beady went on. "JJ will sit on one side of me, being the only son. Who shall I have on the other?"

"What about your favourite vicar?" suggested Jonty.

"Yes, or Harry, my old bridge partner," Beady said.

"I've arranged an appointment at the hairdresser for you," Serena interjected. "How about a manicure too?"

"Not sure I want my hair primped up," replied Beady warily.

"You'll look lovely, Mum."

Beady hated being organised. "I'll have to think about it," she mumbled.

Benjie waddled into the kitchen, arms outstretched to Serena. "Mama."

"He's a poppet, isn't he?" said Beady.

"You take him, Mum, I've got to dash out for a client," Serena said handing him to her mother and hurrying out of the room.

"Poor little fellow being left alone," said Beady, hugging Benjie.

*

Forty-eight hours later, the day of the party finally arrived. Serena woke at 6am and glanced at her long to-do list.

"I must take Mum to the hairdresser at 9am. That'll keep her away while we lay the tables and place mats."

As she drew back the curtains she saw it was drizzling. *Thank God we've got a marquee,* she thought.

Alicia teetered into the room wearing Serena's purple high heels. "Can I have these for the party Mummy?" At that moment she lost her balance and fell on the floor. "Ow!" she cried.

Lang came through the door covered in shaving foam. "What's going on?" he asked.

"I'm trying to be like Mummy, but the shoes hurt too much," wailed Alicia.

"Breakfast is on the table!" Maggie called up.

Beady was already tucking into a bowl of fruit and yoghurt. Freddie was dripping syrup round his porridge and the table, while Benjie sucked butter off his toast.

"As it's Mother's party tonight, Maggie, will you get the children to clear up while I take her to the hairdresser?"

"Yes, Miss Serena. I thought it would help if I took them to the park, so you could get on with the food." Maggie smiled as she wiped the butter off Benjie.

"Good idea. Oh, and Vivi's coming to collect them all for lunch," Serena added.

Twenty minutes later, having dropped Beady at Kool Kutz, Serena strode into the marquee holding all the place names (which had been agreed with Beady the night before). As she began laying them out, Lang brought in the glasses with two bottles of wine for each table. There was no gaiety in him at all, his mind was elsewhere.

Suddenly there was a warbling from his breast pocket,

"Hello Jonty. Yes, she's here." He handed Serena the phone.

"What's the matter with him?" began Jonty. "He sounds very fed up. Anyway, we've got all the veg and cheese and will be with you about 4pm. Is that okay?"

"Yes, great. Could you bring two pots of your homemade horseradish?" Serena asked as the doorbell rang. "Hang on a sec, JJ." She dashed through the house, then yelped, "Oh, the cake looks fantastic covered in flowers! Oh but now I'm not sure this seating plan really works."

"No doubt Beady will change everyone round during the courses much to everyone's annoyance," Jonty observed. "Serena, you're doing a great job, stop fussing. Anyway, listen, I must go, I've got to iron Cheryl's dress." They both laughed.

Shortly after 11am, presents for Beady arrived. Several plants and bouquets came by special delivery. A fascinating, heavy parcel arrived from Harrods. Serena put them all in a cupboard under the stairs before Beady returned from the hairdresser.

"You look very chic, Mum."

"Oh, it's all so tight! They put too much spray on," moaned Beady, trying to separate the strands across her forehead but thankfully, by mid-afternoon though she was in a more upbeat frame of mind.

"Now, what can I do to help, darling?" she enquired, breezing into the kitchen and wrapping an apron round her dress.

"Could you peel some potatoes ready to roast later?"

"Oh, haven't you got a more interesting job for me to do than that?"

"Alright, could you lay the left-hand side marquee tables and fold some napkins? Which you always do so well," Serena added, as she did the other tables in half the time.

"Hi Beady," said Lang, carrying a large tray with yet more

glasses into the marquee. He then reached up to hang some trailing flowers round a pillar.

"That's charming, Lang. My friends will love the place. I think I'll have a rest before it all gets exciting." Beady walked back into the kitchen taking off her apron.

"I'll come up with a cup of tea at 6pm," Serena called. Having reached the top of the stairs Beady heard a familiar voice at the door.

"Hello Father Paul. Do come up and say hello. I'm about to have a rest," she called down as Serena showed him into the sitting room, leaving his case in the hall.

Beady was rather miffed that he didn't come straight up to see her, though by now she was lying down under the duvet.

"Would you like tea or something stronger?" asked Serena once the priest had settled himself comfortably.

"I'll have whisky with a dash, please. This *is* a beautiful place."

They chatted for ten minutes then Serena said, "Shall I show you upstairs? Your bedroom is on the first floor next to Beady's. There's a new shower in the bathroom."

"Oh good. Is there time for me to have one before the party?" he asked.

"Yes, of course. Here we are Father Paul. This room has a lovely view of the garden. See you later."

As Serena closed the door her mobile rang. "Hi, how are Freddie and Alicia? Was lunch a success?" she asked Vivi.

"Yes. Everything's fine, but I had an idea. Why not leave them here for the night? Bella can put them to bed."

"That would be a great help, but you might need to warn

her that Freddie falls out sometimes. Oh, but I suppose Alicia will want to be here for the party."

"Don't worry. Georgie's decided they're going to have their own imaginary one, dressing up in my clothes for a midnight feast," said Vivi laughing.

"Thanks so much, darling. See you about 7pm—don't forget the salmon." Serena turned to see Beady standing by her door.

"Has Father Paul come up yet?"

"Yes," whispered Serena. "He's having a shower."

As the grandfather clock chimed 4pm, the doorbell rang again and Jonty and Cheryl staggered in carrying four trugs overflowing with vegetables. There was a distinct smell of cheese from Cheryl's handbag.

"Phew! What a journey," said Jonty. "The leeks fell out onto the platform at Paddington. Several people had to help us rescue them. Here, take the beetroot, they'll need baking for an hour. Oh, and open your bag Cheryl. Here's some homemade brie."

"Thanks JJ, I'd better put that in the fridge," said Serena.

"No, no! You must let it breathe at room temperature," enthused Jonty.

Serena smiled. "Right you are. Okay, well I'll deal with all that later. For now, why don't I show you both upstairs?"

A minute later they all passed Beady standing at her bedroom door looking glamorous in full makeup, but still in her dressing gown. There were hugs all round, then she whispered, "I think Father Paul is still in the shower. The water's been running for ages."

Just then Maggie came running upstairs. "The two young helpers, Issy and Tim, are here. What shall I get them to start on?"

"Jugs of water on all the tables. Fruit juice on the side, then wash the lettuces my brother brought. After that put the olives and crisps out in little baskets," said Serena, mentally ticking items off her list. "Thanks Maggie."

Serena went to her bedroom and showered briefly with a fragrant honeysuckle gel, then slipped into a long silk dress. She felt Lang's hand slowly caress her back as he zipped it up.

"You look stunning my Fig Tree." She sank onto the dressing table stool as Lang kissed her deeply. "Have you chosen a shirt for me?"

"Yes, it's on the bed. Shall we give her our presents now with a glass of Champers?" Serena wove blue eye-shadow round her lids and frilled her lashes with mauve mascara.

"Not too strong on the lips darling, just think of all those guests you'll be kissing!" Lang laughed. He suddenly saw the similarity between mother and daughter vis à vis their use of bright lipstick. *They'll both be doling out red blotches tonight*, he thought.

Serena ran into Father Paul descending the stairs with Beady in tow who was asking for all the gossip she'd missed while away.

"Mum, let's go into the drawing room," she said.

Just then Lang walked by carrying a crate of Champagne and Serena introduced him to Tim and Issy. She then guided everyone into the warm, lamp-lit lounge where a pile of gifts lay on the table.

"Ooh, this is exciting. I don't like getting old usually but being here with my family is such fun. It's almost worth turning seventy for!" said Beady, ripping open Cheryl's beautifully wrapped present—a home-knitted cardigan. "My favourite colours! Oh Jonty, isn't she clever?"

Beady hugged Cheryl, slightly marking her cheek with scarlet lipstick.

"This is ours, Mum," said Serena.

"A handbag full of my favourite cigarillos! How divine and so thoughtful." She pecked Serena on the cheek, leaving her mark again and smiled at Lang.

"These others are from the children. You'd better open them tomorrow when they're here," Serena suggested. Instead, Beady turned to another pile of presents. "Oh look! Two CDs. Theo playing my favourite Rachmaninov and Chopin. Darling, you must be so proud of him."

"He's sorry not to be here," said Vivi. "He is packing for his next tour."

Everyone was feeling quite bubbly as the first guests arrived.

Sir Ron Duncan, a great admirer (with bad breath and sandals) walked slowly towards Beady. "Hello, my dear girl. You look as wonderful as ever," he muttered, kissing her hard.

Behind him came Sheena Peet, hobbling with the help of one stick.

"I remember you sitting in your father's office chatting so fast I couldn't hear his dictation. You were quite demanding but delightful. Happy birthday!"

Everyone settled round Beady, sinking into sofas and cosy armchairs.

Laughter welcomed Ramsey Baldwin (her eye surgeon), who was handsome with thick white hair and a tanned long face. Handing Beady a book he chuckled, "I think you'll enjoy this experience."

"Oh, Ramsey, how good to see you."

They laughed warmly, holding hands.

Hairdressers Sam and Benny arrived with a tray of Beady's favourite hair colour and shampoo, both wrapped in gold paper.

"Goodness! How exotic!" Beady hugged them both.

Music filtered into the room as the string quartet began their first Mozart piece. A surge of guests arrived, all bearing gifts.

Lady Sircombe swooped in bearing an enormous plant.

"This will look glorious in Madeira by your pool—just smell the leaves." Beady did so as Lady Sircombe clutched the pot. "Aren't they divine?" She plucked several leaves to smell them.

"Yes. What an amazing scent. Thank you my dear."

Serena stood poised by the marquee. "Do all come and sit down for dinner."

As she guided Beady to her seat between Jonty and Father Paul, the birthday girl looked across at an empty seat.

"Who's missing?"

"Henry Bond hasn't arrived yet Mum," said Serena.

"It will be good to see him. We used to play bridge often. Do you remember him, Father Paul?" Beady asked.

"Yes, a big jovial man, ginger beard, owned a shoe shop, came to church twice a year," replied Father Paul.

Issy and Tim served foie gras to all the tables while Lang helped with the wine. After a short gap filled with buzzing chat, the main course arrived on huge serving dishes. Most ate slowly, almost overwhelmed by the variety of vegetables picked fresh for the party from Jonty's land.

The doorbell rang during the quartet's rendering of Mozart's tender Sonata No. 22, unheard by everyone except Lang. Answering it, he welcomed Henry Bond and the two of them slowly walked towards the marquee, making small talk as they went.

Just as they were about to reach the party, Henry tightly gripped Lang's arm and suddenly fell across the marquee's entrance. Lang gasped as the elderly man's arm slid away from his own.

Serena rushed over, whispering urgently, "Is he alright?"

Lang felt Henry's faint pulse, then listened to his chest. "No."

"Oh my God! What can we do?" gasped Serena. "We must call a doctor at once. Get Tim to help move him into your study. Hurry, for God's sake, the party must go on without Beady knowing or she'll be destroyed. I'll go and call Dr Howe. You help with Henry. Make sure he's covered up with the rug on the sofa."

Lang hoisted Henry up and headed off to the house.

Luckily, Beady's table was at the far end of the marquee away from the entrance and several people were getting up to chat to her and offer their presents. But Beady noticed the empty chair again.

"I wonder where Henry's got to? He's normally very punctual. I hope he comes soon." She turned to Jonty, "Get Cheryl to come and sit with us."

Jonty went over to the next table where Cheryl was avidly telling Lady Sircombe about her riding school.

Just as he caught her eye, Serena came and whispered to him about Henry's accident. "Keep Mum occupied at all costs. Just suggest that Henry must have forgotten the date. After all he is. . . was. . . eighty-one."

"Well, she's just off to the loo," Jonty pointed to Beady gliding through the tables, eagerly chatting to the guests.

As she came into the kitchen, her eyebrows rose. "Hello Dr Howe! How nice of you to come. Do go through."

"I've just got to see a patient, but I'll pop over later," he replied as Beady made an exit to the toilet.

Meanwhile, Serena had discreetly given Father Paul a note

to come immediately to the study without Beady knowing. He disentangled himself from Ramsey, but as he was about to open the study door, Beady tapped him on the shoulder.

"That's the wrong room if you're looking for the cloakroom, it's through that door," she said, pointing to the hall.

"Ah yes, thank you."

Beady wove her way back to the top table. Everyone had finished the scrumptious main course. Tim and Issy cleared the plates ready for the birthday cake that would be followed by speeches.

Meanwhile, having felt for Henry's pulse and listened to his chest, Dr Howe closed his eyes and murmured, "I'm afraid he's dead. The ambulance will be here shortly. I've told them to come to the side door with a stretcher and *not* ring any bells. There was nothing you could have done."

"Oh no, this is awful." Serena ran her hands through her hair. "I need a drink. Would you like a drink Dr Howe?"

"Thank you, a glass of wine would be ideal."

Serena turned to her brother. "You better go back to Mum, because the birthday cake is about to arrive. I'll follow you in when we've lit the candles."

The quartet started playing 'Happy Birthday' as the whole marquee became a blaze of candle light. Jonty carried the cake in proudly to his mum who was trembling with excitement and hardly able to stay sitting down. Everyone stood with a glass of Champagne singing lustily and cheering Beady. Jonty gave her a knife to cut the first slice, holding her quivering hand gently.

"Oh, look at those wonderful flowers on the cake, I can't bear to spoil them." She was radiant. The air was filled with laughter.

Serena poured herself a glass of wine and swallowed it in

one go. She noticed her hand was shaking and attempted to pour herself another drink but the wine spilt over the sides of the glass. She closed her eyes for a few seconds and took in a deep breath before grabbing the bottle and a spare glass and heading back to Dr Howe.

Serena heard the back door slam and wondered if Henry had been carried away. She spotted the doctor sitting with his head in his hands and Henry was nowhere to be seen.

"I got you a drink," Serena said and Dr Howe looked up.

"Thank you," he said, taking the wine and glass. "Henry is with the ambulance. Poor fellow. Are you alright?"

Serena hugged herself and nodded. "It was just a shock."

"I understand but you did all you could," Dr Howe said gently. "You should see to your mum."

"Yes, I will, thank you doctor," Serena said.

She re-joined the party and was relieved to see Beady chatting happily with her friends. Quite a few were looking flushed, so Serena asked Issy to offer coffee.

Just before midnight guests began to leave. Despite Henry's unfortunate 'departure,' Serena felt pleased the party had been a success. As she warmly kissed everyone goodbye, Lang smiled at the little red blotches on everyone's cheeks, especially Ron Duncan and Ramsey Baldwin who had a kiss from Beady as well as Serena and now looked like clowns.

Finally, the door closed.

"Thank you, my dears, for a glorious party," said Beady, sitting down with a blissful sigh. "It was very good to see so many friends, but I did miss Henry. I'll give him a ring tomorrow."

Serena opened her mouth and then closed it. She would tell her mum about Henry tomorrow.

PART TWO

Chapter One

Moscow

Theo's fleeting visit was all too brief. Having done his utmost to comfort Vivi and reassure her, their poignant goodbyes were difficult. As Vivi was at Beady's party, he himself was preparing to return to Russia for urgent pre-St Petersburg rehearsals.

When he was in the taxi to Heathrow, hee glanced back at the house and saw Georgie's sobbing face waving to him from her bedroom window. He hated leaving home and felt Georgie's soft kiss still lingering on his cheek, but then an even stronger wave of excitement washed over him.

No, I have to go. It was the right decision, Theo thought

Sergei met him at the airport on a fine, warm afternoon, bubbling with enthusiasm over their schedule for the next ten days.

"There are big posters outside the Philharmonic Hall in St Petersburg announcing your debut, plus a very handsome picture of you at the piano," he said, as they embraced, then walked outside towards his green Audi in the car park. "How is Vivi? I bet she's excited about coming to see you play. Which reminds me, I've booked you both into a charming hotel. There's a room upstairs for your Baba and I'm next door to her."

"Thank you, Sergei." Theo patted his arm then sighed. "If only Georgie was old enough to come too. It breaks my heart to leave her. We must try and get some future bookings nearer London."

"Yes, Paris and Vienna are both distinct possibilities," enthused Sergei, before his face grew more serious. "To more immediate business though. Ivan, the pianist you are replacing, is a local boy, so you have to win over your audience with an outstanding performance. Outstanding, you hear?"

Sergei revved up the car and zoomed into the lunchtime rush hour.

"I won't disappoint you," murmured Theo.

"Ah, there's your mother." Sergei waved out of the window.

"What time shall I see you tomorrow?" Theo asked, feeling the need to reassuringly touch Sergei's arm.

"Your usual studio at 9am," replied Sergei, as they drew up outside Baba's apartment block.

Later that evening, Theo showed Baba photos of the children and reminded her of Vivi's imminent visit.

"She's such a wonderful person," he said. "I'm glad you'll both be with me in St Petersburg. Sergei seems to be organising all my time leading up to the concert."

"Yes, he really is devoted to you. He talks proudly to everyone about your talent," enthused Baba.

Theo paused for thought. "Yes, he's a caring man. Now Mama, I must be up at 8am. It's time for bed."

"Sleep well," she said as they hugged.

Theo drifted off to sleep imagining he was in Vivi's arms, the scent of her body teasing his nostrils.

*

As he entered the Conservatoire the next morning, Theo could hear the other musicians playing odd phrases, having a joke and tuning up. It was like coming home. Glad to be back, he walked through to his rehearsal room. The glistening piano was tuned to perfection as he tried out a few notes.

"So, are you in good form, my friend?" enquired Sergei entering the room.

"You tell me!" Theo smiled, then began vigorously playing the opening movement of Rachmaninov's Piano Concerto No.2.

He became so immersed that he didn't notice a small audience of his orchestral colleagues standing transfixed as he reached a climax of searing emotion; before tenderly beginning the slow movement. After fifteen minutes of thunderous chords and the most sensitive interpretation, his enthralled audience applauded, surprising him by their presence. Exhausted, he slumped forward, drained of all passion.

He felt an arm round his shoulders and looked up. The audience had disappeared.

"That was incredible." Sergei's eyes were moist.

"Yes, but now I've got to go back and work on the detail," said Theo.

Two hours later they left the room together in silence.

"Shall I walk home with you?" Sergei asked.

"No, I'd like to think about tomorrow."

"Murel will want to see you about rehearsals with the whole orchestra. You're to meet him about 9am."

Sergei outlined the arrangement, which involved five days of rehearsals with Murel and the Moscow orchestra, three days of solo practice, the flight to St Petersburg, and finally one day with the Petersburg orchestra and Murel. It was going to be one of the biggest weeks of Theo's career.

*

The next morning, the conductor was waiting in the hall to welcome Theo back. They chatted about the tempo of the first movement.

"Let's begin," urged Theo, longing to start work with the orchestra again. They rehearsed until 1pm.

"This afternoon we'll start the slow movement. It's beginning to be very special already." Murel put an arm round Theo as they walked off the platform.

Sergei was waiting by the door. "Come, maestro, I've booked a table at our local café."

Theo turned to Murel. "Would you like to join us?"

"Another time perhaps. I have to work on the score." The conductor walked hurriedly on ahead of them.

Sergei and Theo enjoyed a chatty lunch together. The Russian, as always, boosting his protégé's confidence, which distracted Theo's thoughts about home for a while.

The afternoon rehearsal developed into a very emotional interpretation of the sonorous second movement. It rose and fell in waves of passion, greatly pleasing Murel.

Chapter Two

City of London

Lang's office

Lang's phone rang just as he was going to a lunch meeting.

"Mr Wantage of Parker Insurance for you," said his secretary.

"Good heavens! Where have you been?" asked Lang, picking up the receiver. "Why don't you pop round here and we can grab a bite together?"

He sat down again, and tidied some papers, remembering all those years ago when Bill Wantage used to help him revise for endless stockbroking exams. He recalled how he had got quite angry with him once for flirting with Serena at an office party.

Ten minutes later his secretary knocked on the door. "Mr Wantage for you."

A tall, broad-shouldered man walked in and boomed, "Good to see you Ling Lang. Director's office! I'm impressed."

"Nice to see you as well. Still with Parkers, eh?"

"Yes, I've been with them for over ten years now. I think we still have an account with you, but we've not done any business recently." Bill's voice seemed louder than Lang remembered.

"Do you still sing in the choir?" he asked.

"Yes, I love it, gets rid of all my tension. I bellow and relax." Bill laughed.

As they left just after 3pm, Bill said, "Would you like to buy 50,000 shares for our Staff Pension fund? You've got the details."

"Thanks very much," replied Lang in a surprised voice. "I'll call you as soon as we've dealt."

Bill looked pleased. "I've got some more suggestions to talk about next time," he said. "But I must get going now because Sophie and I are going to hear our granddaughter Annie sing madrigal in her school choir."

"Actually, I'm off for a week in Italy with the family. Let's meet once I get back," Lang suggested.

Satisfied by the order he hurried back to his office to execute it.

*

"You look happy," remarked Serena when he got home, the children babbling their welcome.

"Yes, I met Bill Wantage who actually gave me some nice business," said Lang as he picked up Benjie.

"Oh yes, I remember him," said Serena, pulling a face. "Let's have a drink to celebrate you being on holiday at last!"

The children started chasing each other, shrieking with delight.

"When are we going to Dilly?" asked Freddie, swinging on Lang's foot.

"Italy," corrected Serena. "Sunday, in the middle of the night. You'll wake up by the sea."

"Where's my spotted bathing suit?" asked Alicia.

Maggie came in, bouncing Benjie on her shoulders. "Do you want to take him up to bed, Mr Lang?" Receiving a nod, she chased the children upstairs.

"Come on Alicia and Freddie, race you upstairs."

A swoosh of pattering feet was followed by several thuds as everyone fell into the bathroom.

Chapter Three

South of Naples, Italy

The children scampered down to the sea's edge in blazing sunshine. They were staying at their friend's villa, just south of Naples and it had its own beach.

The first few days were the happiest Serena could remember as she saw Lang unwinding. Candlelit, wine-fuelled evenings outdoors seemed to renew their physical bond.

On Thursday, Lang went shopping and returned with English newspapers and a very solemn face.

"What's the matter darling?" Serena put an arm round him that he shrugged off.

"I don't like the markets falling like this and I'm worried about my dealing company," he said before he went off alone to the summerhouse.

All that relaxation gone in a trice, thought Serena. She slowly followed him.

"Why don't you talk about your worries to me? Why heap them up inside? It's spoiling our holiday!" she complained.

Lang swallowed hard and was just about to reply when there was a piercing scream, and Freddie ran towards them holding a very red hand.

"Something's bitten me! It's hurting," he cried.

"It looks like a wasp sting, poor darling." Serena carried the wailing boy into the kitchen and sprayed his swollen hand. All thoughts of Lang went to the back of her mind.

*

The next day, Serena almost revved up to her usual hectic speed by organising several family events to keep the children absorbed. She knew that Lang's sudden change of mood could spoil their spontaneity.

During a boozy taverna lunch, they met some old friends who shared a long table. While the children had water fights and pushed each other off their lilos, Benjie fell asleep on Serena's lap and a lot of laughter revived the atmosphere.

Later than evening by the pool, Lang rolled over to stroke Serena's bare, browning back. "How I wish we didn't have to go back on Sunday." But Serena was fast asleep.

On Saturday they hired a dinghy and went fishing for several hours. Lunch was the highlight of this glorious day because every mouthful not eaten was plopped overboard and gobbled up by hungry fish. Then suddenly a puff of wind blew Freddie and Alicia's sun hats into the water where they merrily bobbed away, much to the children's amusement.

Alicia started singing, "Row, row, row the boat," as she rocked it from side to side which frightened Freddie.

Chaotic fun continued until they reached the marina.

Chapter Four

Aylesbury

"Tea time! Where are you all?" called Cheryl.

Georgie and Jonty were hiding on a big haystack near the house. Cheryl went on calling as Jago giggled in her arms.

"Cooee!" called Georgie softly. "Here, come and find us!"

Cheryl looked up. "I can't get up there with Jago in my arms. Come down. I've made scones with strawberry jam."

A screech of delight followed Georgie at great speed down the bales of hay. Close behind was Jonty looking like a scarecrow.

"What a sight!" exclaimed Vivi, taking a quick photo as her brother galloped round the yard with Georgie on his shoulders.

Teatime was a riot. Cheryl had left out a bowl of flour and water so the children could make dough balls which they threw in the air for Jonty to catch and juggle.

Vivi relaxed in an armchair beside the Aga enjoying the laughter and remembering one time when her brother chased her when they were younger—he had spiked a dried cowpat on a stick. She'd run so fast but could only escape him by climbing a tree.

I wish Theo could see the children now, she thought wistfully.

*

Cheryl took Georgie for an early ride before the students arrived for their horse riding lessons. Jonty took Jago to a barn where three kittens were suckling their mother. Entranced, he lay down in the hay and stroked his favourite, which had snow-white fur. All morning Jago clasped the white kitten inside his anorak, bringing him to the kitchen where Vivi was making her special bread.

"Look what I've got!" he boasted, lifting up the kitten.

Georgie looked thrilled. "Can I hold him, please? Let me see his little face. Where did you find him?"

"We've been in the barn," said Jonty. "The mummy's got three kittens. . . you can have one if you like."

"Ooh, yes, I'd love to have a kitten to look after, but won't its mummy cry if we take it away?" asked Georgie.

"No, she's always having babies."

Vivi thought for a while and suddenly realised that the children might not miss Theo so much if they had a pet.

"Yes JJ, we'd love to take the kitten home."

Georgie rushed over flinging her arms on Vivi. "Mummy, thank you. I will love it so, so much."

*

"I wish we didn't have to go back to London. These few days have been heavenly Cheryl," Vivi said as she looked around the glorious surroundings.

"You know you can stay as long as you like. Do you think Georgie would like to stay on as it's half-term?' Cheryl suggested.

"Well, Mum's coming to stay shortly. She was heartbroken when she found out about Henry's death so it would be good for her to be around the kids. It will cheer her up. Then I go to St Petersburg for Theo's concert. Another time though, I'm sure Georgie would love to stay."

Vivi turned to see Georgie pushing the kitten in a toy wheelbarrow.

"You must miss Theo, sis. He seems to be away so much." Jonty put an arm round Vivi and gave her a hug.

"I do. Georgie misses him dreadfully too. It's even affecting her school work," Vivi said sadly.

Jonty frowned. "We didn't realise that. Why not come down more often?"

"I can't. There are always clients to see on a Saturday."

Bella welcomed Vivi and the children home three hours later with a big apple pie and ice cream.

"I *have* missed you all. Mr Theo phoned. He sounded very tired but said everything is going well," Bella said and Vivi sighed.

"Oh, I wish I had spoken to him! Did he say when he would finish his rehearsal?" Before Bella had a chance to reply Georgie interrupted, "Look what I've got, my own little kitten, Bella."

"Our kitten!" Jago corrected indignantly.

Chapter Five

St Petersburg

Theo lay on the ornate couch in his dressing room fifteen minutes before the concert was due to begin. His nerves were like little stabs in his stomach.

What a magnificent building this is, Theo thought. *A theatre of astounding proportions.*

Yesterday, after Vivi had arrived, he'd walked into the Philharmonic Hall to see a long, wide stage with seats stretching in a rectangle beneath tall, white columns. Boxes hung draped at each side of the stage.

There'd been a few problems adapting to the new orchestra, but he felt confident they'd all be resolved in the dress rehearsal. Such amazing acoustics!

There was a faint tap on the door and Vivi came in looking radiant in a red satin gown, her hair swept back with a flower coiled into the knot.

"Oh, my love, how are you feeling? Have you done the breathing I suggested?" She kissed him deeply and they held each other.

"I'm ready. Oh, how ready I am," said Theo with a tremor. "Ivan's injury's given me such an opportunity. This could be a turning point in my career. I have to prove myself to a big new audience *and* the critics tonight."

"Be calm," Vivi said, softly putting her hands round his head and massaging both temples in a circular motion.

Sergei, Theo's manager, came in hurriedly as the loudspeaker announced, "Five minutes please."

"Hello, Vivi, you look wonderful. You have to go now, I'm afraid. It's nearly time. Good luck Maestro," Sergei said, giving Theo a quick hug.

Vivi blew kisses as they swept off. Shortly afterwards, Theo walked gracefully up the podium steps to scattered applause. He flipped his tails over the piano stool and settled himself.

Everyone fell silent, then suddenly Rachmaninov exploded throughout the great hall. Theo's fingers flew across the keys with amazing energy. You could sense the audience becoming electrified. No one stirred. Seven minutes later, as the slow movement began, there was a palpable hush that became contagious.

It was the first time Vivi had seen Theo perform in Russia and she was transported. Later the mood changed as the third movement began languidly, mounting to a rapturous crescendo. The ecstasy was almost painful. An ovation burst out as the final notes died away.

Theo looked down to see Vivi's moist eyes meet his soul. Baba, Theo's mother and Sergei were wrapped in an emotional hug. The audience stood up as thunderous applause greeted his second return to the platform.

After a wonderful supper with family and friends, Vivi and Theo ambled back to their hotel beside the canal. Relaxed at last, they stood gazing at the water in silence. Theo kissed Vivi tenderly. As they walked slowly into the reception area several staff and guests cheered.

"What a surprise. Thank you so much," Theo said bowing

to them all. "Please forgive me but we must go to our room. My wife has to leave early tomorrow."

They climbed the steep stairs leading into a charming candlelit room. A second surprise awaited them as they stepped out onto the balcony where shimmering light reflected from the beautiful canal below. A bottle of Champagne was on the side table.

"Oh darling, what a magical evening," whispered Vivi. "You've certainly captured St Petersburg. I'm so proud of you. I've never seen you play like that." She put her arms around him. "Just look at those beautiful hands," she said, gently caressing them.

They talked, sipping Champagne, then collapsed onto the enormous double bed, giggling with warm laughter.

*

Early the next morning, they went by taxi to the airport, both deeply reluctant to say goodbye.

"I'll be back soon once I'm done with the next concert. Tell Georgie and Jago I'm longing to see their little kitten!"

Tears coursed down both faces. Vivi couldn't look back to wave.

Once she'd disappeared from view Theo turned to see Sergei beckoning him.

"Thought I'd find you here. Come! We have a press conference in an hour. Let's have breakfast first."

He put an arm round Theo and guided him to the car where they talked avidly about the previous night's performance.

The press conference was daunting. If Theo had expected

praise after a brilliant performance he soon realised things weren't so simple in St Petersburg, where the journalists and critics were wary of newcomers, especially those replacing their own favourite soloists. He sensed some hostility in their questions but was later rewarded by applause. He left the room accompanied by Sergei who patted him on his shoulder.

"Great! You managed those hounds well. Let's celebrate."

Chapter Six

Kensington

Serena was busily trying to hurry up the family breakfast. "I've got my first day at the Qatar Embassy," she said, closing Freddie's sandwich box.

"You're looking splendid in that red suit, darling. I'm sure they'll treat you like a queen," Lang said. "See you all tonight."

The children rushed over to hug him as he opened the front door.

At the school gates, ten minutes later, Serena saw Vivi parking.

"Hi sis, you're looking very smart!" called Vivi.

"It's for some new clients at the Qatar Embassy. I don't quite know what they want me to do," said Serena anxiously. "How was Petersburg?"

"Fantastic! Theo played amazingly. I'll ring you later. Mum's having fun with the children," said Vivi, waving before rushing off.

Fifteen minutes later, Serena hopped out of her car to be met by an official who offered to park it for her. She was shown into an enormous hall with ornate urns and vast baskets of hanging flowers.

"Come this way, madam. Abdul Tendri is expecting you."

Serena almost gasped as she followed the tall, elegant Arab into another enormous room with a mosaic tiled floor and long windows adorned with rather drab velvet curtains. There were six vast sofas in faded gold, red and yellow brocade and as many large armchairs. Lots of carpets were scattered around under huge chandeliers. Ancient sculptures were placed on pedestals amongst more exotic flowers.

"Miss Mayne, how good to see you." Abdul Tendri stretched out a hand and shook Serena's firmly. "I've heard a lot about your interior design work through a friend of mine. It seems you have a flair for colour. His Excellency would like some re-furnishing done in this room and the reception hall. He thinks the curtains could have more interesting colours and the upholstery will need to match."

"Oh yes, of course. Now I've seen the two rooms I wonder if I can bring some samples of different materials. I'd be delighted to suggest a new colour scheme," said Serena confidently.

*

"What a day. What a place!" Serena was dying to tell someone about her visit to the Qatar Embassy as she rushed in to her office.

Gems was answering two phones at once. Serena signalled for her to put them down so she ended both calls abruptly, saying there was a sudden emergency.

"It's unbelievable, Gems. . . just a billionaire's paradise. Five floors of opulent rooms. Rich Persian carpets—so beautiful. No one seems to get up until midday. The head guy seems to wander round in a long robe with slippers on. I peeped into the kitchen, which looked like a circus with masses of people chopping, peeling, grating, cooking and baking; it was amazing! It felt as though the only aim of the help as to pamper everyone. I've never seen such a vast reception room with tons of sofas and lots of beautiful, ornate chairs. Long velvet drapes at the windows and—"

The phone rang.

"Yes, hold on please." Gems handed the phone to a radiant Serena, mouthing 'It's *them!*' as she did so.

"Hello? Yes, Mr Tendri, I'll bring some more samples tomorrow. I'll see you at midday as arranged."

"I've never seen you so happy, Serena," said Gems.

"Well, it's quite a challenge," replied Serena breathlessly. "I'll have to work like a racehorse to achieve their deadline. They want the best of everything. At least I've finished Poppy Le Harvre's penthouse. The others will have to wait."

Gems kept quiet, knowing that her boss's drive would be uncontrollable.

Serena continued, "Oh, and I must give you a raise. Things are going to get hectic around here!"

She arrived home longing to tell Lang her news, but rang Vivi instead, knowing he wouldn't be back until late.

The children were climbing all over her for attention. Vivi listened avidly to her sister's enthusiastic descriptions.

"Don't wear yourself out and ignore the family," she said cautiously.

"No, of course not! You know me, bags of energy," Serena replied. The front door slammed and Lang appeared looking ashen. "Must go—I'll ring back later." Serena put the phone down and frowned at Lang's pale face. "What's the matter darling?"

"Think I've got food poisoning, I've been so sick." He hurried upstairs.

Serena shuddered inside as she heard him retching. Her enthusiasm evaporated.

The children were running upstairs to see Daddy, then back down again to get Serena's attention.

"Leave your father alone, he's not well. Please sit down. Your tea's ready." They followed her into the kitchen where Maggie had placed a large pizza on the table. "You serve it please, Maggie, I've got to make some urgent phone calls." Serena plonked Benjie into his high chair.

"Mummy, I must tell you what happened in class today," said Alicia agitatedly. "We found a poor little frog hopping along the window sill and—"

"Tell me later, darling." Serena hurried to check on Lang but got distracted by some samples of exotic materials in the hallway that she had collected from Peter Jones on her way home.

This purple and cerise shot silk will be splendid for the curtains, she said to herself.

"What *are* you doing?" asked Lang leaning over the banisters. "Could I have a cup of tea please? I feel awful."

"Sorry darling, I'll bring one up straight away."

As Serena went back into the kitchen, Freddie was standing on a chair with his mouth wide open while Alicia threw Hula Hoops towards his face. Benjie was giggling, trying to blow bubbles through his jelly, and Maggie was trying her best to control the mayhem.

"Come along, your Mummy's here now," she said, still smiling. "What are you doing? Freddie, get down at once. Alicia, stop throwing Hula Hoops."

"We're practising circus taming. Freddie's the lion and I'm the lion trainer." Alicia laughed.

"Maggie, please go and bathe Benjie, Freddie can jump in afterwards. Alicia, have you done your homework? And your piano practice?"

Serena stood waiting as Alicia rushed past into the sitting room and started plonking through a Mozart minuet with great speed and quite a lot of mistakes.

A few minutes later, Serena walked slowly into the bedroom where Lang lay inert looking extremely pale.

"Here you are," she said, putting his tea down.

"I've asked Dr Williams to pop in as I've got a bad pain in my guts," Lang said quietly.

"Oh you poor darling," replied Serena, stroking his forehead tenderly. "Shall I get you some dry toast and Marmite?"

"No thanks," Lang whispered.

Dr Williams arrived half an hour later. He walked down the stairs with Serena, saying it was a nasty viral infection. "Try to keep the children away. It's very catching but should only last about 24 hours."

"Thank you for coming at such short notice."

"Of course. Your man is looking very thin," the doctor added as a parting shot. "You must feed him up."

"I will doctor. Thank you again."

Shutting the front door, she heard a loud shriek from upstairs, she rolled her eyes and raced up to the bathroom where Freddie was emptying his wellies into the bath, which was overflowing.

"Oh Freddie, must you? Mummy is very busy. Come on, let me dry you. It's past your bedtime." Serena sighed, wishing she was back at the Qatar Embassy.

Chapter Seven

Chiswick

"How relaxing this house is compared to Kensington. Serena is a dear, but she's always on the run," said Beady, rocking Jago in her arms.

"Why don't we go for a stroll in Kensington Gardens after dropping Georgie off?" suggested Vivi. "It's such a lovely morning, although I must be back for a client at 11am."

Georgie started singing in the car, teaching Granny a song while Jago clapped hands singing, "Ah, ah, ah."

"There's Serena driving off. She must be going to her Embassy job," said Vivi who went on to describe Serena's new job at the Qatari Embassy.

"I didn't realise she was working for such important people these days!" said Beady proudly.

They drove through heavy traffic and parked in a side street near the entrance to Kensington Gardens.

"What a lovely sight seeing the road leading up to Kensington Palace. It reminds me of poor Diana," Beady said as they strolled along five minutes later.

The sun radiantly lit up an avenue of large chestnut trees. Jago began chasing the pigeons for a while, then plucked some daisies, which he handed to Vivi, broken stems and all. Vivi held a hand to her chest and made a big deal of smelling the flowers much to Jago's delight.

They strolled towards a fountain, swinging Jago up and down

between them to squeals of delight. Suddenly, he broke free and rushed to the fountain, splashing his hands in the water.

"Want a drink, Mama?"

"No, you mischief!" Vivi laughed and picked him up, swinging the boy round in circles, then hugged him.

"Oh Vivi, you look so happy with the little fellow," said Beady. "It's amazing how fast dear Georgie is growing up. Such a sweet-natured child, so eager to do everything. She tried to make my bed yesterday. I said to leave that for Bella to do but she said that Bella's is her friend and she should help her."

"Yes, she's very caring and sensitive," Vivi agreed. "That's why she misses Theo so dreadfully. They are very close. He's not here long enough to see her progress, and I'm worried that her work is being affected by his absence."

"Yes, I can see she misses him by the way she says, 'Daddy would do this if he was here.' Look how little Jago's growing too; such a bright, cheeky boy."

"I'm going to write a long letter to Theo telling him he must give us more of his time," Vivi declared. "And I'll ask Sergei to book concerts here or in Paris. After all, it's not just the kids who miss him."

"You're a wonderful, generous wife, dear Vivi. He's lucky to have you. When your father was alive he used to say, 'Keep that flame cherished in little Vivi, she has a rare soul'."

"I wish I'd known Daddy more, but he was always away, just like Theo is for Georgie," said Vivi sadly, squeezing her mother's arm.

Just after returning home Jago fell asleep, just in time for Vivi's client, who she led upstairs for their counselling session. Once Vivi was done with her second client, she made a light lunch. Jago was pushing cars under her feet and running them along the grass and up her leg as they chatted at the garden table.

"It's so warm today, just like Madeira. I wish you'd all come out and stay with me."

"You sound lonely Mum."

"Well, I am when I come back and see you all," Beady confessed.

"We'll definitely come over and stay this summer. The children would love it. Even if Theo is still busy in Russia or Europe, we'd all benefit from some sun, and we could teach Georgie to swim in your pool. Maybe Jonty and Cheryl might come? It depends on how his forest is growing. Come on, let's ring him now," suggested Vivi enthusiastically.

They each spoke in turn to Jonty. Vivi filled him in on Serena's wonderful new job.

"Goodness, she'll be designing Buckingham Palace next!"

"Listen JJ, what about you and Cheryl coming out to stay with Mum in July when we're there?"

"That's an interesting thought, but I'm not sure when the big riding school opens," he said. "Oh, and I'd have to get someone to look after the trees in case there's a heat wave. I tell you, it's worse than having kids."

"Oh Jonty, do try; it would be such a treat for Mum."

"I promise I will try," Jonty said. "Especially after Henry. Is she doing any better?"

"She is, thankfully. She understands there was nothing anyone can do but feels guilty that she didn't know about it at her birthday. I told her to stop being so ridiculous."

"Too right," Jonty agreed. "I'll come and spend some time with her soon."

Chapter Eight

Moscow

As he drove west out of the city, Sergei chatted non-stop to Theo who was gazing at the sparkling birch woods that stretched for miles. They shimmered in the May sunlight like tinsel. The light was so brilliant. Theo suddenly recalled the slow movement of Shostakovich's Piano Concerto No.2. The sheer beauty of the forest captivated him.

"What are you going to work on for the Vienna concert?" Sergei asked.

"I'm already thinking of Shostakovich No.2 plus a few Chopin waltzes which should suit a Viennese audience. I can't wait." Theo smiled, glancing at Sergei's deep sparkling eyes.

"My mother will be happy to greet you. She loves me bringing people to her dacha and enjoys cooking wonderful dishes. The only problem is I don't have a piano there for you to practise on, but a neighbour has. People in the country are so friendly. They'd leave it in a field for you to play if you wanted!"

Theo stretched his arm across Sergei's shoulder. "You look after me well," he said, patting him. "Ah, these magnificent birches—they're *so* beautiful!"

As they came out of the forest the warm sun dazzled them.

"Here we are. Look! There's my best girl waving by the gate."

A stocky lady of about fifty-five with a coiled plait came out to greet them. She didn't speak a word of English.

Two hours later, sitting round the dining table enjoying an

enormous bowl of borsch, Sergei realised how relaxed Theo was. Sergei's mother hummed a song, which he took up and began swaying to.

Laughter and hand-clapping resonated round the wooden house as vodka flowed. A full moon stretched through the open door. Overwhelming tenderness flowed between them.

"Tomorrow we have a banya party in the back garden," announced Sergei after the meal. Theo looked perplexed. "You don't know what that is? Oh, then I'll explain. All the men in the family pop in and out of our wooden sauna outside. We drink vodka and have fun beating each other with birch twigs. You'll love it!"

"It sounds great," Theo said. "But I need to practice for the concert."

Sergei shook his head. "You need some time off away from work and family. Just relax and enjoy this beautiful country for once."

"I don't know. . ." Theo said, feeling guilty. He should be home with his wife and children.

Sergei placed a gentle hand on his shoulder. "You work hard, Theo. Just let loose and enjoy yourself."

Theo gazed out of the window. He did work hard and all the travelling took a toll on his body. He never did have a chance to just relax and enjoy the moment. He turned back to Sergei.

"I look forward to the banya party."

*

Theo woke slowly, forgetting briefly where he was. Stretching both hands, he felt the urge to get to a keyboard. He got up, stood by the window and watched Sergei help his mother move garden furniture around, then pick some flowers, which he handed to her.

What an amazing person he is and so caring. I'm lucky he's my agent and a good friend too, thought Theo as he walked out to join them.

"Here's the sauna for our lunchtime fun. You'll meet a lot of friends today." Sergei laughed.

"Can I use your neighbour's piano for a few hours?" asked Theo, the sunlight making him blink.

"Yes, it's only an upright, but I'm sure they'll welcome you. Come, let's go through here."

A few hours later, Theo returned tired but satisfied with his practice. People started arriving around noon. Vodka and caviar on blinis were consumed freely. Eventually, everyone started undressing.

Sergei's mother had gone indoors to prepare the evening meal and various naked figures sat on the benches in the sauna, laughing and languorously tossing back more vodka before clambering outside the hot wooden box to roll in the last snows of spring. Almost to his own surprise, Theo ended up enjoying himself a good deal.

*

The following morning, Sergei took Theo on a long walk through the nearby forest. Occasionally a warm shaft of sunlight penetrated the dense foliage. When they came to a clearing Sergei talked excitedly about Theo's future, his ambitions and plans for the next six months.

Theo listened and began to feel a certain security about the plans and recognised how reliant he was becoming on Sergei. It was reassuring that no anxieties seemed to be in the way of his very calm, warm feelings in Sergei's presence.

They sat in silence, feeling the sun caressing their backs. Sergei lay on the earth, legs splayed out, whilst Theo perched on a stump head raised to the sunlight.

Later, they ambled back to the dacha. A strong smell of herbs lingered in the kitchen where a huge mixed salad with various coloured leaves had been prepared.

Theo turned to Sergei. "This is such a beautiful weekend, thank you. But I am missing a real piano, I'm afraid."

Sergei laughed. "Don't worry. We'll drive back in a couple of hours after I've helped Mama stack the logs. I'm glad you came Theo. I haven't seen you this relaxed. . . well, ever!"

Chapter Nine

Aylesbury

Jonty was busy examining saplings and pleased to see they were free from blight. He looked up to see Cheryl gently guiding a long trail of ponies with giggling riders across the field to the paddock. He waved but she was too absorbed to notice. How he loved his Cherry Berry.

Later, when they met for a picnic lunch of local produce, he said, "You had a big class this morning. I waved but you didn't see me."

"Yes, there were some nervous ones, but even they have such courage," Cheryl replied. "If they can't do something they go on and on trying."

"It's wonderful what you do. I don't know how you have the patience," Jonty said hugging her.

*

Jonty heard an urgent rapping on the kitchen door at 7am and tiptoed downstairs, half dressed, with his face covered in shaving cream.

"They've gone," said Jacob anxiously.

"Who's gone?" asked Jonty.

"Them sheep in Top Field—just vanished! The gate was open."

"Wait while I get dressed," replied Jonty.

The two men walked off up the hill to an empty field.

"Stolen, I reckon," said Jonty, clenching his fists. "Look at these tyre marks, it must have been a big van."

"I didn't 'ear a thing," said Jacob worriedly.

"I must ring the police."

Jonty dialled while pacing round the tracks.

"Are you covered by insurance?" asked the desk officer when he got through.

"No, I didn't think it was worth the cost," Jonty replied. Then, a minute later, "Yes, we'll wait for you here."

After giving them directions he called Cheryl. "Bring us a thermos, love. We've not had breakfast, so a couple of bacon sandwiches would be welcome too. All the sheep in Top Field have gone—every single one. We're waiting for the police."

"Oh no! That's awful," cried Cheryl.

Half an hour later, two officers arrived in a Range Rover, just as Jonty and Jacob were finishing their sandwiches.

"There's been a series of sheep rustlings in Buckingham-shire," said one of the policemen. "We haven't caught anyone yet. Some abattoir must be making a lot of money out of these thefts."

"What a fool I was not to have insured them, but the premium was very expensive," moaned Jonty.

"Yus, I was really fond of 'em sheep but at least the ones who'd already lambed are flourishing in Middle Field down by the forest," Jacob said trying to reassure his boss.

"I've got an idea," said Jonty. "You know that old wooden caravan up in the corner of the yard. Would you mind sleeping in it for a couple of nights if we pulled it into the Middle Field by the wood?"

"Yes, Mr Jonty, I wouldn't mind stopping them rustling anymore, and I'll take my gun, too, if only to give 'em a fright."

"I'll get a good breakfast sent up to you each morning." Jonty laughed.

*

Jacob woke to see the headlights of two vehicles slowly coming up the track. It was 4am. He scrambled to the caravan door, gun in hand, as it crept up the track. He jumped down and yelled, "What the 'ell are you doing here? This is private land. I'm calling the police!"

The vans revved up, turned around and went back down the hill.

"K744 RLM," repeated Jacob to himself.

Breathless, he ran down to the farmhouse to tell Jonty what had happened.

"Well done Jacob! It's lucky they didn't harm you. Let's ring the police right away. They might catch them on the main road if they're quick."

Cheryl appeared in a patchwork dressing gown. "What on earth's going on?" she asked.

"Clever old Jacob caught them trying to steal from the Middle Field and he's got down the number of the truck," explained Jonty.

Cheryl hoped the sheep rustling would be resolved before Beady arrived, she couldn't imagine how his mother would react to the idea of thieves on their land.

By the time he'd finished with the police, who promised to

be in touch with any leads, Jacob went back up to his caravan, while Cheryl had fallen asleep in the armchair.

Dawn broke as Jonty walked down towards Middle Field. The sun peeped above the old barn roof and began to spread over the paddock. He could see someone had cut another chain on the gate and their tyre tread was very similar to the previous marks.

Fancy coming back for more so soon, he thought to himself.

Chapter Ten

Notting Hill

In her office, Serena was rushing to assemble various materials for the Qatar Embassy job. She'd bought a vast amount of brocade and silk, which was already being made into curtains and loose covers for the sofas. Abdul Tendri hadn't yet paid the agreed advance and her outstanding bills were mounting up.

She was beginning to flag but was determined to remain cheerful. After all, the last thing she wanted was to upset Gems when there was so much work to be done.

At home, Serena was on a short fuse through sheer exhaustion, snapping at the children and argumentative with Lang who had recovered from his virus and back at work, but she felt he still had a deathly look to him. She couldn't remember the last time she had seen Lang with a spring in his step.

"You mustn't do any more work until they've paid you the agreed advance," he stressed. "Explain how you've had to fork out for all the materials. Don't get yourself into money problems."

She knew Lang was giving her good advice but was fearful in case they withdrew the contract and she was left with heaps of expensive material.

"Mummy, I haven't seen you at teatime for days now. Poor Freddie cries himself to sleep even though Maggie reads him *three* stories and only reads me one," said Alicia sadly. "*And* Daddy comes back so late we never see him either."

Serena put her arms round Alicia, realising how she'd forfeited the school run and her usual time with the kids because of the Embassy job.

"Darling, I'm sorry, I've been so busy, but Mummy has an important job that has to be finished in two weeks. It's like you being asked to do a week's homework in one night," she said, stroking Alicia's forehead. "Come on, let's play our favourite duet together."

Just as they finished, Freddie came in and threw himself onto Serena's lap, thumping hard on the piano.

"Who'd like toffee ice-cream?" Serena asked.

As both children rushed to the freezer, Lang wandered in from the garden.

"Oh Daddy, you're here too. Will you read me some more Jungle Book stories?" Alicia asked.

The doorbell interrupted everyone.

"I've got a letter for Miss Mayne," explained a courier. "Could you sign here?"

Serena read the letter and exploded. "The Embassy want to change the gold velvet upholstery on the two large armchairs to a maroon and gold brocade. It will be impossible to complete the contract on time if these changes are made now."

She hurried to her laptop, dashed off a reply and added a demand for the overdue progress payment.

As she pressed 'Send' and flopped back in her chair, Lang put an arm round her shaky shoulders and murmured softly, "Let's have a drink in the garden before I go up to read to Alicia."

He kissed her on the top of her head and Serena smiled warily.

*

Serena picked up the curtains, which looked superb, and proudly delivered them to the Embassy. Several staff were summoned to hang them for His Excellency to see at lunchtime.

Serena arranged the drapes until they fell elegantly, then stood back and waited with everyone else for the arrival of the Ambassador and Mr Tendri.

"My goodness, these curtains are splendid," said the Ambassador. "What an improvement, Miss Mayne."

"You certainly have a flare for colour," added Abdul Tendri, handing an envelope of money to Serena. "And thank you for accommodating our. . . how shall I put it? Our last-minute change of mind about the loose covers."

"I'll be bringing them in a couple of days," she said calmly, pleased with the elegant curtains, which gave the room an almost regal effect.

Back at the office where Serena was handed a page of messages, she immediately rang the upholstery team in Birmingham to ask when the loose covers would be ready.

"There'll be a slight delay as we're short staffed," the manager replied regretfully. "But we should be able to deliver most of them by Saturday, or perhaps Friday, if it's urgent. The two large chairs won't be ready for a week. They're more like thrones and we've got to use special stitching."

Serena put the phone down and turned to Gems. "They're impossible people to work for! I've only been paid for the materials so far, but I guess it's good money compared to my usual clients." She drew breath. "Now, I must dictate some urgent letters, Gems. So many people are clamouring for quotes and ideas. That article in Harpers about me working at the Embassy has certainly propelled me into the big time."

"Yes, it's exciting. You've had so many new people asking for appointments," agreed Gems.

"It is exciting, isn't it?" Serena said, smiling. "I'm not going to stress out about the Embassy. It will all work out, I'm sure."

Chapter Eleven

City of London

Lang's office

"Hello Mr Mayne. Could you drop in and see Mr Calder at 10.30am tomorrow?"

Lang hesitated at the end of the telephone line. "Err, yes, I think I can manage that," he replied to Calder's secretary.

He couldn't sleep that night worrying about what his boss wanted to speak to him about and he got himself into a panic.

The next morning, he tentatively knocked on Calder's door.

"Ah, morning Lang. Come in and sit down. With this market so rotten we've got to make sure all our accounts are paid up and the loans are well covered. Have you sorted out that client of yours who's been so slow in paying?" he asked bluntly.

"Yes, I think so. I'll check and make sure."

"I want everyone to check all their clients and we'll go through them at the next board meeting."

Lang left the office feeling extremely anxious. He knew that his boss was suspicious.

A few hours later, he arrived home edgy and agitated. Serena was out. Maggie was feeding the children. Benjie was screaming.

He walked into his home office wishing he could talk to someone about his problem, but he knew he couldn't. Serena would be so disappointed in him and he couldn't deal with that. No, he was going to sort this out himself. But how?

Chapter Twelve

Moscow

Theo had begun practising the first movement of Shostakovich's Piano Concerto No. 2; it needed extra attention due to the tricky rhythm. After an hour, he found himself getting cross with his fingers and decided to go and listen to the orchestra's rehearsal.

"What's up? You're looking worried," said Murel, breaking off at the sight of Theo's dejected face.

"I don't know. I can't get into the 1st movement," he replied.

"Well, listen to us for a while. . . give your head a rest," suggested Murel, the ever-inspiring conductor.

His charm soothed Theo as he sat and listened to the orchestra for an hour, then walked more serenely back to his studio.

Sergei wandered in some hours later and sat quietly to one side.

"It's not going well today. I need pushing." Theo sighed. Sergei put his hands on his client's shoulders and gently massaged them. "Ah, that's good. I'm beginning to rely on you for everything."

The afternoon rehearsal was a challenge as Theo had to perform the 1st movement and synchronise with the orchestra who hadn't heard him play that particular concerto before. Murel urged him on and by that evening, the 1st movement was powerful and much improved.

When he got back to Baba, Theo flopped down onto the sofa.

"Phew, what an exhausting rehearsal. My fingers just didn't behave today."

"You're working too hard," Baba said bluntly, as the mobile rang in his pocket.

"Hello, dear Vivi, how lovely to hear you. What? Clever girl, coming top in Maths and singing, let me talk to her," said Theo. "Hello my girl, you *are* doing well at school."

"Yes, and I'm singing a solo lullaby at assembly," explained Georgie. "I made Mummy a chocolate cake with flowers on it for her birthday today. Auntie Serena's taking her out so Alicia's coming over."

"Can you put her on again? Hi Vivi. I've got a surprise for you. Two seats in a box for the Vienna concert."

"Oh, how wonderful. Who's the other seat for?" Vivi asked excitedly.

"Georgie, as it's holiday time and I miss her," Theo said. He smiled as Vivi audibly passed this information on.

"Beady is off to stay with Jonty today by the way. We've had a lovely time," said Vivi.

"I'm really sorry to have missed her. Maybe she'd like to come to the Paris concert?" asked Theo.

"She might enjoy that, I'll ask her. I must go darling, I think Jonty's just arrived to pick her up."

Vivi put down the phone.

"Daddy didn't wish you Happy Birthday did he?" said Georgie.

Vivi took in a deep breath and forced a smile on her face. "He's very busy darling," replied Vivi.

Ten days into rehearsals, Theo felt much more confident.

Sergei made sure he wasn't driving himself too hard and lent him some of his favourite CDs of opera and poetry to help him relax.

Meanwhile, the Vienna concert hall had asked for information about Theo's career which Sergei rapidly supplied, eager to promote his new prodigy and to attract a large audience.

There were also rumours that a big agent in Vienna had shown interest in poaching Theo which made Sergei anxious.

Theo invited Baba to Vienna too. She beamed when he suggested it, especially at the chance of seeing Georgie.

Chapter Thirteen

Aylesbury

Jonty listened to his mother's chatter all the way down to Aylesbury. She'd clearly loved staying with Vivi and the children but was sad not to see Theo, saying she would have loved to hear him play, especially Rachmaninov.

Cheryl was waiting in the drive, waving as she opened the gate.

"Ah, what lovely air," said Beady, breathing in deeply. "I've got lots of herbs and, of course, tomatoes and lettuce, but you've got everything here already I see."

"Yes," replied Cheryl. "We both enjoy working hard at our produce."

After an omelette and salad, Jonty proudly brought out their new cheese, which he had aptly named 'Aylesbury Croft'.

"How delightful, I must take some back to Madeira with me. How is your riding school, Cheryl? I hear you do wonderful things for the children."

"She's a marvel. The kids have to deal with disabilities and learning difficulties but Cheryl gets them confident and full of courage to try new things," said Jonty proudly.

"Well, I just love helping the children to be honest. It's extraordinary how the ponies seem to sense these youngsters need extra support and attention," added Cheryl.

"What about your wood, JJ? It sounds like an enormous project. I'm longing to see it, but I'd like to have a little rest in my room first if I may."

"Yes, of course Mum, let me take your case. Your room looks out to the Chilterns from over the front porch."

In the late afternoon, refreshed from an afternoon nap, Beady and Jonty ambled down toward the woods.

"These are chestnuts and the beeches are further down. There are some other varieties across this clearing. We had a virus on the maples but discovered it early and had to cull quite a few. Prince Charles' office has been most helpful with advice," explained Jonty.

"I was so proud of you when I read The Times article. What a great legacy to leave the next generation," said Beady.

"Yes, Serena and Vivi's children will see them fully grown," said Jonty, drawing Beady over to a bench. "I love being down here. It's very peaceful just quietly walking around."

"Yes, you've always loved nature since you were a little boy and grew enough carrots in your garden for two meals. When you were ten you were climbing trees and would sit in them for hours." She smiled. "And do you remember me hauling your lunch up on a pulley?" They both laughed.

"How are you feeling about Henry?" Jonty asked delicately.

Beady shrugged. "It's just shocking, but at the same time, it's not, if that makes sense. Obviously I know Henry was elderly but dying like that, in the middle of a party. So upsetting. I hope to die in a better way."

"Mum!"

Beady chuckled. "Oh love, it will all be our time one day."

They sat for some time in silence. As the sun went down it became chilly and Jonty led his dear old mother back to the house.

*

Cheryl took Beady to the new riding centre to see the extension being built.

"I'm going to give you both a cheque towards your wonderful ventures," Beady said enthusiastically.

Suddenly, a bus packed with noisy children drove round the corner.

"Here's my other family," said Cheryl laughing. "They've all come for their lessons. Do you want to watch them?"

"Oh yes, I'd love to," said Beady excitedly.

"I'd better get you some wellies, it's very muddy in the paddock."

Beady watched entranced as some of the more fragile children were lifted up onto their docile ponies, each one excited and laughing. There was a chubby little boy with one leg who looked just like Jonty when he was seven with blond curls falling over his face and a cheeky giggle.

Beady longed to help, then suddenly had no choice in the matter.

"Here, hold this rein!" Cheryl called to her, thrusting the pony's reins in her hand to guide the little boy around the paddock.

"My name's Tom," said the curly haired boy. "I like to go fast."

"You must wait for the others I think," Beady told him wondering how she would keep up.

By the end of the morning, Beady had assisted, along with the other helpers, several groups of children. She enjoyed seeing their eager spirit respond to the activities.

"You were a great help this morning," said Cheryl afterwards.

"Well, it was wonderful to watch the youngsters responding. Some are so brave, you can see they are in pain," replied Beady sadly.

Chapter Fourteen

Chiswick

Vivi heard Georgie rush down to tell Bella about Vienna.

"Wonderful! Now give your little brother a hug," replied Bella as she held Jago in outstretched arms.

Vivi smiled as she followed the excitement. "Yes, Theo's arranged a wonderful surprise for us both, tickets to his concert! Will you be alright looking after Jago on your own? It's only for a couple of nights. Perhaps Benjie can come over one afternoon with Serena?"

"Yes, of course I can manage, Miss Vivi," Bella said.

"We'll be going in two weeks on Friday." The doorbell rang. "Ah, that's for me. Perhaps you could take both of them to the park? There's a puppet show on by the café."

The puppet show was quite a violent Punch and Judy act, and little Jago clung tightly to Bella every time Punch bashed Judy on the head. After the show, Georgie bumped into a school friend who invited her to lunch.

"Can I go home and ask Mummy if I can go?" she asked.

All morning Vivi worked hard with some troubled clients and was quite exhausted. After they left she sat on the floor doing a little yoga to refresh herself.

Suddenly, she could hear Georgie calling and a minute later heard a whisper outside her door, "Mummy, Anya has asked me for lunch. May I go? She only lives up the street. I met her in the park and. . . "

"I'll be down in ten minutes, darling," said Vivi quietly.

Walking downstairs, Vivi heard shrieks of laughter from the garden.

"Mummy, can I go with Anya?" asked Georgie. They were both swinging from the climbing frame.

"Yes, of course, have a good time," she called after them as they scampered through the front door.

Vivi wandered into the garden and sat on the swing thinking about what Theo might be doing. This continual separation was sapping their relationship. She kept meaning to write a letter expressing her sad feelings—maybe now was the time to do it.

Bella came out with Jago.

"Mama!" he called, running up to hug her knees.

"Hello, my lovely boy." Vivi picked him up, tickled his toes and put him in the swing. His laughter warmed her needy feelings.

"He's going to lunch with Tom next door," said Bella.

With both children away, the house was empty. Vivi sat down to write to Theo, choosing her words carefully. She mustn't deliver an ultimatum because he had to fulfil his passionate ambition, but there could and should be alternatives that would allow them to be together like any normal family.

After all, although he was very attached to Russia, the orchestra, his mother, and Sergei, he was also wonderful at home. The children needed stability. They needed their father.

A tear fell on the page. Vivi put her pen down and sobbed. She was always telling her clients to let go and express their feelings, yet she couldn't do so herself. . . not to him.

An hour later, the letter remained unfinished when Bella quietly appeared.

"Are we going to have a party next week for Jago's birthday, Miss Vivi?" She put a cup of mint tea on the table.

"Oh yes. He'll be two already! A 'Thomas the Tank Engine' cake would be fun. I can't decide what to give him. He has so many toys. Perhaps a scooter?" Vivi suggested.

"I'm giving him a singing CD. He loves songs," said Bella.

What a generous girl, thought Vivi. Back in Indonesia, Bella came from a poor family and had eight siblings.

"I must do more nursery rhymes on the piano with him and try and find a singing class," said Vivi.

The doorbell rang.

"I've had an enormous burger for lunch, Mummy. Anya wants to play duets on the piano," said Georgie excitedly. "She's got an uncle who lives in Vienna. Could she come and see Daddy play?"

"I don't think so because there aren't any tickets left this time," Vivi said.

The girls ran off distracted by the piano. Bella went next door to collect Jago who arrived hand in hand with his friend Tom.

"He wants to stroke our kitty cat," announced Jago.

The two little boys ran into the garden where Tinky was fast asleep under a shrub.

The house was full of laughter again, Vivi felt happy and wanted in their young lives. How she loved them.

Wouldn't it be lovely to have another one? she thought.

The phone rang and startled her.

"Hello Mum, how good to hear from you! Glad you're having a busy time with JJ."

"I wondered how you were, Vivi. I get worried seeing you alone so much," said Beady.

"Actually, I don't feel great, but we'll talk about it another time."

Chapter Fifteen

Kensington

"This really is crunch week. The Embassy must have everything ready for next Friday. They've only sent me one cheque, all the overtime is costing extra and I haven't even given you a bonus yet, Gems," said Serena anxiously.

"Don't worry, you can give it to me later. The main thing is for you to deliver the goods," said Gems. "You might be asked to go out to the Middle East, just think of that! I'd love to see you in a burqa!"

"Don't be silly, they don't want me out there," replied Serena. Her mobile rang. "Who? The Sun? Yes, that's me. What? Well, I don't know if I'll be at the Qatar reception. Yes, I've designed a lot for them recently. No, of course I can't discuss my payment, that's a private matter. I'm afraid I must go to a meeting—goodbye." Serena switched off her mobile, saying, "Maybe not all publicity is good, they're like leeches. Those journalists are so tenacious."

A few anxious days passed, then early on Friday a delivery of loose covers arrived at the office to be inspected before delivery to the Embassy.

Serena was pleased to find the work flawless and directed the courier to deliver them to the Embassy. She knew they would be blown away by the covers and hopefully a cheque to cover her expenses—and her fee—would follow swiftly.

Chapter Sixteen

City of London

Lang's office

A week later, Lang left his office deciding to have a quiet drink at the Tower Bridge pub fifteen minutes from his office. He felt heavy from the worries bearing down on him and utterly depressed. What a dreadful mess he'd got himself into.

The fact that he was deceiving Serena and Calder made the stress so much worse. He realised he couldn't get the money to repay the dealing loss no matter how many times he told himself it would get sorted somehow or another.

Lang leaned over the river wall watching the murky water as the high tide slowly turned and started sluicing out to the estuary. Despite achieving so much in his business just one error of judgement had doomed his future prospects. There was no way out. He began to tremble.

What would happen to my family? Will I end up in jail? Lang leaned further over the wall.

"You alright mate?" Someone touched his arm as he bent over.

"Leave me alone, I'm fine," replied Lang, tears coursing down his cheeks.

"You look as though you need a drink," the thin-faced man said.

Lang walked away ashamed of his tears, his dilemma, his

shuddering body. As he paced slowly along the Embankment he remembered Alicia asking him to play solitaire before bedtime. There was no answer to his problems and no reason to stay away from home longer.

His clothes were damp with drizzle as he walked through the front door to find Alicia and Freddie sitting on the stairs waiting.

"Oh Daddy, at last!" Alicia stood up. "Freddie's missing Mummy and you promised solitaire before bedtime, so let's play now. Your coat's wet. Have you been crying?"

"No, of course not, it's the rain. Come on, let's play on the floor."

Freddie jumped on Lang's back as Alicia kissed him on his damp cheek. Maggie walked in carrying Benjie.

"Say night, night," she instructed.

Lang hugged him. "Good night my lovely boy."

After a fun round of solitaire, Serena suddenly burst through the front door, breathless.

"Hello kids. Hello darling, pour me a drink please." She flopped into an armchair.

"We've been waiting for you for ages Mummy," complained Freddie.

"Yes, we have," said Alicia, crossing her arms.

"Sorry guys, I've been so hectic with the Embassy," Serena replied.

"Supper is ready children." Maggie came in to pick Freddie off the floor.

"Lang, you look ashen. Are you feeling alright?" Serena asked, glancing at the crumpled man sprawled on the floor.

He ignored her. "How was your day?" he asked.

"Oh, it was incredible. They loved everything! I was introduced to the Ambassador himself. He's a huge man dressed in white and gold robes. Lots of people bow to him. He shook both my hands to show his approval and spoke through an interpreter. The reception's tomorrow night." Serena was bubbling. "And there will be more to do later."

"I've had such a heavy day at the office—let's watch a video together later," Lang suggested.

"I'll see the children into bed, then you can read to Alicia. I've got a few more calls to make."

"Can't you leave the office alone tonight, Fig Tree?" he asked as she left the room.

Lang sat staring into space. *What am I going to do?*

He could hear Serena's voice and he pulled himself off the chair. He found her gushing on the phone to Vivi about her embassy job.

She rang off when she saw Lang's gloomy face.

"I was just telling Vivi about—"

"I heard," Lang said miserably.

She shot him a sharp look. She almost resented being dragged down by his gloom.

"Will you come with me to the big reception party tomorrow night?" she asked animatedly.

"No, I won't, but you go. You've worked hard for it," he said quietly. "I'll go read to Alicia." And he walked away before she could stop him.

Chapter Seventeen

Moscow

Theo was deeply immersed in Shostakovich's Piano Concerto No.2. The slow movement was akin to his soul. He wove into the tender emotions as his rippling fingers caressed the keyboard.

Briefly, he looked up to see Sergei sitting at the far end of the rehearsal room. Each lyrical phrase grew more and more passionate. His whole being lingered on each sequence of notes. Poetic harmony sank into the keyboard as each cadence rose and fell until the final drifting note finished and Theo rested his hands on the piano, eyes shut, head bowed in silence.

A minute later, he felt a soft stroke on his neck that sent a warm quiver down his back, then a gentle caress round his shoulders. Theo's heart was racing as he felt Sergei's soft fingers. Theo stretched his head back and Sergei tenderly cupped the pianist's face. He opened his eyes and saw Sergei looking at him adoringly.

What am I doing? Theo abruptly rose and walked out of the door.

Chapter Eighteen

Aylesbury

"Prince Charles' secretary just rang to ask if he could visit the plantation next Wednesday," announced Jonty.

"Oh, how splendid! I'll still be here, I'd love to say hello," Beady said enthusiastically.

"Well Mum, he may not have time to come to the house. We'll see."

"Should I cancel the children's' classes that day?" asked Cheryl.

"No, my love, just keep them riding. I'd better tell Jacob to make sure all the trees are tidied up and labelled."

"What time is he coming? Will he want lunch?"

"He'll only be here a couple of hours," answered Jonty.

The sound of laughter rolled up the drive and a bus load of children pulled up outside the riding school.

"Can I help again today?" asked Beady.

"Yes, of course. I think Tom would love to see you. Come and give me a hand with their hats and boots."

It was a beautiful, sunny morning. Cheryl loved hearing the children's excited voices as they got ready for their riding.

Little Tom called out, "Hello!" when he saw Beady bringing a riding hat for him.

Soon the paddock was packed with docile ponies. Beady led Tom round while Cheryl instructed, "Hold the reins tightly, straight back, slow walk." She smiled as she watched Beady's pleasure guiding Tom, and the way they chatted away to each other.

*

The next day, Cheryl showed Beady the dairy, where some Aylesbury Blue was being made. The matriarch was impressed and also delighted when her daughter-in-law handed over an entire new cheese.

"How should I pack it when I go back to Madeira?" she asked.

"We'll organise a special box for you with air vents, so it doesn't sweat," suggested Cheryl.

"This is a splendid place. I don't know how you find time to manage it all," Beady said, holding Cheryl's arm.

"I just love home-made produce, I suppose," Cheryl replied. "Have you ever tried my gooseberry and rhubarb relish?"

"Perhaps I'll take some of that home too!" Beady laughed.

"Ah, there you are," said Jonty with an armful of beetroot. "St James's Palace rang to say the Prince will be here around 10.15am on Wednesday for an hour before he has to inspect some architectural designs at Aylesbury town hall."

As her son talked, Beady began to wonder if coming back to England might not be more appealing than life in Madeira.

How much would I miss my friends out there? she wondered.

Chapter Nineteen

Moscow

Theo ambled through the front door exhausted. Baba gave him a hug as usual, happy to see him, and babbled away, but Theo didn't respond.

"What's the matter? You don't want any food and you're anxious. I suppose it's pre-concert worries, is it?" she asked.

"No, Mother, I just want to think. I'll go and play some music upstairs. See you in the morning," Theo mumbled, hurrying to his room, ignoring his mother's sad face.

*

At rehearsals Sergei came into the studio. "I was so carried away by the music, your talent, the expression on your. . ."

"I can't listen to this now," Theo interrupted furiously. "For God's sake, my head will explode, it's all too much! My wife and daughter are coming out soon for the concert. What do you think could possibly happen between us? We must never talk of this again." He walked to the piano, raised its lid, and played several loud chords.

Sergei watched him for a few seconds then left the room. Theo found it hard to concentrate but an hour later was challenged to join Murel and the orchestra for their first run-through.

When Theo returned to his practice room, he found a

hurriedly scrawled note on the concert hall piano about his train departure to Vienna and the coming week's schedule, including the arrival time of Vivi and Georgie at the station. Information Sergei would usually deliver to him personally, but he was nowhere to be seen.

Chapter Twenty

Kensington

Serena had received a very exciting phone call from an Italian count called SanTranto. He said he'd read about her in a *Times* article and wanted to know if she'd consider a makeover of his Rome office.

"How much would he pay you?" asked Gems enthusiastically. Serena told her the incredible amount and Gems whistled, clearly impressed. "Wow! Your reputation could become European-wide after this."

Serena nodded, but then sighed, thinking about Lang and the children coping without her. She tapped her chin with a highlighter pen.

"I won't mention it just yet. We're off to a 'do' in the country tomorrow. Maybe I'll talk to Lang on Sunday. He may say yes, or absolutely not, depending on his mood."

*

Serena felt vibrant in a backless, mauve, silk dress on Saturday morning while Lang looked suave in his pearl grey morning suit. They'd been invited to a wedding in Sussex. The reception was to be in a huge barn. Alicia and Freddie went to stay with Vivi and Benjie stayed with Maggie.

The wedding took place in a field with a long table instead of an altar. The bride's dress blew in circles round her legs and she had to keep pulling it sharply down. At one point the groom even tried to tread on the dress to keep it anchored.

Luckily, it was a short ceremony, slightly spoiled when the wedding ring blew off the table in a sudden gust. All the guests had to go on hands and knees searching for the wretched thing. It was finally found by the cherubic page boy, embedded in mud.

The reception was Indian-style, with cushions and throws on the floor, draped scarlet curtains and incense sticks scenting the air. All kinds of spiced dishes had been prepared; chicken korma, poppadums and basmati rice. Everything looked and tasted amazing, while soft music came from the rafters.

The barn had an atmosphere of highly charged expectancy and was festooned with hanging candles. Flowers and fountains of purple water were positioned at each end.

After meeting various friends and enjoying the free-flowing drinks, Serena found herself quite tipsy. Guests reclined on cushions as dancers performed sensuous contortions. Serena and Lang ambled out of the barn with Serena swaying slightly. She ran her fingers slowly up his arm and Lang squeezed her waist.

On the way home, Lang drove up a remote country lane and began to hurriedly undress Serena as soon as the car stopped.

Oh, how good it is to have him back in a good mood.

He began kissing her avidly and threw his clothes onto the furrows of a ploughed field. He lowered Serena onto his crumpled jacket and passionately made love to her in the moonlight, producing groans of deep pleasure.

Afterwards, they lay happily in each other's arms. It was after 3am on Sunday morning as they entered their sleepy household, relaxed, slightly muddy, and giggly, shushing one another.

Chapter Twenty One

City of London

Lang's office

Lang's firm was bubbling with news of a startling mining report and the fact that some Australian nickel shares were rocketing. Returning from a meeting, he found a message from Calder waiting for him.

Please come to my office as soon as possible.

Lang felt his stomach drop. The phone rang, making Lang jump.

"Darling, I've had a marvellous offer from—"

"Serena, I can't talk now," Lang interrupted. "I've got to go and see Calder. Ring me later."

"But darling—" she said to nobody, as he put the phone down.

Lang walked anxiously along the corridor and knocked on Calder's door.

"Come in Lang. Sit down. Now you told me that the debt for Sunrise Investment Co. was settled, but it isn't, is it?"

"No, sir," murmured Lang rather lamely.

"Is this company anything to do with you?" asked Calder quizzically.

"Well, err. . ." Lang faltered.

"I want you to tell me who owns the company and why it hasn't paid up," said Calder angrily.

Lang put his head in both hands and said, "I'm afraid it's me."

"You?"

"Yes. I own it and I haven't the funds to pay off its debt."

There was silence for several seconds, then Calder stood up. "In that case I think you should clear your desk. Stay at home and you'll hear from our solicitors shortly."

Pale faced, Lang rose and hurriedly left with tears in his downcast eyes.

Arriving home, Lang dreaded seeing the children, but there was no avoiding it. As soon as he crept through the front door Alicia ran towards him.

"Hello, Daddy." He pushed her away. "Why are you crying?"

Lang marched off and slammed his study door.

Maggie put her arm round Alicia in an effort to cheer her up. "Look at your poor kitten," she chuckled consolingly. "Benjie's sprinkled flour all over its head."

Freddie came in wearing a papier-mâché spider mask. "Look what I made!" he shouted.

"Don't go near Daddy," Alicia told him. "He's very sad and cross."

Half an hour later, Serena rushed in while talking on her mobile. Alicia sat on the stairs waiting to hug her, but the conversation went on and on in another language. Freddie circled round and round on his scooter.

"Shh kids, go into the kitchen." Serena waved them off. Eventually she finished talking.

"Daddy's cross," said Alicia sadly. "He didn't even say hello."

Serena hugged her and kissed Freddie on his mask. "I'd better go and see him then, hadn't I?"

A few moments later as Serena gave a soft knock and walked into the study she saw Lang sitting slumped at his desk. "What's the matter, darling?"

"I've been kicked out," he replied bluntly. His voice muffled.

"What do you mean?" Serena frowned.

"It's a mix-up over money," he snapped.

"I don't understand." Her eyes roamed round the room, then returned to his face. "How will we live?"

"I have absolutely no idea," mumbled Lang, putting his face in his hands.

Chapter Twenty Two

Vienna

Murel had given the orchestra a serious talk about what to expect in the Austrian capital, and Theo realised it would be an even bigger challenge for him than St Petersburg. A long rehearsal with many interruptions ensued, which annoyed him. He wanted to surge through all three movements and attack the problem phrases with the orchestra.

After lunch, a complete run-through restored his confidence.

"Bravo, Theo. Your tempi are excellent!" said Murel.

"A wonderful finale," added Sergei, appearing from behind the piano.

"I'm going to the studio," murmured Theo. "Please get me some black coffee and a sandwich, Sergei."

One hour later, just as he was leaving, his mobile rang.

"Hello darling, how are you?" asked Vivi.

"Exhausted, but longing to see you and Georgie next week," he replied softly. "Sergei has organised the hotel and your box. We'll meet you at the airport."

*

The next morning, Theo woke to a tense neck and shoulders. He didn't quite know what he was saying, but shyly asked Sergio for a neck rub. He half expected him to point blank refuse, but Sergei agreed, although he was more withdrawn as he tenderly rubbed his client's shoulders this time.

There was a hasty knock on the door and Murel walked in with a plump bearded man carrying several cameras.

"This is our photographer who's going to take some promotional photos," he announced.

Pulling on his jacket and scraping a comb through his messy blond hair, Theo sat poised at the piano.

"Now play, please," instructed the photographer.

Once they were done, the photographer wanted to come to the rehearsal to take pictures of the orchestra.

Theo was getting impatient about the waste of time. Soon Shostakovich was piercing the walls of the auditorium. The rehearsal went well and was up to the standard Murel hoped for. As the orchestra drifted away, Sergei asked Theo if he wanted a lift to the airport.

"Thank you," said Theo, avoiding eye-contact. "That would be very helpful."

They drove in a tense silence and at the arrivals barrier, Theo and Sergei could hear yells of "Daddy!"

Georgie almost fell onto her father, while Vivi followed serenely. Sergei drove them all to a small hotel near the opera house where everyone was to stay.

Georgie stood beside Theo on a tiny balcony and stared at the cityscape below in great excitement, talking non-stop.

Sergei handed him a schedule for the next day. "Rehearsals begin at 10am prompt. I'll pop in later."

Vivi linked arms with Theo and Georgie. "This is all so wonderful" she beamed. "Let's unpack, then go down and have something to eat."

The hotel restaurant was full of elegant mirrors, chandeliers and gold statues. Georgie, wide-eyed and full of laughter, gasped at everything. Vivi looked radiantly at Theo as they exchanged news.

"At some point I'll show you where Mozart lived, but you must go to some of the galleries and museums while I'm rehearsing," Theo said.

"Are you all enjoying yourselves?" asked Sergei approaching the table tentatively. Then spotting that Vivi and Georgie most certainly were added, "If you'd like me to drive you around tomorrow morning while the Maestro's rehearsing, I'd love to show you some of the sights of this magnificent city."

"Oh, that would be perfect," said Vivi excitedly.

"Thank you," said Georgie.

The two men glanced at each other meaningfully. Vivi noticed this and remarked, "I'll leave you two to chat while I put Georgie to bed."

Later that evening, Theo and Vivi fiinally got some peace and space, just the two of them. They sat on the balcony above the soft flowing Danube.

"What a spectacular view," exclaimed Vivi. Then, after a moment's pause. "How are you feeling about the concert?"

"Nervous, but it's good to have you and little Georgie here." He kissed her tenderly.

*

The reflections from the water shimmered on their bedroom ceiling as there was a gentle knock at the door, followed by Georgie bounding in wide-eyed and expectant.

"Where shall we go first?"

"Let's wait for Sergei to suggest places," said Vivi drowsily, then added after a yawn, "Do your concert clothes need pressing, darling?"

"I'll leave them for the valet to do."

Breakfast arrived a few moments later, much to Georgie's delight. Theo was restless to start rehearsals.

"I'll meet you this afternoon at the Café Central," Theo told them.

Half an hour later, Sergei took Vivi and Georgie on a tour along cobbled streets to several museums, then they went on a water taxi along the Danube.

"It's so beautiful," Vivi called to Sergei, sitting in the bow.

"Isn't it?" he agreed. "This wonderful river flows for miles and miles and finally goes into the Black Sea."

"Wow!" said Georgie. The boat rocked as she stood up to try and touch the bridge they were passing under.

"Careful!" called Sergei, then smiling at Vivi. "I'm so glad she's enjoying herself. Which reminds me, I thought we could all go to the Mozart House with Theo tomorrow after he's finished rehearsing."

While Sergei continued talking, Vivi thought she'd prefer to go on alone with Theo.

"The cafés here are popular and have always been a meeting place for artists and writers. The Café Central has an extraordinary wax figure of Peter Altenburg, a homeless poet and sketch artist who was an oddity and almost lived in the Café. His wax model sits in the window table and he is shown reading a newspaper. That's where we're meeting Theo shortly."

Vivi noticed every time Sergei mentioned her husband he smiled. It was nice that he clearly was so fond of her husband.

"Oh, this boat trip is so fun. I love the pretty houses," enthused Georgie. "Are we going to see Daddy now?"

"Yes," replied Sergei. "Right now!"

As they arrived, Theo was sitting in a corner seat looking very tired.

Vivi kissed him on the brow. "You look exhausted," she murmured, sitting down whilst Georgie jumped on his knee.

Sergei walked up to Theo. "I'll see you in later in the theatre dressing room. Try and get a little rest before the concert. I'll show you to your box at 7.15pm, Vivi."

Chapter Twenty Three

Kensington

Serena was frozen in fury and abject fear. "What are we going to do? Why has this suddenly happened? What went wrong? We seemed so safe and you were making good money, especially when you were promoted."

With his head in his hands he whispered, "We'll have to sell this house and pay off the mortgage. I'll never get another job in the City."

"Why? Tell me what's happened!" she cried.

"My dealing company made a big sale of shares which it didn't own. The price went up and I had to buy them back. I've defrauded the firm. There's no way I can pay the loss—I'm finished."

Serena was totally stunned. "Where will we go?"

"Perhaps Jonty might have a cottage or know of one we could rent," Lang suggested quietly.

"That would mean I'd have to commute. I must continue my work as it's going so well. Oh God! I want to scream! Wasn't there any warning it was going to happen? And what about the kids' education? How could you be so stupid, Lang?" she said angrily.

"We'll have to find them a state school wherever we live," replied Lang, turning away from her.

"And poor Vivi. If we move she'll be lonely."

"Oh, stop going on and on. First thing is to ring the bank,

the solicitor and your brother. We may have to sell the furniture. If we can get more than £1.5 million for this house at least that would pay off the mortgage and leave a bit over."

Black despair gripped his guts. The shame, the utter shame, stripped him bare. Lang's throat tightened as the bile rose.

He began to tremble as Serena left the room shouting, "Why the hell did you have to gamble our lives away?"

She sat on the stairs and wept convulsively. How she hated her husband right now. She took a deep breath and dialled Jonty.

"Hi, Cheryl, can I speak to JJ? Oh, is he? Well, in that case could you get him to ring me back as soon as possible," she said quietly, before climbing the stairs to her spacious bedroom. She looked at the garden where the children were playing hide and seek with Benjie.

I wonder how they'll be affected if we have to move, leaving all their friends? thought Serena. She felt as though steel bands were constricting her body.

"Pull yourself together, girl," she said, wiping the tears away. Her mobile rang. "Hi Jonty. Something terrible has happened. Lang has lost his job. He's actually been sacked and owes a lot of money. We'll have to sell the house and find somewhere. . ." She broke down crying. "Somewhere smaller. Sell the furniture and. . . oh, it's quite ghastly, JJ."

"Shall I come up and see you?" he asked anxiously.

"Oh yes, please do. I think Lang's breaking down. He's in a frightful state. I don't know how to help him. Please don't tell Mum about it yet."

Alicia burst into the bedroom and flung her arms round Serena. "My friend said she thinks you're the prettiest mum in the school."

Serena rang off and hastily wiped her eyes.

"Have you been crying Mummy?" Alicia asked studying her face.

"No, I was just talking to Uncle Jonty, darling."

"Is Daddy alright now? I want to play snap with him."

"No, don't bother him now," said Serena, stroking her daughter's long hair. "Come and help me bathe Benjie."

Freddie wandered in. "Daddy's gone out and wouldn't play football with me," he said grumpily.

Chapter Twenty Four

Aylesbury

Prince Charles arrived in a black Daimler promptly at 10.30am with an assistant carrying a large notebook. Jonty and Cheryl shook hands just as the children were arriving.

"That's a happy bunch of youngsters," said Prince Charles smiling.

"Yes, they're regulars at my riding school," said Cheryl shyly.

"Let me lead the way to my ten-acre plantation, Sir," suggested Jonty.

He and Prince Charles walked downhill in radiant sunshine with the Prince asking many questions about how the idea originated. He was enthusiastic about the long-term benefit to the environment. They also discussed the maple disease. After looking closely at a withered leaf, Prince Charles wondered if the virus was the same as that which had affected his own trees. A few minutes later he started talking about some of the produce that Jonty and Cheryl grew.

"We're quite self-sufficient here," replied Jonty proudly.

"Yes, so am I with the Duchy of Cornwall Estate. It's very rewarding growing simple produce from the land. As I said before, I'd like my Trust to make a donation to your excellent project."

"Oh, thank you very much, Sir," replied Jonty, a little red in the face as they both ambled back up the hill, with the Prince's assistant following a few paces behind.

Cheryl walked towards them carrying some pieces of Aylesbury Croft on a wooden platter.

"This is our latest cheese, Sir. Do try a piece." She presented the plate.

"Delicious! It has a good crisp tang and a lively mixture of herbs.

Just then his assistant leaned over. "Excuse me Sir, but we have to go now. We're due at a farmers' meeting where they're discussing pig-breeding."

Prince Charles sighed. His visit had been all too brief.

Five minutes later, Jonty looked towards the drive where Beady was opening the gate, looking rather over-dressed but happy as she waved the royal party off down the drive.

"I do wish Mum hadn't waved," he muttered and led Cheryl back to the garden seat.

"Well, that went well," Cheryl said, sitting down. "He has such enthusiasm for other people's ideas. It's refreshing to hear him offer advice and very generous of him to give us a grant." Jonty didn't respond. "What is it?"

Jonty stared into his hands. "I'm afraid I had a call from Serena just before Prince Charles arrived. Lang's been sacked from his firm for malpractice. He's got a huge debt and they think they'll have to sell up and move to a new house. I said I'd go up and talk to them. It's pretty urgent, they're both in a terrible state."

"Oh my God, JJ, what are they going to do? Those poor children will be so upset to leave their schools," said Cheryl.

"First things first. Can you give me a lift to the station? Oh, and we mustn't say a word to Beady yet," he called over one shoulder as he walked towards the kitchen.

Chapter Twenty Five

Vienna

The large Wiener Musikverein Concert Hall was packed with an expectant audience. There was a throbbing buzz as people waited for the concert to begin. Sergei took Vivi, Georgie and Baba to a box near the stage.

Georgie stared round the enormous gilt concert hall. "Oh Mummy, this is so exciting."

Baba smiled at her granddaughter's animated face filled with delight even though she couldn't understand most of what the girl said.

The lovely sound of the orchestra tuning up gave Georgie plenty to stare at. A few minutes later, Murel strode onto the podium. There was an instant hush as Theo, head erect, walked to the grand piano and bowed low to the audience. Vivi held onto Georgie in case she stood up if he looked at her.

Shostakovich burst forth. Theo's power swept across the piano, the wonderful acoustics reflecting his brilliance. Vivi was totally spellbound at the magnitude of his playing. Baba seemed enraptured and on the edge of her seat. Georgie watched Theo's fingers race across the keys. It all seemed very loud as they were almost on top of the orchestra.

What an experience! The lyrical slow movement reached a peak of such tenderness that made Vivi cry inside. BANG! The bubbling final movement erupted from the keyboard, on and on, until the last chords were instantly drowned by a huge ovation. The audience cheered and even stamped their feet. After four rousing returns to the auditorium, Theo put his hands up, indicating an encore, and settled to play several Chopin etudes.

All at once Vivi realised the enormity of Theo's talent in a way she'd never done before. All his senses were there in his beautiful playing. As the Chopin finished, Theo gave a special bow towards their box and Georgie blew him a kiss, Baba waved, and Vivi looked deep into his eyes.

Sergei collected the family from their box and took them to Theo's dressing room.

Georgie ran to him. "Oh, Daddy, Daddy!"

Vivi kissed and hugged him, then he embraced Baba warmly.

"Well, the audience loved you," enthused Sergei. "I've arranged a long table at the restaurant next door when you're all ready."

It was a happy gathering and although Baba could understand very little, Sergei was able to translate most of the conversation for her.

"So, tomorrow!" said Theo at one point, taking Vivi's hand. "I thought the three of us could go to Mozart's house before you catch your plane home."

Sergei glanced at Theo but said nothing.

*

They entered Mozart's house. Theo glanced at the ancient church next door. It was the oldest in Vienna and where Mozart had first rehearsed The Marriage of Figaro. It had perfect acoustics.

Up some narrow stairs, a beautiful spinet stood in a sparsely decorated room. Various ancient scores were placed near the keyboard. There was also a wooden piano which looked odd, while on the walls hung several beautiful pictures of Mozart wearing a grey wig and velvet jacket.

The room had a wonderful feeling, as various arias were piped through concealed speakers. It was like walking back into the Eighteenth century.

"This is so beautiful. I wish we could stay longer," said Vivi.

Arriving at the airport, affectionate hugs made Vivi and Georgie unable to leave Theo. He tenderly nudged them towards the barrier.

"I'll be home in a week," he reassured them. "It will fly before you know it."

Chapter Twenty Six

Kensington

Serena fell into Jonty's arms as he arrived on her doorstep in the morning.

"Let's go into the garden," she whispered.

Jonty put an arm round his sister's trembling shoulders as they sat under the huge chestnut tree. Maggie had tactfully left some coffee on the table.

"Lang's in his study and will be off to see the bank about our mortgage in half an hour. It's all such a shock and quite devastating. I never thought he'd do such a thing. I'm scared Jonty. Do you think he'll go to prison?" she asked in a whisper.

"I don't know enough about it. Let's be practical though. Where are you going to live? A good friend of mine who's got a dairy farm has a cow-man's cottage that's empty. I'll ring him and ask if he'll consider renting it. It's quite big, I think. You can store your furniture in one of our barns if you like. Of course, it'll take some time to sell this, and it'll be a real change of lifestyle for you being in Aylesbury instead of. . ."

"But I'm not going to live there full-time!" interrupted Serena. "I'll have to commute. My work is becoming very successful. I've just been invited to go to Rome, for heaven's sake." She paused. "Although. . . I suppose I can't really go now, can I?"

"Don't be crazy, you must. You're the breadwinner now," Jonty exclaimed.

Lang suddenly appeared at the kitchen door. "Hello, JJ. Darling, I'm off to see the bank." He looked ashen and dishevelled.

"Shall I come with you?" Jonty asked unexpectedly.

"You mean now your brother-in-law's a crook?"

Jonty ignored the remark and walked over to Lang. "Come on, let's face the melt-down together."

He looked back at Serena for a moment, then guided Lang towards their front door.

At the meeting, Jonty was able to fill out Lang's monosyllabic explanation. Luckily, it emerged that there would be no difficulty in paying off the mortgage when the house was sold.

When they got home two hours later, they walked into the garden where Alicia, Freddie and Benjie were all splashing in the paddling pool. Serena was pacing up and down the kitchen talking to Gems, organising her Italian trip.

"She'll always be in the fast lane, even when she's ninety," said Lang despondently. "Let's have a drink JJ. Oh, and thanks for being here today— it was quite an ordeal."

Finally, all three adults sat round a bottle of wine with the occasional splash of water from the kids in the pool.

"Who were you on the phone to, Fig Tree?" asked Lang wearily.

"Well, since you ask. . ." Serena glanced quickly at Jonty, then braced herself. "I've been invited to Rome to do a wonderful job for five days. The money's amazing."

Lang was silent for a moment. "But you can't possibly go to Italy at such a dreadful time. We need you here."

"Lang, you must let her go. You need everything she can get now," stated Jonty.

Lang got up and walked inside, slamming the door behind him.

"Was that cruel of me?" asked Serena quietly.

"No. Just necessary," murmured Jonty.

At that moment there was a second loud slam.

"Was that the front door?" asked Serena anxiously.

"I think so. Listen, you must go to Rome," said Jonty. "Leave it to me and I'll talk to him later tonight. Tell your client you'll be catching the 7am flight."

"Thanks JJ, I'm so grateful. I think it will be a big opportunity for my business. I'm getting an advance of £15,000. I'll go and phone him now."

"Lang's gone off in the car," she called from the hall a minute later.

"He'll come round," JJ said confidently and he prayed that he would.

Chapter Twenty Seven

Chiswick

Vivi had just said goodbye to a client and was surprised to see Lang walking slowly towards her.

"Hello Lang, come in. Is anything the matter?"

Lang slumped onto the sofa. "Oh Vivi, I've been such a fool. I've been sacked. I'm finished."

"Now calm down and tell me slowly what's happened," she said softly.

Lang recounted in detail how he'd started speculating but the losses got bigger and bigger and the whole business spiralled out of control. He began sobbing.

Vivi went over and put an arm round his shoulders, letting him cry.

"I'll never be able to work in the City again. No one will trust me. We'll have to sell the house to pay off the mortgage and the rest will go to my firm. We'll never be able to live in London again. Jonty's trying to find somewhere to rent near his farm. Christ, I feel so ashamed. Poor Serena can barely look at me. She must hate me for letting her down. She's going to Rome tomorrow. Oh, Vivi, I want to die. To be swallowed up. I don't know if I will go to jail—the sheer humiliation and guilt."

Vivi let him unburden himself. She was not only shocked but very sympathetic to see Lang, normally a self-controlled man, bent double in despair. The phone rang.

"If that's Serena, don't say I'm here," he whispered.

"Oh, I must," Vivi replied. "Hello, JJ. Yes, I've heard the awful news. Can I ring you later this evening?" she said and put the phone down. "I think you must have something to calm you down. Will you come with me to see our doctor if I ring him?"

"How will that help? The damage is done. I've ruined my reputation and my family's lives," he cried.

"I think a sedative will help you. Please come with me," she begged.

Lang flopped limply on the sofa while she called Dr Falcon.

Vivi talked to Lang in the car after they'd seen the doctor. "I think you must go home now, Serena will be wondering where you are. She knows you're in a bad state. If she goes off to Rome tomorrow, please try and support her. She's going for both your sakes."

Lang bit his thumbnail. "Yes, I'll go to her now."

"I'll ring Serena tonight and maybe you and the kids could pop over at the weekend? Come and see me any time, won't you?" Vivi said as they arrived back in Kensington.

Lang dragged his feet to his front door. Jonty was on the phone in the hall. Serena was feeding Benjie as the other children ate supper.

"Hello darling," she said in a subdued voice.

"Daddy, Daddy, Daddy," squeaked Alicia and Freddie in unison.

"Let's have a game of hide and seek before we go up," asked Freddie.

Lang put an arm round Serena's tight shoulders. "Is that okay with you, Mummy?" he asked, looking at Serena.

"Yes, of course. You go and hide first, Alicia."

Jonty walked into the kitchen smiling at Lang as the children whirled out of the room.

"I've been to see Vivi and told her about the awful mess," he confessed.

"Ready!" shouted Alicia.

Lang called, "I'm coming!" and slowly walked out of the sitting room.

"Cheryl's coming up tomorrow lunchtime and will stay two nights to help with the kids, so there's no need to worry," announced Jonty.

"Thank you, dear JJ," said Serena; then, after a moment's thought. "Will Mum be alright on her own?"

"Oh, she'll love helping out at the riding school. I think we'll have to tell her soon though," said Jonty.

The conversation was strained at supper. Television alleviated the tension as Lang and Jonty watched a football match.

Serena rang Vivi in the hall, then sat on the stairs, choking down a few tears. They talked for over an hour. Vivi offered to have Lang, Alicia and Freddie on Saturday night. She promised to keep in close contact with Lang and said she'd taken him to a doctor to get a mild sedative.

"Oh Vivi, it will be so awful if we move to the country away from you," said Serena sadly.

"Yes, it'll be a big wrench for me too, especially as Theo's away so much, but I'll pop down often. I'll commute at the weekends." She laughed. "Theo's flying back next Sunday. The concert in Vienna was just amazing. I'll tell you more when you get back. Have great success in Rome, you clever girl!"

Chapter Twenty Eight

Aylesbury

Cheryl and Beady had a wonderful lesson with the children. Beady's little boy was improving his trot daily. After some work in the farm shop, Cheryl took Beady in the car to the highest point of the Downs with stunning views all over Buckinghamshire. She brought out a thermos of tea and some homemade scones.

"Beady, I have to tell you some bad news."

"Oh my goodness, what is it?" queried Beady.

"Lang has been sacked from his firm due to some dodgy business and—"

"How dreadful," interrupted Beady. "What will happen?"

Cheryl described the situation and noticed the high colour mounting in Beady's face, alarmed in case it would lead to a stroke.

"Perhaps I'd better give poor Serena some money. I always felt Lang was a weak man," said Beady, shaking her head.

Cheryl looked anxious. "I've said I'll go there later on to help with the children because Serena has got a wonderful contract in Rome for five days and it's worth a lot of money. Hope you don't mind if Jonty and I leave you here for two days?"

"I'm sure I'll be alright," said Beady. "But seriously, Cheryl, what will happen?"

"They'll have to sell the house and Jonty is looking for a cottage around here."

Beady gasped. "Oh my God, how dreadful. Sell that lovely house. I can't bear it!" She started blinking uncontrollably. Cheryl put an arm round her thin bony shoulders.

"We'll all manage together," she said soothingly. "We've got a great family, Beady, and we must all pull together during this dreadful crisis and not be angry." Cheryl squeezed her hand.

"Yes, of course." Beady sat bolt upright. "Yes, of course," she repeated, then shook her head bitterly. "Although Serena probably hasn't helped. She never stands still. Never did, since she was young. Maybe that's what drove Lang to strive so hard. More money! It's all too much!" she cried.

"Beady, I'm serious—try not to think too badly of them. After all, you've often said how much Serena's like her dad."

This provoked a short bark of ironic laughter. "Yes, she is. He was like an arrow. Zoomed everywhere, but he went too fast. It killed him in the end."

When Cheryl left for the station, Beady walked up to the stables and waited for the children. She helped Jane, Cheryl's assistant, get the riding hats ready.

"Wonderful lady, Cheryl. I love the way she runs this place. She does so much for the kids," said Jane.

"She certainly is a marvellous teacher with great patience," replied Beady, waving to the bus as it came up the drive.

Meanwhile, Cheryl arrived at Kensington around lunchtime.

"I left your mum eagerly going off to the stables," she told Jonty, who gave her a big hug.

He replied, "Serena went off at 5am this morning to catch her flight to Rome. Lang's here, but Benjie is at the park with Maggie and Jonty.

"Good to see you," said Lang, giving her a peck on the cheek.

"Now, what can I do that's most useful?" asked Cheryl. "How about I make a lasagne for supper and some meringues for the children's tea?"

"That would be splendid," said Lang quietly.

Cheryl and Jonty were a huge help to Lang and he started to feel not entirely himself, but in a much better place than before. Soon it was the weekend. Lang and the children waved goodbye to Cheryl and Jonty at Turnham Green tube station, then drove on to Chiswick where Vivi welcomed everyone.

Lang walked in with Benjie on his shoulders. Alicia and Freddie tore through the house to find Georgie who was hiding up a tree.

"I thought we'd all go to the zoo. Yours have never been," suggested Vivi.

"Err, no they haven't. Shall I stay here?" he said.

"No, you're coming with us. This will be your first step in looking after the children more, now you have the time."

Chapter Twenty Nine

Moscow

After Theo and Sergei arrived back in Moscow, they realised the Vienna concert had produced several enquiries and offers of even greater opportunities. There was even interest from London's Festival Hall, and one of Paris's leading concert halls had asked Sergei if Theo was free to play a Tchaikovsky concerto at the end of June.

Theo discussed the latter offer with Murel who thought it possible to have the 1st Concerto ready and the orchestra could rehearse the Pathetique as well. Sergei was also negotiating about a possible recording contract for Theo.

After an animated discussion over lunch, Theo and Sergei walked through the park, chatting and laughing enthusiastically.

"I must go back and pack. I'll be off to London in a few hours," said Theo.

Sergei checked his watch. "Yes, you must," he confirmed, clearing his throat and gazing at a nearby bench.

"I shall miss it here." Sergei's eyes widened and Theo added, "I mean the orchestra and Baba."

"Oh, of course," Sergei said, looking at the floor.

"And. . . you, of course."

They locked eyes. Theo felt his heart begin to race and he turned away not wanting to see Sergei's hopeful face.

Chapter Thirty

Chiswick

Arriving at Heathrow, Theo got a taxi to Chiswick and quietly opened his front door. He heard soft music coming from the sitting room and found Vivi humming a quiet lullaby to sleepy Jago in her arms. He stood transfixed by their beauty.

Looking up, she smiled. "Ah, you're back at last. He's not feeling very well so I'm trying to lull him to sleep."

They kissed tenderly, then Theo gently took Jago upstairs and waited for Vivi in their bedroom.

In the morning, Georgie and Jago raced into the room. "Daddy, Daddy, you're back!" yelled Jago. They all lay in bed chatting about Russia, school, and Vivi's work.

"Sergei's asked me to meet someone from the Festival Hall at 10am. After that, where shall we all go?" asked Theo.

"We went to the zoo yesterday with Uncle Lang and Alicia," piped up Georgie.

"You should see the chimps, they're such fun, and the lions were just sleepy and didn't move," said Jago, laughing.

"Breakfast time!" called Bella.

After the children had left the room, Vivi started to tell Theo the awful news about Lang. "Serena's in Rome on a wonderful job for five days, so we had him and the kids here last night. He's in a bad way. It's so sad for them all."

"Oh no, I hope it all works out for them."

"Me too," Vivi said, then she smiled. "I'm so happy you're

home my love. Hey, how about we drive into the country, have a picnic and get away from it all?"

"That sounds good. I'll be back here by 11.30."

"I'll organise some food while you're out. Goodness, I shall miss Serena when they move away."

"Well, maybe I'll be home more often by then," said Theo. "Depends if this morning goes well."

It was a glorious May afternoon as Theo drove the whole family down to a lovely wood near Oxshot.

Georgie started singing Frere Jacques. "Come on Daddy, join in!"

Everyone muddled along, then there were peals of laughter as Jago tried to sing. An hour later they arrived at the edge of a small wood with a nearby field filled with sheep. A tiny stream trickled across it.

"This is beautiful," said Vivi, spreading out the picnic rug.

Jago walked over to the sheep, making 'baaing' noises to them.

"Let's explore the woods, Daddy," said Georgie, dragging Theo off towards the largest trees.

Vivi laid out the food and fed Jago some yoghurt with a banana sandwich.

"You're such a happy little fellow," Vivi kissed his cheek. She could see Theo and Georgie running down the hill towards her. "Food's ready!"

"Ah, this is really peaceful," said Theo, tilting his head back and closing his eyes. "I remember coming here years ago with some cousins. We all slept in a big tent and had a huge camp fire."

Vivi watched Theo relaxing and wished he was always around

instead of going to Russia so often. She chatted to him about Serena's job in Rome.

Suddenly Theo's mobile rang out, interrupting the fun.

"Just had some great news," bubbled Sergei. "The EMI recording manager is coming to Paris to hear your performance."

"How exciting," beamed Theo.

"Can you come back to Russia a little earlier?" Sergei asked.

"It's not easy. Anyway, I'm having a picnic with the family. I'll call you when I get home. The Festival Hall meeting went well by the way. Speak to you in a bit."

"I assume that was Sergei ringing from Moscow?" queried Vivi.

"Yes, he said the EMI recording manager is going to Paris to hear my performance. Isn't that splendid? Sergei is fantastic. I couldn't do half as many performances without him."

Vivi looked away without saying a word.

As they drove home, Vivi couldn't help pondering on the relationship between Sergei and Theo. Sergei obviously adored her husband and kept him busy but why always so far away from home? Something didn't feel right.

"Why doesn't Sergei organise concerts for you in London or nearer to where you live?" she suddenly asked.

"He obviously has more contacts in Russia and Europe," said Theo quietly.

Vivi didn't respond.

*

Jonty rang to ask Vivi and Theo to a family supper at Kensington. He sounded very domesticated, stressing, "You can't come until the children are bathed and Cheryl has read them stories. She's already made the supper. Honestly, it's amazing, she's loving the family routine." He sounded delighted.

They arrived at 7.30pm and sat round the garden table. It was a beautiful evening. Theo tried exchanging news with Lang but found him very subdued.

"How's work, Theo?" asked Jonty, his voice upbeat and trying to make conversation easier. Theo recounted his news about Paris and the possible EMI recording.

"I think we might take Beady to Paris," suggested Vivi. "She's never heard my dear husband give a concert abroad."

A few minutes later, Serena excitedly rang from Rome. "The place is huge with marble floors, wonderful long windows and shrubs on balconies. It's a real challenge for me. The Italian Count is very courteous and enthusiastic about my designs, but he flirts too much."

"Does he indeed?" mumbled Lang.

"How are my chicks? Is Alicia doing well?" Serena asked fondly.

"Everyone is fine," Lang responded.

"Yes, yes, everyone is enjoying a busy time, Serena," said Cheryl. "I'm loving being here. Benjie does keep asking for you though."

"Give him a special cuddle from me. Anyway, I'll be back shortly. Must dash, I've got to go to the Count's party. I might pick up more work. Who knows!" Serena rang off.

Everyone became more relaxed as the meal progressed and the wine flowed. Then, just as they were finishing the dessert, Beady phoned.

"Jonty, someone called Bill Thane rang to say there's a

cottage to let up the hill near his hay barn. I don't know what he's talking about. Would you contact him as someone else is already showing interest?"

"Yes, I'll ring him tomorrow. He's a lovely old man who has a big farm near Oving. Thanks so much Mum. How are you getting on?" he asked.

"The house seems a bit empty but the kittens keep me company and I've been helping in the farm shop. How's Serena doing in Rome?"

"She's having a great time and my Cherry Berry's being a good substitute mother. The children love her." Jonty smiled at his wife.

Lang chose not to speak to Beady. He hadn't faced his mother-in-law yet.

"She sounded happy enough," Jonty said, when he hung up the phone. "Mind you, I've got a hunch she's thinking of returning to England full time."

"Yes, she hinted the same thing to me last week," said Vivi wistfully.

*

Lang took the kids to school and came home to find a letter from the estate agent asking to show a potential buyer round the house.

"That's pretty quick," he said to Jonty, showing him the letter.

"Well, it's a nice house and the area's always in demand. You should be able to sell quite easily," replied Jonty.

"Serena's due back this afternoon. It's been such a help having you both here," said Lang.

Cheryl smiled. "I've loved it, especially bath time. Jago seems to be a bubbles fan. Did I tell you what happened. . . ?"

There was a loud bang on the front door. Lang went to open it.

"I'm back! I've lost my key, everything fell out of my handbag and I've got a headache." Serena fell through the door, hair flopping over her tanned face. "Phew! What a gathering." She laughed as everyone stared at her in astonishment. "Where are my chicks?"

"Still at school, except for the tiddler, of course," said Lang quietly.

"Let's go together and pick them up," Serena suggested. "How are you Cheryl and JJ? Thanks for being here."

"Mummy!" Benjie ran and hugged his mother's knees. She scooped him up and covered him in kisses.

"Well, since you're here now, I think we'd better be off," said Cheryl.

"We'll drop you at the tube station," said Lang.

"Thank you and say goodbye to Alicia and Freddie. I will miss them."

"You've been so helpful with the kids, thank you."

Lang pecked Cheryl on the cheek. Ten minutes later, Serena stopped their massive car outside Turnham Green Station.

"See you soon Jonty, hopefully with the removal van at your barn next week." Serena waved as JJ and Cheryl walked into the station.

As they drove off Lang mumbled, "I suppose you'll want a divorce now that I've completely messed up our lives and let you down."

There was silence for a while, then glancing at Serena he

saw her eyes were full of tears. He handed her a hanky as her nose dripped onto the steering wheel.

"Whatever happens, we've got to stay together for the children's sake. Somehow, we must comfort them as they move home and change schools. You should have told me what was happening from the get-go, so as for us—"

They were cut off by Alicia and Freddie rushing out of the school gates and hugged Serena. They both burst into chatter about school news. She watched their eager faces vying for attention. Arriving home, they fell into their usual routine of tea, homework, then play.

"Early bath time for everyone tonight, I've got a lot of phoning to do," called Serena. She laughed as they all chased her upstairs, squealing with delight.

"Is Daddy coming to read us a story?" asked Freddie, padding around, covered in soap.

"Not sure," said Serena. "Why don't I read you one?" They snuggled round her on the bed. Little Benjie lay on the pillow.

A few minutes later Lang appeared. "Someone from Rome's on the phone for you."

"Ask them to ring back in ten minutes, thanks."

"They said it's urgent," he replied.

"Alright, you take over the story."

Lang hesitantly lay on the bed and soon found himself wrapped in wriggling arms and legs.

Later in the evening, over supper, Lang told Serena about the estate agent's visit on Tuesday.

"Gosh, that's quick; we haven't got anywhere else to live yet." Her voice was anxious and brusque.

Supper was fairly tense. Neither Serena nor Lang knew how to handle the situation and she was still in shock.

"I don't know how we're going to decide what to keep, or what to pack, or what to sell," she said sadly.

"I'll help with it all, once we've found a place in the country. Shall we make a list of all the furniture going into storage at Jonty's?" said Lang.

Ignoring this question Serena suddenly announced, "By the way, I may have to go back to Rome—it's part of the contract, and we certainly need the money now."

"When will you know?" Lang said anxiously. "Only someone's coming to look at the house tomorrow."

"I'll leave you to show them round. I can't bear the thought of anyone living in our beautiful house," replied Serena tearfully.

Maggie popped her head round the door. "Little Benjie's crying, and there's an Italian on the phone for you, Miss Serena."

"Thanks Maggie. Lang, you go to Benjie please, while I take the call from Rome."

Having comforted Benjie, Lang disappeared into his study, praying that he could make it up to Serena—somehow.

Chapter Thirty One

Moscow

Theo's week with the family came to a tearful end, as Georgie hugged him desperately, begging him not to go away again. Jago clung to his knees and Vivi bravely waved him off in the taxi.

"I'll see you in Paris, darling," Theo called out to her, as the car disappeared from her view.

Vivi sighed, then brightly suggested, "Let's go to the park—that'll make us all smile." She didn't want to cry in front of Georgie and Jago.

Five hours later, Theo arrived in Moscow. Sergei was patiently waiting, eager to see him.

"I'm dying to get back to the piano. I've not had a chance to practice much at home," said Theo.

"Well, Maestro, the orchestra is keen to rehearse too."

Theo arrived at his familiar and welcoming studio to work on the Tchaikovsky Piano Concerto all morning. Murel came in briefly to suggest the orchestra rehearse with him in the afternoon. After lunch, various players gave a cheer as he walked in. Murel was quite strict with Theo during their three-hour session.

When the rehearsal was over, Sergei walked in as Theo sat at the piano. The Russian lent his tall, lean body over Theo, enthusiastic as ever, and told him how well the rehearsal had gone.

"Shall we have a meal at our usual restaurant?"

"Yes, I'm famished."

Without thinking Theo wrapped his arm around Sergei's waist. He watched Sergei carefully who slowly smiled. Theo felt his heart quicken. It felt like the most natural thing in the world to be so close to Sergei.

"I love working for you," said Sergei. "And watching you gain confidence in your wonderful playing."

En route to the restaurant, Theo glanced at Sergei who was whistling as he walked. There was something about him that just made him feel. . . good.

I don't understand, I've never felt like this before, he thought.

"Come on Theo," called Sergei. "I'll order your favourite pie."

Theo walked on, disturbed yet elated, by his feelings.

Chapter Thirty Two

Aylesbury

Jonty and Cheryl found their house unbearably empty after being with the children fulltime. Jonty arranged to meet Bill Thane at his Oving farmhouse that afternoon. Cheryl came too as she didn't want to listen to the silence of her home.

Bill was a charming, elderly, rather deaf man with a long beard. The cottage was set in an orchard surrounded by fields and grazing sheep. It had three bedrooms, a kitchen with an Aga and several outhouses.

"They could be turned into more bedrooms if necessary," said Jonty.

"Oh yes, you can do what you like with those old barns," replied Bill.

"I think my sister will love the place. I'll give her a ring and let you know when she can visit."

When they got back to the farm, Jacob was standing by the back door with two dead rabbits.

"I reckon them poachers 'ave been 'ere again. They must've been disturbed. I found these near the oak trees."

"You take one home," Cheryl said.

Meanwhile Jonty rang Serena to tell her about the cottage. "Could you come tomorrow? It's very nice. I think it might be just what you need."

"Well I could come in the morning with Lang, after I

drop the kids at school and get there by midday," said Serena hesitantly.

*

Jonty, Serena, Jago and Bill walked up the hill to see the cottage lit by the afternoon sun. Serena walked in first, followed by Lang, and felt an immediate cosiness. Thankfully it was bigger than she'd expected. The previous tenant had added an extension.

"We could put the upright piano in here and make it a big playroom," she said, as her phone rang.

Meanwhile Bill, Jonty and Jago walked outside.

"Yes, of course," she murmured a few moments later while Lang stood looking at her. "But I can't possibly get a plane until tomorrow evening." Her husband frowned. "I'll ring you as soon as I've got a flight."

She hung up as Lang asked moodily, "You're off again?"

"Lang, I have to work. We have no bloody money because of you! I've got to work non-stop so we can survive. You've left me no alternative. I have to be the earner and you'll have to help with the kids more. I'm under contract for the Rome job so I must fulfil the work."

"What am I going to do about the furniture?"

"You can surely sit in the van and guide it into Jonty's barn, can't you? I'll be off tomorrow night anyway for about five days. Do you want Jonty and Cheryl to come up? If so, ask them now," Serena said emphatically.

Lang remained silent.

"Come on, let's have proper a look around," said Serena and Lang followed behind her, staring at the floor.

They drove back to the farm to discuss the cottage and Serena's job. "Well, at least Jonty's coming up to help me," said Lang despondently.

"You shouldn't need anyone. You ought to be able to cope with your own children," Serena retorted.

"You have Maggie," Lang shot back and Serena shot him a hard stare.

"Well, because of you, I won't have her anymore." She crossed her arms. "Whether we like it or not, we're taking the cottage, so we have to make a list of what's going into storage."

*

Serena awoke the next morning to a call saying that the evening flight to Rome was cancelled. She groaned loudly. She needed to get some space away from Lang.

Chapter Thirty Three

Chiswick

"You look furious! What's happened?" asked Vivi, when Serena arrived at her door with a tear-stained face.

"You can't go on blaming him forever," Vivi said twenty minutes later after Serena had vented her frustrations. "His weakness drove him, and the shock has devastated you, but Sis, somehow you've got to ride the storm. It's no use being angry with each other. You've got to try and build a new life for the children's sake. Pick up the pieces. You're a creator—come on."

After a few sobs Serena hugged Vivi. "Yes, yes, you're right, but I wish I was calm like you."

Vivi chuckled. "Well, let's face it, you never will be. You'll always be running in the fast lane. That's what your talent is. Let's go out for a coffee in the park, it's such a lovely morning and the fresh air will be good for you."

Chapter Thirty Four

Kensington

Lang opened the door to a beaming middle-aged lady dressed in yellow and a short man in a city suit standing behind her. After a short conversation, Lang showed them all over the spotlessly clean house (Maggie had been up at 6am polishing and tidying everywhere). The couple loved its long elegant sitting room, and the master bedroom, upstairs.

"The garden is simply divine—it's got such character. I love that big oak tree," said the lady.

"My children play hide and seek there," said Lang.

"We don't have children. Only dogs and my elderly mother," said the man.

"Quite a convenient area for shops and for you to get to Mansion House," said the lady in yellow.

Lang cringed. Later that morning, he showed three more couples round the house. It got easier each time as he answered the same questions.

Serena came back at midday. They had a brief lunch with Jonty who'd arrived to help out before Serena left a few hours later for a re-scheduled afternoon flight.

Lang had received a summons to the Financial Conduct Authority, which filled him with anxiety, but the next few days with Jonty lifted his spirits. Alicia and Freddie played up a bit, and Benjie missed Serena a lot, but Jonty always managed to get everyone laughing. The day before Serena's return, Jonty was left to do school runs and homework. He loved it.

On Friday, Lang was so terrified that he was incapable of seeing the kids, so he left early for his meeting in the City. Sitting on the crowded tube he realised what an outsider he'd become, no longer belonging to the business world and saddened by the chaos of the commute. He was deeply upset and incredibly alone.

As he walked towards the tall imposing building, he became so agitated he had to stand still for a moment, while a choking sensation rose in his throat.

Suddenly a hand patted his back. "Morning, dear boy! How nice to see you."

Lang turned to see an old friend. "Hello Adrian."

They exchanged small talk for a minute, then Adrian said, "Must dash. I've got a meeting at 10.30, but let's meet for a drink sometime." He touched his friend's elbow and disappeared.

The interview was merciless and lasted about an hour. Lang left the room wrung out and dejected.

"Christ, I hope this doesn't lead to a gigantic fine," he muttered to himself, striding towards the lifts.

He limped home, relieved that Serena wasn't there to interrogate him. As he came through the front door, he could hear screams of delight in the garden, and found Jonty crawling round on all fours pretending to be Nana, the dog in Peter Pan, while Alicia and Freddie swung from a tree pretending to fly. Lang fell into the study and wept.

After a couple of minutes Maggie knocked on the door. "Mr Jonty wondered, would you like to come and see the children while they have lunch?" she asked tentatively.

"Yes, of course." Lang put on a smile and ambled into the kitchen, where Freddie was standing on a chair, blowing through an empty loo roll while Alicia banged a saucepan lid and Jonty clicked two spoons together.

"Here's Daddy—now play him our tune."

It was riotous and ridiculous and it made Lang laugh. He felt like he hadn't laughed properly for months.

They'd all eaten shepherd's pie and were ready for Maggie's surprise pancakes. Each one flew onto a plate. Maggie juggled two, calling Lang to put his hands out. He caught them both.

"Oh Daddy, you are clever," said Alicia, rushing up to hug him, making Lang beam.

After the meal, Lang and Jonty sat down to discuss the most difficult morning in Lang's life. As always Jonty had an amazing capacity for listening and did his utmost to comfort his brother-in-law.

"Well, it'll certainly be the start of a new life for you both, living in the country," he said. "Days will drift, not rush, by. It will be good for Cheryl and me to have you living so near."

Lang welcomed those cheerful thoughts, but what about Serena? *She never sits still and is happiest on the go. Will she be happy in the country?*

Chapter Thirty Five

Moscow

Murel was waiting patiently as Theo entered the rehearsal room. "We'll be starting with the last movement, then doing a complete run-through," the conductor announced.

The rehearsal was vigorous, with constant stops so that Murel could improve phrasing and tempi. Theo was exhausted as the final climax ended with his fingers racing across the keys. Sergei took him back to Baba's house to rest.

"I'll pick you up at 7pm for the cinema," he said.

As Theo walked into the sitting room, Baba was lying on the floor.

"Oh Mama, what's the matter?" he exclaimed in Russian.

"I just collapsed. I can't get up," she whispered. Theo bent down tenderly and lifted her onto the sofa. "Oh the pain," she cried.

"I'll call the doctor."

He came an hour later and diagnosed a possible stroke. Theo rang Sergei to cancel the film and instead spent several hours in the central hospital where it was discovered that Baba had indeed suffered a small stroke and needed to be kept in for a few days.

Theo was distraught about his mother and would not go out anywhere, despite Sergei's suggestions. He even cancelled two rehearsals. Murel urged him back, due to the upcoming visit to Paris. Sergei had arranged for his cousin to take care of Baba at home while Theo was working. She was an ex-nurse and very caring.

Even though it gave Theo some comfort that Baba was in safe hands, he'd hoped to get home before Paris, and now it was completely impossible. He needed to see his wife. Vivi helped him sort out the muddle of feelings he had whenever Sergei was around.

Chapter Thirty Six

Kensington

Serena arrived home in a flurry, having successfully completed her designs in Rome. The Count wanted her back in a month's time. At the office, Gems had coped with various requests for Serena's consultations.

"Phew, life's really getting hectic. I see the Qatar Embassy wants me to do the top floor, and what about the Russian millionaire in Princes Gate wanting a new banqueting room designed?" exclaimed Serena.

"I know. How's home?" asked Gems.

"What's left of it," muttered Serena. "The house... oh, my lovely house is being looked over by people I don't know—it's a vile feeling. I won't show them round. I can't bear it, so I make Lang do that. I resent what he's done to us—it's unforgivable. To think one's husband can cheat like that, it's chilling."

"Perhaps he wanted to make more money for you and it just went wrong," said Gems quietly.

"It bloody well did! What on earth are we going to be like in the country? Anyway, I'm absolutely going to commute, even stay overnight when necessary," Serena said bitterly.

"What shall we say to the Qatari Embassy? Could you start next week? Or would you rather contact the Russian millionaire?" asked Gems.

"I think it would be interesting to work at Princes Gate. Get me the number and I'll speak to Mr Orlensky."

Serena spoke at length to her potential new client and was immediately challenged by the oligarch's requests. She arranged to meet him the next day at Princes Gate. He suggested a fee which was double anything she'd ever earned before.

Returning home to bedlam, Serena relaxed as she watched Jonty swinging from a branch dressed in a rug pretending to be Mowgli, while Alicia and Freddie rolled on the grass. They stopped their game and rushed up to Serena, welcoming her with hugs of delight.

Lang wandered into the kitchen surprised to see her. "Hello, Fig Tree." He put an arm round to hug her.

"Hello," said Serena stiffly and Lang moved his arm away.

"Can we finalise the list of furniture going to Jonty's barn next week?" Lang asked.

"Well, the only problem is showing people round the house. If half the furniture has gone, the place won't look good. Let's postpone the removal van until next month," Serena suggested.

"All right, but we'd better decide on the list tonight before you go away again."

They had an amiable drink and went through every room in the house. Serena couldn't bear to sell anything so at least half would have to be stored. The smaller items would go to the cottage.

"I've got a fantastic new job at Princes Gate with a Russian millionaire called Mr Orlensky, so I'm not going away for a bit," said Serena enthusiastically.

"Oh good, but you won't be here much either, so I'd better carry on doing the school runs, hadn't I?"

"Yes, of course, because they're sending a car to pick me up every morning and I won't be back until late. This is a big contract, Lang, I've never had such an offer," Serena said excitedly.

"I'm glad for you," said Lang truthfully.

"It's for us, for our survival."

"Yes, I realise. I do realise it's all my fault," Lang said sharply.

"Excuse me, Miss Serena. Freddie's calling for you," Maggie said anxiously.

"Poor boy, he's having such nightmares lately," said Serena, hurriedly going up to comfort him.

Chapter Thirty Seven

Aylesbury

Jonty returned home from Kensington exhausted. He recounted all his adventures to Cheryl and Beady who were greatly amused at his imagination with Alicia and Freddie.

"I knew they were missing Serena, so I had to entertain them. Lang's not in a good state either."

Beady asked various questions about his firm and how much money Lang owed. "Might there be a big court case? Or could he even go to prison for fraud?" she asked.

"No, I don't think so, but every penny from the house which doesn't go towards paying off the mortgage must go to the firm. Then somehow he must pay back the deficit," explained Jonty.

"Poor Serena. She's having to work so hard now," said Beady, she waited a beat. "I was thinking about Madeira. I'm wondering whether to move back to England. Vivi's offered to build a flat at the end of her garden but she would need to discuss with Theo once he is back. I must admit I do feel lonely out there sometimes."

"Well, that sounds like a splendid idea if you really want to leave Madeira, Mum. We'd all see so much more of you," Jonty said.

"I was thinking about the money from selling the house. I'd want to give all three of you a share, but maybe slightly more to help Serena," said Beady.

"That's a fantastic idea. You must suggest it to them now, it'll certainly alleviate some of their anxiety. Do you want to ring tonight when Serena gets back from work?" suggested Jonty.

After supper, Jonty rang Serena asking how the Princes Gate job was, then passed the phone to Beady, who suggested selling her Madeira house. "Some of the money would help your dreadful situation, darling."

"Are you sure? Goodness, that would be marvellous because the sale of our house won't be enough to pay back the wretched debt. Thanks Mum! What a fantastic offer. It would be lovely to have you back, especially living at Vivi's too," Serena said happily.

"Well, I'd better return to Madeira and put the house up for sale now, hadn't I?" Beady chuckled.

Chapter Thirty Eight

Moscow

Baba was recovering well. The young nurse had been encouraging her to walk and do special exercises. Theo was working all hours to perfect Tchaikovsky's Piano Concerto No.1. He felt more nervous than usual about this piece, and Murel sensed it.

"Come on Theo. Push yourself. You can play this so well. Where's your spirit gone?" he asked gently.

"I just don't know. I can't get into it." Theo sighed. "Let's sit down quietly together and go through each part in turn."

They spent a whole day in the studio, playing through each movement. No one was allowed to disturb them. After several hours, Theo gained confidence and began to play with greater enthusiasm.

A massive problem for Theo was that Murel would not be conducting in Paris. He was frightened of the artistic interpretation being different with another conductor, Gilberte.

That night, Vivi rang up for a chat and soothed his anxiety (as she always did) and suggested that Beady come back to London and live with them in a garden flat. Theo had always liked his mother in law so had no issues with it.

"We're so excited to come to Paris!"

"I can't wait for you see hear my performance. Is Serena going to come? Will she have time with this contract?" asked Theo.

"She's working Saturdays on this particular job, but I'll see if she can get the time off," said Vivi. "Georgie's composed a piece for the piano called 'Happy Daddy's Day.' It's being played in school assembly. We'll make a recording of it."

"How exciting, I knew she was musical like me. Give her a good luck hug."

"I will. How's Baba now?" Vivi asked.

"Much better. The nurse caring for her is wonderful—she'll come and live here while I'm in Paris. She's a cousin of Sergei's, actually. If all goes according to plan I hope to come home after Paris for a while."

"Oh good, I hope it's for a nice long time," said Vivi.

*

The next morning Sergei bounded into the studio. "Great news! EMI are definitely going to be at the Paris concert. You'll show them, Maestro."

"That's wonderful news, even though I'm rather nervous of practicing with the new orchestra and Gilberte. I've been so spoilt with dear Murel."

"If all goes well EMI might offer you a London recording soon after the Festival Hall," said Sergei.

"Wow! That would be amazing." Theo opened his arms and hugged Sergei.

Chapter Thirty Nine

Paris

After a hectic week, Theo and Sergei arrived in Paris. Sergei had booked four rooms at the Hotel d'Angleterre where Theo would meet his family later that Saturday afternoon.

After lunch, Theo met Gilberte at the Salle Pleyel. The rehearsal started nervously, but during the second movement there was a mutual surge between the piano and a thrilling finale. Theo inwardly exploded. The whole orchestra stood up.

Walking back to the hotel along the Champs Elysée, Sergei pulled Theo round to face him.

"That was fantastic, I'm so proud of you."

Theo grabbed him round the waist, holding him close.

"My God, we make a fabulous combination, don't we?"

They walked with linked arms back to the hotel along the Seine.

Vivi, Jonty, Cheryl and Lang arrived at the hotel in the early evening and met Theo after he'd had a rest.

"What a pity Beady isn't here too. Serena couldn't make it because she's working late," said Jonty.

"It's lovely to see you all." Theo said, hugging them one by one. "I have to go in about ten minutes for a run through and to do some press interviews, so we'll meet up again after the concert. Sergei's arranged dinner at a lovely restaurant by the Seine."

The Salle Pleyel was buzzing as Theo walked into his dressing room. Vivi had brought a tiny framed photo of Georgie and Jago.

"Good luck, my darling." She kissed him tenderly. As she was leaving, a photographer came in.

"Just a quick photo of you both," he said.

"Oh, me too?" said Vivi surprised, putting an arm proudly round Theo's shoulder.

Gilberte walked onto the podium followed by Theo, to a round of applause. Tchaikovsky's Piano Concerto No. 1 rang out through the beautiful concert hall. Vivi and the family were sitting in the second-row stalls spellbound by Theo's performance. Gilberte was sensitive to Theo's interpretation and the orchestra rose to the occasion, which was greeted at the end by thunderous applause.

After the performance, Theo and Vivi sat at the centre of a big table adorned by flowers with Lang on one side and Jonty and Cheryl on the other.

Sergei had organised a wonderful feast but was not present. He wanted to give Theo space with his family, although Theo wished Sergei could have been there.

All the family glowed together in response to an extraordinary, overwhelming evening of seeing their Theo perform. The maître d'hôtel presented him with a large bottle of Bollinger.

"Cheers to Theo!" Jonty said, standing up proudly.

"We're missing Serena and Beady," said Lang. "But I know they would have been so proud of you. Congratulations, Maestro, what an achievement."

Every hotel Vivi had stayed in for a concert seemed to sit alongside a river. The Seine was certainly the most beautiful. She sat with Theo on their balcony for a while without a word, with her head on his chest. Their legs were outstretched on a chair.

"Oh Theo, this is such a memorable night," she said, before lifting her face up to kiss him.

*

"See you in about a week," said Theo fondly as he waved his family goodbye. "Just got to sort out Baba's permanent care and then I'll be home."

Sergei suddenly appeared as he walked out of the airport, clearly he had been waiting for Theo's family to depart.

"The performance was moving indeed, Maestro," he said. "I think EMI will have been impressed. Shall we go and have lunch?"

"Yes—take me somewhere that you've enjoyed. After all, it's my first time here, and you're the Paris expert."

Sergei smiled. "In that case, prepare to be amazed."

Chapter Forty

Kensington

Vivi returned on Sunday to pick up Georgie. She recounted Theo's success and described to Serena the beauty of Paris.

"How I'd love to have stayed on a bit with him. I don't know what or where his next concert will be. He says he's coming home in a week, thank goodness. How's work? Is Princes Gate a huge job?"

"Yes, it's an enormous challenge, and going to take a lot of ingenuity to complete, but I've never had such a generous contract. It should keep us going for some months," said Serena. "Lang came back full of praise for Theo's concert. Did him good to get away I think."

"How are things between you?" asked Vivi.

"At least we're talking to each other now, which is easier," replied Serena.

"Lucky you. I don't know what's going to happen to *us*," Vivi said sadly. "I'm wondering if Theo will ever settle in London. Russia seems to have such an attraction for him. The children really need their Daddy around."

"It must be so difficult for you. Does he ever talk about the future or when he might come back for good?" asked Serena quietly.

"No, he seems to evade the future and it worries me. Family time is so inconsistent. I try to remain calm because he's an artist, yet a part of him seems so distant. I love him dearly but I'm wondering if there's something I don't understand."

*

Lang picked up the children from school. He was beginning to enjoy ferrying them to and fro. Their vivacity staved off any pangs of depression that haunted him. He even enjoyed putting them to bed since Serena often didn't return until 8.30pm or later. Then he would sit down for a drink with Serena and he was relieved that they were now talking, albeit leaving many things unsaid.

"Now, two possible offers on the house seem definite. Which are we going to choose? I quite understand you're reluctant to see it go, but realistically we've got to pay back the firm," Lang said solemnly.

"You decide," replied Serena quietly.

"Well, the Buchans seem very keen and they'll willingly pay extra for fixtures and fittings—they love the carpets, and raved about the curtains," Lang replied.

"Oh God, I wish we didn't have to go!" said Serena, near tears. Her mobile rang. Serena glanced at the screen for accepting the call. "Hello Gems. Yes, of course, I'll pop in on the way to work early and sign the papers. Sorry I haven't seen you for days, but I'm working flat out at Princes Gate. Okay. . . no problem. . . speak to you later." Serena put the phone down.

"I'll ring the estate agent and tell them we're definitely accepting the Buchans' offer then, shall I?" Lang asked.

"Do what you want," Serena said, storming out of the room.

Chapter Forty One

Aylesbury

Jonty's plantation was now surrounded by wire fencing to keep the deer and rabbits out. They'd previously done a lot of damage, nibbling the bark of the young saplings.

Cheryl's riding school had suffered a dramatic happening when someone deliberately opened the stable doors and two ponies had bolted. She, Jonty and Jacob searched all morning for them, and found one had fallen in a ditch while the other had vanished.

Cheryl rang the police to alert them and Jonty did his best to comfort her.

"It's such a terrible thing to do to our children's stable. How can people be so destructive?" she sobbed.

"Oh Cherry Berry." Jonty wrapped his arms round her. "We'll get another pony from Jacob's friend."

"That's not the point, Jonty," Cheryl said, wiping her tears with her jumper.

"Look the police are here."

The two policeman looked solemn when they saw how distressed Cheryl was.

"We think it's a group of two or three youths who've caused havoc on several farms. One pony got trapped in a cattle grid and broke a leg. The vet had to shoot it."

Cheryl gasped. "How dreadful"

"I suggest you put padlocks on all stable doors now," suggested the police officer.

"Living in the country used to be so peaceful and safe, now we're all being threatened," said Jonty sadly.

"It's our empty-headed local lads, got nothing to do but destroy anything they can," stated the police officer. "We've got to go too Tentram Farm where a whole lot of pigs have been set loose."

"Thanks for coming," said Cheryl. Once the policeman had left she focused on the task ahead of her. "The children will be coming soon."

"I'll ring Jacob's friend to see if he can lend us an extra pony. You could choose one this afternoon," said Jonty.

"Thank you," she replied.

A few hours later they arrived at a large paddock full of various ponies. Cheryl looked around trying to find a docile one suitable for the children. A small head nuzzled under her arm.

"This is the one," she said to Jonty. She smiled as she stroked his head.

Chapter Forty Two

Paris

Theo was amazed and overawed by Paris. He felt guilty for letting Vivi believe he was going back to Russia to look after Baba rather than staying in Paris for a break with Sergei, who had taken him to many vibrant places. He knew he shouldn't have lied, but he knew there was no way she would have approved of him not coming home with them unless he had a good reason to stay away longer.

The Louvre was full of wonderful paintings. They walked slowly together absorbing each gallery, sometimes just looking, sometimes discussing their feelings about the work. It was a new dimension to his emotions because he'd never really looked at paintings like that before.

Sergei took him to the gallery café where they enjoyed a coffee and croissant, chatting non-stop. Later, they drove round the Arc de Triomphe and down some beautiful tree lined boulevards.

"I must go back home soon to see Vivi and the children. When will we hear about the EMI recording, do you think?" asked Theo, the guilt becoming almost too much.

"Maybe in about a week."

"Now, the other big question I have is, will my mother be alright left with the present carer? It seems she's getting stronger, but you never know if she might have a relapse."

"Don't worry, I'll look after her like I nurture you." Sergei smiled. "How long do you intend to be in London?"

"At least two weeks. After all, we've not got anything to work on at present," said Theo.

"Our next engagement will hopefully be at the Festival Hall," said Sergei. "I shall miss you a lot." Theo blushed. "Will you miss me?" Sergei asked tentatively.

Theo nodded, then sighed. "I do feel close to you. . . but I just don't know what to do about it or how I should feel."

Chapter Forty Three

Kensington

Lang had received a letter from his firm in the City. The lawyers were demanding payment immediately for his outstanding debt, so that no further action need be taken. He shuddered as he read the letter and rang his lawyer straightaway, who suggested he send an e-mail stating the sale of his house was almost complete and the surplus equity would be sent within a month.

He went to the school gates to pick up the children filled with anxiety.

"Daddy, Daddy, why are you so late picking us up? I start ballet in ten minutes," said Alicia crossly.

"And it's my first time at judo. I can't be late," exclaimed Freddie.

"I'm sorry, it was bad traffic," muttered Lang. "Have you got your ballet things with you?"

"Yes, of course, Daddy. Hurry up! I can't be late and remember, both classes are at Kensington Town Hall."

Lang delivered the children to their after school clubs, parked the car and waited. Even with the sale proceeds there still might not be enough money to pay the debt after deducting the mortgage.

Where on earth was I going to get the rest of the money to complete the amount owing?

"Daddy, are you asleep?" asked Freddie, hammering on the window an hour later.

"Where's Alicia?"

"She's talking to her ballet friends. I'll go and tell her you're waiting." Freddie ran off.

"One of the girls pushed Olivia over when she was trying to do her arabesque, so I had to comfort her," said Alicia when she finally got to the car, with her brother behind her.

When they reached home, both children rushed into the kitchen.

"Ah, there you are!" said Maggie. "Sit down quickly. The pasta is ready and Benjie has finished his."

Lang went straight to his study to contemplate his problems but he was disturbed a short while later by his children. It was homework time. Freddie always needed help with his maths. Benjie sat on his father's lap while Lang read out the questions for the Maths test. Alicia was practising the piano as Serena appeared.

"Hello, Mummy! You're nice and early." Alicia hugged her.

"Where's Daddy?" Serena asked.

"Doing Freddie's homework."

"You're home early," said Lang, entering the room.

"Yes, I've got a migraine, I need to lie down," she said quietly, very reassured to see how well everything was going in her absence.

A few hours later Lang walked into the darkened bedroom to see how Serena was.

"Would you like a cup of tea or iced juice, darling?" he asked tenderly.

"Yes, I'd love a cup of Darjeeling, thanks." As he returned with the tea she said, "Do draw the curtains, my head's a bit better now. Children all in bed?"

Lang nodded, then sat on the bed and asked how her work was going.

"It's an enormous project but somehow I'll complete it."

Lang then recounted the demand from his firm and what his lawyer had suggested about the imminent house sale.

Serena could see how upset he was and played down the urgency. "There's plenty of time. We're lucky to have had an offer so quickly. Beady phoned to say she'd put her house up for sale and will help us out over the excess money needed to pay back the firm."

"That's very generous of her, especially as I know how disgusted she must be with me," said Lang feeling a massive surge of relief after all his worrying. "As soon as the Buchans have signed the contract, we can organise a removal van to collect the furniture for Jonty's barn."

Chapter Forty Four

Chiswick

"Daddy's coming home today," Vivi announced, as the children jumped up and down excitedly. "Shall we go and meet him?"

"Yes, yes!" Georgie yelled.

It was a beautiful June morning with hardly any Sunday traffic. At Heathrow airport, Jago was very excited to see all the planes. Georgie was amazed at the Duty Free. Suddenly, Theo's blond head appeared in a crowd coming through the exit doors of the Arrivals lounge.

Georgie rushed up to him. "Daddy, Daddy!" she shouted, followed by Jago pushing his way through lots of legs. Vivi embraced him.

"What a lovely surprise," he said, grinning as he lifted Jago up into his arms.

The journey home was full of laughter.

"It's so good to be back," he said, putting an arm round Vivi as she half turned from the wheel to kiss him.

Lunch in the garden was a huge plate of vegetables and aioli dressing which Bella had lovingly prepared for them all.

"Good to see you home, Mr Theo," Bella said.

Ah, this is how it should always be, thought Vivi.

Everyone settled back into a warm family routine.

"It'll soon be holiday time. Shall we go to Cornwall, France or maybe Madeira to see Mum?" asked Vivi.

"Let's go to Madeira for some sun and sea," said Theo. "It'll be the last time I guess seeing as it's up for sale."

"I can take ten days off from work."

"I shall miss my piano but never mind," said Theo. "Georgie you must play your piece to me."

All thoughts of Sergei were at the back of his mind.

Chapter Forty Five

Kensington

The children had cupcakes in a tent pitched in the garden, while the adults chatted over Lapsang Suchong and scones. Vivi announced the holiday arrangements and Serena wished she could join them, but work came first.

"Why don't you go over with the kids, Lang? It would be such fun. Mum would love it," suggested Serena.

"Well, err, I'm not sure I can leave selling the house at present. It depends on the dates," he murmured. "Let's see if the Buchans can pay cash since they urgently want to complete. If it all goes smoothly, though, then we might be able to go."

"Shall we ring Beady and see if she likes the idea of a family invasion?" suggested Vivi.

Of course, she was thrilled to hear her daughter's voice, and excited to learn of their visit.

"I've had one offer already for the house. Being near the sea makes it popular. I had an excellent sale last week of pictures and garden furniture. I made £4,000!"

"Jolly good, Mum. You're doing well," said Vivi.

Serena then related the latest news of their house sale but hadn't got very far before there was a wail from Freddie as he limped in with blood oozing from one knee.

"What have you done?" she exclaimed, scooping him up.

"Mummy, I fell on the rockery being chased by Georgie who was a lion about to eat me," he sobbed.

Chapter Forty Six

Chiswick

Vivi enjoyed having Theo at home for a week. While she worked most mornings, he practiced for a few hours, then they'd have pleasant lunches in the garden with Jago before collecting Georgie from school.

Theo loved being with her. Somehow the child's enthusiasm refreshed him. On Friday evening he took her to Britten's 'A Young Person's Guide to the Orchestra.' Georgie was enthralled and seemed to understand all the instruments in their different moods.

The following week, Georgie's school invited him to give a master class for the senior pianists. It was a very popular event. Georgie was so proud of her father that she sat spellbound, watching every movement or direction Theo gave to the pupils. At that very moment she decided she wanted to be a pianist herself.

That same evening Vivi decided it was time to do a pregnancy test. She had been feeling off colour for a few days, and it was only when she checked the calendar that she realised she could be pregnant. The little blue line confirmed her suspicions had been correct, but unlike the previous occasions, something stopped her from rushing to tell Theo. *Would it affect their present relationship? How would I manage with him away all the time?*

She rang Serena to ask for advice.

"Wonderful news," said Serena. "That will keep him home more, instead of going to Russia all the time."

Vivi wasn't sure it was quite as simple as all that.

A few days later, enjoying a quiet moment together in the garden on a warm June evening, Vivi felt an overwhelming warmth running through her and the news burst out.

"Theo, I'm carrying your baby," she whispered.

There was silence, then Theo beamed. "How wonderful. I never thought we'd have a third. I wonder if it will be a cellist instead of a pianist."

"It's so good having you here for a longer time," enthused Vivi. "It's so important for the children."

"Yes, being here with the children is really invigorating. Georgie's so full of exciting ideas. I'd like her to start violin lessons, or flute, to expand her musicality," said Theo.

"And what about little Jago? Shall he start the recorder or the trumpet?"

"We'll be able to have trios when the new one arrives!" Theo said, kissing her.

*

Theo took Georgie to school and met Lang at the school gates.

"I'm going to be a father again," he announced.

"Wow! That'll be busy for you!" said Lang.

Just as Theo was driving off, his mobile rang. "Sergei, how are you? What? EMI wants to start recording in how many weeks? Will Murel be conducting? That's great news! Speaking of which, I'm going to become a father again."

"Oh," said Sergei, then there was silence.

"How's Baba doing?" Theo eventually asked hoping to change the subject and lighten the mood.

"She's still rather fragile but loves her carer. There's always great laughter when I pop in to see her," replied Sergei. "I must go; I've got to speak to Murel. Bye."

Theo was disturbed. He knew Sergei wouldn't be too happy about the baby, but he could have at least said congratulations.

Home was life without the piano, without the pressure. Here he was needed and loved. Yet, he also relied on Sergei for so much in his professional life. Where did his priorities lie? There was a severe conflict between his family and the Russian. Each intruded on the other's emotions—neither belonged together.

Theo drove home slowly and was welcomed by the sight of Jago hosing the front garden under Bella's supervision. He turned the spray to face his father.

"Daddy! Shall I water you?" yelled the little boy.

Theo laughed. "Come on you rascal. Let's get the train set out."

A few minutes later, Theo lay on the floor with trains puffing round him—his mind miles away in Moscow.

At lunchtime, Vivi walked in looking quite beautiful. "One of my clients has offered us tickets for the Barbican tonight, Shostakovich and Prokofiev. Shall we go?"

"Oh yes, that would be interesting to hear," replied Theo. "By the way, EMI have asked me to do a recording in two weeks' time. It's very exciting, but it means I must practice every morning and go to rehearsals next week. We're doing the Rachmaninoff Piano Concerto No.3 and some Chopin sonatas. Sergei has organised it all and will come here to oversee proceedings. He'll stay in a hotel near the EMI studios," said Theo excitedly.

"He's a busy man, does he *have* to come to London, too?" inquired Vivi.

"Yes, I'm his number one client. Plus, he keeps me calm. I couldn't possibly perform without him," replied Theo.

"Couldn't you?" asked Vivi.

"No I can't." Theo walked into the garden wishing to end the conversation before it got too intense.

*

Simon Rattle was conducting at the Barbican, which was packed. For once Theo was in the audience, which gave him such a different perception of the pianist's performance. It was obviously difficult not to be critical of the Shostakovich concerto he knew so well, but he was most impressed by the orchestra's interpretation, especially of the second movement.

Later they had supper overlooking the Thames where Theo met various fellow musicians. Vivi loved every moment of the evening and was pleased to see him integrating socially with the London concert scene—wishing Russia could be forgotten.

Chapter Forty Seven

Aylesbury

Cheryl's riding school was holding a summer fête to raise money for new equipment. Each child showed off their skills in front of a huge crowd who cheered them on. There were tables full of home-made produce from Cheryl's shop and local farmers sold some of their fruit and vegetables, bread and cakes.

The Mayor of Aylesbury gave prizes to the 'best rider' and the 'cleverest pony.' Jonty was so proud of Cheryl's organisation. They raised nearly £3,000 towards the new riding school. The Mayor was most impressed and donated a personal cheque to round off the total.

Cheryl also got a huge regular order for produce from a local stately home, so it was a very successful day indeed for her. Jonty noticed that the new pony had settled in nicely and was trotting around happily.

When they'd cleared up, Jonty took Cheryl to his Land Rover.

"I'm going to show you a charming place where we can peacefully enjoy a little supper," Jonty said. "My Cherry Berry has worked so hard."

He drove alongside a canal and parked outside The Barge Restaurant in Aylesbury. The garden had lots of tables beneath some amazing hanging baskets. Jonty had pre-booked a table right on the edge of the canal.

"This is enchanting," said Cheryl, looking around in awe. "What a lovely surprise."

Over supper, Jonty asked Cheryl if she'd like to spend a week with Beady and the others on holiday in Madeira.

"Of course, if I can leave the stables with reliable help. What about your plantation though? Can Jacob cope on his own?"

"I don't see why not." Jonty shrugged. "It would be nice for all of us to be there since she's selling it soon."

"Okay then, let's go. I need a rest," she admitted suddenly feeling tired from her chaotic day.

Chapter Forty Eight

Kensington

A removal van was booked for 10am the following Friday to take the first lot of furniture down to Jonty's barn. Serena had told Lang what should go but could not bear to be there when the van came.

Her Princes Gate job had become increasingly hectic. She had an army of people making curtains and covering walls with rich brocade. The ceiling had a beautiful velvet canopy with two chandeliers on either side.

The Russian, Mr Orlensky, was a perfectionist and came in every few days to see what progress had been made.

A London interior design magazine had written an article on Serena and she had even started working Saturdays, which was having a negative effect on her and the children, especially Freddie, who refused to go to bed until Mummy came home.

Alicia had a busy social life to distract but moaned to Lang, "Mummy isn't a mummy any more, she seems to like making curtains more than looking after us."

Lang realised he had been left to deal with family life entirely because of Serena's work and questioned whether this was some form of punishment dished out by Serena to make him realise how hard juggling work and family commitments could be.

Before he lost his job, Lang really had left the majority of the parenting duties to Serena during the working week, even though she too had a job—although it wasn't quite so full on as it had become.

Sometimes, the anxiety over his debt and meeting the children's demands was almost too much to cope with, but guilt forced him to give as much time as possible to the children. In a curious way their love eased his sense of trauma and seeing them happy in his company certainly wasn't punishment—it was a privilege.

Nevertheless, he missed being close to Serena and the major breadwinner. There was never time together any more, let alone chats, as she just fell asleep when she finally got to bed.

How our roles have changed, all because of my stupidity, he thought sadly to himself.

Chapter Forty Nine

Chiswick

Theo's family time came to an abrupt end with four hours' practise every morning at home then meeting the orchestra at a stuffy rehearsal hall in preparation for the EMI recording session.

Sergei had arrived earlier in the week to ensure the orchestra was settled in and that Theo had his schedule organised.

They met on Monday evening in his hotel room, greeting each other with a warm hug. Sergei lifted his face towards Theo as if to kiss him but Theo drew back at the last second.

"I've missed you dreadfully. I can't go on hiding my feelings any more. I love you Theo," whispered Sergei, sitting down beside him on the sofa.

Theo's guts tightened. He froze for a moment, before saying cautiously, "I've always known I meant a lot to you professionally."

Sergei stroked his client's long fingers and nodded. "But it's not just that," he murmured.

"I know," whispered Theo. "I do understand as I have strong feelings for you too. It's complicated though. Vivi's carrying our third child. God, I'm so confused. This has never happened to me with another man before and—"

His mobile rang. Vivi's name flashed on the screen and he silently gave a prayer of thanks as he answered it. He didn't know what he wanted and talking about it only made him feel more troubled.

"Hello darling," Theo said cheerfully, and Sergei stood up and walked out of the hotel room.

*

Theo arrived home subdued and emotionally taut.

"What's the matter?" Vivi asked. "You seem exhausted."

"Oh, it's nothing, I'm just worried about the recording session," he replied distractedly.

"Life has been so happy recently. You've been home more often, there's not been too much pressure. Now it's all starting again. Why?" asked Vivi tenderly.

"I don't want to talk right now," replied Theo abruptly.

"Theo!" Vivi exclaimed.

"I'm sorry," Theo said, rubbing his forehead. "I just need to rest."

He hurried up the stairs before Vivi could respond.

Chapter Fifty

Notting Hill

Serena dashed into her office. "Hi Gems. Sorry I haven't had a moment to pop in before. How are things?"

"Quite busy. You've got more enquiries since your article was mentioned on TV," Gemma said excitedly.

"Oh that's amazing! But I'm having problems finding a suitable carpet for Princes Gate."

"What about those Persian shops in Piccadilly? They're very exotic," suggested Gems.

"Yes, yes, of course. You *are* clever. I'll dash there now. I've given you a bonus in your monthly cheque by the way. You work bloody hard all alone here. I do appreciate it," said Serena.

"Oh, thank you. By the way, how's home? Is Lang coping with the kids and house sale?"

"Yes, he is actually. Wish I could say the same. I get back so late sometimes, and find the children sitting on the stairs waiting for me, refusing Lang's attempts to take them up to bed. I explain to them I have to work hard, but they say why can't Daddy do it?'" Serena said sadly.

"It must be very difficult trying to make them understand," said Gems.

"Yes, it's all a great strain at present. Anyway, I'll dash off to Piccadilly. Get me a taxi please," said Serena hurriedly.

Chapter Fifty One

Kensington

The following Friday, Lang was still relaxing after the school run with a cup of coffee when the removal van arrived earlier than planned. The men carried out various items of furniture covered in cloths to transport to the countryside. Lang felt the inevitable remorse coming over him again, especially when he saw his desk and a large box of books being loaded.

He decided to go with the van, meeting Jonty and Cheryl outside the barn. It was huge, empty and, thankfully, watertight. As he watched the removers unload the furniture, Cheryl gave him a mug of tea while he expressed his anxiety over talking to the children about the move. He'd have to explain why his desk and so many other things had vanished.

"Yes, it's a difficult event for kids to understand. They don't like change. Perhaps you could get them a pony to ride when you move down?"

"That's a great idea, Cheryl. They both love riding. This is only the first removal load, Jonty. There'll be another next week if that's alright?"

"Yes, that's fine, Lang. I'll see you whenever you arrange it," said Jonty.

Lang got back to Kensington just in time to collect the children from school. Alicia was full of excitement having been chosen to lead the end of term gym display, and Freddie was in a relay race, which he wanted to practice with his sister and Lang after tea.

The phone rang as they came through the front door. Freddie rushed into Lang's study, too excited to question why the phone was on the floor instead of on Daddy's desk. He hoped it was his mum.

"Hello Mummy, I'm in the relay race! When are you coming home to join in?" he asked eagerly.

"Oh, darling, I can't come back yet. Is Daddy there?" she asked, and Freddy hollered for his dad.

"Hi love."

"Hello Lang, I just wondered how the removal went?"

"Well, except that it seems very empty in my study without the desk and books," he said rather quietly.

Freddie, who was still listening, interrupted, "Where's your desk gone, Daddy?"

"Not now, Freddie, I'm on the phone." Lang waited until he had gone, then said, "We'll have to tell them about what's happening soon, now the furniture is disappearing."

"Yes, let's take them for a picnic on Sunday, or even better, go down to Oving and show them the barn," suggested Serena.

"That's an excellent idea but how do I explain where my desk has gone? What on earth shall I say to him?"

"Tell him its gone to be mended. Must dash. See you tonight." Serena rang off abruptly.

After tea Lang and Maggie joined Freddie and Alicia in a relay race round the garden, and Lang told them his desk was being fixed—a story they accepted with ease before continuing their games.

Chapter Fifty Two

Oving

Sunday arrived amid great excitement.

"We're off to have a picnic!" squealed Alicia.

"We might pop in and see Uncle Jonty and Auntie Cheryl too," Serena said and the kids cheered.

They all sang songs in the car, arriving at the Oving farm mid-morning. Lang got out the picnic basket and blankets and walked into a nearby field.

"Look at those little lambs!" Freddie laughed.

"Come on kids, come and have some orange juice," said Serena. She waited until they were sitting down, then said, "Now, we've got a surprise for you. We're all going to move to a little cottage just over there."

"What do you mean, move?" asked Freddie.

"We're going to live in the country, *and* we might get a pony," said Lang.

Alicia burst into tears. "Move from London and my school? We can't!"

Serena cuddled her daughter. There was a loud toot as a Land Rover drew up. Jonty and Cheryl got out.

"Well timed," muttered Lang thankfully.

"Let's go and see the barn," said Cheryl, taking Alicia's hand. They strolled through a lovely orchard, then into the converted barn.

"It's very small," moaned Alicia.

"Could you build a tree house for me, Daddy?" asked Freddie excitedly.

"Where could we keep the pony?" asked Alicia.

"You'd have to keep it out of the orchard, because he'd eat all the apples." Cheryl laughed.

"Let's go upstairs and see the bedrooms," suggested Serena.

"I bagsy this one. It looks out on the sheep," said Freddie.

Jonty and Cheryl kept the excitement going by suggesting a big playroom at the end of the barn. After a picnic lunch they all went back to Jonty and Cheryl's farm where Alicia and Freddie enjoyed a pony ride.

"I think your appearance saved the day," said Lang. "They seem to have accepted the move better than we predicted, which is a great relief, although Alicia will find it difficult without all her friends. Kids are so resilient. I hope they'll be happy."

"It will be lovely having you nearby and we can all help each other out," said Jonty. "By the way, how's the house sale going?"

"Fingers crossed we'll be able to complete soon. They're very nice people and adore the house. We're so lucky to have sold it quickly," said Lang.

"Right kids, come on, time to go back to London!" Serena called to the hay-loft behind the stables.

"Here are some fresh eggs," said Cheryl, handing them to Lang.

"Thanks and I'll see you next week with another removal van," he said.

Their journey home was full of questions.

"But what about my friends?" Alicia wailed.

"They can all come and stay. Besides, you'll make different ones at your new school," Serena said.

"What about my relay race? And my good points list at school?" asked Freddie.

"We won't move until you've finished this term. Then you might go for a holiday with Granny Beady," said Serena.

"And with you, Mummy?" they asked.

"No, with Daddy, because Mummy has to work."

"Why can't Daddy work like he did? Then you could come too," asked Freddie.

They reached Kensington to find Benjie in the paddling pool, with Maggie pushing two wind-up boats round him.

"Miss Vivi rang to ask you to lunch, but I told her you'd gone for a picnic," Maggie said.

"Thanks, I'll ring her now," said Serena.

"We've been to see our new house," stated Alicia.

Indoors, a minute later, Serena quickly updated her sister on the Oving trip, then asked, "How's the bump?"

"Oh, just a little morning sickness, but I'm feeling sad now Theo is back practising like a fiend for the EMI recording. We've had a lovely fortnight of family life and love. Georgie's flourished having her Daddy around. Now it's like he's back in Moscow, only he's still in London, and he's moody too. We see very little of him. Sergei is around organising his daily schedule all the time," said Vivi sadly.

"Poor love, must be hard. Shall we meet for lunch tomorrow? I'll take you to a lovely bistro near Princes Gate," suggested Serena.

*

At the bistro both sisters had a good old moan and laughed

a lot at some of their clients' behaviour at work. Again, Vivi mentioned her anxiety about Theo's moods.

"He seems so fraught when he's working now. He never used to be like this. Something has changed in him," she said sadly.

"I had the same worry over Lang before he told me about the debt. He was so tense and gloomy when he came home, I nearly went mad trying to guess what was wrong. They just never tell us what's going on inside their heads!" said Serena.

"We're not in debt!" Vivi snapped. "It's—it's something else but I don't know what."

"I didn't mean to suggest—"

"Oh, I know," Vivi said, smiling sadly. "Ignore me. Must be my hormones."

Chapter Fifty Three

Central London

EMI Studios

Theo was glad to be back with the orchestra. Murel greeted him warmly.

"This is going to need a lot of repetition. Have you done a recording before?"

"No, I'm a little nervous about it," Theo said truthfully.

"Well, don't be. It will spoil your interpretation," said Murel.

Sergei handed them both a coffee as they went on discussing the first movement.

After the morning session there was a long break so Sergei took Theo to lunch at an Islington restaurant renowned for its celebrity clientele, then drove him back to rehearse on his own. Lunch was intimate and fun, extravagant and expensive. Sergei did his utmost to relax Theo.

The first recording session seemed to go very well, but sadly the balance between Theo's playing and the orchestra wasn't good, so they decided to record again the following day. Sergei tried to calm him down, but Theo was frustrated by the session and rushed out as soon as the recording was over.

Chapter Fifty Four

Chiswick

On arriving home, Theo stomped over to the piano. He'd put a 'DO NOT DISTURB' note on the drawing room door, practiced for about two hours, then lay on the sofa feeling utter despair.

Vivi came in despite the notice, and found Theo face down asleep on the sofa.

"Hello my love," she said, stroking his head.

"Go away," grumbled Theo.

"What's the matter?" Vivi asked.

"What isn't?" cried Theo. "I can't do anything. Even my playing today wasn't good. We have to record again tomorrow."

Vivi ruffled his blond hair. "What's worrying you? Have you lost your confidence?" she asked.

"Yes, I have. Everything is such a muddle."

"We're all right, aren't we? Surely our family gives you love and fun," asked Vivi.

"Yes, of course it does, but my music has suddenly become confused," he said.

"Why don't you talk to Murel about it? Give him a ring and ask him over."

"Yes, perhaps I might. Actually, that's a good idea," muttered Theo.

Murel arrived by taxi later that evening and was immersed with a dejected Theo. Successfully, so it seemed, as afterwards

Vivi enjoyed a surprisingly light-hearted supper with them both. She was fascinated by Murel's ideas and philosophy towards music and musicians. It was a stimulating evening. Theo was visibly relaxed and happier.

The week progressed well. Each day's recording blended into the next. Sergei told Theo his playing was wonderful, and this confidence boost gave new depth to his work. They saw little of each other during the recording week, mostly because Theo was exhausted and went home early, where Vivi did her utmost to keep him calm and happy.

Murel arrived very excitedly one morning to say he had a possible offer from the Royal Festival Hall, so Sergei went along to talk to the management. By the end of the week the recording was played back to the orchestra and Theo. They were surprised how good their performance was. Murel was very proud indeed. The future was looking very bright for all of them.

Chapter Fifty Five

Aylesbury

Cheryl had tripped over some fencing near the paddock, gashing her leg badly so Jonty took her to the local doctor who dressed it.

"No riding for a while, I'm afraid. You can teach it, but don't ride," said Dr Williams.

For the next few days, Jonty would bring a cup of tea to her in the afternoon, whilst in the evenings he cooked supper, which they ate in the kitchen. One day he even brought in two tiny kittens he found in the hayloft in an attempt to cheer her up.

"They must be Hettie's, being that marmalade colour. They're in need of your loving care, she's deserted them, I think." He put them in a basket by the Aga with a bowl of milk.

"Anyone there?" called Jacob a couple of hours later. "I found this poor little owl in the woods. Looks like it fell out of its nest. Can you give it some milk, Cheryl?"

"Yes, I'll put it next to the kittens."

"What have you done to your leg?"

"Oh, I tripped on a bit of loose fencing by the paddock. It's just taking ages to get better" she replied.

"Sorry to hear that. Get well soon," Jacob waved them out.

"Lang will be coming down with another load this week," said Jonty. "I'm glad they've told the kids about the move."

"Me too," agreed Cheryl wondering how her lounge had become an animal hospital so quickly.

*

Two days later Lang arrived with the removal van.

"We haven't brought the piano yet as Alicia needs to practice for the end of term concert. Oh Cheryl, what's happened to your leg?" he asked with concern.

"Just fell over a fence. It's on the mend though finally. How's Serena?" she said, handing him a mug of tea.

"She's going to be interviewed on ITV. The children are very excited. But she's working such long hours. Alicia and Freddie are missing her like crazy, and Benjie wakes up calling for her," said Lang anxiously.

"She's certainly in the fast lane," said Jonty.

"You can say that again! Anyway, I must be off now, I think the removal men have finished. See you next week." Lang kissed Cheryl goodbye.

*

Jonty received a disturbing phone call from the police saying they'd caught the sheep stealers, and asked him to come to the station to make a statement. He was very nervous about going, so Cheryl—almost back to normal self after her week out of action—went with him.

Apparently, the culprits were two young men from the local village who'd stolen hundreds of sheep and exported them to France. Because he hadn't been insured, Jonty had lost quite a lot of money. To Jonty's relief, they would probably be jailed and fined heavily.

He still needed to replace the sheep though, so the following week he decided to go to a local livestock market where there were regular auctions. There were the usual dealers, one a friend of Jonty's, who suggested a dozen from a well-known farm. This time he insured them and put chains on all the drive gates and made sure they were securely locked.

Chapter Fifty Six

Central London

EMI Studios

The EMI recording was complete and Murel felt a great sense of achievement with Theo and the orchestra. They were both anxiously waiting to see if the Festival Hall offer would come to fruition.

Theo called Baba on his break, to check in with her, but was surprised that her carer picked up instead.

"She's what?" he asked confused.

"She had a fall. I did leave you a message. She has been asking for you," the carer said.

Theo sighed and rubbed his head. Vivi would be livid that he had to leave the country again, but Baba needed him. A week would be enough time to spend with his mother and make sure she was getting the best care.

"Everything okay?" Sergei appeared and rubbed a hand across Theo's back.

Theo shook his head. "Baba had a fall. . . I have to go and see her."

"Oh, I'm sorry Theo," Sergei said. "I'll come with you to check on—"

"No," Theo said, more sharply than he intended. "I'll go alone; besides it might be good for me to have some space to think."

He stole a glance at Sergei who reluctantly agreed with him.

Chapter Fifty Seven

Moscow

Theo arrived at Baba's apartment and found her more fragile and limping with a walking stick. She was so pleased to see him.

"I want to visit my dacha and breathe some country air," she said.

"Oh, Mama, I think you're not strong enough yet," said Theo gently.

"I want to go! Ask your friend to take us," Baba suggested.

Theo anxiously considered whether to ask Sergei. His complex emotional involvement was tearing into him, but for Baba's sake he decided to ring his manager and explain the situation.

Sergei arrived two days later and was pleased to organise the trip, leaving the carer behind. The car journey took a few hours. Baba slept part of the way but was overjoyed when they arrived at the little house. Sergei unpacked while Theo made soup for lunch.

Baba hobbled round the garden after managing a few spoonfuls of soup, then Theo tenderly helped her to bed as Sergei prepared a special salad for the two of them that evening. They talked for a couple of hours, and Sergei suggested various potential venues and a new orchestra to play with in order to stretch Theo's virtuoso performances.

"It's so exciting to see you improving your style and achieving recognition in so many places," said Sergei eagerly.

"I want to push you to the limit. I know you can reach greater heights, Maestro."

"Don't push me too much. I haven't the energy at present. Our situation's exhausting me, I'm in a turmoil about it."

"Just do what feels right." Sergei smiled. "We have deep love for each other."

"Yes, we do." Theo's voice broke on the last word as he admitted his feelings out loud, and he started to weep.

Sergei hugged his trembling body and stroked Theo's hair softly. They stood entwined for some minutes, lost in the peace and tranquillity of the countryside, far away from Kensington, Moscow and real life.

Chapter Fifty Eight

Kensington

Serena had gathered the children around her as Lang put the television on to watch the design show.

"There you are, Mummy!" said Freddie excitedly.

"Ssh, listen!" said Lang.

Serena came across as a bubbly, enthusiastic personality full of new ideas and colour schemes.

"You do look pretty, Mummy," Alicia said matter-of-factly.

Lang was very proud to see how captivating his wife was on TV. It was also lovely to see the whole family sitting round together for once.

"Mummy, you're famous! I must tell all my friends," said Alicia excitedly.

"Right, bedtime kids, it's late." Serena chased them upstairs, as Lang said, "You came over so well, darling."

"I did, didn't I?" Serena laughed. "Thank you love."

*

A few days later the Buchans' lawyer arranged completion for three weeks' time when the children's school term had finished. It was a very upsetting time for Alicia and Freddie having to say goodbye to friends and teachers. Alicia had played well at the concert but was devastated that it would be her last performance with her friends.

Serena was working so hard she was hardly aware of the imminent move. Fortunately, because of her job, they were able to keep Maggie on and she agreed to come with them, much to Lang's relief.

His biggest problem was fending off the firm's demand for the balance of the debt. He wrote explaining that it would be settled on the sale of his mother-in-law's house, begging them to be patient.

"Thank God for your huge barn, Jonty," said Lang after overseeing the arrival of a third removal van the following Friday. "All this moving is causing a lot of upset to the children and Serena."

"Yes, it must be awful seeing your favourite items disappear. Oh, and talking of moves, I've just heard from Beady who says she's had an offer from someone for the house. They've offered cash which is very exciting."

Lang smiled, visibly relieved. "That's quick isn't it? Mind you, it's in a lovely position near the sea."

"We're all meant to be going there next month, aren't we?" asked Jonty.

"Yes, depending on how the move goes."

"Surely you can arrange to come out with the kids? It would be so nice for Mum to have all her grandchildren out there one last time."

Lang sighed. "Yes, it would, but moving is a big issue, especially since I have to organise it all while Serena's so busy."

"It must be very difficult," agreed Jonty.

"It is but I know I brought this on myself," Lang said. "I'll try my best to get us to Beady's."

*

The following weekend, the whole family spent the day at the barn, having taken down a selection of their favourite things to start putting in their new bedrooms, plus bicycles, train sets and TVs. Lang made it an adventure.

The kids played in the orchard, while Serena cleaned the Aga. Lang mowed the lawn at the back of the house and planted three favourite roses he'd brought down from Kensington. Serena put pots of herbs by the kitchen door.

"Can I bring a school friend down sometime and have a picnic?" asked Alicia.

"Yes, let's do that next week, as you've finished school. We'll bring Maggie and Benjie too," said Lang.

"Will Mummy be working?" asked Freddie sadly.

"Yes, Mummy is doing a very important job, earning money for the family." Lang tried to reassure him.

"I know! Let's bring Georgie and Auntie Vivi too."

"Alright," agreed Lang.

Chapter Fifty Nine

Chiswick

Georgie and Alicia had fun sleeping in the tent in Vivi's garden one night the following week. Vivi had given them a picnic plus two torches beside their sleeping bags. Their whisperings and giggles went on until nearly midnight.

The next day two sleepy faces called out, "What's for breakfast? We're starving!"

"Come on, get dressed. We're going on a pleasure steamer down the Thames in half an hour," Vivi said.

"Whoopee!" cried Georgie.

Vivi said goodbye to Jago and Bella then drove the girls to Chiswick Pier, where they boarded the pleasure craft excitedly.

"It's like a history lesson," called Alicia as they passed the House of Commons, then onto Tower Bridge, and the Thames Barrier.

"Greenwich looks like a huge palace," exclaimed Georgie.

Suddenly, Vivi's mobile rang. "Hello Theo darling. How is Baba? I can't hear you too well. I'm opposite Greenwich on a pleasure boat with Georgie and Alicia. It's a treat for the school holidays."

"Well, she's in the dacha with us, but she's very frail," said Theo, not commenting on the family life he knew he was missing out on back at home.

"You poor thing. Any idea when you'll be able to come home?"

They chatted on for a few more minutes about nothing in particular before Vivi pensively turned off her phone.

"Is Daddy okay?" asked Georgie.

"Yes darling, he's fine, absolutely fine," she replied.

Lang phoned that evening to ask if he should collect Alicia.

"Let her stay another night, they're having great fun together. Georgie's doing what she calls a 'sing song play,' Jago's a lion and Alicia's a witch."

"Well, if you're sure. It gives me more time to get the new home up and running. How are you Vivi?" Lang asked.

"I'm enjoying being pregnant and the baby has started kicking, but I'm fed up with Theo not being here, especially now it's holiday time," said Vivi crossly. "I have my own work to do, after all."

"Yes, it must be very hard for you, especially when the children are at home all day. Why not let Georgie come back here tomorrow? And I'll take them to the boat lake? Also, will you all come down to our cottage next weekend?" Lang asked.

"Oh, that would cheer me up. Yes, on both counts," said Vivi.

"It'll be a bit of a crush, but I'm sure we'll manage somehow," chuckled Lang.

Chapter Sixty

Oving

The country weekend was a great success. The children raced around the fields. Serena had even managed to finish early on Friday. Vivi so enjoyed her time in their barn and just being all together, especially when they visited Jonty on the farm. Alicia and Georgie helped him groom the ponies. Cheryl cooked a huge Sunday lunch and everyone felt happy and at ease for the first time in a long while.

Despite the happy feelings, Vivi suddenly felt resentment that Theo wasn't with them all at such a happy family weekend. *Why was he always away and why was Sergei always with him?*

They discussed dates for the Madeira holiday, as Lang felt the move would soon be finalised.

"Shall I book the flights?" suggested Serena. "It's very sad I can't come but this Princes Gate job is worth every penny in terms of our future. Also, I've got the Qatar Embassy to return to. The rooms upstairs have to be totally re-designed."

"Yes, we understand that, dear Fig Tree," Lang replied, putting an arm round her shoulder, which visibly stiffened.

Chapter Sixty One

Moscow

Sergei stood in the doorway of the little cottage. "Do you want to practice on next door's piano? You seem depressed. Maybe you need to work?"

"I'm so confused I don't know what to practice. You've not found a new venue for me," replied Theo.

"Well, I'm wondering what to do myself. I am questioning if I was wrong to promote your music and fall in love with you. It's an impossible situation for us both which seems to have no future. How can our relationship flourish with all your guilt and indecision? I've put my whole life into yours. What is it you want?" Sergei pleaded.

"I don't know!" Theo protested. "What am I meant to do with all these feelings? I love you. I love my wife, Vivi. I have enough love for both of you but. . ." Theo stopped yelling and walked out.

Sergei found him at the bottom of the garden. The setting sun cast long shadows across the rooftops on the horizon.

"I must go to London. We'll take Baba back home tomorrow," Theo said, sitting up.

The next day, Theo said goodbye to Baba and her carer and Sergei drove him to the airport. It was a cool parting, neither said a word as he went through the departure gates.

Sergei wandered back to his flat alone and lonely. The strain of his relationship with Theo was becoming too fraught.

All his previous relationships had been fairly short, but this passionate friendship was so complicated. He'd never felt such love before, but he was beginning to realise Theo could never be completely his.

In New York a close liaison with a famous conductor had been fairly intense but nothing as deep as this. Then there was the Italian tenor who wanted to move in with him. Sergei had found his eagerness overwhelming. He started to worry the tables had turned and he was the one was being overly eager with Theo.

He'd moved away from home before his parents realised he was gay, and soon got entrenched in the musical world, then became an agent, then a promoter. His career had gone from strength to strength but at the cost of a long-term relationship. His warm charm, understanding and ability to encourage people was greatly sought after. . . but the only man he wanted was Theo.

Chapter Sixty Two

Kensington

The last official day in their Kensington home had arrived. Alicia and Freddie were intrigued as they watched the removal men carrying the final pieces of furniture out of the house.

As he walked into the long sitting room, memories flooded his mind. He walked slowly up the uncarpeted stairs into their bedroom, pausing at the vacant space where the bed had been—their love nest.

Lang couldn't bear to go into the children's bedrooms. As he stood sadly in his empty study he gulped. Lang stood against the door and wept.

"Ten years at our happy house, lost to someone else."

An overwhelming sadness engulfed him. The children were yelling from the front door. He brushed a tear away.

"Come on, jump into the car. Maggie, you sit in front."

He drove the children down to Oving where the remaining furniture was already being moved into the barn. They thought it all quite an adventure, directing the removal men to their bedrooms.

Maggie had brought provisions down for supper. Cheryl and Jonty arrived, much to Lang's relief. They'd brought fresh eggs, homemade cheese, bread, and some vegetables.

"This is great. I forgot about doing a shop before we left," said Lang, rubbing his forehead.

"You're well moved in already," said Jonty, looking around.

"I suppose we are," said Lang sadly. "I wish Serena was here. She'll be coming down by car later this evening."

"Why don't you pop over for lunch tomorrow?" said Cheryl.

"Oh, yes please!" chimed Freddie and Alicia.

"Shall I stay here with Benjie?" Maggie asked.

"No, you must all come. You've not seen our farm, Maggie," said Jonty.

Serena arrived about 9pm. "Did the move go well?" she asked. "It all looks quite cosy. Once we've taken the last removal sheets off, our new home will be complete, I suppose."

"Mummy, come and see my room," said Alicia excitedly. "I've got a little fireplace and a wash basin all of my own."

"That's lovely, darling. How are you doing, Freddie?" Serena asked.

"The train set won't fit in my room. It's too small!" wailed Freddie.

"Don't worry old chap," said Lang. "We're going to build a playroom. The piano and your train set will have plenty of space in there."

As both children ran out of the room, he turned to Serena. "Benjie's asleep. Cheryl and Jonty came around earlier armed with veg and eggs. We're going to have lunch with them tomorrow."

"Sounds great."

"Supper's ready," said Maggie. "I made the Shepherd's Pie in London. You've got a lovely Aga here."

*

Serena left at 7am for the station, much to the sadness of the children and Lang.

"Mummy's never here anymore," cried Freddie.

"Come on kids, let's help Maggie unpack all the crockery, then we'll get the bikes out for a ride and discover some new places," said Lang hurriedly, worried by Freddie's repeated outbursts over Serena.

After hour's unpacking they went off on an adventure ride to explore the area around their new home. Freddie met two boys at the next farm, fishing in a little stream.

"Want to find some tiddlers with us?" called a fair-haired boy of about eight.

"Can't at the moment. I'm going for a bike ride with my dad," replied Freddie.

"Maybe later on today?" suggested Lang, knowing it was just what he needed, to make new friends.

That night, Freddie crept into bed with Serena and refused to move.

Chapter Sixty Three

Chiswick

Theo arrived at lunchtime to passionate hugs from the children and a warm embrace from Vivi.

"You looked splendid. Let me feel the baby." He placed both hands tenderly round her stomach. "Oh, it's lovely to see you all." He kissed Vivi and held her close.

"Look what I've made for you, Daddy. It's a picture of a grand piano with little mice playing the music. They're singing, 'Hello Daddy.' Do you like it?" said Georgie. She threw herself into his arms while Jago circled round his ankles waiting to be picked up.

For the next few days, Theo spent every moment with his family, taking Georgie to museums and concerts, which she loved; Jago to a miniature railway, which made the little boy squeal with delight, while with Vivi he cherished every precious minute, especially in the bedroom. He also found time to practice on his beloved piano each day.

On Thursday, Beady arrived unannounced.

"Mum, what are you doing here?" said Vivi, astonished.

"I just suddenly felt an urge to see you all. Is everything alright?" Beady asked.

Theo felt slightly disturbed remembering his other life in Moscow.

"Yes, of course it is Mum. The baby's kicking well and Theo has just returned home at last," said Vivi warmly. Theo pecked Beady on the cheek.

"How's the piano?" Beady asked.

"As wonderful as ever," replied Theo.

"Let's all have a drink," suggested Vivi.

Georgie made a great fuss of Granny and little Jago clambered on to her lap.

"One of the reasons I've popped over is for a family gathering about the distribution of funds from my house sale. I'd like Jonty and Serena to come here one day," Beady stated.

"Gosh, that's going to be difficult for Serena. They've just moved to the country and she works like a Trojan; never gets home until at least 9pm and leaves before the children even wake up," said Vivi.

"I'm sad that lovely house has gone. What's the cottage like?" Beady asked rather curtly.

"Enchanting," said Vivi. "It's surrounded by fields. Perhaps we'd better all meet on Sunday—Serena's only day off?"

"Yes, I love it down on the farm," said Beady.

"You must come and see your special flat at the end of the garden, Granny," piped up Georgie. "I'll show you."

She took Beady's hand and pulled her out to the garden. Meanwhile, Vivi phoned Jonty, then Serena at work, to arrange the following Sunday.

Chapter Sixty Four

Aylesbury

Three days later everyone arrived by midday. The children rushed to the stables, followed by Cheryl, who gave them each a pony ride, holding onto Freddie's pony firmly. Family lunch was full of laughter and a wonderful spread of vegetables, roast chickens, garlic, and masses of bread sauce.

Afterwards, Beady decided to assemble everyone in the drawing room so they could all hear her ideas. She settled on the sofa.

"I'm advancing an extra amount to Serena and Lang due to their present urgent circumstances. The rest of you will be compensated in my will, of course. I hope this allows Serena to see more of her family, who I feel are quite stressed by her daily absence."

"Oh Mum, that's incredibly generous." Serena hugged Beady warmly.

"Thank you so, so much," Lang could only whisper. Inwardly, he was ashamed all over again.

"I've virtually sold the house, so you'll have the money soon." Everyone fell silent for a moment.

"Will you come and see our new home, Mum?" asked Serena.

"Yes, I'd love to," said Beady.

"Leave the kids here," said Jonty. "I'll take you over."

Beady was enchanted by the farm and its potential, much

to Lang's relief. He felt enormous gratitude for her generosity and hoped so much that as a result of it Serena would ease up and come back to the family. The children were being badly affected by her absence, which still felt like a punishment to him because of all the mistakes he had made in his own career.

At one point Beady took Serena aside.

"Darling, you must give a little more time to the family now I've helped you financially. I noticed Freddie seems subdued—not his robust self. I hear he misses you dreadfully, poor little fellow. As for Madeira, you'll have to take a week off. I've got something very special to show you. I'm sure the Princes Gate chief would let you have a rest. Shall I speak to him?"

"No! For heaven's sake Mum, don't interfere. I'll ask him for some time off. Believe it or not, I'd quite like a holiday too. I'm working hard but it's not just for me, it's for my family," said Serena emphatically. "I'll mention it to the client tomorrow. By the way, we're hoping to build an extension here for the children's playroom—plus an extra bedroom for when you come to stay."

Beady was amazed at Serena's practical approach to such a big change and questioned how she really felt, but sensed it wasn't the time to discuss it.

"Let's go back to the farm," suggested Jonty.

When they got back, Cheryl was helping the children do potato prints in the kitchen.

"Do you want to stay for a bit, Mum?" asked Jonty, putting the kettle on.

"No, I can't. I'm flying back tomorrow. I only came over to see you all, mostly because of Serena and Lang's financial problems," Beady said.

"You're a great mum," Jonty said, hugging her.

Chapter Sixty Five

Chiswick

Theo showed Beady to her room on their return. "Do you want a little lie down?" he asked.

"Yes, I might have fifteen minutes."

After her two-hour-long nap, Beady enjoyed playing with the children. Jago especially loved making her draw funny pictures and Alicia proudly played her piano composition, which Beady thought was marvellous.

The next morning, Theo and the children took Beady to the airport while Vivi saw several clients.

"See you all in a few weeks!" Beady called, waving goodbye.

"Let's go to the little farm and see the piglets, Daddy," suggested Georgie on the way home. "It's not far."

Ten minutes later they were watching the piglets rolling in mud, while the goats stood on their hind legs, begging for dandelions to chew on. All this was directly under the flight path of the enormous jets coming in to land. Georgie picked up a baby rabbit and gave it to Jago who nursed it tenderly, then dropped it as the next plane roared over.

Suddenly Theo's phone rang.

"Hi. The EMI recording is selling well," said Sergei eagerly. "Several interviews have been arranged and the Festival Hall called at last."

"Hold on a minute," said Theo, racing over to stop Jago

crawling under a fence to play with the lambs. "Yes, go on, you were saying about the Festival Hall?"

"They want you to play in three weeks, just before I go away."

"Who am I replacing?" Theo couldn't hear the reply as a huge 747 flew overhead just then. "Listen, I'm near the airport, I've just been dropping my mother-in-law off. I'll call you from home in an hour or so, okay?" he yelled. Theo felt a buzz, hearing Sergei's voice.

Alicia was sitting beside a fence letting her fingers be sucked by the little lambs. "I wish I could have one Daddy, can I?" she asked.

"Come on you rascals, let's get an ice cream," suggested Theo excitedly.

When they got home, the children were bubbling with fun describing all the animals.

"Lunch is ready," called Bella. Vivi came down from her work exhausted, but avidly listened to all the fun.

"The sheep were sweet, Mummy," said Jago.

"Well, I must do some practicing this afternoon. Sergei rang to say we've got a concert at the Festival Hall two days before we go on holiday," said Theo.

"That's very exciting darling. We can all come and hear you in London. Oops! The baby just kicked—it obviously agrees!" Vivi laughed before adding, "Actually, if you're going to be busy every day I think Georgie can go to gym club. You're longing to join, aren't you?"

"Ooh yes, Mummy, two of my friends are going," enthused Georgie.

Theo suddenly felt an urge to speak to Sergei again. "I must go and practice now," he said and pecked Vivi on the cheek.

"Tell me more about the concert. It's great to hear your voice," he murmured two minutes later in his study. Sergei explained how a Russian pianist had cancelled due to a wrist injury and that Theo had been suggested as a replacement. "Could Murel conduct?"

"No, I'm afraid not," Sergei said. "But don't worry, I'll be coming over from Moscow on Sunday night, we'll talk about all the details then."

"How's Baba?" Theo asked.

"Just the same. My cousin took her to the park yesterday. She loved feeding the ducks, but her appetite isn't good."

"Do give her a hug from me."

"I will. I'll see you Sunday," called Sergei before he hung up.

A little figure had snuggled onto Theo's lap. Jago lay gazing up at him. Theo took both his hands and played a nursery rhyme. They sang together for a few minutes. "Off you go. Daddy has to work now."

That evening, Murel arrived for supper, much to Theo's surprise. Vivi had asked him and his girlfriend, together with two other mutual friends. It was a warm, balmy evening. Theo gazed across at Vivi who looked absolutely radiant in the candlelight, touched by her thoughtfulness.

Murel was thrilled about the Festival Hall but sad not to be conducting Theo. "I'm in Paris, unfortunately, but Woolsey is a great conductor. You're playing Rachmaninoff's Theme of Paganini and several Chopin Sonatas, all of which, by the way, you do splendidly,"

"I'm glad you think so," murmured Theo proudly.

The evening's conversation ranged across music, politics and lots of orchestral gossip. Vivi was pleased to see their first dinner party in a long time go so well.

The rest of the week Georgie was away all day at gym club. Theo practised each morning then went off to rehearsals, whilst Vivi saw her clients every morning and rested in the afternoons.

On Wednesday Theo didn't return until late. Sergei had persuaded him to go back to his hotel where they discussed his forthcoming Festival Hall concert and media interviews before cuddling on the sofa. The moments they stole together were becoming increasingly precious to them both, and they loved being able to shut out the world from the safety and comfort of the hotel room.

Chapter Sixty Six

Notting Hill

"Gems, could you get me a ticket for the family's flight to Madeira? I've spoken to the Princes Gate officials and told them I'm going away on business for ten days and that I'll leave work for the various departments," Serena said.

Gems looked wistful. "Fancy you having a break! I've hardly known you stop work in these last five years I've been working for you. . . even on Christmas Day."

"Well, it's the last time Mum will have all the family in Madeira as she's sold the house. Lang is getting the benefit of my share of the proceeds to sort out his bloody debt to his firm, then it's finally over. Poor Freddie is missing me dreadfully and I'm going to have to take Saturdays off to be with him." Serena's worried voice concerned Gems.

"Once they're back at school it'll be easier, won't it?" she said.

"Yes, but we've still got seven weeks of the summer to get through." Serena gnawed her bottom lip, then picked up a heap of paperwork. "Anyway, let's do the bills. Any letters or emails need replying to?"

They worked for a couple of hours before Serena rushed off to catch bedtime in the country.

Chapter Sixty Seven

Oving

Serena arrived home to hear Freddie wailing under the wooden staircase.

"I'm back, Freddie!" She snuggled him tenderly on her lap. "I've got some happy news, I'm coming to Madeira with you! We'll have such a fun holiday." She stroked his forehead.

The wailing subsided as he slowly went upstairs to bed with Serena.

"Hello darling, you're early," said Lang who'd just emerged from his study. He pecked her on the cheek.

"Does this go on every night?"

"Yes, quite often I'm afraid," replied Lang.

"Hello, Mummy!" Alicia rushed up and hugged her. "Can my new friends Tom and Sarah come and stay tomorrow if you ring up their parents?"

"Just let me see Freddie to bed first," Serena said.

Supper was on the table half an hour later. Alicia was allowed to stay up a little and was delighted to hear that Serena was coming to Madeira after all.

"How can I thank you and your mum for being so generous?" he asked.

"I really don't know. But it would be a help if you could try and get a consultancy job of some sort. I'd be pleased to see you working again, although you seem to be managing the kids quite well instead of me. Speaking of which, I thought perhaps we'll ask one of Freddie's friends from London to come down next weekend. It might help his insecurity a bit."

*

The barn was soon buzzing with children. Alicia's friends slept in a tent outside, screaming and laughing until late. Freddie's best friend, Col, slept in the lower bunk bed.

In the morning, Lang took them all to Cheryl's for some riding and a high tea. He pondered on Serena's suggestion and wondered how he could ever show his gratitude to his beloved Fig Tree. A lot of repairs had to be made before he could get close to her again.

"Look at the puppy, Daddy!" Alicia called, holding a bundle of fur in her arms. "Can we have one?"

He was jolted out of his despair by the gaggle of excited children running amongst kittens and chickens.

"Maybe some time later," he said.

Just then, Cheryl called the children to the stables to help clean up and put the ponies to bed. Lang had a problem dragging them away and only a promise of pizza got them into the car.

Returning to the cottage, Lang found Freddie had taken a baby chick under his anorak to put in his bunk bed. Serena came back just as the chaos was getting out of hand. She took the baby chick and put it in a box by the Aga, leaving the cat outside, and tucking all the children into bed.

*

The following day Lang took everyone to see a hot air balloon display. Gently, the multi-coloured orbs floated up, interrupted by blasts of flame heating the air. There must have been more than a dozen of them in the still blue sky. The children stood in awe of their magic and wanted to go up in one.

When they got back to the cottage, Maggie had laid out a big picnic in the orchard. While everyone ate the delicious fruit salads and sandwiches they heard an angry bellow. It was the farmer who owned the field next to the cottage.

"Which one of you lot opened the gate and let the sheep out?" he shouted. "Now you come and help round 'em up."

"We didn't open the gate," Alicia protested.

"Come on, Flash," he called to his dog who raced towards the bewildered sheep in the drive. The children circled round laughing and trying to guide them back. "You stand in a line by the fence, while Flash and I round 'em up."

A few minutes later the sheep were safely back.

"It might have been Benjie," whispered Freddie. "Look, he's swinging on the gate again now." They all went back to the picnic laughing.

Serena and Lang were asked to dinner by their new landlord, a very wealthy friend of Jonty's. He'd invited a local couple who had children of a similar age. The husband, James Holt, was a partner in an investment management firm whose name Lang recognised. His wife, Penny, ran a private nursing home for the elderly. Jonty and Cheryl knew the couple well.

It was the first time Lang and Serena had been out together for over a year and both were a little subdued until Penny mentioned needing some interior design work done. Serena got carried away with lots of suggestions.

As they drove home Lang laughed. "I've not seen Jonty

tipsy before. It must have been that potent home-made wine!"

"Yes, he looked quite red in the face. Nice people, weren't they?" said Serena.

Lang leaned over to kiss her.

"Look out, we're nearly in the ditch!" she laughed, and Lang righted the car. "The children have really settled in well, haven't they?"

"Yes," agreed Lang. "And what about you?"

"It's taking me a long time to accept leaving London," Serena admitted. Lang stopped the car. Serena looked at him. "What are you doing?"

"I can't go on saying 'sorry' all the time," he suddenly blurted out. "I can't undo my terrible mistake, and I can't expect you to forgive me. I've ruined our life together, the most precious thing I have. Let me try and help by doing everything for the kids, allowing you the freedom to work as you want. I realise you're the earner but on top of that I'll try and get some kind of job where I can work from home. Oh, Fig Tree, give me a chance! I do love you." Lang drew her to him, tears falling on her hair.

"Give it time," whispered Serena.

Lang drove slowly home with her head resting on his shoulder.

Chapter Sixty Eight

Central London

Sergei's hotel

Theo recorded an interview at Classic FM that was to air alongside a selection of pieces from his latest London performance. They also promised to play excerpts from the EMI recording, which would help to increase sales.

Afterwards, he and Sergei went back to the Russian's hotel where they discussed the immediate future.

"Now, your priority is the concert. That's all. Nothing else matters. This is the highlight of your career," said Sergei enthusiastically.

Theo clutched his arm. "I hope I can do it."

"You've shown us several times the passion you can give to your performances," Sergei urged.

"But it isn't just a question of the music, is it?" said Theo. "It's us, too. I'm being torn between you and Vivi. I just feel so confused and muddled. I need to focus on the music and at times it's so hard."

"You cannot let anything get in the way of the music, Maestro." Sergei's eyes bored into Theo's. "I don't know what our future holds but if we are meant to be, then Theo, we will."

Chapter Sixty Nine

Chiswick

"Are you always going to be late after talking to Sergei?" asked Vivi crossly when Theo arrived home at midnight. He jerked his head back in surprise at her tone. "I've thrown away your supper. It wouldn't keep for more than three hours and I ate alone. Let's talk about him, shall we?"

Theo slumped on to the sofa exhausted and unable to think of a decent enough reason to get out of the conversation.

"Why are you always with him? Can't you see your mother without him? Can't you rehearse without him? Can't you live without him?" Vivi stared at her husband with a passion he could hardly believe.

"He controls my musical life, that's all." Theo said, staring at the floor.

"Darling, what is it? Talk to me. Our baby is arriving soon. What is your priority? Music or our child?"

Theo drew her to him. "I love you," he whispered.

"Do you?" she asked quizzically.

"Of course I do," Theo said, holding her hand. "I will be here for our child, I promise."

Vivi stared at him from the corner of her eye, feeling her heart race. *Why didn't he answer any of my questions about Sergei?* His blatant avoidance made her even more fearful of what was happening to her marriage. She knew something was wrong, she just couldn't work out what.

Chapter Seventy

South Bank

Rehearsals were tough, especially with a conductor who was new to Theo. He learnt different phrasing and tempi. The orchestra was very sensitive to his interpretation. Sergei had organised some excellent publicity and secured a lot of bookings.

After his rehearsal, Theo decided to visit the Festival Hall. He crept downstairs into the Auditorium. Cleaners were sweeping the floors preparing for an evening performance. A slim woman dressed in jeans and an elegant jacket was humming through her solo with a pianist. Theo took a deep breath and stared at the stage.

I'll be there soon. He smiled, then ran back up the steps and out of the Hall, passing a poster of himself by the box office. He rang Sergei.

"I've just popped into the Festival Hall and feel so excited to be playing there."

"Shall I meet you somewhere?" asked Sergei.

"No, I must go home. There was a row last night about me getting home so late."

"Oh, I see," Sergei replied stiffly.

"But I did enjoy spending time with you. You know that, don't you?" Theo asked, hating Sergei's distant tone. "What's wrong?"

"This," Sergei said in the same tone. "You having me and your wife. It isn't fair to me or her."

Theo sighed. "I know. . . I'm sor—"

"See you at rehearsal tomorrow," Sergei cut in, before hanging up the phone.

Chapter Seventy One

Notting Hill

"There's a crisis at Princes Gate. A fire has burnt some of the curtains," said Gems urgently as her boss swept into the office.

"You're joking! I'd better go over there at once," said Serena, rushing back out.

Lots of people were milling around the big banqueting hall where the charred drapes lay on the floor.

"How did this happen?" she asked the manager crossly.

"I think it was an electrical fault, madam."

"What a futile waste of all my work. It'll take weeks to replace these, and they were all dyed to match the walls!"

Serena could hardly contain her anger, especially as most of the staff stood staring blankly at her. The butler arrived and apologised profusely for the accident, reassuring her about replacements. Serena thanked him and left.

Returning to the office she spent hours reordering the material and dye colours.

Finally, she turned to Gems. "I forgot to ask if there were any letters to sign."

"Yes, about four. There's also an enquiry from an official at the Saudi Embassy. They want to see you."

"Is there?" gasped Serena.

"When are you free?" asked Gems.

"Sometime next week I suppose, but I can't take on any more work for months. Come on, let's go out and have a coffee."

"Yes, that would be nice," said Gems, a little flustered.

Just as they were leaving, an enormous bouquet arrived from Princes Gate with a charming note of apology.

"You'll have to keep these in the office, I can't possibly take them on the train. I'd look like a walking florist's shop!" Serena laughed.

"They can sit on my desk," enthused Gems, eyeing the beautiful arrangement.

Whilstdrinking their coffee, Gems suddenly placed one hand on her boss's arm. "I'm getting engaged!" she blurted out. "It's all very sudden, I'm so excited."

"How wonderful!" Serena hugged her warmly. "Is he that guy I met at the door with your car keys once?"

"Yes, that's Gully. We've known each other for six years, but don't worry, after we get married I'll still work for you, Serena." said Gems genuinely.

"Oh, that's a relief, I couldn't possibly do without you. You're so patient with me and all the trauma in my jumbled old life. I'm so happy for you, Gems."

Chapter Seventy Two

Oving

Lang was lying on the floor, feet in the air, swivelling Freddie like a helicopter. Squeals of delight from the boy propelled Lang's feet faster and faster. They were both unaware of Serena watching until Freddie fell down.

"Oh Mummy, I'm the fastest helicopter," he yelled, rushing up to hug her.

"Yes, you are! Lang, where's Alicia?"

"In the bath with your best bubble lotion and singing away."

"Little minx! And how's Benjie?"

"Has a bit of a cold. Maggie's up there now."

Serena felt an unusual warmth returning home to laughter and for the first time, realised she was pleased to be in the peaceful countryside, away from the rush.

She went up to comfort Benjie, then popped into the bathroom where all she could see in the tub was a great, white, mound of foam.

"Where are you Ally-Pally?" she called.

Alicia erupted out of the bath covered in foam. They laughed together as Serena dried her.

"Why don't you get in Mummy? Do you ever have time for a bubble bath anymore?"

"Sometimes," said Serena hurriedly.

"Do you have time to think of us? Do you have time to

think of Daddy at home all alone?" Alicia was suddenly very serious which caught Serena unawares.

Unable to answer she pulled Alicia towards her, hugging her tight, soaking her own clothes.

Chapter Seventy Three

Princes Gate

The banqueting room was humming with activity as Serena arrived. All of the carpets had been sponged, windows cleaned and remnants of charred drapes thrown away.

She took a deep breath and started to examine the damaged corner then called two assistants who'd helped her do the original drapes. Together they copied every detail to match the colour scheme. Serena thanked the assistant for the bouquet and he handed her an envelope.

"For you," he said. "From His Excellency."

Serena opened the envelope on the train home and was stunned to see it contained a generous cheque.

Brilliant! That'll pay for the Madeira trip, she thought.

Chapter Seventy Four

Chiswick

The following day Vivi was feeling rather low and decided to call Serena.

"It's Theo's endless absences," she explained. "Now he's rehearsing for the Festival Hall, he's tense and distant. What a mixed-up person he seems. Being an artist he's naturally moody, because all his thoughts are deep in the music, but when he comes home he's so remote now, even with the kids. He was wonderful when he first came back. Now it's as though he's been taken over. The other night he came back at midnight having been with Sergei. I was furious. They seem to be together all the time."

"Just remember after this concert, he will be home to focus on you, the kids and the little one."

"I hope so," Vivi mumbled.

Just then the front doorbell chimed and Georgie came in.

"Hello darling, how did you get on today?" asked Vivi.

"It was great," replied Georgie. "We did loads of somersaults."

Vivi went to the kitchen, sitting Jago down for tea. "Georgie, would you like to go and stay in the country with Alicia for a few days after gym week has finished?"

"Ooh yes. Will you come too, Mummy?" Georgie asked.

"No, I can't darling, I have to see clients every day," Vivi said.

"Can't they do without you for a while?" asked Georgie.

"No, they need my help," Vivi replied quietly.

"Why is Daddy out all the time now? He took me to so many fun places when he first came home."

Vivi rolled her eyes. *Yes, and now he's AWOL all the time.*

With a forced smile, she said, "He has to practise with the orchestra, so he'll play well at the concert we're going to. You know how important his work is."

Chapter Seventy Five

Kensington

Vivi and Serena met for lunch just off Kensington High Street.

"Poor Vivi, you do look tired." Serena gave her a hug.

"I'm not surprised, the baby was kicking all last night.," Vivi said, rubbing her belly softly.

"Just think, we'll all be on holiday soon, with Mum."

"Yes. I hope Theo will be more relaxed with us all once the concert's over," said Vivi quietly.

"I'm sure he will be. Oh, I didn't tell you, I had a ghastly drama at work. All my specially dyed drapes caught fire in the banqueting hall alcove. It'll take ages to re-do," Serena said brusquely, grabbing her mobile as it rang loudly.

"Freddie's fallen off his bike and cut his knee badly. He wants to talk to you," Lang said.

"Hello, my lovely boy. Has Daddy put a dinosaur plaster on it? Yes, I'll be home later. Be brave. Auntie Vivi sends you a big hug. Bye." Serena rang off, then said with relief. "Lang's coping very well, I never thought he'd be so patient."

Chapter Seventy Six

Aylesbury

Jacob knocked on the kitchen door.

"Did you hear them two shots? Bloomin' poachers. They got a rabbit and a pheasant. I was passing on the tractor and they ran off into the wood. Don't know if they had a car. It's bloody dangerous with them guns."

"How ghastly," said Cheryl anxiously. "They could have got any of us."

Jonty put an arm round her. "You're quite safe with your ponies, love. There's no way of stopping those poachers. We must keep vigilant."

"Anyway, do 'yer want this pheasant?" asked Jacob.

"Yes please, but you keep the rabbit," said Cheryl.

"You know we're going away in a few weeks' time, Jacob. Can you manage on your own? Or shall I get Will to come and help?" asked Jonty.

"That ain't a bad idea."

"I'll talk to him tomorrow. You can cope with the vegetable garden. Help yourself to anything you fancy. The stables are looked after by Cheryl's friend, as you know. Shall we go down and look at the forest? We've not checked all the trees lately," suggested Jonty.

They walked together through Jonty's plantation.

"I hope them bloomin' rabbits 'ave been kept out," muttered Jacob.

"Yes, they are a problem," agreed Jonty.

"Why not get some of them CCTV cameras," suggested Jacob. "Several locals are thinking about it."

"That's a good idea. I'll look into it."

Chapter Seventy Seven

Moscow

Sergei received an urgent phone call from Moscow during the morning rehearsal. Baba had deteriorated, and her breathing was very shallow. Sergei's cousin had called the doctor who suspected another stroke and suggested she go to the hospital. Sergei was in a panic. *When should he tell Theo? How much rehearsal could he miss at this vital time before the performance?*

Before he had time to decide, Theo walked out of the rehearsal room.

"Maestro, I don't know how to tell you. Baba has weakened and been taken to hospital."

"I must go to her." Theo started running outside.

"Stop! Let me help you," called Sergei, grabbing Theo's sleeve. Tears were streaming down the musician's face. Sergei embraced him. "I'll book a plane tonight if I can and will explain to Woolsey and the orchestra what's happened."

"I'm going home to tell Vivi and pack," Theo said, breaking free and rushing along the street in a blind panic.

Vivi was in the garden when Theo hurried in.

"Baba's very ill. I have to fly to Moscow tonight."

"Oh, you poor darling." She hugged him. "How can I help?" She stroked his tearful face.

"I know she's dying." Theo sobbed.

"You go and I'll make arrangements to join you later," Vivi said, trying to reassure him.

Just then his mobile rang.

"I've booked a flight this evening and will come with you. I can take you straight to the hospital," Sergei said calmly.

"Thanks—I only hope we get there in time."

As they arrived at the hospital gates in Moscow late that night, Sergei's phone rang.

His cousin was crying. "I'm afraid Baba has just died. I told her Theo was coming and she smiled and just closed her eyes."

Sergei put the phone in his pocket. "We're too late, Maestro."

Sadly, the pair walked into the hospital and found her looking peaceful with a small smile on her lips. Theo fell onto the bed wailing. He kissed and stroked her still face. He lay there for some time while a nurse talked to Sergei about funeral arrangements.

*

Three days later, Baba lay in an open coffin in the nearby church. Several friends came to pay their last respects. Vivi had arrived the day after her death and was a great support to Theo, especially during the poignant service.

At the Orthodox church everyone held a lighted candle and walked round the coffin, tenderly kissing her goodbye. There were more than thirty friends and neighbours at the service who found it deeply upsetting saying farewell to such a special lady.

Theo clung to Vivi, occasionally glancing at Sergei and his cousin, who were on the other side of the coffin.

At the cemetery, Theo sobbed uncontrollably as Baba was lowered into the grave, each person throwing a handful of earth onto the disappearing coffin. One of her friends screamed in pain when it was covered.

An hour later, everyone gathered at the apartment. There was a large picture of Baba on the table beside a slice of black rye bread. In turn they each gulped down a small glass of vodka and touched the bread in her memory. Vast amounts of food were consumed amongst tears and the babble of people reminiscing about events in Baba's life.

Theo was bewildered not knowing any of her friends but smiled as people spoke her name. By the time he and Vivi returned to their hotel, he was emotionally drained.

"I have to stay on to sort out the will and her apartment. I'll return as soon as possible. I must practice for the concert, too. Give a big hug to Georgie and Jago for me." Theo held Vivi in his arms tightly. "Oh! The baby just kicked me!" He lingeringly kissing Vivi. A tear slipped down her cheek.

Over the next few days Sergei helped Theo sort things out in the apartment and took him to a lawyer. It was a time of emptiness for Theo who found it hard to cope with any of the practicalities. Sergei looked after him as far as the musician would allow. Theo's fingers were itching to practice.

Once they had sorted out everything, they flew home and Theo went straight to the rehearsal rooms. Woolsey quietly welcomed him back and they all began to play enthusiastically. It was such a comfort to be deep into music again. Theo felt inspired as the Rachmaninov grew within him.

This concert was going to be for Baba.

Chapter Seventy Eight

Oving

Georgie was having a wonderful time with Alicia. Every morning they went to help with the riding lessons, then they were allowed a long ride with Cheryl who encouraged them to gallop after a few canters. The girls loved grooming the ponies and Cheryl enjoyed watching them.

Lang arrived in the early evening to collect the girls and found Freddie looking like a scarecrow.

"I've been driving a tractor all morning with Uncle Jonty," he shouted.

"You're giving my family a lot of fun," said Lang.

"Do you fancy a glass of home brew?" asked Jonty.

"That would be a treat," replied Lang.

"We'll soon be on holiday all together. Mum's really looking forward to it. Don't know how she'll cope with so many hungry mouths though." Jonty laughed, as they sat watching the kids, holding a glass of brew each.

"It's great that Serena's coming too," added Lang. "The children will so love being with her. She's working very hard on the banqueting room. And I think there's been a call from a Swiss banker for her to advise on his home in Wiltshire. Can't imagine how she'll fit that in as well. We'll see even less of her."

"It must be so hard for you," sympathised Jonty, laying an arm on his brother-in-law's shoulder.

Lang shrugged. "It's our new normal, I suppose."

*

Lang drove the carload of muddy children home.

"Right. Everyone in the bath, then supper afterwards."

"Your wife rang to say she'd be late. Something about a new client," Maggie said as Lang handed her a heap of dirty riding gear. "It's bangers and mash tonight. I've fed Benjie. He'd love to see you."

Lang read a short story to Benjie, then tucked him into bed, and finally got the other three children downstairs for supper in their night clothes.

Serena arrived home even later than usual to find Lang half asleep in the sitting room.

"You're late," he said softly.

"Yes, I had to meet this Swiss banker chap at a hotel in Knightsbridge. He's called Oleg Paranosky, is absolutely loaded, apparently! Got a lovely estate in Wiltshire *and* houses in New York and St Petersburg. He's quite a young man. His wife is charming with blond plaits coiled elegantly round her head," said Serena. "There are several four-poster beds to be upholstered plus bedroom walls covered in silk and heavy old tapestry curtains."

"I wish I could find some way of contributing to our finances," Lang said anxiously.

"You're doing a great job with the kids. It's lovely to see them settled so quickly into country life. You too, for that matter," Serena added. "It's a big help, Lang."

"It is?"

Serena nodded. "I appreciate it and you for that matter."

Lang felt his heart skip a beat. He finally felt like him and Serena were getting back on track.

*

Lang phoned a number of his City friends to see if they had any ideas for part-time work. No one came up with anything positive. They all chatted and exchanged gossip, but he felt completely out of the loop. When Lang finally put the phone down, he once again felt rejected and depressed. How his life had changed.

The mobile rang.

"Lang, can you come over and give me a hand? Jacob's gone to the market and one of the plantation fences needs repairing urgently," asked Jonty.

"Yes, of course." Lang was relieved to get out of his despondency.

Half an hour later, he felt increasing calmness in the plantation while he worked with Jonty straightening the fence. It was very peaceful amongst the saplings.

"Goodness, how beautiful this place is. There's something tangible in the air." He sat down on the grass as Jonty finished tightening the wire mesh.

"Yes, I often come here and amble through the trees. Imagine how magnificent it will be in the future. Just think of Alicia in forty years looking at the huge, mature oaks spreading out to the sky."

Lang wiped his sweaty brow and followed Jonty up the hill. "Have you any idea what I could do for a part-time job? I'd like to contribute. . . take the pressure off Serena somehow."

"Well, I don't see how you could manage anything else. Besides, you're doing a splendid job with the kids, I've never seen you cross with them—you're a natural," said Jonty.

"But they're missing their Mum such a lot and I'm missing work terribly."

"Would you go back to work in the City?"

"That's all I know," Lang said. "But none of my City friends have any work. It's just strange being so far away from my former life."

Jonty wrapped one arm around Lang's shoulders. "Something will come up soon. Don't lose hope."

Chapter Seventy Nine

London

The Festival Hall concert was getting near. Preparations were hectic with only a few days to go before rehearsals in the Hall itself. Woolsey felt the orchestra was at its best, and Theo was excelling.

When the big night arrived, the concert hall was buzzing with excitement. All the family, including Alicia and Georgie, were sitting in the third row and cheered as Theo walked in. Rachmaninov's Variations on a Theme of Paganini filled the Hall with passion.

Theo knew he was playing for Baba, so his emotions were doubly intense. Everything melded into an astonishing climax. *Perhaps I overplayed the end?* he thought.

There was a moment of silence, then the audience gave a standing ovation. Theo looked down at Vivi and his family clapping wildly. He couldn't see Sergei anywhere.

Walking off stage, Woolsey patted his shoulder. "What a performance, Theo. Your best ever."

"A great reception, Maestro." Sergei was waiting in the dressing room and hugged his client proudly. "Never have I heard you play so well."

"Yes, Baba was here willing me on," Theo said, glancing up at the ceiling.

There was a knock at the door.

"Oh, Theo. What a wonderful performance," Vivi said tearfully. "I'm so proud of you." She kissed him.

"Daddy, I watched your fingers going so fast I thought you'd fall off the stool!" Georgie laughed. "Do your hands hurt now?"

"That's what I call a marathon," said Lang.

"Oh Theo, it was so moving." Serena hugged him.

As usual, Sergei had arranged a wonderful celebration dinner. The whole family was full of laughter and enjoyment at being together. Many bottles of wine were consumed.

"We'll all be in Madeira on Friday," said Jonty, very flushed.

"I think we must be getting back, I've got an early start," said Serena around 11pm. "Jonty and Cheryl, you're staying with Vivi aren't you?"

"Yes, if we can stand up!" Jonty laughed.

"Thank you for coming all the way from Oving," Theo enthused. "I haven't even seen your new house yet!"

"Come over as soon as you can," said Lang.

*

Sergei rang early to say Theo had received amazing notices in The Times and Guardian, 'A Maestro is born.' But there was a disappointing review in the Telegraph, criticising the performance.

"Oh, that's an awful one," said Theo.

"Never mind. You've got to move onto the next challenge," enthused Sergei. "I suggest you come to Moscow after your holiday. Shut yourself away in the studio and practice all day and all night if necessary. This recording is going to be one of the peaks of your career."

"Let me have a think about it while I'm away. Will I see you before we go to Madeira?" Theo asked quietly.

"Let's have lunch on Friday," suggested Sergei.

Chapter Eighty

Chiswick

Jago rushed into the bedroom, jumping on Theo.

"I'm a jellyfish Daddy, and Mummy's a whale. What are you?"

"Where's Georgie?" asked Theo sleepily.

"She's asleep. I can't talk to her!"

Theo smiled. Family life was beginning to involve him again after a long absence. Vivi now looked visibly pregnant, her usual serenity a little marred by maternity tiredness. They lay in bed exchanging news, Theo stroking her tummy, eager to feel the baby kicking.

Georgie floated in. "Come on Daddy, get up. You've been away too long with the piano."

"I know," Theo agreed ruefully.

"Are you going to be here when Mummy has the baby?" asked Georgie.

"Yes, of course I am. I'll drive her to the hospital," Theo assured her.

"I wonder if it will be a boy or a girl. What would you like to call it, Daddy?"

"Leo or Oscar maybe," said Theo.

"Mirabelle or Katya you mean!" said Vivi. Jago began jumping up and down on Theo which drove everyone out of bed quickly. "Come on, breakfast time, get dressed. I've got to start packing for our holiday this morning."

"Whoopee, we go tomorrow," said Georgie.

The house was full of excitement all day. Theo helped by taking the children out to the park leaving Vivi to assemble all the holiday gear.

Bella helped pack the toys and beachwear. "I'm going to miss you all. It'll be so quiet around here."

"Do you want your friend Lara to come and keep you company?" suggested Vivi.

"Yes, actually I am a bit anxious at night here on my own," she replied truthfully.

"I understand, " said Vivi, thinking of the night they were burgled. "Call Lara and see what she says."

*

The taxi arrived to take them to the airport. Georgie babbled all the way to Heathrow while Jago was enthralled by the planes taking off. The children took a baggage trolley and whizzed it about, narrowly missing other passengers, including Serena and Lang who were there already and came over to greet Vivi and Theo.

Cheryl and Jonty arrived in a fluster having been held up. Apart from Benjie, screaming with earache as the plane descended, the flight was peaceful.

Beady was waving excitedly as they came through customs. She'd ordered several taxis and directed Vivi's family to her own car.

"It's so warm, Mum, and what a glorious blue sky. I'm so glad to be here at last," Vivi said stroking her bump.

Chapter Eighty One

Madeira

Beady's spacious villa was welcoming, with plants everywhere and flowers in each room. A long refectory table was invitingly covered with various plates of cold meats, cakes, stuffed eggs and masses of local fruit.

"I'm starving," said Alicia.

"Me too," agreed Georgie.

"I'm longing for a swim," said Serena.

"I thought we'd take a picnic to the beach," said Beady, delighted to see all the family together at last.

"This is such a big house Granny," said Georgie, looking around in awe.

"Yes, Grandpa bought it hoping all the family would come and stay. It's a pity he's not here to see you all," Beady replied. "He loved watching the stars at night. I must show you his telescope."

Soon everyone was relaxing in the midday sun. Georgie and Jago were busy making sandcastles and burying each other. Serena strode off towards the sea, anxiously followed by Alicia and Freddie.

"Where are you going, Mummy?" they called.

"Just for a quick swim. You play with little Benjie and Jago, I'll be back in a minute."

Cheryl was rolling a ball into a little pool for Benjie who loved splashing in the water.

"Why has Mummy gone swimming alone?" Freddie asked.

"Perhaps she felt hot. Come on, let's all have an ice cream," Cheryl said.

They ran after her and were soon sitting at a table enjoying huge cornets. Benjie's face was covered in chocolate.

"He looks like a clown," Alicia said pointing at him.

"Can we go swimming with Mummy now?" Freddie asked.

"I don't think so, because Granny said the waves are very big, but we can go over there to the children's pool," Cheryl replied.

"Yay!" said Freddie.

"Finish your ice creams first," said Serena, wrapping a towel around her chest.

"Mummy, you're back," he shouted, running up to her.

Serena and Cheryl spent an hour beside the pool watching the children jumping in and out. Lang came over to join them and brought a message from Beady. The picnic was ready.

Alicia and Georgie skipped and paddled their way towards Granny, followed by the others. Beady sat in a low deck-chair handing out sausages which were devoured in seconds. Vivi gave each child a juicy slice of melon. It was a languid afternoon.

"We're all unwinding at last," Jonty said, quite red in the face.

"I think we should go to the flower market tomorrow," suggested Serena.

They ambled back to the house as the sun began to lose some of its intensity, then asked Beady which rooms they'd be sleeping in.

"Now Serena, you and Lang are in here," the matriarch replied, revealing a huge double bed alongside some big double doors leading onto the balcony, Vivi and Theo, I've put you in here overlooking the sparkling sea," Beady said, then turning the corner, "Jonty and Cheryl, you're here in the annex."

Everyone started unpacking.

"I'll go and supervise the children downstairs," Beady announced.

Beady interrupted the children's squealing hide-and-seek game and got them all to draw the beautiful sunset.

Afterwards, she went upstairs and knocked on Serena's door. "I must show you something special, my dear." She opened the wardrobe and took out an exquisite patchwork quilt. "This was made by your great aunt and I'd like you to have it." Beady smiled as she unfolded it.

"Oh Mum, it's so beautiful. I'll treasure it."

She hugged Beady who then said, "Now you know why I wanted you all here. I'm giving Vivi and Jonty some other family items later."

"Yes, you did say and that's wonder—" suddenly Serena noticed the time. "Oh my goodness! I must get the children to bed, they've been up for hours. Come on, bedtime!"

"Hooray, Mummy's putting us to bed," squawked Freddie.

"We're *all* going to sleep together," said Georgie.

Serena organised them into their sleeping bags.

"Quiet now, I'm going to read you a story," she said. "Some more of the Famous Five." Alicia and Freddie snuggled up to her.

*

The following day, Serena arranged for everyone to visit the Funchal flower market. Vivi decided to rest at home so Theo stayed too, as did Jago and Beady. The house fell quiet as soon as everyone else went out. Beady sat on the veranda and read Jago a story, while Vivi and Theo dozed on the loungers.

"Isn't this peaceful, just the two of us?" murmured Vivi, flicking her long dark hair over the top of the seat.

"I'm beginning to unwind slowly, and you are looking radiant, dear," he said softly.

"The children are loving you being back, especially Georgie."

"I thought of taking her to a concert in Funchal. I think she's old enough to appreciate composers like de Falla and Rodrigo," Theo suggested.

"Oh, she'll love that. Hello, Jago, have you had a nice walk with Granny?" asked Vivi.

"Mummy, I saw big, big fishes eating flowers."

Theo whisked him up and threw him in the air to shrieks of delight.

"Shall I help you prepare supper, Mum?" enquired Vivi.

"Yes, that would be useful. I'm doing a fish pie. If you could peel some fruit for a dessert, darling."

As they chatted in the kitchen, her daughter revealed the stress of Theo being away so often and his increasing moods.

"I'm so worried that I can't help him emotionally, and when the baby comes I'll need him around more."

"Have you talked about it together?" asked Beady.

"No, he's so stressed half the time it's difficult to get near him."

"Well, I'll be there when the baby arrives."

"Thanks Mum," said Vivi, hugging her.

Serena and Cheryl returned with Alicia, Georgie, Benjie and Freddie close behind.

"I'm starving. Can I have some crisps, Gran?" asked Alicia.

"Actually no!" Vivi handed them each a banana. "These grow here. Have you seen the bunches of them dangling from those tall trees?"

"Come on, let's read a story," called Lang, putting down the newspaper he'd been flicking through.

A few minutes later the children were settled on the sitting room floor as Lang started reading Treasure Island aloud. Even little Benjie became absorbed.

"Shall I hand round drinks, Mum?" asked Jonty from the kitchen.

"Yes, please do."

"I'll lay the table," offered Cheryl. "The flowers were fantastic by the way."

Half an hour later the whole family were devouring fish pie, followed by fruit salad and ice cream.

"Tomorrow I'm taking everyone on an exciting trip," Serena announced.

"Where to?" asked Jonty, raising his eyebrows.

"Wait and see," replied his sister in her usual bossy way.

*

After breakfast, everyone followed Serena to the nearest bus stop, except Vivi, Theo and Jago. As they neared the centre of Funchal, she pointed to the cable car.

"We're going on the funicular all the way up to see the tropical gardens."

The children were very excited as they jumped off the bus. Jonty and Cheryl walked on ahead to stand in the queue. They boarded the car whilst it was stationary and held tight as it gripped the cable again and started up the steep mountain. The cabin swayed a lot and Cheryl looked very anxious as Serena pointed at various exotic trees on the way up.

They arrived at a fantastic forest with wonderful tropical flowers. Long steps wove deeply down into the wooded valley and a stream trickled alongside the cobbled paths.

"Go and explore," called Serena as the kids raced on ahead.

Lang suggested they all meet by the nearby Geological Museum in two hours. He followed the children, holding Benjie by the hand. Jonty and Cheryl were amazed by the variety of the shrubs, trees and flowers and trundled off on their own.

Meanwhile, Vivi had taken Jago to the beach for a paddle. Theo was in a sombre mood, reading on the veranda, and Beady was bustling round the house tidying up the debris.

Theo answered his mobile as soon as it rang.

"Hi Sergei, what's new?" he asked.

"Well the recording date has been arranged. We'll have three weeks to practice in Moscow, and Murel is already rehearsing the orchestra. Are you having a nice family holiday?"

"Yes, it's relaxing, but I'm missing *you*, of course." At that moment Beady slid back a glass door and appeared on the veranda. "Anyway, I'd better go. Bye!" said Theo abruptly.

"Oh, sorry. I didn't realise you were on the phone." Beady grimaced. "Would you like a coffee?"

"Yes, please, that would be lovely," Theo replied, hoping Beady hadn't heard anything.

A few minutes later Beady put the coffee down. "I am so sorry that your mother died Theo. You haven't any other close relatives in Russia, have you?"

"No, only a distant cousin."

"Now you'll be able to stay at home with Vivi and the children more," suggested Beady.

"Yes, I hope so, but it does depend on my work. I have a big recording session coming up soon after we return. I haven't told Vivi yet," said Theo quietly. "Sergei only arranged it recently and has just told me the dates."

"You seem to rely on him for everything. Poor Vivi will be upset to hear you're going away again so soon, especially so late in her pregnancy. She's worried about you," said Beady anxiously.

"If the work takes me to Moscow, I have to go."

"But you never used to be away so much," Beady persisted.

"I know, I know, but I can't help it," Theo whispered.

"Can't help what?" Beady frowned.

Vivi walked in with Jago carrying a bucket cutting their conversation dead.

"Look at my baby crab, Daddy." He plonked the bucket onto Theo's lap.

"He just loves the beach. You must come with us tomorrow," said Vivi.

A few hours later, Serena arrived back with everyone else, Lang carrying Benjie on his back. They all flopped onto the sofas.

"It was a magical place," said Jonty.

"I took lots of photos, Mum. The stalagmites were amazing and there were so many beautiful crystals in the Geological Museum," said Serena.

For the rest of the week, the family spent each day on the beach. Georgie loved her concert outing with Theo and was fascinated to see guitars in the orchestra.

"It's brilliant going out with you, Daddy. I do wish you didn't go away so much."

"I have to go where the concerts are, darling," he replied, hugging her. "I hope you'll play in a concert one day."

"Me too," she replied.

*

On their last evening, Beady and Jonty set up some fireworks on the veranda. All round the town huge rockets were exploding. The children were very excited, except for the two little boys who hid indoors, scared of the noise.

Beady opened a bottle of Champagne for everyone.

"Well, this is goodbye to the Madeira house. Cheers to my new Chiswick one," she said with a huge grin.

"It's been such a relaxing holiday," said Cheryl. "Thank you so much, Beady."

"Even Serena has got out of the fast lane for once," commented Lang.

"Mummy's been here all day long," piped up Freddie.

Theo said little, his thoughts already in Moscow.

*

The next morning, they all waved goodbye to Beady and the children were in tears.

"Now, don't you work too hard, Serena. Remember your family," said Beady sternly.

"Yes Mum, don't fuss," Serena replied annoyed.

"It's a mother's job, darling! And you too, Vivi, take care of your dear self."

"I will, Mum."

"Oh, and don't forget I'm coming back out to help with the removal, Ma," said Jonty, kissing her on the forehead. 'This was a much-needed break."

PART THREE

Chapter One

Chiswick

Back in London, Maggie welcomed them all home. "I did miss you," she said.

"Thanks," mumbled Theo, who was already wondering how to tell Vivi he would be going to Moscow again. He waited until they were alone at supper and Vivi responded as he predicted.

"Must you really go off again?" Vivi said tearfully.

"This is a most important contract. I'll have to practice all day and all evening. Murel will conduct and we'll do the actual recording in about a month," he said quietly.

"When are you ever going to stay with us longer? And be a proper father to your children? And a husband to me for longer than a few days at a time? You see more of Sergei than you do of us. Have you forgotten that I'm pregnant? I'm due in a few weeks. Just get out, Theo."

As soon as he left the room, Vivi remained in a heap. Her whole being saddened by the news, especially after such a happy holiday together. Their early years of marriage had been so peaceful. It seemed the more successful he became, the more he went away. She walked slowly upstairs to the empty bedroom.

Theo remained in the study, anxious at how upset Vivi was, but also wretched and emotional about his own situation.

Chapter Two

London

Serena left Aylesbury refreshed and full of energy. From Marylebone Station she rushed off to Princes Gate where slow progress had been made with refurbishing the stateroom during her absence. She decided to recruit one more assistant to speed up the sewing involved and was keen to move on to the next project down in Wiltshire.

She entered her office to find Gems was talking on two phones at once.

"Oh, Serena, I'm so glad to see you, there are so many queries to answer. Did you have a good time in Madeira? You look lovely and brown."

"Yes, it was great to spend time with the kids."

"Well, it's been non-stop here while you've been gone. The Wiltshire people are keen for you to start. Then the Qatar Embassy is asking when you'll return to do the upper floors," said Gems.

"I'm in for a hectic few months I think," said Serena. "Get me Oleg Paranosky in Wiltshire. I'd better meet him again tomorrow and find out more about his project."

Chapter Three

Oving

Lang felt rather alone. His wife had fled to the office, the children had been collected by Jonty, and Maggie had gone shopping with Benjie. He was walking through the orchard when he spotted a man with a shotgun tucked under his arm strolling towards a nearby van.

"What are you doing on my land?" Lang called out.

The man turned to look at him then started running, tripped and dropped his gun, before finally reaching the van and droving off at speed. Lang went into the house and immediately phoned Jonty who suggested he didn't touch the gun.

"Let the police deal with it."

"I thought the countryside was a safe place," mumbled Lang anxiously.

"Don't let the children or Maggie know about it," suggested Jonty. "Did you get the number plate?"

"Sorry, no," Lang said shakily. "I didn't even think—"

"I'll be over in a bit."

Lang was relieved to see Maggie and Benjie appear with a car full of shopping.

"Hello, Mr Lang. Benjie's been such a good boy helping me today that I bought him a small football. He wanted a toy gun, but I said the ball was safer," she said.

Jonty arrived quickly and they went to inspect the shotgun.

"I presume you've already called the police?" said Jonty.

Lang shook his head, still in shock. "Let's give them a call and explain to Maggie what happened. Come and have lunch with me and we'll bring Benjie. Gosh Lang, you're shaking."

"It was all just very sudden," Lang said quietly.

They headed back to the house and Jonty took Maggie aside to explain the situation. She gasped and ran to the window. When she saw the gun on the floor she clutched her chest.

"I'll call the police right now," Maggie said, picking up her phone.

Cheryl was surprised to see them all. Jonty quietly took her aside and repeated the story in more detail. She helped ease the atmosphere and kept the conversation light and jovial while they waited for the police to call back.

"Hello, Daddy," exclaimed Alicia, "I didn't know we'd see you so soon!"

"The girls have been so helpful," said Cheryl. "They've led some of the children round the paddock and helped with their tack. Alicia is very good with saddle soap!"

"Wasn't it relaxing in Madeira? Mum really loved having us all. I think she'll miss her social life out there," said Jonty.

"Oh please, she'll be too busy helping with Vivi's baby; loving being a hands on granny at last," said Cheryl.

"Serena's got a very opulent new client, some Russian guy who has a mansion in St Petersburg, a flat in New York and an estate in Wiltshire," said Lang. "She's going to refurbish all his four-poster beds. We won't see her for dust."

"That's a funny thing to say about Mummy," exclaimed Alicia.

"It's just a jokey Daddy phrase," reassured Cheryl. "The gymkhana is Saturday week. Will you bring them, Lang?"

"Let's see if we can get Mummy in the Parents Race," added Alicia.

Chapter Four

Chiswick

Theo was packing a small brown case when Georgie rushed in and sat on it.

"I won't let you go away, Daddy!"

Theo sighed. "Come on Georgie, help me pack. Don't make it difficult for Daddy."

Georgie peered at him. "Why are you so serious?"

"Go and start your piano practice and I'll come and play a duet with you in a few minutes."

"Okay, but let's play some fun music for a change." Georgie stomped out of the room.

Jago ran naked through the bedroom with Bella chasing after him. "Come on, Jago, it's your bath time," she called.

I'm going to miss the family chaos, Theo mused, as he walked into the drawing room where Georgie was playing a jazzy tune. They both liked Scott Joplin and she laughed when Theo made mistakes on purpose.

Vivi walked in smiling and plonked Jago on Theo's lap. "He's had a bath and wants to join in the fun. I wish I could, too," she said, sinking into the sofa.

Theo's mobile buzzed in his jacket pocket, but he paid no attention, knowing it would be Sergei with arrangements for the following day. He was well aware of Vivi's feelings and knew his departure would cause more upset, but couldn't prevent his visit to Moscow, and Sergei.

＊

Apprehension and sadness hung over the whole family. Theo was eager to go quickly, but his taxi was late so everyone hung about in the hall, with Jago trying to roll his tractor down the banisters. The phone rang.

"It's for you, Miss Vivi," said Bella.

"Hello? Oh Mum, how lovely to hear you. We're just seeing Theo off; can I ring you back?" said Vivi quietly.

Georgie was in floods of tears when Theo eventually left. Bella gathered up both children and suggested the local swimming pool. She hastily took them out, leaving her tearful employer alone.

After a busy morning with three clients, Vivi went down to the kitchen to prepare lunch. The house was unbelievably quiet. The baby kicked and she stroked her tummy.

"I can't wait to meet you," she said softly.

Chapter Five

Moscow

Sergei embraced Theo as he came through the arrival gates.

"It's good to see you, Maestro," he said. "But you look stressed and tired."

"I am," Theo replied.

Chatting non-stop, Sergei drove him to Baba's house where he'd brought produce and some of his favourite chicken soup, which was laid out ready in the kitchen.

"It feels strange to be without Baba. I miss her," Theo said sadly.

"Come now, let's talk about work to take your mind off it," suggested Sergei, who proceeded to describe the week's busy schedule. "Murel is determined to make this a memorable recording. Come on Theo... where's your enthusiasm?" Sergei urged.

"It'll return once I'm with the orchestra. What time do I start in the morning?"

"8.30."

"Well in that case I think I'll go to bed soon," he said. "Thanks for organising everything as usual."

"Will you be alright alone here?" Sergei asked concerned.

"Yes, it's fine. Goodnight, dear Sergei."

They hugged and Theo waved as the car drove off.

*

Theo awoke wondering where he was, forgetting he was in

Baba's house. It had an empty feeling without her. He dressed himself hurriedly, drank a quick cup of coffee and rushed off to the rehearsal.

A resounding welcome greeted him as he walked in.

"At last you've returned." Murel gave him a brief hug.

Theo felt it was like coming home. He worked tirelessly with the orchestra, perfecting each movement for the next four hours.

Sergei took him out to lunch. "How was it sleeping in your Baba's house without her?" he asked.

"A bit strange, but I might get used to it. Anyway, it's great to be back with the orchestra."

"Yes, I'm sure it is. Will you have supper at my place tonight?" asked Sergei. "I've bought some of your favourite fish."

"Well, that would be nice. I've never been to your apartment before. Shall I come over straight after the rehearsal?" Theo suggested. Just then his mobile rang. "Hello darling, how are you? Yes, I've settled in and the orchestra gave me a great welcome. How are things at home?"

"We're all missing you so much, but Georgie especially wants to talk to you now, I'll put her on. . ."

"Hello Daddy," said Georgie, "I want to ask you something special. I do love you, and I know you love us and the piano. Which do you like best?"

Theo felt a lump in his throat and was stunned. "I love you all best, my darling girl," he replied, tears stabbing his eyes. "I tell you what, will you compose a tune for me? A laughing tune, and I'll compose one too."

"Oh, that's a great idea, I'll start mine now." Georgie put the phone down.

That evening, a cosy supper accompanied by a generous

amount of vodka calmed Theo's fraught emotions in Sergei's apartment.

"You're an excellent cook," Theo said and Sergei blushed. They chatted contentedly until it got late, and Theo yawned. "I think I'll go to bed. Thanks for this. I'll see you in the morning."

"Don't go yet," Sergei said, putting an arm round Theo, as he went to stand.

The Maestro pulled away. "I must." He walked out of the room, towards the front door. "I'm going to walk home. I just have a lot to think about."

*

The week was musically fulfilling in every way. During rehearsals, Murel was tough yet inspiring. Theo and Sergei spent most evenings together. Sometimes the Maestro's moods prevented Sergei getting near him.

At the end of the second week, Theo suggested they went to Baba's dacha since it was going to be sold.

"It'll be our last weekend here," he said as they arrived.

Relaxing in each other's company on Sunday, Sergei suddenly put Theo on the spot. "Do we have a future together or not? We walk round each other like two tentative bears, hardly touching. Where are you, dear Maestro? With me or your wife? Can't you decide?"

Without a word Theo got up, walked out of the front door and disappeared for two hours. He returned on the doorstep covered in snow, bedraggled and calling out to Sergei. "You can't ask me to choose!" He fell into his arms sobbing.

"You're soaking. Come, take off your jacket and get warm."

Theo began to tremble. Sergei wrapped a rug round his shoulders, sat him down close to the stove and leant against his knee.

"I'm getting warmer now," Theo said quietly. "I think I'll go to bed."

"Sleep well," muttered Sergei, more confused than ever about Theo's inability to answer his direct questions.

*

The pair went for a long walk in the nearby forest. They hardly spoke, instead they simply enjoyed each other's company.

After lunch, Theo went to practice at the next door neighbour's house as he had before, returning three hours later to find Sergei preparing supper. It was a comfortable, reassuring scene that he took great pleasure in.

"I wish we didn't have to go back tonight," said Theo.

"Me too," agreed Sergei sadly.

They talked non-stop during the car journey back to Moscow.

"Coming in for a drink?" asked Sergei, stopping outside his apartment.

"Yes, I'd love to," said Theo, ruffling Sergei's hair.

"Do you want to stay the night? There's a spare room," added Sergei.

"Yes, I do," said Theo. "And thank you for being so understanding. I do love you but I'm not ready to. . ."

"I understand," said the Russian.

Once indoors, they listened to some beautiful recordings, both sprawled on the sofa, sharing the emotions of Shostakovich's Piano Concerto No.2.

*

Having slept well, Theo woke up keen to get going at the rehearsal. It was an important run-through of the whole piece. It went fantastically well. He felt as if his playing had never been more fluid or technically precise.

The rehearsal finished at midday and as he walked out of the hall, he glanced at his phone messages and saw there was one from home. He dialled the number and was surprised to get Bella.

"Miss Vivi has been rushed to hospital. Ring her, Mr Theo. Maybe it's the baby. I am here with Georgie and Jago, who are asleep," she said in one long, rapid sentence.

Theo searched his diary for the maternity hospital number. After endless minutes, he was put through to a Sister who told him that Vivi had been rushed in at 10.30pm with her contractions increasing.

The doctor tried to prevent the baby coming out early but a seven weeks premature boy had arrived at 3.30am. Both of them were in intensive care. Vivi had lost a lot of blood and the baby's breathing was very weak.

"Oh my God! Please, please give her my love. I'll catch the next plane home," he said agitatedly, tears running down his face.

He phoned Sergei immediately and explained the urgency of the situation, begging him to book a plane as soon as possible.

While Theo packed his brown bag, Sergei stood rigidly watching him. Theo's mobile rang. It was Serena.

"Have you heard the news? For God's sake, come back now! Poor Vivi's alone and in a terrible way. So is your son. I'm off to see them now and Jonty is coming up in a couple of hours."

"Oh Serena, tell her I'll be there as soon as the plane arrives.

I can't imagine how she must be feeling. I feel so guilty that I wasn't there when it happened." Theo rang off as Sergei picked up his case and walked out to the car.

"I know you have to go now, but what about us? You can't keep ignoring my questions" begged Sergei.

"We can discuss all that when I return. Vivi and the baby are what matter right now—they need me."

Theo abruptly slammed the car door and Sergei drove them the airport in complete silence.

A grey drizzle dampened the tarmac. Theo deftly wove in and out of the crowd at Arrivals and got to the passport stand first.

A surly woman examined his Russian visa, delaying his anxious wish to race to the taxi rank. A few hours later, Theo ran to the reception at Queen Charlotte's Hospital. He dashed to the nearest lift and jabbed the 'up' button repeatedly.

"It's out of order, that one," said a porter.

"Where can I find my wife? She's been put in intensive care," Theo urgently asked a nurse who was standing by the other lift.

She gently directed him to the private wing where a bustling sister with a clip-board approached him.

"Can I help?"

"Oh. I hope so. My wife, Vivi Hanover, has been brought into intensive care. Where can I find her?"

"Room five. She's just had a transfusion."

Theo pushed open the door, his anxiety almost exploding as he checked himself and gently moved towards Vivi who was propped up on several pillows. Her eyes were shut, her hair hung limply round her pale face. The oxygen mask rose slowly up and down.

Theo leaned towards her forehead, kissing it tenderly.

"Oh, Vivi darling, I'm so sorry not to have been here when all this happened. Can you hear me?" He stroked her hand as she slowly opened her eyes.

Vivi raised her mask slowly. "Have you seen our son?"

A Scottish nurse reapplied the mask. "Please let your wife rest now. I'll take you to the premature clinic."

As Theo entered the warm room, he saw ten life-support machines between masses of pipes, each attached to incubators containing tiny babies who'd arrived too early. The nurse pointed to his fair-haired, sleeping son.

Theo had an overwhelming urge to hold him, but the nurse in charge said he was on steroids to develop his lungs and must remain in his cosy incubator. He stroked the baby's precious round head then reached in to fondle his son's miniscule yet exquisitely long fingers.

"It's pure magic: a miracle," he whispered. "Just being here with him. I don't know how he sleeps with all these bleeps and wires."

"They sleep all the time in this unit," the nurse replied. "Let me take you back to your wife, she needs you so much. We nearly lost her at one point she was haemorrhaging so badly, and she's still weak, but I'm sure she'd like to know that the wee boy is fine and looks just like his daddy."

Vivi lifted a hand to greet him. He slid onto the bed beside her and whispered, "Our son is beautiful, but I couldn't see the colour of his eyes because he was asleep."

Her arm entwined in his, but she didn't open her eyes.

"Your wife needs to rest. You can come back at lunchtime tomorrow," the nurse said gently.

"Yes of course." Theo kissed Vivi on the forehead. "I'll see you soon."

Chapter Six

Chiswick

Just as he reached the front door, Theo's mobile rang.

"Hello, it's Beady. How's Vivi? She is not answering her phone."

"I've just come back from the hospital. She's lost a lot of blood, but seems to be stable. She won't be answering her phone any time soon though," said Theo.

"Well, I'll go and see her now," announced Beady.

"I don't understand. . . where are you?" he asked.

"I've just arrived at Heathrow, so I'll catch a taxi. It's room five isn't it?"

"Err, yes, but she's very tired and can hardly talk," Theo said. "I was told to come back tomorrow."

"I understand that, but I'm her mother and I *must* go to her."

As Theo opened the front door, he heard screams of laughter and found Jago dressed as Batman, chasing Georgie and a friend who were covered in sheets, bouncing down the stairs.

"Oh Daddy!" Georgie rushed over and hugged him, followed by Jago. "Have you heard about poor Mummy? Have you seen our new brother? Have you—"

"Yes, my lovely girl. I've seen Mummy and your baby brother. They're both doing well." Theo poured a large whisky and sank into an armchair.

"Hello, Mr Theo. It's really good to see you," said Bella. "The children have been so good. Is Mrs Beady coming later? Shall I do a chicken pilaf for you both?"

"Yes, she will be here this evening. That would be splendid, thank you Bella," said Theo, who suddenly felt exhausted. "If you could just feed the children now. I just need to rest for a bit."

Beady arrived by taxi looking very jaded to find Theo in the living room, rubbing the sleep out of his eyes.

"Poor girl," she said. "And for this to happen when there was no one there to comfort her. Mind you, she's always been brave, and your son looked very peaceful." She paused and smiled. "Anyway, you're back, that's what matters."

The phone rang.

"Theo, are you in London?" demanded Serena.

"Yes, I've just got back from the hospital."

"Oh, thank God! What's the latest?"

"She's very fragile. I was shocked to see her on oxygen and hardly able to speak," said Theo quietly. "I wish I'd been there when it happened. Your mum's just arrived. Here, have a word with her."

He handed the phone to Beady.

"Yes, the babe has one special nurse looking after him twenty-four hours a day and he's so tiny, but they said he's doing well. Poor Vivi, what an awful time she's had, I wish I could help her. Mind you, the nurse said she'll be stronger in a few days."

"Oh, thank heavens for that. Listen, I'm at the office, why don't I pop over?" Serena asked.

"Yes do—I'd love to see you."

Serena arrived half an hour later and they discussed arrangements for the children during the coming week and visiting times for Vivi. Serena suggested Georgie stayed in Aylesbury with Alicia. She could help Cheryl get ready for the gymkhana.

Chapter Seven

London

Serena visited the hospital every evening at 5pm. She could see Vivi gradually recovering. One day the oxygen mask was off. The next day she was sitting up in bed.

"Any little tasties you'd like me to bring you next time?" she asked.

"Yes, I'd *love* some smoked salmon."

"No probelm." Serena got up and pulled on her silk pashing. "Oh, by the way, Georgie and Alicia are having a wonderful time helping to prepare for the gymkhana. Cheryl's giving them lots of jobs and keeping them busy. Georgie sends you a thousand hugs and is missing you."

"I miss them too," groaned Vivi.

"I'm sure. And what about the new one? When are they going to let you see him?" asked Serena.

"Tomorrow, with any luck. Oh, and did I tell you, Theo's suggested we call him Sebastian."

"Very stylish," said Serena.

"Do you think so? I rather had my heart set on Felix."

"Felix!" Serena pulled a face.

A week later, Vivi was walking back from the Premature Baby Unit just as Theo arrived.

"How lovely to see you up and dressed. You look much better my darling."

"Do you want to go and see little Sebastian? I do wish

he could sleep beside me here, but he's not strong enough yet. At least I'm expressing my milk for him, so he gets all the nourishment. Oh, Theo, I wish you'd been here. I felt so helpless, I couldn't stop him coming early. The contractions overwhelmed me. I so needed to hold on to you. Don't go away again till he comes home—please," Vivi begged.

Sergei's face flashed through his mind. *How will I tell him that I won't be back anytime soon? I miss him but I can't leave Vivi. Not now.*

"Of course not, darling." He kissed her tenderly on the lips. "Let's both go and say hello to our beautiful son."

They took it in turns to hold his tiny hands and stroke his blond head. The nurse in charge chatted encouragingly to them, saying his breathing was getting much stronger and Theo and Serena caught each other's eye and beamed.

Chapter Eight

Aylesbury

"This is your great day," announced Jonty, giving Cheryl a big hug.

Lots of children were arriving as Alicia and Georgie helped put on their boots and hats and showed the visitors where to wait. Cheryl had three volunteers to help with the small jumps and to control the selection of young teams.

Quite a large crowd of parents, carers, and visitors stood excitedly round the paddock all waiting for the local MP to arrive for the prize giving. The buzz of children's laughter echoed across the fields.

Soon the ponies were led into the paddock. The riders with the most severe disabilities raced first, proudly trotting towards Cheryl at the finishing post. A nine-year-old girl won. All the children cheered.

Before long, eight groups had taken part in the races. Then it was time for some events that involved small hurdles; a few ponies were stubborn and refused to lift their chubby legs over. One or two children fell off, laughed, and were helped on again.

Towards the end, Georgie, Alicia, and a few other helpers wearing fancy dress costumes galloped round blowing giant bubbles for the other riders to catch amid squeals of laughter.

Lang sat next to the local MP and chatted jovially to her throughout the event. Jonty had a list of winners, plus several rosettes ready for the prize giving which was very moving.

Some of the children couldn't walk to the table, so the ponies collected the badges amid cheers for each child.

Alicia and Georgie got a rosette each for 'best assistants' and were beaming as the MP pinned them on their jackets. Everyone celebrated with homemade cakes and scones.

The MP, Mrs Welling, gave an enthusiastic speech, praising Cheryl for a marvellous new riding centre and for all her excellent work. "The enthusiasm and pride of all those riding in the competition is rewarding indeed, and this is the best event I've been to locally in a long time. My congratulations to you all," she said. She walked around meeting and chatting to the children.

"What a fantastic afternoon my Cherry Berry," Jonty said kissing her.

A little boy who had limited hearing and sight walked up to her, helped by his Mummy, with a bottle of Champagne. "Here you are, Miss Cheryl."

"I wish Mummy was here," whispered Alicia to Lang.

"Yes, mine too," said Georgie pensively.

"Thanks for your wonderful help, girls. You too, Lang." Cheryl kissed them all. "We must go up and see Vivi and the baby soon. How about next Tuesday?"

Chapter Nine

Wiltshire

Serena left earlier than usual to meet Oleg Paranovsky at his Wiltshire home. She arrived at a beautiful Jacobean mansion set amongst elegant lawns and formal gardens. As she drove up a long drive surrounded by cornfields, a huge lake appeared on the right with a pair of graceful weeping willows dipping into the water. It was a breathtakingly serene place. A large studded wooden door opened.

"Welcome, Mrs Mayne." The Russian seemed taller than before. "If you could please follow me."

They climbed up a broad staircase to the first floor. "Now, this is my master bedroom." He opened the door to reveal an enormous four-poster bed with faded tapestry curtains. A log fire was glowing under an ornate mantelpiece. "This is where my wife does her writing sometimes."

He pointed to an antique bureau close to an elegant standard lamp. Several silk-embroidered armchairs stood beside the fireplace.

"I'd like you to choose the wallpaper and replace the bed curtains to match it in any exotic materials you choose. We have another, smaller room, along the corridor with a similar bed. I'll show it to you."

A door opened on to a smaller room.

"This needs lighter walls as it's north-facing, maybe ochre? The four-poster maybe in light grey and green brocade, perhaps?"

Serena was amazed at the opulent rooms.

"Perhaps you would consider designs for the dining room later? Let's go down and discuss the contract."

His wife met them in the hall. "This is Serena Mayne who is going to change our lives in the bedroom." He laughed.

"Hello, I'm Marisha, I've heard a lot about you." A tall lady with blonde hair in a chignon held out one elegant hand and guided her into the vast drawing room.

"What a beautiful space," exclaimed Serena. "I love that big samovar. Did you bring it from St Petersburg?"

"Yes, it reminds us of our home in Russia," Marisha replied.

Oleg Paranovsky wrote out the suggested contract and handed it to Serena. "I've increased the original fee, which I hope meets with your approval. Can you start preparations this week?"

"Yes, I'll be here on Thursday, I just have to finish a job in Kensington during the next few days." Serena read through the contract and thanked him for the increased fee, far beyond anything she'd expected.

"I'll send a car for you every day if you'd like that?"

"Thank you very much."

Serena drove off feeling very pleased with the new prospect of working in such opulent surroundings. It was a great challenge too. She was longing to tell Lang. She could finally see the light at the end of their financial trouble. Soon they would be able to get their dream home again.

Chapter Ten

Chiswick

Vivi was finally well enough to go home but also upset that she couldn't take Sebastian with her.

"You can see him every day when you bring in his milk," reassured the nurse. Theo put his arm round Vivi who was weeping as they left the unit.

Jago bounded up to her as Vivi entered the house. "Mummy, Mummy, I've missed you! Have you left the baby behind?" he asked anxiously.

"Hello, my lovely boy," she replied, hugging him. "Yes, your little brother has to grow bigger before he can come home."

"Oh Vivi, you're home at last—looking better too," Beady said.

They all sat down to lunch. Bella was clearly thrilled to see Vivi home.

"Lang and Serena rang to say they'll bring Georgie back tonight. I've missed her," said Theo.

That evening, Georgie rushed in with Serena. "Oh Mummy, it's lovely to see you." She squeezed Vivi tightly. "Where's my new brother?"

"You'll can see him tomorrow," said Theo.

*

Family life returned to something akin to normal. The following day Vivi took Georgie to meet Sebastian.

"Why is he in that cage with all those pipes sticking out?" asked Georgie.

"That's his incubator and all those pipes help him breathe. You can stroke his hand if you like." Vivi guided her daughter's hand through the window.

"Oh, he's so tiny, like one of my old dolls. Will he grow soon?"

"Yes darling."

At home, Beady rounded on Theo. "I hope you're not going to fly off to Moscow suddenly. Vivi desperately needs you here. We don't want any urgent phone calls from that man who seems to manage everything for you and all the concerts. He appears to have little consideration for your family life here."

"I'll have to return to Moscow in a few weeks to finish an important recording. The orchestra is waiting for me," he said quietly.

"Isn't Vivi more important to you? She's such a wonderful girl and has been through hell and too many lonely times," Beady said angrily. Theo was almost crumbling. This woman would never know how desolate he felt with a jungle of feelings churning inside him. "Well? Shouldn't she be your number one priority?"

Theo began to stutter. "I—I—love her so much."

Tears poured down his ashen face as he got up and slowly walked out of the room.

Jago met him in the garden. "Can I have the paddling pool water Daddy? I want to splash you."

Theo slowly trickled a hose into the pool as Jago splashed him. He sunk into a chair and just watched this bundle of fun shrieking with laughter. Beady stood by the kitchen door watching them with her arms crossed over her chest.

"Hi Daddy, isn't Sebastian dinky? He'll take a long time to grow, won't he?" Georgie said excitedly on her return.

"He's put on weight and those lovely eyes were open," Vivi said. She noticed Theo's sombre face. "Are you alright, darling? You look rather strained."

"Yes, I'm fine." He lied.

*

Jonty and Cheryl came for lunch later in the week and Vivi took them to hospital to see Sebastian. Cheryl was moved to tears seeing all the humming incubators, then holding tiny Sebastian's hand.

"He looks so like his daddy," whispered Cheryl.

"It's a milking parlour in here." Jonty laughed. "Speaking of which. . ." He passed Vivi a photo of one of their calves. "*He's* called Sebastian too."

"Oh Jonty," Vivi said, playfully hitting his arm.

Back at home the family enjoyed Cheryl's home-made scones with cream and jam.

"We wondered if you'd be godmother to Sebastian?" asked Theo.

"Oh yes! That would be very special. I'd love to," Cheryl glowed.

Beady chatted to her while Jonty played hide-and-seek at the bottom of the garden. Eventually he found them all and tipped each child into the paddling pool amid howls of laughter. They retaliated by soaking Jonty in return.

"Can you stay the night?" asked Beady.

"Yes, let's take the new Mum out to supper at that nice bistro round the corner," replied Jonty.

Theo suppressed his on-going turmoil and was cheered by Jonty's garrulous fun. Vivi was calm again, less stressed and enjoyed having all the family around.

Chapter Eleven

Notting Hill

"Gems, I've just finalised an amazing contract with Oleg Paranovsky. His place in Wiltshire is stunning. I've never seen such huge four-poster beds," Serena said, sitting down at her desk. "The curtains must make them awfully hot in summer. Oh! Princes Gate is nearly finished. The team have worked hard to complete everything, so I'm starting on Wiltshire on Thursday. Are there any letters or emails to sign off?"

"Yes, this pile of about sixteen things that need your approval and signature." Gems handed them to Serena. "How is the new baby getting on?"

"He's a poppet, just like his dad and getting bigger every day," Serena replied proudly. "Vivi is stronger and enjoying being home again but she misses Sebastian who is still in intensive care. Thank goodness Theo is around, and my mum is good with Jago."

"There've been a few enquiries as to your availability, but I said you were very busy at present and could they ring back in three months," Gems said.

Serena spent a long time on the phone ordering samples and materials to show Paranovsky on Thursday. "It's a huge job. I'm going to get a few assistants to come down and help me. Could you ring George and Cathy and see if they could meet me at Salisbury station on Friday at 9am? I'll reimburse their fares," asked Serena hurriedly.

Her phone rang. "Hello, Vivi darling, is everything okay? Sorry I can't possibly do lunch. . . yes, I'd love to see Jonty but I'm beginning a big new project this week and wondered if you'd have Alicia for a few days? She could see Granny too. Oh, thank you darling. I really appreciate it."

Chapter Twelve

Aylesbury

Serena arrived home to hear Freddie screaming vociferously outside the downstairs loo. "What's the matter darling?"

"Benjie has dropped my electric train down the loo AND it's covered in his poo," wailed Freddie.

"Come on, I'll get it out and clean it up in no time." Giving him a hug, Serena fished out the mucky engine, poured disinfectant over it and gently washed it again in washing-up liquid. "Help me dry it, love—come on."

"Ugh! Ugh! I can't touch it, Mummy," he shouted. Suddenly the train started running round the hall again, much to Freddie's surprise. "I can hear Daddy calling you. I want you to bath me Mummy."

Serena rolled her eyes. "Well, come on then." She chased him upstairs to find little Benjie already immersed in green bubbles.

Lang walked into the bathroom and hugged Serena from behind. "How was your day, darling?" he asked.

"Hectic, but exciting. I'll tell you the news over supper. Where's Alicia?"

"She's making meringues with Bella as a surprise for you," said Lang.

"Come on Freddie, jump in. Could you read both of them a story while I see what's for supper?" Serena asked.

"Mummy, shut your eyes," called Alicia when Serena entered the kitchen. "Now open!"

There was a marvellous mound of meringues, oozing with cream and jam.

"Darling, what a clever girl to make all those," said Serena happily.

"They're for our supper," exclaimed her animated daughter.

"Would you like to stay with Georgie for a couple of nights? You could see Granny too," enthused Serena.

"That would be fun, and perhaps I could see my new cousin?"

"Yes, of course. You'll visit him as well."

Later than evening, Lang was telling his wife all about the various activities he'd organised for the children that day. Serena couldn't contain herself any longer.

"I must tell you about Wiltshire. Oleg Paranovsky has a huge Jacobean mansion surrounded by fields and gardens. He's asked me to start on the two main bedrooms with spacious four posters and rather decaying velvet wallpaper. The job will take weeks to complete, but he's offered me a fabulous contract that will pay the rent on this house for more than a year. Unfortunately, it'll mean that from this Thursday I'll have to spend a few late nights at the office in order to collect and prepare all the materials to be delivered."

"Well done love. That is exciting news. It's just. . . it's a bit tough on the kids. Freddie keeps asking when you'll be home."

"I know, but I have to do this!" Serena snapped. "Once things get up and running I'll be going from here by car and will see them much more. I've asked Alicia if she'd like to see Georgie for two nights, so I thought you could take the boys to Jonty's for a tractor ride, then swimming another day in the new activity pool outside Aylesbury, or ask Freddie if he'd like a friend to stay in the tent one night."

Lang huffed; Serena's tone irritated him. "It's all very well you giving me things to do with the children, but there must be some time you can be here for them?"

"Lang, you know I have to grab every job I'm offered; there's no other money coming in. This new job will cover all our outgoings and rent, then perhaps I can be with them more," she said in a patronising tone.

"Most unlikely, you've got your house husband now," he grumbled.

"Well, whose fault is that?" she retorted. "I'm trying to help this family."

"And so am I!" Lang yelled.

Maggie walked into the room, to clear the plates and was holding a large bowl of strawberries and meringues. The pair fell silent and Maggie smiled. "Hope you enjoy Alicia's cooking."

"It looks great," Lang said, with a strained smile. Serena glared at him.

*

Lang dropped Serena off to meet Vivi. They didn't speak the entire journey. Vivi took her to see Sebastian on the way home. She reacted with amazement at how small her new nephew was, but she didn't like seeing all the incubators and noisy machines.

"When will he come home to you?" she asked.

"Hopefully in a couple of weeks when he's breathing well on his own. I miss him as soon as I leave the hospital."

Meanwhile, Lang met up with Jonty.

"I was going to ask you if the boys would like to come and see the sheep being dipped," Jonty asked.

"Yes, that would be fun, they're at a bit of a loss today. Serena has just told me she's going to be away for three days at this new palace in Wiltshire. Anything to occupy the boys would be great, especially Freddie."

Chapter Thirteen

Chiswick

Theo was practicing in the drawing room. One of the Chopin sonatas was proving difficult. His phone rang interrupting him.

"Hello, Sergei, how is everything? It's great news that Murel is rehearsing a new programme for a concert over here next week."

"Yes, we have a visiting pianist playing Mussorgsky," said Sergei eagerly.

Theo was taken aback, realising he'd almost been replaced.

"When are you able to return for the big recording Theo? In three weeks?" Sergei asked. "We must get back into the studio, the orchestra is in peak form."

"I just can't come until Sebastian is home from hospital. He's so fragile. I'm longing to play the concerto and see you all." Theo's voice sank almost to a whisper.

"Well, ring me next week after the concert."

"Oh Sergei, I'm sorry, I can't. . ." The phone went dead. Tears welled inside Theo, all the confusion of feelings returned. *Why was Sergei so distant, and not understanding my predicament?*

*

Beady greatly enjoyed being with Alicia and Georgie, and took them out on their scooters. The girls climbed trees in Chiswick Park, fed the ducks and showed Beady the swans gliding under the bridge to catch more bread. The morning ended up with large ice creams at the Park café. Beady got a bundle of napkins and wiped two chocolate-covered faces.

"It's so hot! I wish we could go swimming," said Georgie wistfully.

"Ask Daddy to take you later," suggested Beady.

After lunch, Beady went to see Sebastian with Vivi, leaving everyone else to go swimming with Theo.

A long two weeks later, Sebastian was allowed home, much to everyone's delight. He settled in and never cried at night. The children wanted to play with him, but the baby just wanted to sleep.

Beady decided to go back to Madeira and start arranging the shipment of furniture. Jonty promised to follow on later to lend a hand.

Chapter Fourteen

Wiltshire

Serena was submerged in samples for the matching four posters and wallpaper. Her assistants worked feverishly. Paranovsky liked the colour schemes and materials. Phone calls to the children during the busy working week were quite painful, mostly because Freddie wailed so much and one night dropped the phone in his pasta.

Lang received a demanding letter from his firm's solicitors. He rang his own lawyer and begged him to fend off their threat of issuing a writ to bankrupt him. Lang was in such a state he asked Serena to come home sooner than planned.

"The children are bathed and in bed, I must talk to you now," he said to Serena, as he paced up and down the room. "I got a letter about the outstanding balance. When do you think Beady's money will be available? Do you think you could ask if it is likely to be before the end of this month? Otherwise, I'm in deep trouble."

"What did your lawyer say?" asked Serena.

"He suggested I told them the sale of the Madeira house was almost completed and hopefully I'll be able to pay them before the end of September," Lang said tersely.

"Well, Jonty is over there now packing up all the contents with her," Serena tried to reassure him.

"Do you think you could explain the urgency to her, darling?" he begged.

Serena picked up the phone. "Who shall I speak to, Mum or Jonty?"

"I think Jonty," Lang replied.

After a twenty-minute chat about what furniture was packed, they finally discussed the completion date which turned out to be mid-September.

"I should let your lawyers know immediately so that they can reply today."

"Oh, what a relief! The guilt will stay with me forever, but at least my frightful debt will be paid off thanks to you and your generous mum," he said appreciatively.

"Well, we're in this together Lang. Did I tell you about Oleg? A charming man to work for. He's already recommended me to a couple of his colleagues, so I'll be in Russian houses for years if I get their jobs." She laughed and hugged Lang, who relaxed into her arms. "All of our money problems will be in the past."

Chapter Fifteen

Madeira

Jonty finished packing the last containers ready for collection the following morning.

"Well, it's goodbye to my lovely house." Beady sighed. "I shall miss the sun and the sea most, but at least I'll be with you all in England. Now we only have to sign the contract at the lawyers before we catch the plane back."

She slowly shut the front door and plucked several hibiscus flowers from a branch. Squeezing Jonty's arm, she turned for a last look at the empty house.

"Let's go," she whispered.

Chapter Sixteen

Chiswick

Theo found Vivi rocking Sebastian in his crib.

"I've had a call from Moscow begging me to do a special recording," he said. "The orchestra is waiting for me. Do you mind if I go for ten days? Your mother will be here tomorrow to give extra help. I know she disapproves of me going back but I'm under contract to perform."

There was silence, finally Vivi sighed. "Oh Theo, when will these disappearances end? Your absence is felt more and more by me and the children. Everything seems to go wrong when you're not here. Georgie breaking her arm, the burglary, Sebastian coming early. When are you going to put us first?"

"I have to earn a living to help raise our family, my love. Please try to be understanding," he said plaintively. "I realise I'm leaving our lovely new baby so soon, but I can't postpone the recording any longer." He walked over to the crib and stroked Sebastian's head. He went to kiss Vivi and she turned her head, so his lips brushed her hair.

"Just go," Vivi said hugging herself.

Theo hesitated. For a second, Vivi thought he was going to say he was staying. Instead, he hung his head and left the room to pack.

*

After tearful goodbyes from the children and a frosty look from

Vivi, Theo reluctantly got into a waiting taxi. He arrived late in the evening in Moscow. He looked for Sergei and saw him standing by the exit. They hugged, then drove off to Baba's house. Sergei was not as animated as usual.

"Oh, I have missed you Sergei," said Theo, tenderly holding his hand.

"Yes, me too, it's been a long while since we were together and we must talk about the situation over dinner one night. How is your new son? Is he home now?" Sergei asked.

"Yes, after a very anxious time for them both in intensive care. He's got long fingers and I expect he'll be a pianist too."

Sergei smiled. "See you at 9.30 tomorrow," he replied, leaving Theo alone to wonder why he hadn't suggested a chat over a drink or supper.

*

Theo walked in to cheers from the orchestra and a welcoming hug from Murel. Within seconds, he began the opening chords on the piano, pounding each one with ever greater emotion.

After an hour and a half of rehearsing, there was a break and Murel gave everyone notes about the tempi. Several players came up to chat with Theo and ask after the baby.

By the end of the week, he felt totally on top of the Rachmaninov concerto and eagerly wanted to start recording,

He rang Vivi each day and she always sounded distant. He reassured her that his trips will be less frequent, but he could tell by her tone that she didn't believe him.

On Friday, Sergei asked him if he'd like to meet for supper somewhere or come back to his place. They ate at a local restaurant and after a few glasses the conversation became both more personal, and more uneasy.

"I'm still in such turmoil over us, but I do love you, Sergei, I am sure of that. I have never felt this way about a man before," stated Theo.

"Maybe you do, and my love for you is strong too, but it simply can't ever work, can it? Your loyalties are to your family, your wife, and now your new son. We can't pretend otherwise." Sergei put an arm round Theo. "You need someone else to look after you and promote your concerts. I have someone in mind who you must meet."

"Oh Sergei, what are you saying?" Tears came as he hid his face on Sergei's shoulder.

"It's not possible any more. We must go on to new pastures. We've had a wonderful time together and learnt and given so much to each other, but I cannot share you."

"But I. . . I want you in my life," Theo said, wiping his wet face.

Sergei smiled sadly. "Me too, but we will just be going in circles. You will never leave your wife."

After leaving the restaurant, they went off talking and walking along the cobbled streets until past midnight, but neither could see a way out for them to both have what they wanted.

"Come and meet Alex Petrov at the studio tomorrow morning," Sergei suggested. They hugged warmly, and each walked off home in opposite directions.

*

Theo was nervous at the meeting Sergei had suddenly set up

for him. He was devastated by the changes that Sergei seemed to find unavoidable. *Why hadn't their love resumed again?*

A tall, bearded man with unruly red hair peered round the door. "Am I in the right place?" he asked.

"Come in, Alex. This is Theo, who we talked about. I wondered if you'd like to be at the recording next Monday?" asked Sergei.

"I'd love to. I saw you play in both Paris and Vienna, Theo. You have a unique gift," Alex enthused.

"Thank you," said Theo. He felt the man had a calm authority, which was the essence of good management.

"I'll leave you both to chat for a while and perhaps we can have lunch in the square afterwards," suggested Sergei.

As Alex and Theo spoke, Theo gradually relaxed and explained his ambitions for the future, including the fact that from now on he'd prefer to spend less time away from his family. He then expressed a desire for new challenges and new composers and maybe teaching some master classes for up and coming music scholars. Finally, he spoke in detail of his family in London, especially Vivi and their new son.

Alex conveyed warmth and sympathy while listening to Theo's description of recent events. Sergei joined them for lunch and was saddened but knew it was the right thing when Theo accepted the inevitable ending of their passionate relationship, both personally and professionally.

*

On Monday, everyone arrived early in anticipation of the first day's recording. Murel's enthusiasm inspired Theo and the orchestra to perform brilliantly. The afternoon session was slower because various phrases needed re-recording.

By Thursday the Rachmaninov was completed and captivated all those in the studio, including Sergei and Alex. The Chopin sonatas would start the following day.

That evening, Theo suddenly panicked as Sergei walked home with him.

"It's nearly over, how can I leave you, Sergei?" He grabbed the Russian's shoulders and swung him round, kissing him passionately.

Sergei withdrew slowly. "Think of your future, your music, your family. You have to live for them now. Don't break down and spoil it all, Maestro." He stood frowning at the pavement before speaking again. "By the way, I'll let you know when Baba's place is sold. I've a friend who's interested in buying it for her son." Sergei stroked Theo's face. "This is the end Maestro."

*

Saturday was full of farewells during the orchestral lunch. Quite a few musicians were leaving to join other orchestras and Murel obviously felt sad losing part of his family and a great pianist and friend in Theo.

"I'm sure we'll all meet up in London again one day," he said hopefully.

Sergei had suggested that some of the musicians went back on the same flight as Theo. It would make his departure less painful and mean there was no opportunity to break down in tears.

Chapter Seventeen

Chiswick

Hours later, Theo arrived at Heathrow to be met by Vivi and the children waving madly at the exit with little home-made flags. They rushed at his weary body, hugging him. Theo looked down to see Sebastian's eyes staring out of the baby-sling on Vivi's chest. Emotion flooded up to his throat.

Georgie jumped up and flung her arms round his neck. "Oh Daddy, Daddy!" she cried, engulfing him with kisses.

Vivi saw a tear roll down his face. "You look exhausted. Did the recording go well?"

"Yes," he whispered. He searched her face, wanting to know if they were okay. She smiled at him and he knew he was forgiven. He kissed her softly, then ruffled Jago's hair.

*

The next few days were very tense while Theo came to terms with his complete departure from Russia and from Sergei. He cried from time to time while practicing, but the children's joy helped him to start thinking of new concerts. Meanwhile, all sorts of things—some familiar, others new—were pivoting round him.

His new manager, Alex Petrov phoned to suggest meeting the following week, as he'd be in London for a few days.

Jonty returned with Beady and helped her settle into the

cottage and distribute some items of furniture to the family. The children started school again. Sebastian began to open his eyes more, and pay attention when Theo played the piano. It was a busy time—almost chaotic, but it allowed some level of distraction from the heartbreak he was feeling.

Chapter Eighteen

Oving

The lawyers of Lang's old firm had replied very aggressively about the debt, stating categorically that they would accept no delay. This caused him great anxiety.

He was soon busy with school runs and introducing Benjie to his first day at nursery proved difficult. And Freddie wailed and clung, repeatedly asking why Mummy couldn't take him to school.

"She will soon, when she is less busy," explained Lang.

Having safely delivered all three children, he decided to pop in and see Jonty on the way back.

"Hello Lang, good to see you," said his brother-in-law. "Let's go down to the plantation."

"Is Beady upset about leaving Madeira?" Lang asked on the way down.

"Yes, she was a bit sad, but she'll be surrounded by family now and will love seeing all the grandchildren," Jonty replied. "How are things with you?"

"I had another very aggressive warning from the firm's lawyers yesterday. Jonty, do you think the money will come through this week?" Lang's voice became agitated.

"I'm sure it will. I'll give Beady's people in Madeira a call later, but you can't hurry them. I'm afraid they're a law unto themselves."

They walked round the woods for a good two hours, Jonty

stopping now and then to admire the progress of the saplings and straightening some of the wire fencing.

"I do love this place. How I wish I could see it in fifty years' time."

They stood in silence for a while absorbing the air.

Lang glanced at his watch. "Oh, I must pick up the little one from nursery. He'll be out at lunchtime. How time flies here! See you later, Jonty." He hurried back to the car.

The playgroup was bubbling with children and mums noisily calling their offspring. Lang caught sight of Benjie sitting on a log holding the hand of a curly-haired girl. He went over.

"Hello Benjie, who's your friend?"

"Lucy," he said. "She's my girlfriend."

"Oh your girlfriend," Lang said, with his mouth twitching.

"She's got silver shoes, Daddy. I'd like some like that." The boy laughed and wrapped his arms around Lang's knees.

Alicia and Freddie raced out of Oving Junior School, babbling non-stop as Lang talked to a couple of parents. On the way home, they stopped at the village shop for a home-made ice cream. Lang was relieved to see Freddie had enjoyed school almost as much as Alicia.

"Let's see who can get their homework finished first," he said after tea.

Suddenly the front door opened. There was Serena with an enormous bouquet.

"Oh Mummy! Look at those flowers," exclaimed Alicia. Everyone gathered round.

"The Russians are very generous. They also gave me these boxes for you." She handed out three wooden boxes with feathers painted on their sides. Inside there were sweets.

"Why are you back so early, darling?" asked Lang, pecking her on the cheek.

"They've got a business party at the house, so I was able to bunk off for once." She laughed. "Now, who's going to tell me first how school went?"

Chapter Nineteen

Chiswick

Theo lay in the garden hammock, thinking about everything that had changed and gone, wondering what Sergei was doing now, this very minute.

Vivi walked over and gently pushed the hammock. "You're looking very solemn today, what's up?" she asked. "Are you missing Russia again?"

"No, I'm just wondering about the future. When I'll get my next job," he said.

"Well, surely Sergei will organise it all as usual?" Vivi said casually.

"No, not now," Theo said quietly. "I'm getting a new manager. Actually, he's flying over next week for a chat. Is that alright?"

"Yes, of course, but what's happened to the great Sergei who never left your side and you couldn't do without? He was almost your mother, the way he cared for you," Vivi said, rolling her eyes.

"It just wasn't working. He was getting overbearing and booking me too much work in Russia."

"Really? You thought that?"

"Yes," Theo lied avoiding her eyes.

Tears suddenly filled Vivi's eyes. Unable to trust herself she turned and walked back to the kitchen.

Theo sunk further into the hammock. Suddenly, he was

swung upwards. Georgie laughingly pushed it again and Theo fell out.

"You can swing me now, Daddy," she called, but Theo walked away. "Why are you cross?"

He ignored her and walked indoors. He leaned against the wall and breathed in deeply. His heart was hammering against his chest. His ache for Sergei wasn't going away.

Chapter Twenty

Oving

During the next three days, Lang was in a terrible state, hoping Beady's money would arrive. He snapped at the children and Serena. He didn't eat and went for long walks alone. Twice he was late to pick up Alicia and Freddie. Finally, he exploded on Wednesday evening as Serena came off the phone.

"Can't you bloody well ring up Beady? Do something! I've only got two days before the deadline," he shouted.

Serena had never seen him in such a state. "Lang, calm down! I'll ring them now." She rang Jonty first and explained the panic.

"Oh yes, Mum said you should get a cheque tomorrow," he said.

"Thank God. He's really distraught. Will you have a word with him?" She handed the phone to Lang.

"Will it definitely be here tomorrow? They'll serve the writ on Friday," he said in a shaking voice.

"Don't forget Mum is here in Chiswick now, you can always give her a call," suggested Jonty.

Lang didn't want to admit that he was still uncomfortable about what he had done especially around Beady, who he knew resented him for how hard Serena worked.

*

The next morning, Lang refused to take the children to school.

He insisted on waiting for the postman. Frustrated, Serena had to alter her work schedule and take them herself, much to the delight of the kids.

Lang was pruning the climbing rose cascading round the front porch when he heard the post van rumbling up the drive. He almost fell off the ladder and ran towards the gate.

"Not much for you today," said Fred, handing him two brown envelopes and a blue one.

Lang grabbed them. "Thanks!" While tearing open the blue envelope, he saw the cheque at last. "Good old Beady—she even remembered to make it out to the firm!"

He felt overwhelming relief as if being freed from his own sentence, and immediately phoned his lawyer to arrange a meeting. Having asked Maggie to pick up Benjie, he rushed off to catch a train.

An anxious Lang arrived at the lawyer's office half an hour early.

"You look as though you need a drink," said his lawyer. "Let's go to the pub."

Lang hadn't been to the old familiar pub in a long time. Luckily, there were no colleagues around and after the second stiff gin and tonic, Lang was able to relax a little but couldn't wait to get back to the country.

"Here's the cheque."

His lawyer checked it and smiled at Lang reassuringly. "It's finally over." And Lang felt like he could breathe again.

From the station at Aylesbury, he drove up to the top of a wooded hill and drank in a breath-taking view across the rolling countryside. A sense of security began to ease his panic. This was what he was part of now. Tranquillity seeped into him.

He glanced at his watch. "Goodness! They'll be coming out of school in five minutes."

Back home, Maggie greeted them all with strawberries and cream. The children were amazed to see Daddy so happy. He became immersed in the bonfire, he set up for the kids and homework was forgotten.

Two hours later, Serena arrived back to find three grimy faces peering out of the bath.

"What have you all been up to?" she asked, smiling.

"We made a huge bonfire and baked potatoes and toasted marshmallows," squeaked Freddie.

"But we left one for you. It's in the kitchen with a fork sticking out. They are delicious." Alicia smiled, rubbing the smoke off her face.

Lang gave Serena a hug. "The cheque arrived, and I rushed it up to the lawyers and the debt is paid off, darling. We're free at last! Thank you so much for your generosity and patience. I'll always feel guilty for what I did and the effect it had on us—forgive me a little."

Lang wrapped his arms round Serena and hugged her softly with warm love. The children were splashing each other riotously.

"Oh, I'm so glad it's over darling." She pulled away from him. "If you ever lie to me again Lang—"

"I won't, I promise," Lang said, kissing the tip of her nose.

Half an hour later the two boys were in bed. Alicia was practicing the piano, while Lang finally spoke to Beady, showing his gratitude for her generosity and his relief. It was all over, and he reassured her he would contribute to the family in every way possible. He handed the phone to Serena.

"Mum, the stress has gone at last, and I do appreciate what you've done. The dreadful cloud hanging over us has gone forever, I hope." Serena listened for a minute, then suddenly smiled. "A party? What a nice idea. Will it be in your cottage? Oh, in Vivi's lovely drawing room, what fun. Yes, we can all come on Sunday next week."

Serena put the phone down. "Mum's having a family do to celebrate her new home."

"Now, let's go out for a drink or even a meal by the canal," suggested Lang.

"That's a bit sudden, darling. Maggie might have prepared supper."

"I don't care even if she has. Tonight, you and I are going to celebrate," stated Lang.

Chapter Twenty One

Chiswick

Theo opened the door to Alex Petrov.

"So sorry I'm half an hour late. The taxi took me to some place called Kew. What a beautiful home you have," Alex said.

"Yes, the tide even laps our front door sometimes," said Theo. "Will you have vodka or a coffee?"

They walked through the hall into the garden. After an hour, they'd both relaxed and started discussing possible future concerts. Alex had already fixed a date in Edinburgh.

Vivi arrived with a tray of snacks. Theo began to feel confident that he could progress under the guidance of a dedicated and enthusiastic manager, but it still felt alien to him that it wasn't Sergei he was talking to.

Vivi asked about the plans and was relieved to hear there were no bookings in Russia at present. She also responded warmly to Alex Petrov and suggested he came over one day for lunch.

Later that evening, Vivi enthused over the new manager. "He's charming and very ambitious for you, isn't he?"

"Yes, I'll see how it works out after he's booked some good concerts," replied Theo.

"By the way, I wondered about having Sebastian christened the same day as Mum's do. What do you think?" Vivi asked tenderly.

"Actually, yes. We'll just make it one big family party at lunchtime, Beady won't mind, will she?" asked Theo.

"I'm sure she won't."

"Oh, and the other thing we need to talk about is godparents. We've only got Cheryl so far. I'd like to have Mark Cooper, that clarinettist I used to work with. Do you remember? He's a lovely person," Theo said.

"Yes, I liked him. And I think Lang would be a lovely godfather too. He's great with the kids, isn't he?" replied Vivi.

"I'll ring them up now."

Chapter Twenty Two

Wiltshire

Three tapestry curtains had just been fitted around the large four poster bed in Oleg Paranovsky's master bedroom. He was pleased to see the work progressing, but Serena stood back and looked at them, then sighed.

"The colour just doesn't work, I'll have to find an alternative. Take that lot off," she said, realising that this job was proving much more difficult than any other.

She sent her assistants home early and then decided to take a long stroll in the gardens.

"Goodness, I'm losing my touch. It's all getting out of hand," she said to herself. "What with the stress of Lang's debt, not seeing the children enough and taking on this enormous challenge, I'm feeling I can't cope."

Just then Serena came to the top of a rise. Below her an avenue of beech trees had begun to turn golden and brilliant red as the sun filtered through their leaves. To the left, a copse of ash and hornbeam nestled at the bottom of a hill near several gnarled oaks which stood beyond a flourishing orchard, bursting with russet apples like the baubles on a Christmas tree.

There were so many autumnal colours melding into each other it was almost like a tapestry in itself.

"I've got the answer! Background dark green with gold and reds threaded through the material."

She walked hurriedly back to the mansion.

A few days later, Serena and her assistants eagerly hung up the altered and now totally successful curtains.

Chapter Twenty Three

Aylesbury

Cheryl was busy helping Jonty with a bumper harvest. Lunchtimes were very hectic, supplying extra helpers with food and drink. Unfortunately, they'd just lost two valuable assistants at the riding school, as they'd gone off to university, but luckily Jacob had asked one of his nephews to help out, which was at least something.

In the evening, she sat beside Jonty on the sofa, crocheting a beautiful jacket for Sebastian to wear at his christening.

"Only ten days to go now," she said, holding it up to the light. "I'm going to get a prayer book for the little fellow too. Just think, in a couple of years' time he'll be coming down to stay with us."

"Yes, I'll teach him about trees and get his lungs filled with fresh, country air," Jonty added.

The phone rang. Jonty answered it. "Hello Vivi. How weird, we were just talking about the party. Yes, of course we'll bring up a variety of our cheeses. What about some homemade cider too? Yes? No problem."

Cheryl took the phone from him. "Shall I make a cake? Do you remember I did one for Jago's christening?" Cheryl beamed as she put the phone down. "I do love these family gatherings."

*

Early in the morning there was an angry shout from Jacob. "Some bugger's let the sheep out! They're all over the place."

Jonty groaned put a coat over his pyjamas and ran off to help him. Cheryl made some bacon sandwiches, knowing it would be a long time before the sheep were rounded up.

Chapter Twenty Four

Chiswick

On the day of the christening, Theo helped to rearrange the furniture so guests could eat lunch in their spacious sitting room.

The children were excited at the forthcoming party but their attempts at helping didn't all succeed. At one point, they even left a trail of twitching goldfish who'd almost died when their overflowing tank was transported across the hall floor. Jago's toy train had become embedded in the carpet.

Theo's patience erupted when Georgie jammed the CD machine and deleted a special recording of his. Vivi asked Theo to take Sebastian out in the pram with the other two while Bella helped to put up trestle tables and hired chairs in the garden.

Helium balloons hung round the big trees and golden Champagne buckets were placed behind the shrubs. Theo's specially composed music for Sebastian was to be played on the piano and broadcast outside on speakers for those sitting in the garden.

Cheryl and Jonty arrived carrying their farm produce.

"You look lovely, Cheryl—is that a new dress?" asked Vivi, kissing her on the cheek.

"Yes, I ran it up specially for the occasion. Where shall I leave Sebastian's presents?"

Jonty put down the cake box. "What about this beauty?" He smiled, opening the lid.

"Oh Cheryl, look at those tiny rabbits dancing around a little boy! You are clever," said Vivi, putting the cake carefully on a shelf above the fridge.

The front door burst open as the children ran into the kitchen.

Following them in a few seconds later, Theo gently picked up Sebastian to take off his coat then handed him to Cheryl, saying, "Here is your wee godson. We must get him changed for the christening."

The sky was blue and clear as they walked to the church up the road. Serena and Lang met them and the clarinettist godfather outside, talking to the vicar.

Beady wore a splendid floral hat. She guided her grandchildren into the church and showed them the font where Sebastian would be christened.

"Hope he doesn't cry when the holy water is poured on his head," she said quietly.

A few minutes later everyone else had gathered round them. The ceremony was about to begin. Vivi placed Sebastian in the vicar's arms, where the babe lay placidly throughout the christening.

Alicia and Georgie wore bright-coloured dresses and eagerly stood by the font waiting for something to happen. Freddie, Benjie and Jago took off round the empty church playing hide and seek in the pews at the back.

Sebastian's little face crumpled as the water cascaded down his face and then bawled in shock before returning to Vivi's comforting arms.

It was a halcyon day as the whole family and a few of Beady's friends gathered in Vivi and Theo's garden for a toast.

Everyone enjoyed the buffet, each taking a moment to hold and admire the sleeping boy.

"That's a lovely jacket you made him Cheryl," said Beady, passing her precious bundle to Jonty.

"I shall enjoy introducing him to our forest," Jonty said, kissing Sebastian's forehead.

"And I will encourage him to enjoy music. Who knows? He may even play the clarinet one day," said Mark Cooper.

"Oh, he's a pianist," Theo said winking at Mark, who laughed.

Beady's friends mingled with the family and were intrigued with her new home.

"What a charming cottage, just far away enough to remain independent," chortled one, a lady with a stick. "My flat's in the basement of my daughter's house so I get no peace at all."

"Yes, I'm very fortunate to run my own life and yet enjoy the grandchildren." Beady laughed as three little heads popped up from behind their chairs.

Vivi walked slowly into the garden carrying the christening cake as Theo's music filtered outside. Little Sebastian's eyes opened wide, as if listening to the harmony. He lay in Cheryl's arms beneath the big chestnut tree.

The children listened quietly as they sprawled nearby in the grass. The music was tender and rippling. Everyone stood quietly gazing out at Sebastian.

Beady was quite overcome with emotion and went into the kitchen for a minute to collect herself. The afternoon sunlight reflected onto the tiles as she gazed out of the window at her family.

"How I wish Jack was here to see all of us gathered together on this happy day. It's so good to be living in my new home surrounded by them all. I'm glad I've been able to help with my children's problems," she said to herself.

"Do you want some christening cake, Gran?" Alicia asked, interrupting her.

"Yes please, darling."

Back in the garden, Theo received a text. To his surprise it was Sergei, saying his cousin has brought Baba's house and to call him when he was free.

Returning him to the emotion and doubts of Moscow, he wished Sergei hadn't texted.

"Daddy, can we have the paddling pool out?" called Jago.

"We're so hot," moaned Georgie.

"Only if you put it behind those shrubs so the guests don't get soaked," replied Theo, dragging the hose out.

"I'll do that. You take Sebastian and join the family," Vivi suggested.

"You're going to be busy with three kids, I know from experience," said Lang, stroking the baby's head. "By the way, how's work?"

"I've got a concert in Edinburgh soon. I've never played there before," replied Theo quietly.

The two men sat under the chestnut tree chatting until Beady joined them to announce her friends' departure.

"They've all loved this place and our party. Do come and say goodbye," she said to Theo.

Lang and Serena left an hour later with three very wet children.

"I must go, I've got an early start in Wiltshire on Monday and need to work on a difficult and new design," said Serena, hugging Vivi and Theo.

Theo didn't find a suitable time to ring Sergei back during the evening so decided to do it the next morning. The conversation was fairly stilted and formal, neither man wanting to stir up past emotions again.

"If you give me your bank details I'll transfer the money to you in London," said Sergei hoarsely. "How's work by the way?"

"I've got a concert in Scotland soon."

"So it's working out with Alex?"

"Yes. Well. . . early days. I'll text you my bank details later." He flipped shut his mobile as Vivi walked into the room.

"Jonty and Cheryl are leaving now," she said. "I'm giving them a lift to the tube. Will you put Sebastian in the garden to sleep? It's another glorious day."

There was no time for Theo to reflect on Sergei or the sale of Baba's apartment, even though his emotions were churning inside him.

Chapter Twenty Five

Wiltshire

Serena and her assistants were completing the wallpaper in the master bedroom when Oleg Paranovsky and his wife appeared in the doorway.

"You are working so hard and the room is going to look splendid. Our bed is so beautiful," exclaimed Oleg.

"We have exciting news," said his wife shyly. "I'm expecting our first baby in four months, so we'll need you to design a nursery."

"Congratulations, what a lovely surprise," replied Serena. "Where will the baby's room be? On this floor?"

"Yes, next to the nanny's room," said Oleg, pointing down the corridor as they left.

"Phew! I feel as though we'll be in Wiltshire forever," Serena said to her assistants later as they finished work. "I must go to the office tomorrow morning. I'll be back after lunch. Will you finish off these two walls?"

She arrived back home to find the barn unusually quiet as she opened its front door.

"Coo-ee!" she called, walking through to the kitchen.

She saw Lang and the children in the garden kneeling by the fence gazing at a sheep.

"Ssh! The mummy is having another baby," whispered Alicia, glancing over one shoulder.

It was an enchanting sight to see her family huddled together, watching something so natural.

Lang turned to greet her. "We've been waiting here for an hour darling."

"Did Auntie Vivi have Sebastian like that?" Alicia asked.

"Not quite the same," said Serena laughing.

"Does it hurt having babies, Mummy?" asked Alicia seriously.

"No, not much," Serena lied. "But it's such a happy moment."

"Supper's ready," called Maggie.

"Can we just see the next baby come out?" asked Lang.

*

Serena spent the following morning with Gems catching up on requests from new clients, her bank, invoices from suppliers, and in particular an urgent message from the Qatar Embassy to finish the work there.

"I'll have to reply carefully to them. There's no way I can do the upper floor until I've finished in Wiltshire," she sighed anxiously.

"Maybe a couple of your reliable helpers could prepare the rooms for you?" suggested Gems.

"No, I'll have to be there. Could you arrange an appointment with the attaché? I must explain the situation," said Serena.

She went on to tell Gems about Sebastian's christening, then left hastily for Wiltshire, arriving just as the last strip of wallpaper was being hung.

"Yes, that does look good," she said to her assistants who looked totally exhausted. "Go and take a break."

Chapter Twenty Six

Aylesbury

"Jacob and I are going down to the forest in a moment to see how the latest saplings are doing," said Jonty. "Are you going to be at the Centre all morning?"

"Yes, I will," Cheryl said.

"I'll see you for lunch then. Should be back about one-ish, my Cherry Berry." And with that he pecked her on the cheek, got up, and strode out of the room.

As he walked down the hill, he saw a white van by the open drive gate and walked over to investigate.

"What are you doing on my land?" Jonty shouted. As he got nearer he heard sheep baaing in the van.

He ran to shut the gate to trap them as the van revved up its engine. The van drove at the gate and burst through, knocking Jonty off his feet.

Jacob had heard the commotion and reached the gate just as the white van disappeared from view. He looked down in horror at Jonty who was lying on the dusty path under the broken gate.

"Come on. Up yer get," he said, putting both his arms under Jonty's shoulders. "Cor, you're heavy." Jonty's body flopped forward. Jacob took off his jacket and lifted Jonty's head onto it. "Them bloody thieves escaped again with your sheep."

Jacob knelt, touching Jonty's ashen face, noticing the blood on the side of his head. "Oh no, they can't have taken you! How can I tell Miss Cheryl? She must get the doctor quick."

Fear gripped the old man to his core. He put Jonty carefully down, turned and stumbled towards their house.

Cheryl was waving. "Where's Jonty? There's a phone call from Aylesbury police warning about more sheep stealing. What's the matter, Jacob? You look terrible."

"I can't speak." He took her hand. "Come with me, it's too dreadful," he croaked, pulling her towards the drive.

Cheryl looked down in abject horror. "Oh, my Jonty!" She let out a wail which echoed around the fields. "Who's done this?"

Cradling his bloodied head, Cheryl lay across her husband's body, sobbing for some time, stroking his face and listening in vain for a heartbeat, then staggered to her feet. She dashed back into the house and hurriedly made three phone calls— to the local doctor, the police, and finally to Lang who arrived at the same time as the police.

Everyone stood in the drive while Phil Connor, the doctor, examined Jonty's body. He looked up and sadly shook his head.

"How can this happen? Even the country ain't safe anymore. He was such a good man," said Jacob tearfully.

The police took a long time investigating and talked to the doctor.

"We've not had a death before with all this sheep stealing," said the sergeant worriedly.

"We'll see what the post mortem shows. I'll ring for an ambulance. I'd like to give Mrs Croft a little sedation for the shock." The doctor then walked back to the house with Lang.

Jacob knelt beside Jonty, his body trembling in despair.

As darkness fell it was as if the whole countryside was mourning Jonty, not a breath of life stirred.

While Cheryl dozed, Lang rang Serena about the tragic news. She was horrified and immediately offered to come over, but instead he asked her to ring Vivi and Beady with the awful news.

"It will save doing it in front of poor Cheryl. I'll certainly stay with her tonight. The police are still here," Lang said quietly.

Serena was still weeping down the phone. "How could they kill such a dear person? How did it happen? Those evil bastards!"

"We've all got to help Cheryl somehow. She'll be utterly lost without him," muttered Lang sadly. "I just can't imagine her all alone. I must go, darling, the police are leaving now."

"Ring me if I can help, my poor, poor brother. . ." Serena said softly.

Later that evening, Lang asked Cheryl if she wanted him to cancel the riding school next morning.

"Yes, that would be a great help. I'll give you the list," she whispered.

*

Having interviewed Jacob already, the police came back for more details of the previous thefts and how many sheep were stolen. The officer spent an hour investigating both incidents.

Cheryl was too fragile to see anyone and remained in bed. Serena, Vivi and Beady arrived and quietly crept up to comfort her. She lay in bed hugging Jonty's dressing gown, her face racked with sorrow and confusion. Beady gently took Cheryl's limp body in her arms, holding her close in a tearful embrace. Vivi and Serena cupped Cheryl's hands in theirs and all four were silent, each crying within themselves.

Meanwhile, Lang answered endless phone calls since the local radio had announced Jonty's awful death. Many riding school parents sent messages of sympathy to Cheryl.

"What a terrible tragedy," Reverend Ashworth said, shaking Lang's hand. "Can I go up and see her? She may like some prayers."

Lang agreed and took him upstairs. The Reverend sat down and laid a hand on her shoulder. Lang left them alone.

The family gathered in the sitting room to discuss arrangements for the funeral.

"Of course, we'll have to wait for the post mortem before we can decide on a date, but meanwhile I'll arrange an obituary in *The Times*," said Serena quietly. "I wonder if that nice lady who helps Cheryl in the farm shop might do the catering for the wake?"

"I think Jacob's in a bad way," remarked Lang. "We must include him in the arrangements. Oh, and I've already told him to let me know about any problems in the forest. Apparently, the thieves took a dozen sheep! The heartless cowards."

Beady's bottom lip was trembling. "Oh my boy, how I loved you,' she whispered, grabbing hold of Vivi's hand.

"I don't know how we'll tell the children. They all adored him. He was always chasing them round the garden," remembered Serena.

Cheryl appeared later in the afternoon. She was calm but

very fragile. "I'm not able to arrange anything for my Jonty, I have no strength. I rely on you all to do the things for me."

"Yes, of course we'll organise the funeral, but you might want to choose some of Jonty's favourite music?" suggested Lang and Cheryl nodded.

A few hours later Lang waved goodbye to Serena and Vivi, who were going to relieve Theo from looking after all the children. Lang and Beady had both decided to stay another night to give Cheryl a chance for more rest.

Lang walked down to the forest, closing his eyes as the wind whipped past him, blowing away the tears that had fallen down his face.

Chapter Twenty Seven

Kensington

The following day Serena got to her office before Gems had arrived. Opening her work diary, she saw that the appointment with the attaché at the Qatar Embassy was at 10.45am.

Gemma was astonished to find her there so early. "You're up with the lark! Your meeting at the embassy isn't for ages." Then, when there was no reply. "Serena? What's wrong?"

"My brother was killed during a robbery. It's just so cruel. I only hope they catch the evil, thieving murderers."

"I'm so sorry, what an awful thing to happen, I can't imagine. . ." said Gems.

"I just can't do it," wailed Serena, tears pouring down her face. "Please just tell them that my brother has passed. Explain to the attaché. Also, please ring Oleg Paranovsky and tell him the situation. I must go home after I've signed these letters. Lang is with Cheryl, so I must pick up the kids from school and help arrange the funeral," Serena said sadly.

"Do let me know if I can do anything else. I'm so sorry, Serena."

Chapter Twenty Eight

Chiswick

Vivi and Theo discussed how to tell their children about Uncle Jonty's death. They decided to wait a few days until the weekend. Little Sebastian was sleeping right through, which gave both parents a welcome night's sleep.

Vivi was greatly subdued by her brother's violent death and cancelled all her clients for a week.

Theo had phoned Sergei on Sunday suggesting that the proceeds from the sale of Baba's apartment be sent to his bank in Chiswick. He was pleased that it had gone to someone he knew, and also that it made the break from Sergei easier and final.

They talked about Murel's new orchestra, and several new soloists including a young Ukrainian pianist who played a lot of modern Russian music. Theo felt a pang of jealousy thinking back to his early days there as the special pianist but showed no emotion on the phone.

"I'm coming to London next month to arrange a tour. We must meet," suggested Sergei.

"Maybe, if I'm here," Theo said distantly. They said goodbye and Theo picked up Sebastian and cradled him tenderly as he walked round the garden.

That evening Vivi rang Cheryl to check up on her and was pleased to hear that she sounded a bit more like her old self.

"I've been overwhelmed by tributes to dear Jonty from

people near and far," said Cheryl. "The pony club children have written a beautiful poem called 'The Tree Man' about him. Have you told the children yet?"

"No, we just don't know how to," Vivi said truthfully.

Just at that moment the doorbell rang. Theo answered it.

"Hello, Daddy!" Georgie jumped up as Jago wrapped his arm around Theo's legs. "This is Sally and her mum."

Theo shook hands and thanked the attractive blonde mother for having his children to tea.

"Nice to meet you, I'm Cathy."

"Do come in." Cathy followed him into the garden. "Georgie tells me your husband teaches music at school?"

"Yes, Alan's part-time because he's the first violin at the Royal Philharmonic," Cathy replied.

Vivi came in offering a glass of wine. The adults chatted while the children raced round the garden and hung on the climbing frame. Theo became very relaxed talking about the music world.

"Why not come to the Phil concert? You could meet Alan afterwards," suggested Cathy.

"That would be delightful," said Theo.

Georgie waved goodbye to Sally as Cathy thanked Vivi and Theo for the drink.

"Let's have stroll round the garden," suggested Vivi to Georgie. Sebastian was sleeping peacefully in his pram.

She walked at a slow pace gently holding Georgie's hand.

"Darling, I have to tell you some very sad news. Dear Uncle Jonty has died," Vivi said quietly.

"He can't have done, we saw him last week," Georgie replied emphatically.

"It's true sweetheart," Vivi said tearfully.

"But how?" demanded Georgie.

"That doesn't matter for now, darling."

"I shall miss him so, so much. He always played games with us," cried Georgie. Vivi wrapped her arms around her.

Chapter Twenty Nine

Oving

Alicia and Freddie were thrilled when Serena picked them up from school. Several parents stopped to offer condolences over her brother's death. Luckily, the children had run on ahead chatting to their school friends.

As she drove back in the low autumn sunlight, Serena went to the top of a local hill and stopped the car.

"Look at this view, kids. Let's walk along the top." Once they got there, she turned to her children and held their hands. "Last week something very sad happened, Uncle Jonty died."

Alicia burst into tears. "I don't believe you! We were playing our special game with him at the christening."

Freddie sank onto the grass. "He was my bestest friend. Why did he die?"

Serena realised she had to tell the truth. "He got run over trying to stop some bad men stealing his sheep."

"How could they kill our best uncle?" wailed Alicia, clinging onto Serena.

"At least he's up in heaven looking down at you both," she replied, trying to soothe both sobbing children. "We're going to see Auntie Cheryl on Saturday. Shall we make some pictures to cheer her up?"

"I'd like to buy her a beautiful dress," said Alicia.

"Alright, that's a great idea. We'll have a look tomorrow on the way back from school."

"I want to buy her a parrot," said Freddie.

"Good idea, only her cat might try to eat it," said Serena, stroking his cheek.

They drove back in silence, both children digesting the awful news.

After homework, Serena got the children to paint some colourful pictures, then allowed them to watch TV while she prepared supper and talked to Maggie.

Lang phoned from Aylesbury to say goodnight. Serena told Lang that they'd all come over on Saturday. Maggie would roast a chicken and Alicia had promised to make some more meringues.

"It's strange at night without you," Lang suddenly said. "I've been with Jacob most of the day. We're discussing Cheryl letting the fields out to a local farmer. He suggested selling the sheep, so we have no more thefts and no more worry."

"That's an excellent idea and much safer," agreed Serena.

"Cheryl has asked if I would consider taking over the management of the forest with Jacob, who'll no doubt teach me a lot, but I said that I must fit in all my school runs for the kids," Lang went on. "The pay is pretty good."

"What a great solution that would be," enthused Serena. "And actually, I have an idea too about the woman who helps out in the farm shop. Do you think she might be prepared to live in and keep Cheryl company? She's a single parent and her son is at university."

Having finished his conversation with Serena, Lang walked slowly down to the plantation with Cheryl and Jacob.

"Jonty's here" Lang whispered.

Cheryl collapsed with an agonised wail. Both men sank down and Lang put an arm round her protectively.

"This is Jonty's forest and we will tender it with loving care forever, Cheryl," Lang whispered.

She slowly rose, clinging onto Lang for support. "Let's walk through this paradise. I want to walk all the way through, I can almost feel him here," Cheryl said.

The two men glanced at each other and strolled in silence. The sun was setting slowly behind the forest and it was very peaceful.

When they walked back towards the house, Jacob left them to feed the sheep and Lang squeezed Cheryl's hand.

"By the way, Serena's bringing the children over to see you on Saturday," he said.

"Oh, how lovely, I do enjoy seeing them. As you know, I'm particularly fond of Alicia. She's a very practical child and learns things quickly."

"Yes, she's certainly bright," said Lang proudly. "I think Vivi's coming down as well, so you'll have all the family around you."

"I hope they all know about Jonty now; I couldn't possibly tell them," Cheryl said.

"Yes, they know," answered Lang quietly.

*

A few days later the farmhouse was buzzing with activity. There were children in the haystacks, kittens being chased by Benjie and Jago, and Jacob was busy showing Freddie how to make cheese.

Vivi and Serena prepared lunch while Cheryl enjoyed talking about the farm with Lang. Theo asked her if she would like him to play a small piano piece at the funeral.

"Oh yes, that would be very special. Jonty loved Fauré and Chopin. He often put a tape on at dusk while we sipped a glass of his wine," she reminisced.

The whole family assembled at a wooden table outside, overlooking some rolling hills beyond the forest. The children babbled away as usual as though nothing had happened.

Alicia suddenly stood up. "Auntie Cheryl, I've got a special present for you." She handed her a large carrier bag. "Open it now. It'll make you happy."

Cheryl slowly undid the paper and held up a colourful green dress. Cheryl felt her eyes welling up. "That's lovely Alicia, how very kind of you."

"I wanted to give you a parrot who would talk and make you laugh," said Freddie.

"I love birds, but the cats would get too excited with a parrot in the house." Cheryl smiled.

Georgie had made some colourful flowers out of tissue paper that she had arranged in a vase, at which point Jacob appeared with three little chicks in a basket. The children jumped down and gathered round him.

Everyone enjoyed Alicia's homemade meringues and chatted away trying to fill the silence. Little Sebastian lay peacefully in Cheryl's arms while the adults finished their wine and beer with the homemade cheese. It was a radiant afternoon even though everyone was missing Jonty dreadfully.

"What's the name of that nice helper who works in the farm shop with you?" asked Serena.

"Yes, she's lovely. Her name is Hilary," replied Cheryl.

"I met her son at the stables helping with the lessons," recalled Serena. "Actually, I had an idea which might involve her. . ."

Lang and the family drove back to Oving. Cheryl took Georgie and Jago to feed the ponies, while Beady and Vivi went upstairs to bathe Sebastian who lay gurgling and splashing his tiny feet in a baby's tub.

Theo hadn't yet seen the plantation. Walking through he felt a profound air of tranquillity and was amazed at the large selection of trees. He sat down on a tree trunk briefly and relished the silence. In his head he began composing the gentle notes of a sonata.

"Daddy, where are you?" he heard Georgie's voice echoing down the hill. Reluctantly he began walking back up to the house.

"My goodness, this place is good for the soul," he said to Vivi who sat in the kitchen tenderly rocking Sebastian. "It's very peaceful, darling, isn't it?"

"I forgot you'd never seen the forest before. You were always in Moscow when we came down at weekends."

Theo briefly recalled the anxieties and glorious musical achievements of Moscow. It all seemed so far from recent events, his new son, and the tragic death of dear Jonty. He went over to Vivi and kissed her.

"While I was deep in the forest I began to compose a sonata on the tranquillity of Jonty's creation. I'll play it to you when we get back."

"I do miss my brother so much," Vivi said, stretching out an arm to Theo who came over to comfort her.

The phone rang and Theo picked it up. "Where's Cheryl? It's Dr Ashworth."

"She's upstairs with Beady," replied Vivi.

Cheryl arrived hastily to speak with the doctor who told

her the post-mortem was finished and concluded that Jonty died from a haemorrhage to the brain caused by the impact of being hit by the van. Cheryl thanked him calmly and put the phone down, collapsing into the old kitchen chair. Theo put an arm round her shoulders.

Georgie and Jago rushed into the room.

"Mummy, we've just seen two rabbits with tiny babies running along the field," Georgie exclaimed.

"Could we have a rabbit at home?" Jago asked.

"Let's go see where Granny is," Theo said, trying to move them out of the kitchen.

"No, don't make them go," said Cheryl quietly. "I promised to show them a bird's nest with three eggs in it. I think it belongs to a thrush."

She took both children by the hand and guided them to a thick hedge by the vegetable garden. The mother bird was sitting on the nest as one chick burst out of its shell, a little wide-open beak gaping for food.

"Oh, it's so tiny," whispered Georgie.

"Will the other chicks pop out now?" asked Jago.

They stood entwined inside Cheryl's arms, totally absorbed for several minutes. Suddenly, the mother bird flew off hurriedly in search of food and returned with a wriggling worm.

"Fancy eating worms. Ugh!" said Jago.

Beady and Lang were standing by the kitchen door, pleased to see Cheryl immersed in nature with the children.

After supper, once bedtime stories had been told, the adults listened to the Fauré excerpt that Cheryl wanted at Jonty's funeral. They discussed arrangements and who to invite.

"It's probably better to have it on Saturday," suggested Vivi.

"I'd like to read something." She took out a piece of paper and tearfully read a poem.

"That's beautiful. Do read it in church," said Cheryl quietly.

*

The following day both families attended church, then enjoyed a pub lunch by the canal.

Serena had to return to Oving. She rushed into her workroom to catch up with arrangements for finishing the two four-poster beds during the week. She phoned Oleg Paranovsky assuring him she'd be in first thing in the morning.

Meanwhile, the Hanovers arrived home with two very dejected children and listened to myriad answer phone messages about Theo's next concert. He had an appointment with his new manager the next day.

*

By the end of the week, the family had prepared for the funeral on Saturday. Jacob helped decorate Jonty's coffin with hay and small sprigs of golden beech leaves along the sides. Cheryl and Hilary had prepared four dozen scones, some cinnamon biscuits and a raft of cucumber sandwiches for the wake.

"Would you mind if I stayed for the next couple of nights?" Hilary suddenly asked. She was a tall, diffident lady who seemed fond of Cheryl, having worked in the farm shop for over five years.

"No, of course not. It would be company for me, and we could do some crocheting together in the evening," said Cheryl.

Both women had lost their husbands and shared an invisible loneliness that gave them ease together.

"My boiler's packed up," Hilary explained. "The room's so cold without central heating and hot water. The plumber can't come until next week."

"Oh, in that case I'll tell Lang he needn't stay the night," said Cheryl. "He ought to be back with his family anyway. Did I mention I've asked him to take care of the plantation? Jonty would have liked that."

Vivi phoned to see how the preparations were going and was delighted to hear that Hilary would be staying the night.

"Can we come and stay on Saturday as well?"

"Yes, it would be lovely to have you all here. The more the better. I love to have the house full," replied Cheryl.

"Theo's composed a beautiful slow sonata for Jonty," said Vivi enthusiastically.

"Oh, how thoughtful of him," said Cheryl. "I'm looking forward to hearing it."

Chapter Thirty

Aylesbury

It was a bright September morning as the family waited for Jonty's coffin to be driven off up the hill towards their local church. As they walked to the front pews, Cheryl was supported on either side by Beady and Vivi, followed by Serena and all the children. They were astonished by the packed congregation.

Jonty's decorated coffin was carried in by Lang, Theo, Jacob, Hilary's son Ed, and two friends.

Theo played his tender adagio, Vivi read her poem, followed by two friends who recounted amusing incidents of their times with Jonty. Serena led the children in the hymn 'All things bright and beautiful.'

Cheryl got up and gave an impromptu eulogy to her dear man. There were gasps, gulps, and sobs after her moving words. She stood poised while speaking to over two hundred faces and finished by saying that Jonty's ashes would be buried beside a tree in his forest.

As the coffin finally slid through the curtains, Cheryl's body trembled. The finality was unbearable for her.

Many people came to the wake. Cheryl was pleased to greet so many familiar faces and there was much laughter in people's reminiscences. Even Prince Charles had sent a representative to pass on his condolences. Cheryl felt a warmness surrounding her and in that moment, she felt a small amount of peace.

"I can feel you," Cheryl whispered, knowing that Jonty was right beside her.

Chapter Thirty One

Chiswick

On Monday, after the school run, Vivi decided to rearrange the drawing room because the piano tuner had said that sunlight was damaging the instrument. Bella heaved it round as Vivi pushed the concert grand toward a shady corner.

"Thanks Bella. That's well out of the sunlight now. Ah, here's Theo's fountain pen! He lost it last week. I'll put it back in his desk."

As Vivi unlocked the bureau her eyes were drawn to a pale blue letter lying open. It was from Sergei. Unable to put it down, she began reading the contents, slowly sinking into a chair. The intimate words made her feel sick. The shock of seeing, 'how I miss you already,' made her shake and to then see more loving words across the page was unbelievable. As she put the letter down she saw that the Russian had signed off with the words, 'Farewell, my darling Theo.'

Beneath that letter was another. Theo had started a reply with the words, 'My darling Sergei. . .'

She began to tremble and hurried upstairs, sobbing. Sebastian let out a loud wail and she looked out of the window to see Theo tenderly rocking the baby in his arms.

"How could you betray me," she whispered.

Theo disappeared from her sight and a few minutes later appeared at the bedroom door.

"Hello, Vivi darling, I wondered where you were. Look, Sebastian's fallen asleep." He laid the tiny child beside her on the bed. "You're looking very pale."

Vivi stared fixedly at a small patch of sunlight on the carpet. "I want to talk about Russia. Now you've got a new agent you won't be going to Moscow any more will you. . . especially not to see Sergei?"

"Probably not. Why do you ask?" Theo looked surprised. She held up Sergei's letter. Theo blanched. "Where did you get that from?"

"I didn't go looking for it. I found your pen under the piano and put it back in your desk. But I must know now exactly what this means. Sergei only wrote this four days ago. 'I miss you so much,' he says. 'Moscow seems empty without you. If only you hadn't been married!' What is he talking about Theo?"

Vivi stood up, staring at Theo as he sank onto the bed. There was a deafening pause.

"Did you have an affair?" she asked. "I've often suspected something was going on by the way you spoke to him so tenderly but I told myself I was going mad." Vivi stared at her husband's crumpled body.

"There was something, I admit. . . a connection. . . but. . ." Theo swallowed hard, unable to speak.

"A connection!" Vivi shouted. Theo let out a wail of despair.

There was another silence before Theo eventually spoke. "I suppose it all began when I was very vulnerable, alone with a new orchestra, and living entirely in my world of music, forgetting my family and flattered by Sergei's boundless attention. In the end, though, nothing actually happened. You must believe me!"

"But, how can I? Look at this letter. Neither of you have finished the relationship, have you?" urged Vivi. Theo looked down. "Theo answer me!"

But instead Theo buried his head in his hands. Vivi shot him a look of disgust before marching out of the bedroom, slamming the door behind her. Sebastien woke with a sharp wail.

Chapter Thirty Two

Aylesbury

Cheryl held a meeting about the future of the farm with Lang and Jacob. Both men listened to her idea of letting the fields.

"I'll be able to help you with the ponies. There's a lot of work keeping them creatures cleaned out," suggested Jacob.

"Yes, that'll be very useful. Now, Lang, I know it's a big undertaking but are you definitely up for looking after the plantation? I know Jonty would have liked you to inherit the job and of course Jacob will help," Cheryl asked.

"Yes, of course, I'd love to work in the woods. I've learnt a lot through being with Jonty. My only stipulation is that I must always be available for the kids, doing their school runs and homework," he said.

Cheryl nodded. "Yes, naturally they're your priority, I quite understand. I'm sure we can work something out."

She went on to outline other ideas she'd had about organising different aspects of the farm. Lang was most impressed by her practical attitude. With help, she was obviously capable of running the whole farm, plus the riding school. He also felt a certain pride in being made responsible again at last.

Chapter Thirty Three

Oving

That evening, Lang told Serena about the meeting and how well Cheryl had organised the future of the farm without Jonty. Lang proudly told her of his role in charge of the plantation.

"Really? The whole thing?" asked Serena, amazed. "What happens if we move again?"

Lang was startled. "How do you mean, move? Where to?"

Serena laughed. "Back to London, of course, darling."

Lang was shocked. "Back there? Oh Serena, what's got into you?"

"I'm earning a lot of money now. I'm one of the top designers in the business. . . we've got no more debt. Wouldn't it be fun to slide back into our busy old London life?" She gazed at Lang's amazed expression.

"I don't understand you. Yes, you're the breadwinner, and you're amazing, but I never thought we'd move back to the rat race. Surely, we're settled here now. The children love the country and so do I."

"Well, I don't," she interrupted. "I always thought we would move back once we had the money. I thought you would be happy."

"Going back to London?" Lang said, shaking his head. "This place is beautiful. Our kids are happy, and they are settled."

"I want to move back Lang. I want our old life back—a big gorgeous house. Just think about it please."

"Maybe if you spent more time here, you will see why me and the kids love it so much."

"Excuse me! I've—"

"I have a job here now," Lang said, cutting her off. "And I'm excited about it. I haven't been excited about work. . . since forever. We're staying Serena, so get used to it."

Serena crossed her arms and glared at Lang.

Chapter Thirty Four

Notting Hill

"Hello Gems, sorry I haven't been here for some days due to all the family problems," said Serena.

"I understand. I wanted to know, how did Jonty's funeral go?" asked Gems quietly.

"Oh, it was the saddest day ever, and all the children were so upset. And did I tell you? The police have caught the two men in the van. One was a local boy of only nineteen!" Serena adjusted her pearl earrings. "Have there been any enquiries about new work since I've been away?"

"Yes, this letter came in two days ago from a well-known footballer asking if you'd come and see his estate in Cheshire. He wants you to create an annexe to the main house. Also, the Qatar Embassy is still nagging you to design the upstairs rooms, and finally a Swiss banker wants to talk to you about organising his new property in Zurich," said Gems.

"Phew! It looks as though I'll be busy for the next few years," sighed Serena. She sat down wearily. "Lang won't be happy. I suggested we might move back to London and he shut me down. Cheryl's asked him to take over the plantation and he seems really involved with country life, but it makes me restless. I miss the buzz of Kensington. We have no social life at all in Oving."

"You're so busy. How could you find time to socialise, even in London?" said Gems.

"I don't know," Serena said truthfully. "Don't get me wrong, I'm grateful for all this success but I just miss my old life. I wish things could go back to the way they were. Lang working in the City without the debts, Jonty alive, our house, and the time I used to have with my kids."

"I think you should hire more people to help. You're only getting busier and busier. That way you can delegate more and see your family."

"You're right! I don't want this train to slow down but I do need more people on board. Okay, let's get the word out. I'm sure you could use some help."

Gemma looked at her desk covered in paperwork and laughed. "Just a bit."

Chapter Thirty Five

Chiswick

It was a gentle autumn morning and the spring tide was halfway over the road as Vivi walked along by the Thames. Anxious thoughts poured through her confused mind.

In all her married years, she'd never felt so shattered emotionally. Her love for Theo had not diminished but somehow felt invaded. Her doubts and a feeling of betrayal now bewildered every part of her. She had always known Theo was weak, vulnerable and insecure. Maybe that's what appealed to her when they first met. She felt able to nurture him and encourage his obvious artistic talent.

Perhaps Sergei had felt exactly the same for this immensely creative human being? In all her counselling she had never come across such a confused love triangle.

The obvious devotion that Sergei had surrounded Theo with somehow nurtured his confidence. How had she failed him? Now she must find a way to fulfil all his needs so that he would never be seduced emotionally again.

Sebastian seemed to have strengthened their marriage. No more concerts in Russia would prevent the agonising absences that had upset her and the children for so many long weeks. Somehow, she knew she had to find the strength to talk openly with him and hear how he felt.

Chapter Thirty Six

Aylesbury

Lang attended his first parents' meeting at the children's new school. A very friendly, rounded lady with curly, red hair sat chatting to him before they met the teachers.

"My twins love Mrs Perks. She seems to be a good all-rounder who captures their interest in every subject. You'll meet her in a minute. You can ask her any questions about your kids' work." She smiled, reassuring Lang of the unknown task ahead.

Serena had always done the parents' meetings in London but was far too busy now to attend any school functions.

Mrs Perks was indeed very effervescent and clearly enjoyed teaching Alicia. "She's an amazing child and very observant too," the teacher enthused.

Lang waited in another queue to meet Freddie's teacher, Peter Mudd, who also liked his son.

"Yes, Freddie's very capable but not very brave. A tiny cut to him is like having a leg off. Mind you, his maths is way ahead of the class. Must be Daddy's influence," said Mr Mudd, not realising the remark chilled Lang to his core after his recent downfall.

Lang returned to find bedlam at home. Maggie was chasing Freddie who had a spider in a jam jar and was trying to catch Alicia, who lay screaming on top of the banisters.

"Hello, Mr Lang, glad to see you back!" she said. "Benjie's

in bed but these two are over-excited. Oh! Mrs Serena rang to say she's still in a meeting and expects to be back late."

After their bath, Lang read a story to both children who snuggled up beside him on the bed, then told them about their good school reports.

"I love my new school," said Freddie.

"I do too, but I miss my London friends," said Alicia pensively.

Serena arrived home late that evening, a full hour after Lang had finished his own dinner.

"Sorry I'm so late, darling," she announced, hurrying into the room. "I've had an amazing meeting with a new client called Lars Elmendorf, a Swiss banker. I had to meet him at the Savoy. He lives in Zurich and wants me to design part of his new home. He'd read about my work and knows Poppy Le Harvre. Do you remember that demanding actress whose flat I did?"

Lang took a deep breath. "You have had a busy time. Well, so have I. Are you going to ask about the parents' meeting at school?"

"Oh my God, the parents' evening! I completely forgot. How did it go?" she asked.

"It was good. The kids are settling in well and their teachers are very nice. Now darling, we must talk of future plans. Firstly, I hope you'll never tell the children about the City incident. You know how I regret it all dreadfully, but our lives have changed since moving to the country. It's less frenetic. There's no rushing about. The children are happy and loving the countryside, it's so much more peaceful except for you, my darling."

Serena stared at him. "Lang, I said the other night I long

to return to London. I'm restless here, yet I do love seeing you and the children so happy and contented, but we have no social life any more. We never see any friends."

"But now your workload is so hectic there's no time for us to socialise, so let's try and change our times together so we can enjoy some fun like we used to. If you could allow weekends for us and the children, it would be so wonderful. We could go away, spend time with friends in London, go to the seaside," enthused Lang, excited at his newfound ideas.

Serena's face relaxed into a radiant smile. "That all sounds rather possible and exciting." She wandered over to sit beside him.

Lang stroked her arm. "I long to lie in bed like the old days," he murmured. "Chat and fondle each other. You're so busy these days. You seem to be in the fast lane all the time, my Fig Tree."

"I'm in it and I love it and I have to keep running, but I'll try and slow down for you guys. I'm going to get more help."

"Really?"

She kissed him, then pulled away and ruffled his hair. "Really."

Chapter Thirty Seven

Kensington

Georgie ran towards Theo. "Daddy, I've reserved a seat for you in the front row just opposite the piano. Where's Mummy?

"She can't come because Sebastian is crying a lot. She sends her love, though," Theo smiled. As soon as she turned away, Theo's smile slipped.

He had a massive argument with Vivi about Sergei. He assured her he would never talk to him again, but he knew she didn't believe him. He rubbed his hand through his hair. He was just thankful that she was still willing to work on their relationship.

Georgie went off to join all the musicians backstage. Theo felt quite emotional seeing the excitement on his daughter's expectant face. He recalled all the various school concerts he'd played solo in. How nervous he'd been until his fingers touched the keys. Then he took off and played with great feeling, even at Georgie's age, often finishing with a surge of emotion.

The bell rang, and the concert began with a duet played by two seven-year-olds. Georgie came on and played a charming Mozart piano sonata. Theo watched proudly, noticing her natural musicality. He realised she was playing just for him. Georgie took a bow and glanced at Daddy who was clapping enthusiastically.

There were some very talented flute players and a feisty drummer aged six. Georgie's ensemble finished the concert with a simplified Beethoven string quartet beautifully played.

Chapter Thirty Eight

Chiswick

Returning home around 9.30pm, Theo tenderly kissed Georgie goodnight as Vivi took her up to bed. Theo handed Vivi a glass of wine, when she came back down to the living room.

'I was really proud of Georgie's playing at the concert. Her interpretation was beautiful," he said.

"Yes, she's practiced so hard lately and was thrilled that you were able to be there," agreed Vivi. "She asked if you were going to be at home more and not go away so much. The eagerness in her face nearly made me cry. I assured her that things would be different now because you wanted to be with us more and your concerts wouldn't be in Russia."

Theo stood up. "But I still might perform in Europe, even America," he emphasised.

"Yes, of course, but hopefully the huge emotional part of you won't be torn in half like before. You might be away from us physically, but your heart will still be here."

"I want that more than anything," said Theo. There were tears in his eyes.

Vivi dried them with her hands. "I know you do," she whispered.

Chapter Thirty Nine

Aylesbury

Beady had stayed on with Cheryl, helping to sort out Jonty's clothes and papers. Just being there together in the evenings was a great comfort for both women. Beady remembered the awful emptiness when her husband had suddenly died.

They reminisced about Jonty's various antics, often expecting him to amble through the kitchen door with hay sticking out of his hair.

Cheryl's sorrow was always worse at night when she missed the hugs and warmth of Jonty's body. During the day, she was so busy with the farm, the pony club, the shop and supervising the cheese parlour.

Hilary had also moved in for a few weeks because her kitchen was in chaos and all three enjoyed knitting jumpers for the shop or doing tapestry.

But it wasn't just the women who were missing Jonty. Jacob too, was missing him and felt glad to have Lang's company down on the plantation. They had prepared a large hole ready for the cedar tree to be planted in the centre of the wood.

On Friday morning, a lorry arrived with the bulky sapling and it took three men to lift it into the prepared hole.

"There, that will be a sturdy remembrance of our Mr Jonty," Jacob said, as they all threw spades of earth over the roots.

"We're bringing the ashes down tomorrow, I think," said Lang. "The whole family will be here."

*

On Saturday, Cheryl, Hilary and Beady had prepared a large picnic table for the family gathering. A white cake covered in little trees was the centrepiece with Jonty's name on it.

Cheryl wanted the occasion to be relaxed for the children's sake. She knew Jonty wouldn't have wanted too many tears as his ashes came to rest in the beloved plantation.

Serena arrived with her children just as Cheryl was feeding the ponies. They ran into the stables to help her. Vivi and Theo walked into the kitchen with Georgie, Jago and sleepy Sebastian.

"I think we'll all wander down to the woods now," Cheryl said, holding the box of ashes.

All the children ran ahead, chasing each other down the slope. Slowly, the family assembled round the newly-planted cedar tree. For a few minutes everyone stood in silence, then Cheryl slowly opened the box and sprinkled Jonty's ashes round the tree.

Beady put an arm across her shoulder as Cheryl whispered, "Goodbye my darling."

Everyone was still, then a little wail issued from the bundle in Theo's arms. "Better get him back to the house," he said quietly. "Come on, kids."

Slowly everyone started walking back up the hill. Vivi and Lang remained.

"Well, we've both got fast lane partners who we can't control, but at least we all have each other. I wonder how we'll survive the years to come," said Lang.

"Only with love," Vivi replied, threading an arm through his as they began slowly to walk away.

All the trees were left alone, whispering in the light breeze.

About the Author

As a child, Lotte lived in Kent with her parents who enjoyed entertaining, political debates and literary discussions with the likes of Charlie Chaplin, Winston Churchill, H E Bates, W H Auden and Benjamin Britten.

She was often lonely and turned to writing (stories, diary, poems and letters) to express her feelings of isolation. In her early teens her commitment turned to ballet and point shoes replaced the pen. She was selected by the Royal Ballet School to dance in the Opera Ballet. When rejected for growing 'too tall' Lotte turned to acting and intermittently to writing.

She finally married aged 38 to her loyal husband Chris (who continues to support Lotte by typing our her hand-written stories). Lotte became immersed in her stepchildren and then her own two girls. When her daughters left home she describes "empty years" filled by illness and family problems. Sadly her parents died before her writing career flourished.

Lotte, who is now in her early 80's, lives in London and has published over 20 books.

For more on Lotte Moore, check out her website:
www.lottemoore.wordpress.com
Follow @Lotte_Moore

Other Books by Lotte Moore

Memoir
Snippets of a Lifetime
Poetry
Sensitive Sounds
Children's Fiction
School Scooter Fun
The Magic Teapot
Wheezy the Wobbler
Dixie and the Doughnuts
Lucy and the Magic Pen
The Invisible Elephant
The Dinosaur Who Ate A Piano
Mobile Crocodile
The Teaspoon Family
The Flying Granny
The Zoo Family
The Moon Tree
Short Story Collections – Fiction
Ten Short Stories and a Long One
Twelve More Short Stories
Children's – Non-Fiction
Lotte's War

*"If you are looking for a reflective and thought-provoking read,
then a book by Lotte Moore is certainly one for you."*
– CUB Magazine –